A MURDER IN MICHAELMAS

Other titles by Jeanette Sears with Piquant:

Pig's Progress (2011), also available as a Kindle edition

For Ralph,

Enjoy

A MURDER IN MICHAELMAS !

Jeanette Sears

with best wishes,
Jeanette Sears.

(First Print Run - 48/200)

Copyright © Jeanette Sears 2012

The moral right of Jeanette Sears to be identified as the author of this work has been asserted in accordance with the Copyright, Designs and Patents Act of 1988.

First published in Great Britain by PiquantFiction in 2012

PiquantFiction is an imprint of Piquant.

www.piquanteditions.com

ISBN for Print: 978-1-909281-01-1

Related ISBN for Epub:978-1-909281-03-5

Related ISBN for Mobi/Kindle: 978-1-909281-04-2

All characters, entities and events in this publication, other than those clearly in the public domain, are fictitious and any resemblance to real persons, living or dead, or to any entities, is purely coincidental.

British Library Cataloguing in Publication Data

Sears, Jeanette.
  A murder in Michaelmas.
  1. Oxford (England)--Fiction. 2. Detective and mystery stories.
I. Title
823.9'2–dc23
ISBN-13: 9781909281011

All Rights Reserved.

No part of this publication may be reproduced, stored in a retrieval system, or transmitted in any form or by any means, electronic, mechanical, photocopying, recording, or otherwise, without the prior permission of both the copyright owner and the publisher or a licence permitting restricted copying. In the UK such licences are issued by the Copyright Licensing Agency Ltd– www.cla.co.uk

Cover Design: Luz Design, www.projectluz.com

Typesetting: 2aT, www.toatee.net

FOR MUM AND DAD
in thanks for all your love and support
over the years

"Thou shalt not suffer a witch to live."
[Book of Exodus 22:18]

"For herein may be seen noble chyvalrye, curtosye,
humanyte, frendlynesse, hardynesse, love, frendshyp,
cowardyse, murdre, hate, vertue, and synne.
Doo after the good and leve the evyl,
and it shall brynge you
to good fame and renommee."
[William Caxton, Preface to Malory's Le Morte Darthur, 1485]

"She hath no loyal knight and true,
The Lady of Shalott."
[Tennyson, The Lady of Shalott, 1832]

PROLOGUE

"O WHAT CAN AIL THEE KNIGHT AT ARMS,
ALONE AND PALELY LOITERING?
THE SEDGE IS WITHERED FROM THE LAKE
AND NO BIRDS SING!"

[JOHN KEATS, *LA BELLE DAME SANS MERCI*, 1819]

"'NOW, JANTYLL KNYGHT, PUT UP THY VYSER!'"

[SIR THOMAS MALORY, *LE MORTE DARTHUR*, 1485]

It was as if the boat had been waiting for her.

She hadn't planned it at all. But there was the boat, just the right sort of boat, to carry her to her 'love'! A punt or a scull wouldn't have looked right. It had to be a wooden rowing boat to be authentic. And there it was. What a pity it couldn't just waft her there by magic, drifting romantically through the early morning mist, without the sweaty effort of rowing.

She hung the old camera around her neck and put the flashlight under one arm, lifting up her long skirts to step into the boat. It rocked and swayed with her weight. Yuk, it was wet! It must have rained during the night. Then there was the dew, and the mist that seemed to hang perpetually over the river at this time of year. It was certainly dark, dark for Dawn, a lot darker than it had been on those summer mornings last term. But Dawn was a good time for what she was about to do.

She wouldn't use the flashlight, not yet, not if she didn't have to. She didn't want to wake anyone now sleeping behind the high college walls above her, behind the lead-paned gothic oriel windows jutting out over the river. She felt quite sleepy herself. It was the morning before Noughth Week, the very beginning of Michaelmas Term at the University of Oxford. What student would want to be up so early if they didn't have to be?

She did apparently... and someone else.

She wriggled on the rough wooden seat and rearranged her black velvet dress. It was the one she had made last year especially, based on medieval patterns - a square neck and tight-fitting bodice, curving down to a dropped waist over the hips and the drooping girdle that so skilfully emphasised the groin. She would embroider it when she had the time. Meanwhile she wore three gold amulets for protection hung low around her neck and two bracelets. The lurid modern badge on her breast was a joke. He'd understand. She took off her long purple shawl, the one with celtic symbols that she'd ordered from a catalogue, and tried to forget it was meant to be a tablecloth. She flung it over her legs and flicked back her long black hair, already becoming damp in the misty air. Leaning back, she undid the padlock on the boat chain with her college key and gently let the chain fall through her hands and onto the muddy bank, making very little sound. She put the key back in her bra. She took a deep breath and lifted up the oars. They fitted into the rowlocks surprisingly easily.

This was it. She was ready to go. It must be time now. Or could she have a cigarette first? No, then she'd never do it.

She inhaled again deeply and began to row, forcefully, rhythmically. Memories of that steady motion came back to her with each pull on the blades. The familiar pain in the small of her back began almost immediately, the pain that had stopped her rowing for college last year. She bit her lip and continued to slowly pull... *pull*... *pull*. If only she'd never been... different - how different life would have been...*pull*... *pull*...

She looked behind her. She would have to be careful manoeuvring out of this narrow inlet, dug out of the earth for the benefit of King Henry Hall. On one side was the thick medieval wall of the original quadrangle, on the other the slightly less large bricks of this Victorian canal way. How convenient it was for the river to be so close. Only Magdalen College was as lucky in its proximity to these tributaries of the Thames, if luck had anything to do with the machinations of the medieval nobles and churchmen who had carved up Oxenforde between them all those centuries ago.

As her boat emerged onto the river itself, she left behind the musty mossy smell of the inlet for the cool mists of the Isis in early morning. The dank air immediately penetrated her clothes. Why hadn't she worn a cloak? That bitch Rowan had borrowed it off her last term, that's why, for some ritual. She smiled at the thought of concocting a spell to get it back.

There was no one else on the water. There was just enough light to see where she was going. The water beneath her was still as black as a void. But it should only take a quarter of an hour to row past the boat houses on the right and then down the narrow stream that led to the 'wayste foreste', as he'd called it in his letter.

How silly of him to sign the letter with that initial! It could only be one person, and she knew who he was. And he knew that she knew! She smiled to herself. He must be a glutton for punishment. It will be fun to torment him again for a whole new year.

Negotiating the boat down the narrow side stream where they were to meet was very difficult. The low branches above and the dead leaves and silt beneath were a double enemy. But as she looked behind her towards the old oak tree that marked the beginning of the 'wayste foreste', she suddenly gasped. He was already there. And in the most fantastic armour she had ever seen! It looked like the real thing - all gothic and spiky and menacing. It was probably even from the right period. He must have stolen it! She whooped with delight and put the oars to rest. She turned round in her seat and lifted up her camera.

'I've got to get a photo of *this* for my collection!'

Through the lens in the mist he looked as if he was walking on water. He was right by the water's edge, no boat in sight, waiting for her. What a re-enactment this was going to be! She took two photos to be on the safe side. Wow, it was almost frightening. It was like an apparition, an exhalation from the earth. That helmet with the pointed metal beak, the spiky gauntlets. This was real gothic!

He was helping her dock her boat now. He held out a metal glove chivalrously to help her ashore. She could hardly speak for giggling. She overbalanced and landed heavily against his breastplate, bruising her chin.

'Ow! Oh, I think I deserve a kiss for that, don't you? You should kiss me better, my gentle knight. Come on, get this thing off...'

She put her hand on the pointed metal visor that hid the knight's face. Another metal glove gripped her hand and forced it down. Then he grabbed the camera strap around her neck and began to pull it together and across.

'What...what...what are you *doing?* This isn't what's supposed to...'

Then she felt his chainmailed hands around her throat. She had no idea he was this strong.

She began to struggle, to try to push his hands away. The steel was cutting into her skin. He didn't seem to care that she couldn't breathe.

No!
Choking.
Choking.
This isn't what's supposed to happen...

CHAPTER ONE

"This Oxford I have no doubt is the finest City in the world - it is full of old Gothic buildings - Spires - Towers - Quadrangles - Cloisters - Groves etc and is surrounded with more clear streams than ever I saw together. I take a Walk by the Side of one of them every Evening and, thank God, we have not had a drop of rain these many days."

[John Keats writing to Fanny Keats, 10 October 1817]

The taxi pulled up outside a group of tall neo-gothic Victorian houses. A small sign, barely visible amongst the trees, said: 'st frideswide's ecumenical college, oxford'.

'Here we are, Norham Gardens. Is this it, love?' the taxi driver called to the girl in the back of his car.

'Yes, this is it.'

'Tons of buildings like this round here, I forget which is which! They all look pretty gloomy. They were all built for university dons, of course, in the last century when they were allowed to get married all of a sudden - dons are professors, not Mafia bosses here - you knew that though? Would you trust a group of crusty old bachelors to build a house for you, if you were a new blushing bride? I wouldn't. You studying here? That'll be four pounds fifty, love.'

'Yes. Keep the change.'

'Thank you very much. I'll get your luggage. You look as if your arms'd break.'

The taxi driver stepped out of the car and went round to the back to decant two cases and a bag out of the boot.

'There, that's the lot,' he said to the girl now standing on the pavement. 'I'll bring them up to the door for you. You take the bag and I'll take the cases.'

'Thank you.'

'Have you got a cold? You make sure you look after yourself. Draughty old buildings.'

They crunched up the short gravel driveway of St Frideswide's College. The driver put down her luggage.

'I'll be off then. All the best.'

'Bye. And thank you.'

The door in front of her was huge and arched in old wood with metal bands across it held in place with ugly studs. A black iron ring was the door handle. There was a carved pattern in the stone around the arch in dark red, beige, brown and blackened brick. It looked like the entrance to a church.

The taxi driver was calling to her cheerily as he put the car in gear:

'Hey, isn't this a vicar factory?'

'What? Oh, yes, I suppose so. Sort of.'

'Is that what you're going to be?'

'Um, no. I don't know. Um, I don't think so.'

She hadn't expected to be quizzed on her sense of vocation quite so soon upon arrival.

'Oh well.' As the taxi pulled away, the driver called back cheerily: 'Remember you Americans are supposed to be optimistic! Don't let the so-and-so's grind you down!'

She sighed with relief when he had gone. An overnight flight from Boston, followed by a 2-hour coach ride from London meant that the last thing she needed was an over-talkative taxi-driver. The 'flu bug she had been fighting for the past week had put her to sleep and deprived her the acclimatizing influence of miles of English motorway and now of the energy to appreciate the beauties of the medieval mecca of learning of which she was about to become a part. She may as well have just arrived from the moon or in a time machine for all the sense of place she felt at that moment.

But first she needed to get into the building that was to be her home for the next year. At the moment it looked more like a prison.

She tried the old iron handle. Nope, obviously that wasn't it. The door could have triple bolts on the inside for all she knew. She was probably too early after all. Her aunt was right. She was ridiculously early. Maybe no one was up! She looked at her watch. It was only 9.10am and it was a Saturday. What if everyone was still in bed? Term hadn't begun yet. Maybe she was the only one there!

It was then she noticed the bell pull at the side of the door. It even had a sign above it with 'Please Ring' in old-fashioned handwriting that had been smudged by the rain. As she obeyed the instruction, she was suddenly reminded of *Alice in Wonderland*. Oh yes, Lewis Carroll himself was supposed to have come to one of these houses to play croquet on the lawn, when the college really was just a collection of Victorian dons' houses and when Lewis Carroll was just Charles Dodgson reading Mathematics at Christchurch. She remembered seeing it in the College prospectus. One of the other parts of the college had been a tiny convent for some nuns who were fans of John Keble, one of the founders of the so-called 'Oxford Movement' of the 1830's (perhaps this part in multi-coloured stone, patterned like the 'fairisle jumper' Keble College that she'd just passed on the right). Another wing of the building had been one of the 'safe houses' for Prince Leopold, one of Queen Victoria's sons, when he had been an undergraduate at the university. Maybe she would get his room!

Then again, maybe she wouldn't get in at all.

She rang the bell and looked up at the sky. It was grey and overcast and was about to start spitting rain again any moment. Oh, *please hurry up!*

The door opened (without the grating and grinding she was expecting). A small pleasant man, who could have been Chinese or Korean, smiled broadly at her and said:

'Do not live here! So sorry! Do not know what to do! Come in!'

'Oh! Um, thank you. I'm Evelyn Merry, uh, Eve Merry. I've come to study here. This is my first day.'

He shrugged his shoulders and repeated 'Do not live here' with the same smile. Was he speaking about his own situation without the usual pronoun, or offering her some rather useful advice?

At least he picked up her cases.

With many more smiles, Eve was led through a small lobby filled with bulletin boards filled with notices, up some stairs and into an anonymous modern room that defied easy categorisation into Entrance Hall, Lobby, or anything else readily recognisable. There were several glass doors leading off it into unknown corridors, another glass door that opened onto a garden, and a few more little flights of stairs that led goodness knows where. The walls were painted white, where they weren't covered with the inevitable bulletin boards, the neon lights looking offensively bright and unnaturally modern after the gloomy exterior of the building.

The Chinese guy put down her cases with a smile and left. Eve was about to call after him but didn't know what to say. She looked round at the myriad doorways and stairs and despaired. If a White Rabbit had chosen that moment to appear or there had been a piece of cake on the table labelled 'Eat Me', she would not have been surprised.

Instead a middle-aged woman with blonde hair appeared at the other end of the garden, making for the glass door near where Eve was standing. Halfway down the garden path she spotted Eve. She stopped and threw up her hands in what looked like horror. She turned and ran down the path again and disappeared into the house opposite. She then re-appeared moments later, carrying a huge pile of sheets and towels and tottered on high heels down the tarmac path. She must have changed in a split second out of the sensible trainers and socks she had been wearing a moment before. She arrived at the glass door and swore.

'Can you open it?' she mouthed. 'I've forgotten my...' and she mimed opening the door with a key - for some reason, because if she had spoken normally Eve would have been able to hear her perfectly well.

'You're early, damn you!' the woman said as she bundled the sheets onto Eve's chest. 'Are you our baby?'

'What?'

'The baby of the college.'

'I'm...my name is Evelyn Merry. But people call me Eve. I'm the, um, Lady Frances Fairfax Scholar.' Eve hesitated to say this in case it sounded like showing off. And feeling that her accent sounded very American.

'That's it. The baby of the college. All the rest of them are in their thirties, you know. Well, not *all* of them. There's a few baby ones in their early twenties. Perhaps you'll get on with them. But I always feel sorry for the Fairfax girls. Although you might find a husband here, you know. Most of the men are married but the American girls usually get the ones that are single. We used to have more American girls staying here every year but they went through the single men like a dose of salts and married the lot of them - *every year!* Caused a lot of resentment with the other women in college - you know, just like the War - "overfed, oversexed and over here!"' she chortled. 'But you'll be better off mixing with the other undergraduates in the rest of the University. Of course, the ones here are undergraduates as well, but they're *old* undergraduates. You'll be wanting to mix with the normal ones your own age,' she said in a motherly voice. 'Now, let's get you to your room. Are these your cases?' She didn't wait for a reply. 'Oh dear, I hope I've got your key. They've been changing all the locks like billy-oh around here. Some are the new swipe-cards or smartcards, I think they call them, and others are still the old locks and keys. You don't know whether you're coming or going. Oh, I'm Allie the housekeeper, short for Alison, Eve short for Evelyn. Perhaps I'll call you Evie. Yes, that's it.'

She reached out from under the towels and the two women shook hands. Allie then marched off through one of the mysterious doors, saying: 'Leave your cases. We'll get some hunky man to move those for us later.'

Eve followed Allie down a labyrinth of corridors, up and down confusing flights of stairs, peering awkwardly round the huge pile of white cotton sheets she had had dumped in her arms. They smelt clean and fresh but not like her ones at home. Every so often Allie would indicate like a tour guide to the left or the right: 'That's the chapel' or 'That's the Library' or 'That's married students' studies'. She then said resentfully: 'You're right at the top, of course' as they began to climb the last of the flights of stairs. Who would have thought the college could be so big on the inside?

They arrived on the top landing. Allie fumbled with a set of keys on her belt, like a medieval chatelaine, and opened the door of Eve's room.

'Number Twelve, Red Lodge,' she announced. 'That's 'cos of the colour of the brick. Although why they call this Victorian stuff "red brick", I don't know. Just looks brown to me.'

Eve walked into her room.

The walls and ceiling were white. There was a large oak wardrobe on the right, a painted white chest of drawers in the far corner, and a single bed on the left hand side. The mattress was a boring beige and cream design and looked suspiciously stained. There was a sink with a mirror behind the bed next to a fireplace with an old gas fire. A large armchair and a small coffee table hogged the centre of the room. In front of her was a sofa covered with a torn candlewick bedspread in an offensive shade of red. Under the window was a desk with a lamp and an office chair.

But the window... *the window*! The window was really two windows, two enormous gothic points reaching up into the air, filling the room with a glorious light from a transformed sky. The sun was shining brilliantly now as if held up by the dark clouds beneath and a rainbow had appeared like a miracle, faint yet distinct, as if for Eve's benefit on her first day. It was a sign! She walked over slowly to the window and thought about God and Noah and the Flood and God's promise to never desert His people that the appearance of the rainbow symbolised. Eve turned round to Allie with a beatific smile.

'Have you got a cold?' Allie asked. 'Your nose looks very red. Throw me some of those sheets and I'll make your bed up. Oh, and there are some tapers and matches there if you want to put the gas fire on. Although it's condemned. Going to be castrated. Got to have its poor little tube cut off. The gas man will come round this week to see to it. You may as well make the most of it till then - if it doesn't gas you first. The heating probably won't be switched on for another couple of weeks. They're getting tight-arsed round here - new budget.'

In a few minutes the bed was made and Allie was gone.

The room was a lot bigger than Eve had been expecting. Her possessions would look lost in it. She shouldn't have let Aunt Barbara persuade her to bring so little. She could have brought Nellie the Elephant and Ricardo the Rat for her bed after all. At the thought of her childhood toys, now stuffed away in Aunt Barbara's cupboards, Eve felt ludicrously tearful. It had been a long day already. She reminded herself that she had been on a plane all night. And she was still recovering from the 'flu. She looked round the room. There was a kettle on the chest of drawers but no tea or coffee. She felt too exhausted all of a sudden to do anything about it. Perhaps a short rest would be a good idea.

So Eve took out the pillow from under the blankets, took off her coat and lay down on the bed, pulling her raincoat over her. Within seconds she was asleep.

'Ah, a fine example of the Lesser-titted Snore Warbler, if I am not mistaken!'

Eve woke up with a jump as if her heart was going to explode. There was the sound of hearty laughter and Eve opened her eyes to see a man gazing at her through a pair of binoculars and another man behind him who was doing the laughing.

'Charlie!' she exclaimed. 'What are you doing here? And you,' she added, as the shorter man with binoculars was still looking her up and down, 'stop it!'

'How are you?' said Charlie. 'Thought I'd come and look you up.'

'Or over,' said the other man, now taking the binoculars away from his face and grinning.

Eve realised that she was looking very crumpled and that she may well have been asleep with her mouth open, thus the reference to snores. And all this in front of the man she had worshipped for the last two summers. And her eyes had gummed up - she had been asleep in her contact lenses. She should have locked her door. Eve was just about to sit up properly when she sneezed loudly instead.

'Whoops! Have you got a cold,' said the other man, 'or is that very belated hay fever? ' Before Eve knew what was happening, he had grabbed one of her hands and was holding it round his throat as if she was strangling him. 'Oh, Charlie, help! She's mugging me! It's alright, it's alright, I surrender! I'll give you everything I own - just don't break my fingers, I'm a pianist!'

'Ow!' said Eve as one of the man's fingernails cut into her as she tried to rip her hand away.

'Sorry', said Charlie. 'I told him you came from America. It's his pathetic idea of a joke, pretending all Americans are muggers. Come on, Martin, leave the poor girl alone. It looks as if she's only just arrived. Let me introduce you. Martin, this is Eve Merry - by name if not by nature at the moment. Eve, this is - let me get this right - Crispin Martin de Beauchamp-Massey, Martin to his friends.'

'Does he have any?' said Eve grumpily as she swung her legs onto the floor and tried to straighten her hair.

'Excuse me, Crispin Martin *Alexander Xavier* de Beauchamp-Massey,' said Martin with mock-gravity. 'You missed out a few. And Beecham's spelt "Beauchamp". Charmed,' he added, and leant over Eve's other hand in a fake kiss.

Who was this fool? And what time was it? She squinted at her watch - it was nine thirty on her first day. She squinted at Charlie and his friend.

Charlie's appearance she knew more than well. It was carved into her memory from several sleepless nights and much languishing over photos taken of him on the two youth camps where they had both been leaders. Two summers ago it had been in Maine and only a few weeks ago in Vermont. Charlie had been there as a soccer coach, even though, as he kept protesting, his main game was rugby. There had also been all those late night Leaders Training Sessions and the end-of-camp Prom where Eve had suffered in silence as Charles Boscombe had wowed every female there with his proverbial greek god good looks. Even when he had asked her to dance she had managed to convince herself that it was only because he felt sorry for her. After all there had been one very good reason that summer why he might...

It did not take long to refresh her memory. Charlie was over six foot of pure rugby-playing muscle with the ample covering of thick fat that rugby players manage to make look like muscle too. That combined with wavy blond hair, friendly blue eyes and a brilliant smile had taken its usual toll on Eve, along with all the others, and meant that the last year, appalling in so many ways, had been made strangely more bearable by the torment of fruitlessly longing for him. Eve had realised he was from a much wealthier background than her. Somehow that hadn't seemed to matter in America. But here now in England she was beginning to think that it might.

She now turned her attention to his friend, who looked as if he might be from the same sort of background but was physically somewhat different, to say the least. Smaller, slimmer, and with wild reddish brown hair that he was trying to smooth back with one hand and a flick of his head in a desultory way. But his clothes were more noticeable than his face, although it was hard to say why. He looked impeccably well-dressed, even though he wasn't. He was wearing jeans and a waistcoat and a brown tweed jacket and was now carrying what looked like a woman's floral umbrella. He looked impatient and energetic, and superior, as if he was going to stride across the room any moment and do something outrageous and supercilious.

Eve took an instant dislike to him.

'Martin is the best Hamlet the university has ever seen!' Charlie was saying as if to prompt Eve's admiration.

Martin blew kisses to an imaginary, and presumably turbulent and awestruck, audience, then said: 'Come on, are we going on the river or not? We're supposed to be giving this young woman her baptism by water. Come on, it's going to rain and we need to buy wine.'

'I thought you said champagne?' said Charlie.

'Sssshhh. She's from the wrong side of the tracks, we don't want to spoil her just yet with high living. You're a corrupting influence. I thought you said she was religious. Practically a nun.'

'What!' Eve exploded, as Charlie protested, 'I never...!'

'A champagne-swigging nun. She'll be doing the can-can next. I saw a photo of nuns playing table-tennis,' Martin chattered. 'Who knows what they're capable of? Just don't leave me alone with her.'

Fortunately before Eve could think of a cutting reply, Charlie butted in with: 'Shut up and get a move on. For all we know the river could be jammed already.'

'You're right, as always. Let us away from this dank spot for an even danker one.' Martin looked round the room. 'Bit minimalist in here, isn't it?'

'I *have* only just moved *in!*' Eve responded aggressively, wondering if she should state the obvious.

'Oh, of course. Expecting trunks of stuff to arrive any moment, no doubt. And here was I thinking it was just your vow of poverty.'

Eve found herself saying, again aggressively: 'Are you always this patronising?'

Martin pondered for a second, then replied: 'Only to Americans.'

He beamed at her. He'd riled her. He'd won.

'Give the girl a break, for God's sake,' said Charlie patiently. 'Do you want to come for a punt, Eve?' asked Charlie, now smiling, looking to Eve like the proverbial breaking out of the sun between the clouds. 'And don't take any notice of Martin, he's acting as usual - playing the trivial upper-class twit.'

'And I do it so well,' added Martin.

Eve sighed. She could have said she'd been up all night on a plane, had had 'flu for what seemed like forever, and just wanted to eat a sofa and then sleep for a week, but instead found herself saying to Charlie: 'Of course, I'd love a punt' with a forced smile, hoping it meant what she thought. She began to put on the raincoat that had so recently functioned as a blanket.

The two men left the room gabbling at full speed, leaving Eve alone to find the room key that Allie the housekeeper must have left for her. Ah, there it was, on the coffee table.

Suddenly Martin popped his head round the door.

'You didn't let me help you on with your coat! What must you think of me!'

'It's OK, I can cope,' Eve replied with another fake smile, putting her bag over her shoulder.

'Good-oh, as Bertie Wooster would say - shall I be like a PG Wodehouse novel for you? Is that what you Americans think we're like? Or should I be all *Brideshead Revisited?* We must give you your authentic Oxford experience. Oh, I hear you and Charles were on a camp together. I'd *love* to see Charles being camp! He's so butch, don't you think? But no doubt you kept him in order.'

Was this another persona of Martin's? What did 'camp' mean - was it another word for 'gay'? That would make sense, judging from the way Martin was speaking.

'Um, no, I...' was all Eve could manage before he interrupted.

'You didn't? Oh, do tell me all the dirt. I'd love to know what Charlie gets up to in the vacs. I'm sure he's absolutely swamped with girls who'd do anything for him - don't you think? You can whisper it all to me in the punt when he's not looking. You can whisper it to me and we'll look all romantic and in love. Come on, I'm in an agony of anticipation.'

Was this his 'Brideshead' bit now? Perhaps he just had multiple personality disorder.

Eve turned round to lock the door on their way out. Her eyelids flickered involuntarily with tiredness as she turned the key. It was going to be a long first day.

Charlie's voice sounded from the floor beneath, telling them to hurry up. Martin ran down the stairs whooping.

Eve followed them, torn between her desire to be with Charlie for the rest of her life and her desire never to see Crispin Martin de Whateveritwas-Massey ever again.

Oh, and her desire not to be alone on her first day in Oxford, in England, on a whole other continent, three thousand miles from home.

CHAPTER TWO

"It is enacted, that scholars (particularly the younger sort, and undergraduates) shall not idle and wander about the City, or its suburbs, nor in its streets, or public market, or Carfax (at Penniless Bench as they commonly call it), nor be seen standing or loitering about the townsmen or workmens' shops."

[Laudian Code, 1636]

"...Oxford in those days still kept a great deal of its earlier loveliness: and the memory of its grey streets as they were has been an abiding influence and pleasure in my life, and would be greater still if I could only forget what they are now..."

[William Morris, *The Aims of Art*, 1887]

'What do you mean, you don't have a bike!'

'Every student in Oxford has a bike. They don't let you in the university without one!'

'How are we going to get down to King's?'

'You mean we're going to have to walk? Oh well, I'm a man, I can take it.'

Eve wasn't prepared for the volley of protest that was to meet her announcement that she didn't yet have a bike. Charlie and Martin were about to unlock their's that they had parked outside

St Frideswide's, chained to some black railings at the side of the college.

'Oh well, I suppose we'll have to walk with ours then,' sighed Charlie.

'I am *going* to get one,' said Eve. 'I'll buy one once my money comes through...'

'You're going to buy one here!' Martin laughed as if this was a huge joke. 'You realise that any bike you buy here will have been stolen from Cambridge University (a squalid little place of so-called learning which we can otherwise ignore). Men in gangs come with lorries at night, cut the chains on everyone's bikes, load them up and take them to Cambridge to sell. They then do the same in Cambridge and bring their bikes here. We buy each other's bikes several times over every year!'

'Oh...,' said Eve, deflated.

'Don't worry, don't listen to him,' smiled Charlie. 'I'm sure it will be alright to buy a bike here. It is a speciality market here, after all.'

'For thieves and robbers,' said Martin.

'We'll walk with our bikes, it's not a problem,' said Charlie reassuringly. 'We've got to drop in at the shops anyway.'

'Are we closer to the Cherwell Boat House up here?' asked Martin. 'Would it be quicker to get a punt there?'

'How near are we, Eve, do you know?'

'*She* won't know, she's only just arrived. We may as well head south. We'll go to the shops on St Giles, especially if we want champagne. They don't sell champagne at the Cherwell Boat House. You'd be lucky to get a cup of tea and an ice-cream.'

Eve thought that sounded much better but thought it wise not to say so. All three of them scowled up at the sky. It was getting greyer and darker by the minute.

The two men walked with their bikes in front of Eve, chattering away about people she didn't know, effectively blocking the pavement for any passer-by or for Eve to join in with them. After two minutes of this treatment, Eve thought: why don't I just swathe myself from head to toe in black! I wonder what their reaction would be if I accused them of gossiping? Men hate to think of their talk as gossip. They like to think it's an objective and dispassionate sharing of information about people, even when they're being bitchy. Just because it's done in deeper voices..., Eve thought maliciously in her tiredness.

They had walked out of Norham Gardens and onto Banbury Road opposite St Anne's College. Wycliffe Hall stood at the end of Norham Gardens, an Anglican theological college that shared some lectures and facilities with St Frideswide's. But Martin and Charlie headed left, down towards the large open road called St Giles, named after the medieval church that stood at the crossroads at the top. The three students crossed over the road behind the church, only just avoiding being knocked down by two cyclists dressed as Robin Hood and Friar Tuck.

They were now at the shops surrounding Little Clarendon Street. Eve's immediate thought was 'These look like shops I can't afford to go in.' She did have some money in her shoulder bag, but what if these rich guys wanted her to go thirds with them on extravagant purchases? She wasn't too keen on blowing her scholarship money on her first day on champagne and caviar. And yes, there were champagne and caviar in the window of the very first shop!

But fortunately the men's disregarding of her also consisted in asking her to look after their bikes while they went into the shops. (Or were they being kind? Eve did wonder for a moment whether they might have taken into account her probable finances, or lack of them...)

She looked in the window of Taylor's. It was obviously a delicatessen, with a colourful range of different types of pasta, wild mushrooms, fancy breads, every conceivable brand of tea and coffee, 'Oxford' marmalade and jams (the jars wearing little 'mortar boards' instead of lids - the flat black hats with tassles that are part of Oxford academic dress), kettle chips and cookery books, and continental chocolate bars. She began to feel hungry and wonder what Charlie and Martin might buy.

When they emerged with enormous grins, laughing at some joke, Martin was carrying a bottle wrapped in tissue paper and had a plastic carrier bag with 'Taylor's' written in gold, full of...?

'Right, I've bought the savouries, you can buy the sweet,' Martin said to Charlie. 'You can be our sugar daddy. Oh, Eve, can you take my bike? My hands are a bit full.'

They went back over Little Clarendon Street, past a cafe on the corner, and arrived at the most stunning display of cakes Eve had ever seen at a patisserie called 'Maison Blanc'. A huge pyramid of profiteroles doused in chocolate sauce and decorated with pink and blue dots of sugar was surrounded by little parcels wrapped in silver paper and tied with extravagant pink, turquoise and blue bows. A tiny plastic bride and groom perched dangerously on the top.

'I'm going to have one of those at my wedding,' announced Martin. 'Sod fruitcake and icing.'

'Twenty of those!' said Charlie.

'No, a few hundred!' said Martin. 'One for each guest! Just a little guest list of a thousand...'

'And you get to eat all the left-overs!'

There seemed to be row upon row of chocolate, cream and fruit confections as far as the eye could see, stretching back into the inner recesses of the shop. There were dainty fruit tartlets - each one a work of art in raspberries or mandarin, glazed over with shining sweet varnish. There was an astonishing variety of chocolate cake, painted with swirling cream and decorated with delicate chocolate leaves, the sponge no doubt soaked with exotic liqueurs.

'Ooooooh, I want *that* one!' cried Eve, her reticence exploded by the sight of so much chocolate in varying forms.

She pointed to a row of cakes labelled *'Religieuse Chocolat'*. Each one was a fat choux bun filled with cream topped with a tiny choux bun covered in dark chocolate.

'You realise you'll be eating a monk, don't you,' said Martin. 'A *religieuse* is a member of a religious order. You can bite a monk's head off. That should appeal to you...'

'I know, I took French in High School,' Eve butted in.

'Oh, excusez-*moi!*'

'Come on, I'm starving,' said Charlie. 'I'll stay with the bikes this time. Just get me one of those little fruity ones. Oh, and you can get me a chocolate monk as well.'

'Perhaps it's a nun,' said Martin. 'Doesn't Charlie look like the sort of man who'd rip a nun's head off?'

'Jeez,' said Eve, breaking her vow never to take the Lord's name in vain, and led Martin into the shop.

The cakes were put into white boxes and tied up with ribbon. Eve wondered how on earth they were going to balance with all this getting in and out of a punt. Perhaps they should eat them now to be on the safe side?

Martin flung back his hair as he was paying for the cakes (in French). Eve wondered why he had his hair so long if it was a nuisance. It all added to the impression that he was rather affected. Was it because he'd done a lot of acting? Eve imagined him as Oscar Wilde, with long flowing hair, a black velvet suit and a floppy tie, with a gold-topped ebony cane instead of a woman's umbrella. Mmmmm. And a green carnation. Was Martin gay? If so, what was Charlie doing hanging out with him? It was hard to imagine a more hunky hetero than Charles Boscombe.

Martin turned round to Eve and made slobbering and smacking sounds with his lips over the top of the boxes of cakes.

'Mmmmmmmm...Yum, yum!!'

Eve tried to imagine him as Hamlet. It wasn't easy.

They walked down the rest of St Giles, fought their way through the hordes of Saturday shoppers on Cornmarket, avoided getting run over by the herds of double and single decker buses and crossed over onto St Aldates.

'I thought this was supposed to be closed to traffic,' said Eve bad-temperedly.

'It is,' said Charlie, 'apart from the buses. Apparently when the routes were privatised, about twenty buses started doing each stint instead of one and the whole thing's been clogged up ever since. Carfax - where we've just crossed - is always either completely static or a death trap.'

'Gosh, I don't think I'd want to bike here after all,' said Eve. 'It looks life-threatening.'

'Oh, it is,' said Martin cheerfully. 'But you can get cycling helmets at a discount from your college. Oh, I forgot, you're not a member of the university are you, at St Fryed's?'

'Um, I'm not sure, we're sort of attached...'

'Look, that's the House! Where a certain Charles Boscombe Esquire has been known to do occasional bits of work. We just need to trot down the road a bit further to my college - which is superior in every way to mouldy old Christ Church, of course - in its antiquity, its architecture, its food, the physical beauty of its undergraduates, its adjacency to the river...'

Charlie punched Martin on the shoulder.

'Arrogant bastard!'

'Well, at least we have decent gargoyles. You don't have any - not one! Oh, apart from that particularly reprehensible-looking porter - sorry, bulldog...'

'Who wants revolting little gargoyles picking their noses?'

'I'll have you know that is the prize possession of King Henry Hall! We intend to build a new quadrangle with the proceeds from the mugs, t-shirts and postcards that that little creature alone rakes in. You're just jealous 'cos all you've got is a mouldy old portrait of Henry the Eighth...'

'*And* John Wesley, *and* Lewis Carroll...'

The two men rattled on as they walked past a church on the right. It was St Aldate's church after which the street took its name, as with practically everywhere else in Oxford. Eve looked at the noticeboard welcoming Freshers to the Sunday services. Perhaps she'd give it a try.

Martin suddenly turned Eve's head forcibly to the right and said:

'Brewer Street! Where Dorothy L Sayers was born. I think we should do homage for a while.'

'Wow, I love her,' said Eve in sudden awe. It was for things like this she had come to Oxford.

The three of them stopped and looked down the tiny one way street lined with walls of grey stone. Martin pointed to a handsome square house.

'She was born there because her father was the Head of Christ Church Choir School.'

'And she was baptised over the road at Christ Church Cathedral,' added Charlie, sounding pleased with himself.

'Only because we were too exclusive at King's,' said Martin in a pretend huff. 'And there we are!'

Martin was pointing to a building on the horizon with another tall tower. That presumably was Martin's college.

'Of course, Christ Church Cathedral is only there because of St Frideswide,' said Charlie, bowing to Eve in acknowledgement, 'and all the rest of Oxford.'

But now they needed to cross over the busy road and pass the Law Courts with St Aldate's Police Station and the Coroner's Court. King Henry Hall could suddenly be seen much more clearly, looking as if its high sandstone walls stretched on forever all the way to Folly Bridge.

'Well, what do you think?' Martin asked Eve proudly.

'It's alright,' said Eve cheerfully. 'But I've been on a plane all night, so my aesthetic judgment might be impaired.'

'I was up at seven and I can still see straight,' Martin retorted, obviously miffed at her blase response. 'By the way, do I detect an American accent?'

'Why were you up at seven?' Charlie asked Martin, oblivious to the needling going on. 'I said I was coming at nine.'

'Oh some prat downstairs was playing heavy metal music, would you believe. I went down to shut him up but he just yelled at me through the door to go away. I couldn't believe it! If he hadn't turned his music down pretty soon I would have called the porter.'

'You're going to have to keep him in line.'

'And what's more, we had a fire drill last night!' Martin continued unabated. 'We'd only just arrived back - the second and third years, that is - and we have to rush outside and line up in the quad. It was a complete fiasco. Guy was pratting about, completely disorganised - he's the Fire Officer this year, poor sod, now he's JCR President - and everyone got furious, slow-handclapping, etc. And we got rained on. I'm telling you, it was not a good way to start the term.'

Charlie sympathised as they walked stooping through a small wooden doorway, seemingly made for medieval midgets, and into King Henry Hall.

'Do you want me to do the tourist bit, Eve?' Martin asked, but before she could reply or even nod or shake her head, he raced on, 'Well, I will anyway. Here we have King Henry Hall, known colloquially as "King's" - not to be confused with the vastly inferior King's Colleges in Cambridge or London, of course. Built in the 1460's by one Sir Edward Chichele, a supporter of King Edward the Fourth in the Wars of the Roses. He had money to burn and particularly disliked the Bishop who was building Magdalen just down the river - William of Waynflete, that is - and so decided to build a rival foundation on an old Saxon tower, to top his old rival. One of the nastier gargoyles is supposed to be the good Bishop Willie.'

'The one picking its nose?' asked Eve.

'No, I think its just plain ugly - oh, and it's wearing a mitre with horns. Not very nice.'

'So have Magdalen and King's been rivals ever since?' Eve asked, in an effort to be polite.

'Oh, absolutely. In Eights Week we bash each other's boats like crazy. And please don't ask what Eights Week is - it's a boating thing in the Trinity Term. That's the third term to you.'

'Why is it called after King Henry the Eighth if it was built at the time of King Edward?' asked Eve, feeling a faint glimmer of genuine interest.

'It was Edward Chichele's family who renamed it after they lost out in the Wars of the Roses. And it's in honour of Henry the *Seventh*, not Eighth, the first Tudor king. The Chicheles thought it wise to get on his right side, if he had one.'

'Is that why there are red and white roses all around here - the Lancaster and the York united at last?'

'Yip. In the flowerbeds, and in stone on the walls. So you *do* know some history.'

Eve stifled the desire to retort and instead made appreciative noises as the three of them walked through a second quadrangle that looked even older than the first, in a beautiful mellow sandstone. They then had to walk through a low narrow doorway on the far side of the quad. Eve went in first while the two men stayed outside chatting.

The low-ceilinged corridor where she now found herself was suddenly very cold as if someone had turned the sun off a long time ago. Even Eve had to stoop to avoid hitting her head on the jagged slate roof. She felt she was now in a much older part of the college, a part that perhaps pre-dated the fifteenth century. If the main tower had been Saxon then perhaps this was too. It even smelt old. It smelt of decay and the river, as if the water beyond had seeped up into the core of the building centuries ago and infected the walls with its dank likeness. Eve couldn't resist running her fingers along the small angular blocks of slate, slotted together with no noticeable means of holding them in place. There were so many shades of grey and black (could you have shades of black?) that Eve thought what a wonderful drawing she could do of them in charcoal. But perhaps the light wasn't good enough. Anyway, where were those guys?

Her two companions seemed to be taking advantage of time aside to gossip in lowered voices while she was out of earshot. She may as well forget about them and enjoy herself. She walked on a bit further down the stone tunnel towards the light at the end. How thick the wall was! The tunnel had to be the length of a room at least and who could tell how wide the wall itself was. Eve smiled to herself, remembering how as a child she used to like to imagine that she could be more in touch with people from the past when she touched old buildings. She felt as if the stones could store the wisdom of the ages or tell you about the men who originally moulded them together into walls that would stand up to the centuries. As Eve dragged her fingers over the ancient stone, revelling in its rough and complicated texture, she wondered how many students had passed this way before, or monks or nuns or aristocrats - had gone before her to the river down this dark tunnel. Perhaps it had been at night, with fiery glowing torches, scorching the stone of the passageway as they hurried to meet with forbidden lovers on a secret tryst. She could just imagine hurrying down this corridor in long skirts, wrapping a warm cloak around herself against the cold night air, the smoke of the torch blowing in her face as the wind from the river tried to force her back. And then leaping into a boat to meet the forbidden lover by night, out in the thick woods where no one would see you!

The raucous laughter of Charlie and Martin called her back to the present. What a pity she wasn't on her own with Charlie now. It could have been so romantic on the river without this wretched Martin. There was so mush she wanted to say to him... So...

Eve then stopped, as she realised she'd just thought 'mush' instead of 'much'. Hmm.

As the two men joined her in the stone tunnel, Martin suddenly cried out, his voice made louder and flatter by the stone:

'Oh no! I've forgotten something!'

He turned round and dashed out of the tunnel, leaving Eve and Charlie alone together, for the first time in months.

Two months, one week, and three days, to be precise.

CHAPTER THREE

"IT IS THAT STRANGE *DISQUIETUDE* OF THE GOTHIC SPIRIT THAT IS ITS GREATNESS; THAT RESTLESSNESS OF THE DREAMING MIND, THAT WANDERS HITHER AND THITHER AMONG THE NICHES AND FLICKERS FEVERISHLY AROUND THE PINNACLES, AND FRETS AND FADES IN LABYRINTHINE KNOTS AND SHADOWS ALONG WALL AND ROOF, AND YET IS NOT SATISFIED, NOR SHALL BE SATISFIED."

[JOHN RUSKIN, *THE STONES OF VENICE*, 1851-3]

"...AND SO LAT MY BED AND ALL MY RYCHYST CLOTHIS BE LEDDE WITH ME IN A CHARYAT UNTO THE NEXTE PLACE WHERE THE TEMMYS YS; AND THERE LETTE ME BE PUT WITHIN A BARGET..."

[SIR THOMAS MALORY, *LE MORTE DARTHUR*, 1485]

There were a few moments of silence - embarrassed moments for Eve who could not think of anything to say to her beloved other than something she might regret for the rest of her life. Fortunately Charlie started commenting on the grimness of the weather and giving neutral sporting anecdotes from his exploits last year that meant Eve could laugh politely and forget about herself. Apart from wishing she had had more time to get ready and put on a bit of make-up, that is. What did she look like after her long journey? She hadn't even been able to look in a mirror! She was wearing jeans, a navy and white floral shirt, a navy cardigan and a taupe trenchcoat, with black shoes and bag. That should look OK, and at least she was still wearing her lenses, even if her eyes were starting to feel a bit sore.

Martin reappeared with another carrier bag with a bunch of flowers sticking out the top ('for the ducks', he explained enigmatically) and an oblong black carrying case.

'What's that?' asked Eve.

'That's my 1936 May-Fair Gramophone. It's the only way to travel.'

'You're going to play records in the rain?'

'It's manual, wind-up, no electrics. It might get a bit rusty, but that's all. I thought we should have some 1930's Blues and Jazz to give you your first authentic Oxford experience as we punt lazily down the river, eating strawberries and quaffing champagne in the warm summer sun.'

'Very kind of you, but we don't have any sun...'

'Or strawberries,' added Charlie. 'Ah, here we are. Let's get that one, it looks the least waterlogged.'

They had now emerged from the old stone corridor and were suddenly next to the river, or a very small inlet of the river. Lined up in ranks were long wooden punts, narrow rowing boats and a couple of canoes or sculls. They were chained to the bank like tame animals who showed no desire to escape but were lazily waiting for their owners to release them to get a bit of exercise. Despite the grey sky, the water was a greeny black, like an old-fashioned glass bottle, made darker by the autumn leaves that had already cascaded into it.

'How convenient, to be so close to the river,' said Eve.

'It's great unless you have one of the rooms on this side,' said Martin, jumping into one of the boats and making it sway violently. 'It's damp and musty. In winter you can get water running down your walls. And it's noisy too in the summer with people using the boats the whole time and getting raucous. You get people making love out here too. The number of nights I was woken by the yells and moans of undergraduates on heat! That was my room, up there, jutting out...'

He pointed up to one of the windows in the wall behind them. It was a small bay window with diamond-shaped panes of glass surrounded by stone frames carved with twining leaves, topped off by a dragon's head on one side and an angel leaning out of the foliage on the other.

'Oh, cool!' exclaimed Eve. 'And I thought my windows were neat.'

'Yes,' said Charlie, 'there's a dragon's head and we were at Dragonshead school together - very appropriate. Now, Eve, hop in. I'll take your bags.'

So that's how these two know each other, Eve thought as she tried to 'hop' into the punt. One of the top private (perversely known as 'public') schools in the country. Eve had looked it up in the 'Guide to British Independent Schools' on the internet when she had first developed her crush on Charlie. All it had done was confirm to her that the two of them came from completely different worlds and that she didn't have a hope of getting together with him.

But here she was with his arm around her, helping her into the punt. Eve nervously left the safety of the bank, stepped into mid-air, and almost fell on top of Charlie as Martin made the punt sway by trying to set up his gramophone.

'There'll be time enough for that later, you two.'

Martin took a large 78 record out of its sleeve and put it on the gramophone's turntable while Eve sat down with a bump in the middle of the punt. Charlie then insisted that they swap places so that Martin was in the middle seat and Eve at the other end, so that Charlie and Martin could easily swap over to do the actual punting. Eve sat down on a wet vinyl cushion as if it didn't matter. It would look too prissy to wipe it first. Charlie yelled for some of the food if he was going to do all the hard physical work while the other two lazed around. Martin handed him the bag of savoury food. Charlie took out a wholemeal pasty with distaste, saying 'Is this vegetarian?', but he ate it in four bites anyway.

Martin had now wound up the gramophone with its portable handle. He moved the arm across onto the thick black disc. Jolly music began, very frantic and crackly, and a woman's voice began singing 'Ain't Misbehavin''.

'Oh, who's that woman?' cried Eve. 'What a lovely soprano voice.'

Martin frowned and looked at the revolving label.

'It's supposed to be Fats Wallah!'

'Oh.'

Martin fiddled with a little lever and the voice slowed down to a gravelly black bass.

'That's more like it,' said Martin with satisfaction. 'Right, Charlie, get cracking with that pole. Oh, I haven't undone us yet. Where's my key? Ah, here it is.'

As Charlie drew up the long metal pole with a clatter that had been resting in the punt, Martin unlocked the chain that had been holding the punt at the bank. With an even louder series of clatters he pulled it through its metal holder and threw it onto the path.

'Ship ahoy! Away, me mateys, Jim lad!' cried Martin in a rasping pirate's voice. 'Begone, all landlubbers! Avast behind! Don't you think Charlie has a vast behind?' he continued in his normal voice. 'Of course it's all muscle. They don't call him Charlie "Buns of Steel" Boscombe for nothing you know... ow!'

Charlie had tipped forward the pole and hit Martin on the head.

'I wonder if it's still trying to rain,' said Eve. 'you can't tell in here with all the trees.'

'Is that all you think about, woman? The bloody weather? Here we are, giving you your first authentic Brideshead experience and all you can do is moan about the bloody weather!'

'I didn't watch *Brideshead*,' said Eve huffily, 'I was too young.'

'Weren't we all, dear. But you can watch it on DVD or online. I think we should. In fact, we can watch it when we get back...'

'Will you shut up,' interrupted Charlie, 'and tell me if there's any traffic when we come out of this bit. I don't want to crash into any other boats.'

'Come off it,' said Martin, 'we're the only idiots out on the river in this weather.'

Charlie pushed the ten foot pole into the river bed and forced the punt by degrees past the 'Head of the River' pub and out into the Isis itself. At first they did seem to be the only people on the river. And there was a red and white sign on the opposite bank saying 'PATH CLOSED' to pedestrians.

It amazed Eve how smooth the ride was, since it seemed to be so much effort for Charlie. Every few feet he had to run the pole up through his hands at great speed and then push it down again firmly and slowly for them to make any headway. He quickly took off his jacket as he had already begun to sweat.

Fats Wallah finished and Martin asked Eve to choose the next record as he was eating a sausage roll. He said with his mouth full:

'Of course we're following the same route as Charles Dodgson on that fateful day when he told the story of *Alice in Wonderland* for the first time to little Alice Liddell. Very dubious relationship. But they did punt from Folly Bridge up river, just like us.'

Eve continued to flip through the 78s in a pocket in the lid of the gramophone. They were mostly in brown cardboard sleeves with adverts for the shops in London where they were purchased, long since closed. Each one looked like a large liquorice frisbee. There was 'Your Socks Don't Match' sung by Bing Crosby with Louis Jordan and his Orchestra, 'Snooky Ookums' by Judy Garland on the yellow and black MGM label, 'Between the Devil and the Deep Blue Sea' by Eddie Duchin, and practically anything made into a fox trot, including such unlikely numbers as 'Old Man River'. Eve was torn between choosing something she knew or 'I'm all bound round with the Mason Dixon Line' by Jimmy McPartland and his Squirrels, when Martin impatiently said: 'Put on "Lady in Red"! Have some food.'

Eve accepted a sausage roll and let Martin put the record on, that had 'Glass Base, Handle with Care' on its cover.

'Oh dear! The champagne! How are we going to drink it?' Eve exclaimed.

'O ye of little faith,' said Martin settling back into his seat. 'I have thought of everything. Ta-daaa!'

With a flourish, he drew a box out of one of the carrier bags and opened it to show two crystal champagne flutes.

'But there are three of us...'

'Really?' said Martin in mock surprise. 'And I thought you wanted to be alone with me. Ignore the man behind me, he's just one of the servants. No, seriously, Charlie can drink out of the bottle, can't you Charlie. Wouldn't be the first time. Although I don't think he should drink and drive...'

'Do you remember that Pimm's party in June?' Charlie shouted. 'How the mint stank out my fridge. But the ducks went wild after it. I had quite a few of them drinking out of my glass.'

'Ha! Squiffy ducks!' laughed Martin. 'Talking of which, here they come. Batten down the hatches! Women and children first! Your sandwiches or your lives!'

A flotilla of ducks in V-formation were heading towards them, closely followed by two swans.

'Oooh, swans, how lovely,' exclaimed Eve.

'Lovely, nothing!' cried Charlie. 'Pick up that paddle and bash them if they have a go at you. They're nasty things.'

'Seriously,' added Martin, 'do it.'

Eve obeyed their request and sat with the short squat paddle over her knees as she waited for the attack.

'Perhaps it's the music. Put something else on. "Rock and Roll Waltz" should do it. That'll slay 'em.'

The ducks made do with just bobbing a few inches away from the side of the punt, their brown beady eyes blank with passive avarice. The swans did look terrifyingly large this close to and on the same level.

'Those beaks can give you a nasty peck,' said Charlie helpfully.

'Let's get them drunk on champagne!' cried Martin.

To Eve's horror Martin shook the champagne bottle up and down, popped out the cork and sprayed the champagne at the swans like a mini water cannon, laughing wildly. Both Eve and Charlie cried out their protests. But it did disperse the birds.

'Ha, they've swanned off! Don't worry, it's all froth,' said Martin sitting down again. 'There'll be enough left for us. Eve, hold the glasses.'

It was now time for the cakes. But just as Eve was about to open the box she felt gigantic spots of rain, plopping like liquid bullets on her arms and face. Martin quickly opened the umbrella and held it over her.

'It's alright for you two,' moaned Charlie.

'You're getting wet any way,' said Martin. 'All that sweat.'

'Too true,' said Charlie and pulled off his t-shirt.

Fortunately Eve was opening her mouth to take a bite of chocolate cake which disguised the fact that her jaw dropped. Charlie was now topless, his muscles pumped up, and he was literally steaming. He wiped the sweat from his face with the T-shirt and carried on pushing down on the pole.

'They ought to make punting a racing sport at the university,' panted Charlie. 'It is at Tubingen - a German friend told me.'

'Then you could get another Blue,' said Martin, 'to add to your vast collection. What is it now? Rugby, rowing, football and tennis?'

'You're not so bad yourself - fencing, orienteering...'

Eve knew that a 'Blue' was a sort of honour or award received when a student represented the University at a sport. They had passed the university boat houses on the left bank of the river - mostly nineteen-twenties buildings painted white that looked as if they belonged at the seaside. Each one carried its college flag and coat of arms.

'We should be up to Donnington Bridge soon,' said Charlie. 'Do we want to stop there or go on to Iffley Lock?'

'In this weather...' Eve began.

'There she goes again,' protested Martin, 'on about the weather. I haven't read any poetry yet. Your Brideshead experience is not complete.'

'But...'

Martin took out from his jacket pocket a slim red leather volume with 'Alfred Lord Tennyson', decorated with *art nouveau* flowers.

'I think this calls for "The Lady of Shalott".'

'Oh no, not again,' wailed Charlie. 'you do this every time!'

'It's only four pages. Hold the umbrella over me, there's a dear. Now...' And Martin began to read in a slow calm voice, completely different to his frenetic tone so far:

> 'On either side the river lie
> Long fields of barley and of rye,
> That clothe the wold and meet the sky;
> And thro' the field the road runs by

> To many towered Camelot;
> And up and down the people go,
> Gazing where the lilies blow
> Round an island there below,
> The island of Shalott.'

Charlie began to howl like a dog in pain. Eve joined in, despite the fact that she was rather enjoying it. But it was obvious Martin was going to carry on regardless and soon the two of them gave up. Martin did have a splendid reading voice and obviously knew the poem well:

> 'There she weaves by night and day
> A magic web with colours gay.
> She has heard a whisper say,
> A curse is on her if she stay
> To look down to Camelot.
> She knows not what the curse may be,
> And so she weaveth steadily,
> And little other care hath she,
> The Lady of Shalott.'

But after a few more lines, Charlie suddenly cried out:

'Hey, that's a.....! Hand me my binoculars!'

'I cannot believe a man like you is into birdwatching,' said Martin breaking off bad-temperedly. 'You'll be into train-spotting next. I will not be friends with a nerd.'

'Shut up, or you'll be punting - no, make that swimming home.'

Charlie lowered the metal pole into the punt and lodged it under a seat while Martin reluctantly pulled the binoculars out of a bag and handed them to him.

'Damn! I've lost it now,' complained Charlie. 'I bet I won't see another for ages.'

'The only man I know who wastes binoculars spotting real birds,' said Martin. 'Now I can think of some much better uses...'

Martin grabbed the binoculars from Charlie and the two of them tussled good-naturedly for a while. Eve groaned and looked up to heaven. So this was the cream of the country's youth. They were more like over-energetic puppies. Soon she'd be with two steaming idiots.

They stopped when Charlie nearly lost his balance on the now slippery end of the boat.

'Serves you right, you bastard!' cried Martin. 'I've already been mugged by a mad American today, I...'

'Let's go back,' said Charlie. 'It's not going to get any better.'

'Do you mean the weather or Martin?' asked Eve.

'Anyway, I haven't had any champagne yet,' said Charlie petulantly. He jumped into the main body of the punt, making it sway violently, and picked up the champagne bottle for a swig. Martin was still looking around with the binoculars. He focused on Eve:

'My what big eyes you have! Oh, and what big teeth you have! Oh and what big...! No, modesty forbids!'

'Oh shut up!'

He swung round to look at the left-hand bank that had a small tributary of the river flowing into dense woodland and undergrowth.

'Oh, there's a boat down there, an abandoned boat.'

'Whoopee,' said Charlie sarcastically, wiping his mouth off on his arm. 'I'm turning us round. This is crazy.'

'No,' said Martin. 'Let's have a look at this boat. I'm sure I can see some... something purple in it. I think there's something in it.'

'Perhaps it's courting couples again,' said Eve.

'Push over to the shore,' said Martin to Charlie. 'Let's have a closer look.'

'Push over yourself!'

'No, come on, I'm serious. I want to see what it is.'

With an exasperated sigh, Charlie complied and the three students were ferried towards the bank.

As they neared the tributary, Martin, still using the binoculars, suddenly swore loudly and staggered backwards, nearly upsetting the punt.

'What the...!! What the hell are you doing!' shouted Charlie, trying to steady the punt and catching Martin with one arm to stop him rolling back into the water.

'It's a woman...a girl... a woman!' Martin gabbled. He took a deep breath as he stood up and said more slowly:

'And she's either a seriously good actress... or she's seriously dead!'

CHAPTER FOUR

"The river running down
Between its grassy bed
The voices of a thousand birds
That clang above my head
Shall bring me to a sadder dream
When this sad dream is dead."

[Elizabeth Siddal, *A Year and a Day*, 1855-7]

'What?!'
'Are you sure?'
'What are you talking about?'
'You're joking!'
'Let me have a look!'

The exclamations came thick and fast from Eve and Charlie to Martin's astonishing announcement. All three of them were now standing up and peering down to where the abandoned boat lay. Without binoculars all one could see was the boat itself, and that not very well. Eve immediately wondered whether it was Martin's twisted sense of humour dramatising an innocuous situation. Charlie, who knew him better, realised that Martin was genuinely serious for once. So he took the binoculars from him and now he too focused them on the mysterious boat and its alarming occupant.

'You're right,' he said. 'She's slightly propped up; she must be lying on the seats in the middle. She's dressed in purple. Or there's something purple on top of her, with black patterns on it. It looks... it *looks* as if she'd got her hands crossed over her chest, you know, like one of those medieval whatnots - effigies - on a tomb or something!'

'Oh God!' exclaimed Eve. 'Are you sure she's not just asleep? She might have fallen asleep...'

'What - out here in the rain?' said Martin impatiently. 'She'd have to be pretty stupid.'

'Well, some people are stupid enough to go out boating in the rain,' Eve retorted.

'Oh, and I suppose it's rain-therapy for her complexion...!'

Charlie intervened.

'I'll take us down there.' And he took up the metal pole once more, stuck it deep into the mud of the riverbed and swung the punt round at an angle so that they could be manoeuvred down the narrow side stream. But it was not long before he was forced to say:

'We're not going to make it punting. We'll have to paddle. Eve?'

'Isn't there anyone who can help?' said Eve looking around. 'We need to get the police.'

'No,' said Martin, sounding tired, 'as you so aptly pointed out, we are the only idiots on the river. We'll have to go for the police ourselves.'

'Throw me the paddle,' said Charlie. 'No, don't throw it - pass it.'

The paddle was passed to him. Charlie sat down in the punt cross-legged and began to drag the paddle through the water, ducking every so often to avoid the overhanging branches from the dense woodland on each bank. Long grasses reached into the boat, threatening to cut faces on their thick sharp edges.

'I wonder where it leads to,' said Eve,' this bit of the river.'

'The water looks pretty stagnant,' said Charlie. 'It's not really flowing at all. It's probably a dead end.'

Martin raised his eyebrows. 'Need I add, possibly in more ways than one?'

There was silence for a while.

'Wow, there's a lot of undergrowth,' gasped Charlie. 'I'm having a problem making any headway. How on earth did she get down this far?'

'Perhaps she was pushed, to be out of sight,' said Eve.

'Did she paddle or was she pushed?' said Martin rhetorically.

The other two didn't reply. It was hard enough work avoiding the low branches and long grasses and reeds. The smell of rotting vegetation was a shock after the clean air of the main river. Here the water was dark and sludgy with old leaves and mud, like a dark brown mirror in which it was impossible to see a reflection.

If only there were more oars or paddles so that Martin and Eve could have helped in their torturous progress. There were one or two places where it was necessary to lie down completely in order to slide under an obtruding branch of an old tree or avoid being flagellated by some strong prickly weed grown out of all proportion in this isolated spot.

'At last!' cried Martin. 'There's a bank here. We can pull in here, near her boat. The trees aren't so thick.'

'Thank goodness,' sighed Charlie.

'Let's not get too close,' said Eve anxiously, lowering her voice.

'Why not?' said Charlie.

'In case we wake her up?' said Martin. 'Isn't that the whole point?'

'No...' said Eve slowly.

'Do you want me to shout, to see if she's on drugs or something?'

'No, I don't mean that,' said Eve.

They had now lowered their voices to not much above a whisper, as if they were indeed afraid of waking her up.

The two men were frowning at Eve, not understanding at all.

'I mean,' said Eve in a forceful low voice, 'that it might be a murder. And if it is, then we mustn't destroy any evidence. We've got to be very careful.'

'Oh wow, of course.'

'Yes, you're right.'

There was a pause while they all digested this. The punt lodged with a jolt in the bank, about ten yards from the abandoned rowing boat.

'Well,' said Charlie, 'are we getting out? Or will that destroy evidence too?'

'I suppose it would create some,' said Eve. 'Our footprints for a start.'

'She could still be stoned on drugs,' whispered Martin. 'We still haven't seen her face. This is ridiculous.'

He stood up and yelled towards the immobile girl:

'Hello! Excuse me! Are you alright? Can we help you?'

There was silence for a few seconds.

'I think her eyes are open,' said Martin in a softer voice. 'Give me the binoculars.'

Charlie handed them to him. Martin put them up to eyes and focused them. He then said:

'Oh my God...' and lowered them almost immediately.

'*What?!*' cried the other two simultaneously.

'Er...er...well, her eyes are open alright,' said Martin uncertainly. He was breathing hard. His friends hardly dared ask another question. 'Er, in fact they're a bit too open. They look really weird. She's just staring into space. But... but... it doesn't look normal. I mean, it's not normal staring. And there's blood... I think. Like streaks of it, as if the rain's washing it down, like red mascara.'

'Oh God, oh God, it's murder,' said Eve, her voice quavering.

'We don't know yet,' said Charlie quickly. 'It could be suicide. Surely we've got to check whether she's still alive? Couldn't she just be unconscious with her eyes open?'

The other two looked dubious.

'Anyway,' said Charlie, 'we've got to get the police. Regardless. I'll go. I'll take the punt, I'm fastest.'

'I'll come with you!' cried Eve.

'I'm not staying here on my own!' exclaimed Martin.

'Well...,' Charlie hesitated, then said decisively, 'Eve, you stay here with Martin. I'll be quicker on my own.'

'But...,' began Eve.

'We need to leave someone with the body and it's not fair to ask anyone to be on their own,' Charlie decided. 'My phone's in my other jacket. No one has a phone on them? Oh, of course, Martin, it's beneath you. Eve?'

'Er, don't have one for this country yet - sorry.'

'No. Typical. So that means you two here, and me going for the police. Thank goodness the police station's nearby. It should take me a quarter of an hour to get there, five minutes there, quarter of an hour to get back - with reinforcements. So you've only go about half an hour here. Don't worry.'

'You can tell he's a rugby captain, can't you,' said Martin sarcastically, 'a commander of men. He who must be obeyed.' He saluted, then said more seriously, 'So this means Eve and I have got to hop out onto the bank after all. I hope that won't put us in the frame for the murder,' he lowered his voice and looked at the woman's body, 'whoops, sorry, if it is one, I mean.'

'I don't believe this is happening,' gasped Eve, as she allowed Martin to help her out of the punt and onto the shore.

'God, I wish I hadn't eaten that cream cake,' groaned Martin. 'It's all coming back.'

'Don't!'

'I'll be as quick as I can,' called Charlie as he took up the paddle again. 'Start me off with a push, will you?'

'With pleasure,' said Martin grimly, and put his foot on the end of the punt while Eve held onto it. The two of them heaved the punt out of the muddy bank together. They watched Charlie paddle back down the side stream, yelling at him to watch out for the branches every so often, but then he seemed too far away. Eve and Martin still gazed after him in silence until he rounded the bend and a few minutes later was out of sight.

Martin and Eve were both breathing heavily, Eve gulping instead of swallowing, trying to hold back the panic. To distract herself, she said the first thing that came into her mind:

'Martin...'

'Mmmmm?'

'How did you know it was a woman? I mean, from that distance, when you first saw her?'

'I think I know the difference between a man and a woman. Have a look at her - you'll see. You haven't looked at her yet.'

Eve shuddered.

'No, I don't want to,' she said petulantly.

'Then you'll have to take my word for it,' sighed Martin. 'She's lying there, covered in a purple sheet thing with Celtic symbols on it, her hands arranged over her chest - her rather ample chest - and you can see long black hair coming down over her arms. So unless it's a transvestite heavy metal fan wearing a false pair of bazookas, I think it was fair to guess it was a female of the feminine variety!'

'Alright, alright.'

'I think I'll take a closer look...'

'You can't! You mustn't! You'll tamper... interfere with the scene of the crime.'

'No more than the police will!'

'But... but...,' and again Eve lowered her voice for the fateful word, as if it was impolite to mention it in front of the body, 'if it is *murder*, then there could well be the murderer's footprints in the mud on the bank near the boat. If you go fooling around there you'll ruin vital evidence.'

'Fooling around! I have never fooled around in my life. Before you are the dainty feet of the most agile fencing champion the university has seen in many a long year. I will steal over there like a cat! No one will know I've been.'

'Of course they will! The police are not going to thank you, I'm telling you.'

'I know, I know - we've all watched too many cop shows on TV.'

Eve was silent and turned away.

Martin sighed then said: 'Look, as you pointed out, we're creating evidence by just standing here on the bank. So what difference are a few more footprints going to make? I tell you what...'

'My father...' Eve broke in.

Martin was silenced. There was an emotional charge in Eve's voice that took him by surprise. He waited.

'My father ... was ... a cop.'

'Oh.' Martin paused then said, 'Was?'

'He... he's dead.'

'Oh. I'm sorry.'

Eve rubbed her eyes which were still feeling sore. Martin gazed at her back helplessly.

'So, er, you helped him out with cases, an' stuff,' he said.

'Not really. Well, a little bit.' She sniffed loudly. 'He wasn't allowed to tell us much, of course.'

'Oh, of course.'

Martin flicked back his hair and looked at the boat again.

'So are you going to help me with this, or not?'

Eve turned around to face him. Her face looked stricken and vulnerable.

'What do you mean - "help"?'

'Well,' he began slowly, 'it seems to me that we could be waiting here for the police an awfully long time. I mean, I know Charlie's fast and all that, but it could take a while to convince the police that he's not a complete loony, and who knows how long it will take the cops to arrive after that. You know how long it took us to negotiate all these trees and things blocking this bit of the river. We could be here at least another hour or so, *meanwhile* vital evidence could be destroyed - just by the weather, an' whatnot. What if it suddenly chucks it down on the girl and washes all the blood away, for example? Perhaps the lividity an' stuff will be altered and we can help establish time of death by viewing the body now!'

'I can see who's definitely watched too many cop shows.'

'I tell you what. I'll use the binoculars...'

Martin put them up to his eyes and trained them on the ground between them and the boat.

'Oooookay. I can see the mud in detail in front of me. Right up to the boat. Yep. Not a footprint, hoofprint, or any other sort of print in sight. So, Ms Merry, do you think it's permissible for me to walk to the boat?'

Eve tussled with all kinds of opposing emotions inside her. She was angry with Martin, she was angry with herself, she was angry with the murderer, she was angry with... her father?

'Oh, do what the hell you want! You will anyway!'

Martin pretended to reel sideways at the strength of her outburst, then said matter-of-factly:

'You're right, of course. I will.'

He cleared his throat and walked the short distance to where the boat was caught in branches next to the bank. Eve at first watched him but since she could see the body of the dead girl behind him she turned to look resolutely at the trees opposite and tried to focus her mind on something else. She wished she hadn't eaten a cream cake either.

'At least the trees have sheltered her a bit. Oh, we'd better write things down,' said Martin. 'I have a notebook and pen.'

He took them out of a breast pocket and threw them to Eve where they landed in the mud. She picked them up gingerly and tried to shake the mud off. She then took a tissue out of her coat pocket and wiped them with distaste, more for what Martin was asking her to do rather than because of the mud.

Martin was just saying: 'Oh wow, oh wow, oh wow,' as he leaned over the boat.

'Do you want me to write that down?' asked Eve acidly.

Martin ignored her. Eve sighed impatiently, pen at the ready, feeling more like a secretary than a detective.

'Well, she's dead, alright. Looks like strangulation to me.'

'Oh? How come?'

'Marks around her neck, by the looks of it. Red - nasty. Bruising too, of course. Perhaps not just strangulation. There are cuts as well...'

'Don't touch anything!' Eve cried out as it looked as if Martin was about to move something near the victim's throat.

'It's OK, I'm not going to. I just wanted to see her necklace. I think it's a cross... and something else. Oh, yuk, her eyes do look awful! It's a pity I can't close them, but then you'd tell me off. They always close them on TV but I bet they don't in real life. Actually...,' he paused irritatingly, 'I think those are cuts above her eyes - gosh, that sounds like T S Eliot: "*those were pearls that were his eyes*". Oh mega-yuk! Gross!!' he suddenly cried out as he peered at her face.

'What?'

'I don't think she's got any eyelids! They look as if they've been ripped off... I think that's where the blood's come from.' He waved his hand over her eyes.

'What the hell are you doing?' Eve burst out.

'Don't know why I'm bothering,' said Martin. 'It's a check for brain death. Seeing if her pupils change with difference in light. But her pupils are enormous anyway. Obviously brain dead. Eyeballs ruptured, consistent with strangulation. There are cuts on her hands too, probably from when she tried to defend herself.'

'Oh, how horrible. The poor girl.' Waves of nausea began to sweep over Eve. She closed her eyes and began to recite the 'Kyrie Eleison' in a murmur over and over again:

> 'Lord, have mercy,
> Christ, have mercy,
> Lord, have mercy.'

Martin continued, as clinically as possible, his voice obviously strained:

'She has long black hair - looks too dark to be real, probably dyed. Don't worry, I won't make any puns about "dying". Her skin's very pale, but that's hardly surprising. Hard to tell whether she was pretty or not. Probably not. I would say she's...', he looked up at Eve, '...oh, shorter than you, but it's hard to tell in this position. Then again, I don't suppose her height is going to alter before the police get here, so I won't worry about that. Huh! She's wearing platform shoes anyway. Oh! On one foot - the left. The right shoe looks normal. How odd. Mmmmm. Anyway, she's wearing lots of rings, all pretty tasteless arty-farty celtic stuff - the sort of mock-historic ones you get at Past Times. There's a bracelet too - got a cat on it. Don't think it's real silver.'

'Does it matter?' Eve interrupted him. 'I don't think I want to hear all this. Let's just leave it to the police.'

'Good Lord, she's wearing a badge. Yes, I know I shouldn't have moved the covering, but I wanted to see what the badge was. Wow, you're going to love this. It says "Witch Bitch from Hell".'

Eve was so amazed at first she didn't know what to say. She then wondered out loud:

'I wonder if it's her's - or if someone has put it on her.'

'Dunno. Your guess is as good as mine. Anyway, we'd better get cracking and estimate the time of death before she decays anymore.'

'You...! What...! Excuse me?!' exclaimed Eve, hardly able to believe her ears. 'What on earth makes you think that's your job?'

Martin sighed and looked into the distance for a while. He took a step back and sighed again.

'Am I getting carried away? Or should I do this?' he asked no one in particular.

Eve wanted to say: 'You're getting extremely carried away' but didn't dare break the silence. The rain was still dripping off the trees, like a melancholy commentary on events. She shivered and pulled her coat round herself. God, what an awful situation. Then Martin began again, in a quiet matter-of-fact voice, as if deliberately trying to keep calm.

'Let's be rational about this,' he said, ignoring Eve's slight 'huh!'. 'The nearer to the time of death that the body can be examined the better. We've got a much better chance of being accurate than the police who might be another hour. There are crucial signs that we can catch that would give a more accurate time of death than if we wait for the police. And,' he looked up, 'if it chucks it down with rain again, that could ruin quite a few things. We've got a better chance now.'

'How...? What on earth do *you* know about it? What can *you* do?'

'Oh, my mother's heavily into crime,' said Martin blithely. 'She taught me everything I know.'

'What is she? In the Mafia!'

'Well, she *is* a Godmother - but only to my nephews and nieces. No, she's a crime writer. Writes detective fiction. I've read her textbooks on this sort of thing - well, not all of them, but enough on pathology and forensics, that sort of thing. And I help her with her plots. Didn't your father teach *you* anything?'

'Oh God,' groaned Eve, feeling completely out of her depth.

Martin flung back his long and now wet hair and grasped his forehead.

'Now, let's see if I can remember.... Er, there's all sorts of stuff about if the body's been outside for any length of time and the temperature altering the *rigor*, an' all that. What do you think the temperature is out here?'

'I've no idea. Getting frickin' colder all the time.'

'Tut, tut, language! And you training to be a vicar...'

'I am *not!*'

'Alright, alright, just be patient - *she's* got to be,' said Martin, indicating the body.

'I don't believe this,' muttered Eve, 'I don't believe I'm in this.'

'So,' said Martin, biting his lips and taking another step towards the body. He looked nervous as he muttered, 'I think the first thing is bacteria and insects...'

'Oh, gross!'

'Don't worry, I'm not going to look. I wouldn't be able to see them anyway. The bacteria will be at work on the inside - enzymes and whatnot - starting to... well, yes, we probably don't need to go into detail on that. And flies will have been laying eggs in her mouth, nose and eyes...'

Eve let out an inarticulate cry of protect and disgust.

'Yes, I couldn't agree more,' said Martin, 'but it is very clever, don't you think? The way insects know - within *ten minutes* of the death - that it's, er, feeding time. And I think it's about twelve hour's later when the maggots hatch... Well, yes, we probably don't need to go into that either. I'm certainly not examining her for maggots, not in this jacket. Anyway, amazing ecosystem, don't you think? Your God was very clever when he designed it all - programmed us to self-destruct so we wouldn't litter the place up.'

'*My* God'? I think 'ashes to ashes, dust to dust' sounds a bit more dignified.'

Martin sighed again and grimaced at the body.

'Gosh, I'm not very good at this. I should be looking for signs of how far the blood's settling in the lower part of the body. The blood will be more purple by now 'cos of lack of oxygen, of course. Em, of course if I were really brave, I'd feel her face and jaw for signs of *rigor*, but... Well, I'm certainly not going to feel her neck!'

'Good grief, you're not going to touch her!'

'I *ought* to... to try and establish...' Martin leant over the boat, put out three fingers and gingerly prodded her cheeks and jaw.

'I don't believe you're doing this!' cried Eve.

Martin stood up quickly and said even more quickly: '*Rigor* begins in the small muscles about four hours after death, possibly sooner if she struggled. It's now...' he looked at his watch, '10.50 am. Take off four hours - come on, quickly, quickly...'

'Er, er, 6.50!'

'Yes, so ten to seven. Take off a bit for the struggle and you get... oh, oh, add it on to the time, er, - just after seven o'clock this morning!'

'Or it could be over thirty hours ago,' said Eve, carried away by Martin's excitement. 'What if the *rigor*'s now fading?'

'But it would end in the big muscles, not the face. No,' said Martin decisively, 'she was killed just after seven o'clock this morning.' He suddenly felt in his jacket pocket. Eve wondered what on earth he was going to do now. Was he going to whip out a scalpel?

Fortunately it was only a university diary. He opened it at the blue ribbon marker.

'Was it light enough? Was it light enough? YES! Sun rise, Saturday the seventh of October - 7.10am!' Martin closed the diary triumphantly, looking flushed. He then wobbled uncertainly, sucked in through his teeth and held his stomach.

'Are you alright?' asked Eve anxiously, stepping towards him.

'Em, no. Actually... I think I'm about to ruin the evidence for sure...'

The last few words were said in a gasp as Martin ran into the woods behind him. Soon retching sounds could be heard. Eve looked around her. Should she follow him? She looked down at the notepad. She hadn't written a thing.

After a few more moments, she could hear Martin swearing to himself. He then shouted in a groan:

'God, I'd forgotten how bad champagne-flavoured vomit tasted!'

'Do you need any help?' Eve called out unwillingly.

'Wow, no,' said Martin, suddenly in a different tone. 'Only if you've got a torch.'

Eve wondered what on earth he was talking about.

'Of course I don't have a torch.'

'Never mind,' came back Martin's excited voice. 'Just come and look at this!'

CHAPTER FIVE

"For these last five or six days, we have had regularly a Boat on the Isis, and explored all the streams about, which are more in number than your eyelashes."

[John Keats writing to J H Reynolds, 21 September 1817]

"Love bites and stings me through, to see
Her keen face made of sunken bones.
Her worn-off eyelids madden me,
That were shot through with purple once."

[Algernon Charles Swinburne, *The Leper*, 1866]

I assume you're not asking me to look at the vomit!' Eve yelled through the trees.

'Only if you desperately want to,' Martin's voice floated back. 'By the way, have you got a spare handkerchief? I've made a bit of a mess.'

'Um, I have some tissues. Will that do?'

'Yes, fine. Come in here and look at what I've found. Perhaps you can make sense of it.'

Eve reluctantly began to part the branches of the trees near her, trying to find a path for her feet amongst the grass and bracken that wasn't too muddy. She could see Martin's reddish hair a few feet away when he yelled:

'Watch it! That's where I had my accident.'

She had only avoided treading in the mess by inches. Martin was now standing a couple of feet further away, holding onto a tree and looking down with intense interest.

'Do you have those binoculars?' he asked.

'Oh! Um, no! I don't know... where did I put them? Did you have them last?'

'Never mind. Throw me a tissue and come and look over here.'

He did need the tissues. There were some rather unpleasant stains on his waistcoat and coat sleeve. As he wiped them off, he pointed down to the forest floor another couple of feet away.

'What do you think of that, or should I say, those?'

'I don't know,' said Eve slowly, squinting in the odd mixture of gloom and sunlight. 'What do you think?'

They were looking at some tracks in the mud that wound around the trees, as if some peculiar object had gone down to or away from the river. But the marks were like nothing the two students had ever seen before.

'They can't be footprints, surely,' said Eve. 'Has something fairly thin been dragged down there? Has the body been dragged?'

'I don't know. Did the body have enough mud on her shoes?' (It now seemed safer just to call the dead girl 'the body'). 'But look! There and there!' Martin pointed with his finger. He went one pace closer and squatted down. 'These look like heel prints. It does look like the back of someone's foot to me. But where's the front of the foot?' His voice trailed off as he tried to find what he was looking for.

'If the body was dragged,' said Eve, 'then perhaps it makes sense that you only get her heel marks every so often, if she was being dragged backwards.'

'Hmmm. Digging her heels in, as it were.'

'If it had been her walking we would certainly have been able to tell. You said she had one platform shoe and another that looked ordinary.'

'Good God!' Martin suddenly exclaimed. 'That reminds me! I think I might know who she is!'

'Oh no, you're kidding! That's terrible.' Then after a pause, Eve added, 'Who?'

'I'm not sure,' said Martin, standing up and flicking his hair back. 'I think she might be at my college.'

'No! But who is she, then?'

Martin shook his head, frowning: 'I can't remember her name, damn it. But there was a girl at my college last year who had a bit of a limp, one built-up shoe. She tried to hide it with long skirts but I noticed it one day when she was going up the stairs ahead of me. I thought 'How ridiculous these platform shoes are' then I noticed she was only wearing one. Yes! I bet it was her! She had long black hair! Oh my God.'

'But you can't remember her name?' Eve asked eagerly.

'No, no. It'll come back to me. I'll be able to check with people at King's, someone's bound to know her.'

'So you didn't recognise her out there?'

'Of course not! She's fuc -, *bleep* unrecognisable! Don't be stupid!'

Eve bit her lip. She didn't know whether he was annoyed with her or with himself for not knowing who the girl was.

But now Martin had squatted down again and was saying meditatively, 'There *was* mud on the shoes... but perhaps not enough. Even so, if she'd been dragged, her heels wouldn't have made marks like that. No. Those are very definite prints. It must have been someone walking. But where's the rest of the footprint? Surely someone wasn't just walking around on their heels?'

He stood up and experimented with his own shoes, leaning back on his left foot and digging his heel in.

'Oh great,' said Eve, looking behind her in dismay at the many other footprints they had added, 'we've really messed up the scene of crime for the police.'

'They've got to expect it,' said Martin. 'They'll only do the same when they come clodhopping in here. They're welcome to take my vomit away in a bag for evidence if they want.'

Eve tutted, and then regretted it when she got an even more supercilious glance from Martin.

'I wonder how long the police will be?' she said anxiously.

'Depends if they come by land or water, I suppose.'

'How can you get here by land?'

'Oh, via Donnington Bridge, I would think. There are steps from the bridge down to the side of the river and a sort of towpath. Then you get to the other side of these trees and it might be a bit more difficult.'

'How thick is this bit of the woods, forest - whatever it is?'

'How should I know? Not very, I wouldn't think, 'cos it wouldn't be many more minutes before we would have arrived at Donnington Bridge in the punt.'

'I wonder... I wonder...'

'What?'

'I wonder where the murderer came from...'

'By land or sea? Yes. Hey, that should be a poem.

'Where did the murderer come from?

Was it by land or by sea?

And what did he use for a weapon?

Whatever it was, don't ask me.'

'Bravo,' said Eve. Then, 'What do you think those thin marks are?'

'You read my mind. I have no idea. I only wish I did.'

They were referring to much thinner lines here and there gouged out of the mud, again as if something may have been dragged along the ground but at an angle to the main ruts, as if someone had taken a pencil and run it along the ground for the sheer hell of it here and there.

Martin walked a bit further to the right, ignoring Eve's remarks to be careful.

'Look!' he said. 'Now *that's* a bit more like a footprint.'

Eve joined him and looked at where he was pointing.

'Shouldn't you be sniffing the ground like a bloodhound,' she said sarcastically, then, 'Oh, you're right. Yes, but an incredibly *long* footprint, if it is one. Who has feet that long? It looks like about two feet, not one.'

'Damn! What the hell is it, then?'

Eve shrugged.

Martin looked at her appealingly.

'I don't suppose you'd let me follow the tracks to see where they lead..?

'You're not leaving me on my own here!'

Martin sighed. 'Oh well, that's that then.'

'What if the murderer's still around? He could be anywhere,' said Eve nervously, looking around at the trees.

'Oh yeah, right. As if the killer's still going to be here four hours after the crime. No one in their right mind would be.'

'Well, he wouldn't be in his right mind...'

'How do you know it's a "he"?'

'Murderers have been known to return to the scene of the crime. It has a sort of sick fascination for them. Sometimes they even pretend to find the body.'

'Oh, so that means it's one of us! Or are you saying Charlie did the dirty deed before he called on me this morning?' Martin was teasing her again.

Just then there was a noise in the distance. There was some activity a few hundred yards away in the wood, the sound of twigs snapping and feet disturbing foliage. Eve automatically clung to Martin's sleeve.

'Ow!' he exclaimed as she pinched his arm.

'Sssshhhh.'

They waited silently as the noise grew closer.

Eve then gesticulated and mouthed: 'Let's go back to the body.'

Martin nodded and the two of them stealthily picked their way through the trees and bracken back to where they began by the river's edge. But the noise of their pursuer grew louder with each step, followed by what sounded like electronic interference and muted voices.

Eve breathed deeply in relief. That was a sound she knew well and it was one that spelled safety. It was a police radio.

As if they were being caught in a well-planned pincer movement, at that moment the sound of motor-boats coming up river added to Eve's sense of relief. She then looked at her hands and sniffed. One of them had obviously gripped Martin's jacket where he'd had his 'accident'.

'Yo!' cried Martin. 'Here's our Charlie with the cavalry!'

The boats had to be very careful chugging down the narrow side stream. Even at minimum speed they were still causing enough waves and disturbance to the water to make the murdered girl's boat bob up and down dangerously. One of her arms slid down slightly from off her chest, making Eve cry out and wave her arms at the police boats to stop them coming any further.

'Oh, stop, stop! Charlie, get them to stop! Don't come down any further!'

Now Martin joined in.

'You'll have to get out there. Get out where you are and walk the rest if you can.'

But this was easier said than done. The area of the wood where Eve and Martin stood was only accessible by much smaller boats and to try and walk there on foot meant clinging to the trees on the bank like apes in a most undignified fashion and easing one's way along the slippery bank very slowly. This three of the police officers now did. Eve was disappointed to see that Charlie stayed safely in the first boat. Although he'd probably had enough physical exertion for one day.

The crunching of bracken behind them stopped as two police officers with dogs and another older man emerged from among the trees. The older man with faded brown hair and a brown waxed cotton jacket stood with his hands on his hips and surveyed the scene with a frown that looked permanent.

'Did you find the body?' he said as he marched briskly up to Eve and Martin as they turned to face him. Then:

'Good God! Eve! What... what are you doing here?'

'Oh!' said Eve. 'Oh, it's you! Yes, of course, it would be you. Well, not *of course*,' she gabbled, 'but I suppose it would be, except I'd forgotten it would be, and... wow..., uh,' she looked round quickly at Martin and thought an explanation was in order, 'yes, um, hello, *Uncle* Andy.'

And Eve had the pleasure of seeing Martin speechless.

CHAPTER SIX

"'ONCE, IT WAS NOTHING BUT SAILING,' SAID THE RAT. 'THEN HE TIRED OF THAT AND TOOK TO PUNTING. NOTHING WOULD PLEASE HIM BUT TO PUNT ALL DAY AND EVERY DAY, AND A NICE MESS HE MADE OF IT.'"

[KENNETH GRAHAME, *WIND IN THE WILLOWS*, 1908]

'Uh, Martin, this is Detective Inspector Andy Andrews,' said Eve, as the two men shook hands. 'He's not really my uncle, he's an honorary one. He knew my mother – my *English* mother – they grew up together. And he worked with my father at one point.'

'Yes, we trained together on a very memorable course with the Boston Police Department,' said DI Andrews with an icy smile.

'And, Uncle Andrew, this is - uh, sorry I can't remember your full name,' Eve apologised to Martin.

'Oh, don't worry, Martin Massey will do. Pleased to meet you, sir. I think we've found some stuff that will be of interest to you.'

'Really?' said Andy Andrews, still with the glacial smile. 'Well, first things first. You need to get together with my sergeant and tell him everything you know.' Andrews then broke off and yelled at the police officers in the two boats: 'Hey, get Nigel down here first, will you? We can't start without him!'

'I'm afraid we tramped around the scene of crime quite a bit,' said Eve nervously. 'We did have a good look at the body - well, Martin did...'

'We estimate the time of death at about seven o'clock this morning - well, between seven and seven thirty!' Martin butted in eagerly.

Andy Andrews eyebrows shot up. Eve's heart sank.

'*Gavin!*' Andrews yelled to one of his officers. 'Get over here!'

'Yes, boss,' came back the breathless reply from one of the men who was negotiating the muddiest part of the bank. With less than simian grace, he swung himself over to where Eve, Martin and Andrews were standing. His green waxed cotton jacket was scratched in a couple of places from the branches as was his face.

'Bloody 'ell,' he said, 'I couldn't do that every day!'

'Eve and Martin - Detective Sergeant Gavin Woolston,' said DI Andrews, making the introductions. 'And this is Eve Merry and Martin Massey. Take Martin's initial statement, will you? Eve, come over here with me.'

Two officers were already taping off the scene around the body with blue and white sticky tape, although with some difficulty because of the trees and the limited space. On the other side, the police launches had now backed away and two rowing boats were coming down, bringing men and women loaded down with all sorts of efficient-looking bags and equipment.

'Morning, Nigel,' said Andrews to one man in the first boat. 'Don't say it was murder getting here. We need photos taking as soon as poss., of course, before it chucks it down. Oh, we're going to need better lighting as well, especially for the wooded bit. And our wonderful soco is here! Good morning Susanne, how's the baby today?'

'She's fine, sir,' smiled a pretty dark-haired woman as she was helped out of the boat. 'Gosh, not much room to manoeuvre here, is there? We'll soon be crammed here like sardines.'

'I'll leave you to get changed,' said Andrews. 'There were three people found the body, so we're talking to them now. We really need the scene covered over as soon as possible, but how we're going to stick a tent in the water, I've no idea!'

'When I've done my stuff we can move the boat further onto the bank, no problem.'

'That'll be great. I don't want to move her any more that we have to at this point.'

'Of course not.'

Andrews manoeuvred Eve to one side as Susanne and a sidekick put on their white all-over suits, gloves and shoe coverings before they ventured beyond the sticky tape.

'She's right about there not being much room here,' said DI Andrews with a weak smile to Eve. 'Hold on, where are those two going?'

He was referring to the fact that Martin and DS Woolston were disappearing into the woods followed by another officer.

'Oh, Martin's probably showing him the footprints.'

'Footprints, eh? You have been busy!'

Eve took a deep breath and told her 'uncle' everything they had seen and found so far. Even though she had taken no notes, she found she could recite it perfectly - how they first saw the victim, what she was wearing, her physical appearance and the slight onset of *rigor mortis*, the unusual shoes and that she may be a student from Martin's college, and then the strange prints and markings in the mud in the woods. Eve carefully avoided drawing any conclusions from any of the evidence as DI Andrews would just want the bare empirical facts. It wasn't up to her to tell him what to make of them.

DS Woolston was now approaching them.

'We've got a lot of work to do in the wood, boss,' he said. 'Gonna need quite a team.' When closer he then added to Eve, 'Your friend can't 'arf talk,' indicating Martin with a jerk of the head.

Eve almost said 'He's not my friend' but thought that would sound ungracious. She dreaded to think what DS Woolston had been subjected to. But he seemed a friendly enough guy. He could take it in his stride.

Eve then sneezed, loudly, three times.

'Oh dear,' said Andrews, 'we mustn't keep you out here any longer. Do your statements at the station, it's slightly cosier there than here. Gavin, we need to get these poor people out of here, they've been standing around in the wet long enough. See to it, will you?'

'Right, boss.'

Gavin indicated for Eve and Martin to follow him to the back where the now empty row boats were docked.

At first Eve thought her 'uncle' was going to ignore her and not even say goodbye, but as they pulled away from the bank, Andrews suddenly turned round as if he'd forgotten something and yelled:

'Oh, Eve! Dinner! Maggie will be in touch!'

They both waved to each other and Eve and Martin were taken to where the motor launches were waiting. The whole side stream had now been sealed off by the police and they had to wait while their names were taken before they could leave. With great relief Eve was helped onto the motor boat by Charlie who had been there all the time. It was all she could do not to fling herself onto his chest and cry. He did give her a hug and said:

'Poor girl. Are you alright?'

'I... I think so,' she said instead, doing what is known as 'smiling bravely'.

'Wow!' Martin whooped. 'this is amazing. What a start to the term. What a start to the year! Oh, Charlie, you don't know about the footprints! Well, I'll tell you...'

Eve was promptly disentangled from Charlie as he leaned forward to listen to Martin's spiel. Probably the boat ride would have been exciting under normal circumstances, but Eve was far too tired all of a sudden to enjoy it. She just wanted to get away from anything to do with water, especially as she was now spattered by spray and rained on again.

They disembarked at Folly Bridge next to the Head of the River pub, much to the interest of passers-by. DS Woolston then walked Eve and Martin and Charlie up St Aldate's again to the smart sandstone police station.

'You related to the boss, then?' Woolston asked Eve.

'Not really. He's a sort of honorary uncle. He was at school with my mother and trained with my dad - briefly. My mother was English – she grew up round here. I think there was some exchange program between Boston and Oxford police at one point, that's where he met my father. But that was years ago - about eighteen years ago, or even more, before I was born. That's why he's my godfather, but I've hardly seen him in recent years.'

'What's he like when he's not at work,' asked Woolston slyly. 'They tell me when the clock strikes midnight he turns into a human being.'

Martin laughed at this.

'I really don't know,' blustered Eve, not wishing to be indiscreet. 'I haven't seen him that much since he got married. That was about eight years ago.'

'Ah yes, the, er, interesting Maggie,' said Woolston. 'I've met her a couple of times. Right here we are,' he said as they walked up the steps and through the double doors of the station.

'We won't keep you hanging around,' said Woolston. 'I'll get people to see you separately and we'll get it over with as soon as possible. Ah yes, these interview rooms should be free. Sorry they're not very salubrious. I'll get someone to bring you coffee.'

Eve was deposited in a plain square room on the ground floor. Everything in the room seemed brown or beige. The neutral shades for some reason reminded her of her 'uncle'. And Martin had called *her* room 'minimalist'.

Within a minute, a friendly woman police officer popped her head around the door and said:

'You're Eve? Oh good, here's your coffee. I'm Gill, PC Watkins. How are you feeling? I heard what happened. How terrible? You must be stressed out.'

As the officer sat down opposite Eve, Eve tried to speak. Instead, as she clasped the warm coffee mug, she hung her head, her face crumpled and the tears began to softly flow.

When Eve had given her statement, blown her nose a lot, and been to the Ladies' room, she was told to go to the bar where her friend was waiting for her. This was up several flights of stairs. She was led into a surprisingly pleasant large room, like a pub or common room where the police officers went to relax.

She looked around for Charlie but he was no where in sight. She sighed. She would just have to sit down and wait for him.

But as she sat next to one of the windows she looked to the right. There was Martin, sitting watching some children's program on the TV with a female officer. He seemed to be making her laugh a lot. She was large and was flirting. Eve thought she could hardly be Martin's type (assuming he was into women at all, of course, which Eve still wasn't convinced about).

Eve coughed loudly. Martin did glance round and then exclaimed as he saw her.

'Must dash,' he said to the woman who waved a friendly goodbye and carried on watching TV and munching her sandwiches.

Well!' he said and flopped down next to her. 'What a day for the old memoirs.'

'Where's Charlie?' demanded Eve.

'Really, you must get over your obsession with that young man,' said Martin, closer to the mark than Eve would have liked. 'He went back to the House. Probably ravenous. He said he'd get his bike from St Frideswide's later. Talking of ravenous, shouldn't we have something to eat? I know just the place.'

Eve tried to hide her disappointment that Charlie - the *bleep, bleep, bleep* swine and light of her life - hadn't seen fit to wait for her, so she said:

'Would they give us some food here?'

There was a bar where drinks were being served along with crisps and peanuts at least, possibly hot food too?

'Pub grub!' exclaimed Martin in disgust. 'What do you take me for? I know you come from the Land of Fast Food but that doesn't mean I have to descend to your level. No, I know a much better place. Come on, I'll take you there. Civilisation beckons! They've finished with us here. Unless you want some nuts to keep you going?'

'No, you'll do nicely.'

'Ha, ha. That's right. Adopt a British stiff upper lip under adversity. Although I suppose it's an *English* stiff upper lip really - the Scots and Welsh and Irish aren't known for it....'

Martin gabbled on and Eve had no real choice but to go with him. It was either that or go back to her room and face unpacking. As she thought of the bare room at St Frideswide's she felt very lonely. Oh gosh, what would everyone there say about her being involved in a murder on her very first day! Not exactly an auspicious start.

Martin had now left the common room and was clattering down the stairs with Eve following. As they walked out into the street, he said:

'Let's see, what time is it? About one o'clock. Great, that means a late lunch. I do think they could have at least given us a doughnut in there, don't you? We need sugar. We've been traumatised. But first we need to go to King's - to pick up my car as much as anything else. But I really should check with the porter who that poor girl is. He's bound to know.'

So Martin and Eve walked back towards the river and into the ancient doorway of Martin's college again. The porter's lodge was on the left just as one emerged stooping from the doorway. Martin nipped inside, had a word with the porter, and ran out again, saying, 'I've got it' in an excited voice. 'We must tell the police. Damn!' He thought for a moment, then said: 'Tell you what. You wait here. I'll take a message back to the station with the girl's name, in case they don't know already (although I don't see how they could). Better than just phoning later. Then I'll come back for you and the car.'

'OK,' said Eve feebly as Martin disappeared through the medieval gateway.

Lots more students were around now, milling around with luggage, running up and down the quad, all looking, to Eve, fit and athletic and full of the joys of life. That was not how she was feeling. She would have leaned backwards against the wall if she hadn't been worried about looking like a vagrant. There was a wooden sign in black and white standing right in front of her saying the college was closed to visitors. Did that include her? She was suddenly worried about a tough little man in a bowler hat suddenly grabbing her by the collar and kicking her out into the street.

Just relax, girl! she said to herself. You're getting far too jumpy. This is far too many experiences to be having on your first day in Oxford. You're just tired that's all, and very stressed out, as that woman police officer had pointed out. Eve's nose began to run again. Oh no, that's all I need, she thought. All I need now is for my 'flu to come back and that's me with post-viral syndrome for the rest of term. The last year's been bad enough health-wise. Ever since... well, *then* (meaning when her father died) she'd been susceptible to every bug around. The whole of the last year had been one cold after another, one clammy and shivery bout of 'flu after another. No wonder she'd felt depressed now and again. And cold - she'd been feeling the cold more too. This draughty stone archway wasn't exactly an ideal place to wait either.

Eve was just about to reach a fever pitch of self-pity and resentment against Martin when he reappeared, looking bright and breezy, flinging his hair back in the way that was now starting to annoy Eve intensely.

'Mission accomplished,' he announced. 'Now for much-needed fodder. The car's this way.'

Eve followed Martin through the quadrangle diagonally and then through an archway on the left hand side that led into another quadrangle.

'That's my room,' Martin said, pointing upwards to the left, away from the river. 'I'm at the top on this side. Room 8, Staircase H, if ever you want to visit.'

Eve was tempted to say 'Don't hold your breath'.

'Not such a good room as last year, of course,' Martin was continuing, 'but at least I'm not near the river. Another year of that and I'd've developed pneumonia and galloping rheumatism - if rheumatics can gallop. Although now I do have the disadvantage of what appears to be a complete bastard living downstairs who plays music - if I can call it that - loud enough to rot the brain. We could be in for a trying time. Do you like heavy metal music?'

'*Me?!?*'

'I only asked. You never know nowadays. Beneath that silent chic exterior there could be lurking a rock chick of the first order.'

Eve's mind was boggling so much over being called 'silent' and 'chic' that she couldn't make up a reply. Anyway, they were now out the other side of the second quad (the Sanderson Quad apparently, called 'Sandy' by the students), past a beautiful cloistered area with carved arches and gargoyles and bright red creeper, and into a cobbled courtyard. This looked like the old stabling area for horses and carriages. Eve could imagine immediately what it must have looked like a century ago, bustling with ostlers and stable boys, unloading the new students' trunks, calling to the porters, the horses blowing hard and stamping on the cobbled stone. But now, at the beginning of the twenty first century, all was quiet.

'There she is,' said Martin, 'isn't she a beauty?'

He was pointing to a very old-fashioned mediocre-looking car, dark green with a beige top. A classic Morris apparently, and made in Oxford.

'Oh,' said Eve, who had naively been expecting this rich young man to have a large flashy car. 'Does it work?'

'"*Does it work?*"' Martin said in mock outrage. 'Well, let's see, shall we.'

'Doesn't that say 'PRINCIPAL ONLY' on the wall above it?'

'Oh, he won't be back for days. He's American,' said Martin, as if they were both an explanation for the Principal's absence and that fact that Martin was using his parking space.

Martin got in the car first, apologising for his lack of chivalry as he could only open the passenger door from the inside. It did take several large coughs in protest from the car before it deigned to 'work', but soon Martin was backing it out of the parking space, jiggling over the cobbles, and driving out of another gateway onto a modern gravel driveway. Eve saw a large blob of blu-tack on the dashboard in front of her. Without thinking she was about to pull it off to play with it, when Martin yelled, swerving the car:

'DON'T TOUCH THAT! IT'S THE ONLY THING HOLDING THE CAR TOGETHER!'

CHAPTER SEVEN

"This is a shameful thing for men to lie."

[Tennyson, Morte d'Arthur, 1842]

'Ha, ha, ha,' crowed Martin, 'that scared you, didn't it?! Ha, hahahahahahahaha!'

Eve did not deign to reply but exhaled slowly and fiddled with her safety belt. Of all the childish, stupid...! But no, she wasn't going to humour him by taking the dangling bait.

'Where are we going?' she said as calmly as possible after a couple of minutes as the car sped down Abingdon Road, a continuation of St Aldates.

'South.'

'Yes, but where?'

'It can be a surprise!'

There was silence now for a few more minutes, until Martin starting humming. They went round an island and down another major road. They were obviously leaving the town behind them; the scenery was becoming more countrified by the minute.

'Oh!' Martin suddenly exclaimed. 'You haven't asked me the name of the dead girl yet. Don't you want to know?'

After a pause, Eve replied: 'Not particularly.'

'Really?' said Martin in astonishment. 'That's amazing.'

There was another silence as Eve tried to concentrate on looking out of the window.

'Well, I'm going to tell you anyway. I'm sure I'm right about it. Her name is - was - Feral Harrison...'

'*Ferrell?*'

'Yes, F.E.R.A.L. - you know, like after a wild cat. It wasn't her real name, of course. I think it was a sort of nickname. Anyway, the porter told me her real name was Fern - Fern Harrison. Her room was to be in Sandy, Staircase K, Room 3. So the police will probably be there now.'

Eve frowned hard as she tried to take this in. Feral. How strange.

'I wonder if that's why she had a cat on her bracelet,' she said finally.

'Ah, so you *did* take note of some things. Anyway, I've been remembering more about her. Not that I ever really knew her - with over six hundred people in college you don't get to know everyone. But I can see her in my mind's eye now. I suppose she was quite striking in a not particularly nice way. She did have long black hair that I'm *sure* was dyed - it was far too black to be real. She had a huge bust and wore lots of ethnicy clothes - she wore black a lot. She used to wear things very tight across the bust - her ample bosom - but then long flowing skirts and lots of layers - probably trying to hide the built-up shoe, let's face it. Gosh, poor girl. Anyway, she did wear an awful lot of make-up, you know the sort of white - wow, I almost said *deathly* pallor. Oh, and the most *hideous* false eyelashes!'

'Eyelashes? Oh, yuck.'

'Mmmm. She didn't have *those* when we saw her last.'

'Oh, how revolting! Didn't you say she didn't have any eyelids at all?'

'That's right. Unless she was secreting them about her person somewhere. She did have the most appalling goggling eyes without them. I think that's one of the main reasons I didn't recognise her.'

'So... so... what do you think happened to them?'

'Someone, er, *removed* them I suppose...'

'But *how?* And *why?*'

'How should I know? The falsies were the most awful Liza Minnelli-type whoppers. Perhaps the murderer was a style fascist.'

'Wow.' Eve tried hard to take this in. But it seemed a bizarre detail that she could make nothing of. Then she said:

'Don't murderers sometimes take trophies?'

'What - sports medallions, you mean.'

'Of course not!' said Eve impatiently, not knowing whether Martin was being genuinely stupid or teasing her as usual. 'No, like Jack the Ripper and so on. They used to remove bits of their victims' bodies as trophies and keep them in jars, and things like that.'

'Oh yes, you're right! What was it with the Ripper? It was their wombs, wasn't it?'

'I think so.'

'Well, I'm glad it wasn't that this morning or I think I'd've thrown up more than a cream cake! Wow, this is really getting interesting. But why would anyone want someone's eyelids? Perhaps it was a woman who was jealous of Feral's lovely lashes and so ripped them off in a petulant frenzy! In which case it will be a simple matter to identify the murderer - I've just got to look round college tomorrow and see who turns up to breakfast in Liza Minnelli eyelashes.'

Eve did tut this time. How could Martin joke about something so horrible and so serious?

'Of course,' she said, 'it might not have been the murderer who took them. It could have been someone who came across the, uh, body before us and, well, stole them after the event...'

'Oh, some eyelid fetishist just happens to be walking through the woods at the right moment, finds the dead body, and whips her lids for his collection! Ha!'

'It's possible!' said Eve stoutly. 'We mustn't rule it out!'

'Oh, I suppose you're right. Oh, look, here's our turn-off.'

Eve looked at the road sign but didn't recognise any of the names of the towns or villages. They were out in serious countryside now. Looking at the trees starting their autumn fade with the beginnings of friendly browns, yellows and oranges made Eve suddenly realise how tense she had been holding herself for the past few hours, that her muscles were literally aching with it, she had been controlling herself so tightly.

She sighed and closed her eyes, feeling some of the tension ooze out of her.

But on the blank black canvas of her eyelids appeared Feral Harrison alive, Feral Harrison standing up, Feral Harrison in full splendour, eyelashes and all, an image of Feral Harrison that Eve's imagination must have been working on without her realising it. Eve opened her eyes again quickly and stared at the road ahead.

'Where... where are we?' she said tremulously.

'Don't worry, I'm not kidnapping you. We're in Great Wilton now and I am taking you to one of the foremost eateries in the country. And if you offer to pay I shall be most offended.'

'Oh, I wouldn't dream of it.'

'Here we are,' said Martin and slowed the car down at what looked like the entrance to a mansion. Huge stone pillars marked the beginning of a driveway on the right which Martin turned the car down. A small discreet sign read: LE MANOIR AUX DEUX CHATS - *Chef: M. Jean-Luc Étoile*. The name sounded vaguely familiar to Eve. Didn't he have a TV program on PBS in the States?

The car meandered down a long lush driveway where the trees were inexplicably greener than on the road. The driveway seemed so long, Eve began to wonder if they were ever going to get there. But then, with no warning, the car emerged from among the trees and a beautiful manor house in mellow cotswold stone appeared before them.

'Oh, how lovely!' Eve exclaimed. 'It looks Jacobean, or perhaps even Elizabethan.'

'Mmm, right on both counts. I think it's an Elizabethan foundation with Jacobean stuff added. And it is lovely. I'm surprised my mother didn't snap it up.'

Eve paused, then said: 'Your mother?', hoping this didn't sound too inquisitive. Was Martin's family really that wealthy?

'Oh, she collects places like this,' said Martin breezily. 'But I'm afraid good ol' Jean-Luc pipped her to the post.'

Martin parked the car in an area marked for the purpose at the side of the house and the two students walked up to the front entrance of the house. There were about five other cars in the car park, so the restaurant was either very exclusive or not very full.

'Oh, I hope they let you in in trousers,' said Martin.

'And you're not wearing a tie,' said Eve anxiously.

Martin produced a tie from a jacket pocket: 'Ta-daaa!'

Eve's lip began to tremble against her will and her eyes began to fill up with tears. She turned her face away. How stupid! She couldn't let this upset her, why was she over-reacting? What on earth was the matter with her? But she suddenly felt lonely and isolated and at the mercy of a lunatic who was putting her in an impossible situation that she hadn't asked for.

'It's alright, I'll vouch for you,' said Martin cheerfully. 'Eve? Eve? Don't turn away. What's the matter? Oh gosh! You're crying! Oh no. I'm only joking.' His voice became suddenly softer. 'Take no notice of me. I'm only joking. Of course they'll let you in.'

He put one arm round her and felt in another pocket of his jacket.

'I know I've got a hankie somewhere. Oh no, I used it when I was sick! It's probably in a plastic bag at the police station, marked 'Evidence' by now!'

But Eve pulled herself away. 'I...I....I want to go home!'

'Look, I'll cover my jacket in sick stains again - then they won't let me in either! No, look, I'm sure it will be OK. They don't mind women wearing trousers. I was only joking. We don't have to go here. We can go to McDonald's if you like.'

But this seemed to make Eve cry again. She didn't know why. It was all against her will. She felt powerless and stupid. How dare Martin imply that McDonald's was more her style!

'Oh dear, that wasn't the right thing to say either, was it. Look, there are people staring at us out of the window. They must think we've just had an awful lovers' tiff. Go on, slap me - make it look realistic! Then I'll burst into tears, throw the car keys at you and go off in a huff! Go on, it'll be fun!'

Eve wiped her eyes and took a few deep breaths.

'I'm sorry,' she said quietly. 'I don't know what's happening to me. I've been on a plane all night and I'm in a new country and I've had 'flu and... and...'

'Yes, I know, I know the rest,' said Martin soothingly. 'That's why we need to eat. You're exhausted. *I'm* exhausted. Don't let my drivelling *bonhomie* fool you - I'm fit to drop. All I want to do is collapse into one of Jean-Luc's well-upholstered seats and eat the equivalent of a sofa - or here, probably a *chaise longue*.'

'I'm sorry,' said Eve sounding every bit as tired as she felt. 'You're hungry. You need to eat. I'm being selfish. Let's go in.'

'Whoopee! I triumph!' cried Martin, and grabbed her hand and led her up the steps to the imposing front door.

Inside the lobby there was soothing violin music playing, piped from somewhere up above. A smartly dressed man inquired after their health, took Martin's name and then their coats. Fortunately one did not have to book ahead for lunch, so they were alright. The warm calm atmosphere was very relaxing. There was a huge fire in an ornately carved fireplace, the carpet was thick and plush and there was highly polished antique furniture arranged tastefully around the room. Eve was very impressed by two large glass cabinets - one full of yellow and green floral china, the other an arrangement of delicate ivory figures.

Martin was speaking to the waiter in French who was leading them to their table. Several other tables were occupied by well-dressed people talking quietly and drinking. Eve tried not to think about what she looked like by this point in a horrendous day and the fact that she was no doubt the only person there in jeans. Another waiter came and gave them the Menu and the Wine List. Martin knew what he wanted without even looking.

While Eve looked at the Menu, Martin looked at her.

He decided that she must be almost the same height as him - so perhaps she's five eight or even five nine. Tall for a woman, anyway. The right height for a model. Slim to the extent of being almost too thin. Right for a model again. Her skin is olive or sallow - hard to tell when she's so wiped out. If she's a bit tanned from the summer then she's very pale underneath - looks rather ill, in fact. *Very* dark brown hair, almost black, in unruly wispy curls as if she can't decide what hairstyle to have. Shortish at the moment, but hard to tell if it's a short cut growing out or a longer cut where the hairdresser got carried away. She frowns and narrows her eyes a lot as if she can't focus very well - dodgy lenses? Nose - a strange upturned knobbly shape that defies description and can look anything from slim and cute to unfortunate depending on the angle of the viewer. Mmmm, front teeth very slightly prominent (that she sucks when she's nervous or daydreaming), again cute or not so, depending on Eve's expression. Unusual for an American not to have perfect teeth. Perhaps it was the English mother's influence. Oh, but her eyes are gorgeous! Just the right shade of brown with soft dark lashes - just like Oscar, my spaniel, thought Martin. Pity about her clothes. She'd look great in high heels. Those thick soled boots look too heavy for such slim legs, as if they'd break...

Eve was sucking her teeth and frowning over the menu. How could food cost this much?! She would be forever in Martin's debt if she let him treat her. Then again, she certainly couldn't afford it herself and it was too late to get out of it now. Oh well, the rich so-and-so could afford it. A bit of redistribution of wealth won't do him any harm. Although unfortunately it would only be redistributed into the pocket of Jean-Luc Étoile, who's probably rich enough already.

'OK, I'm ready,' she said nervously, as if checking in for a parachute jump.

But she had spoken before she realised Jean-Luc himself was walking up behind her. His silent shoes on the thick carpet gave no warning and so when the chef greeted Martin in enthusiastic French like an old friend, Eve yelped in surprise. As Jean-Luc held her shoulder in apology, Eve cringed in embarrassment which unfortunately also looked like fear.

'*Ne faites pas attention à elle,*' Martin said. '*Elle est paranoiaque!*'

The two of them joked about her reaction for a while. Eve felt the eyes of the entire restaurant upon her.

'*Excusez moi,*' she said quietly, '*mais je... je suis trop fatiguée de parler à ce moment.*'

'Well, who would have guessed it,' said Martin, 'There's the High School French making a showing.'

'You are ready to order, mam'selle?' asked M. Étoile. 'Let me see if I can guess what M. Martin wants. You and your father - you are so similar!'

'God, don't say that,' complained Martin. 'I'll see if I can surprise you.'

Martin duly ordered a *Mosaique de Gibiers aux Noisettes et Champignons Sauvages* (Terrine of fillets of Venison, Teal, Pigeon and Pheasant, wrapped in a mousse of their own livers, studded with Wild Mushrooms and Hazelnuts) followed by *Papillotte de Rouget et Dorade aux Petits Legumes* (Fillets of Red Mullet and Sea Bream with Vegetables, scented with Provencal herbs, baked in a paper parcel). Eve was determined to be different. She chose what she hoped was a more modest *'Potage de Cresson au Citron Vert'* (Peppery Watercress Soup with Lime) as *hors d'oeuvres* and then said she would go straight on to dessert without a main course, despite Martin saying she was trying to make him look like a pig.

After a bit more laughing and joking, Jean-Luc went to honour another table with his presence.

'You come here with your father, then?' said Eve, to make conversation.

'Well done, Sherlock! Yes, the old man drags me out here from the sweat of my labours every so often. At least once a term anyway. It's only because he likes it so much. I think he flies out here with guests quite a lot.'

'Flies?'

'Yes, there's a helipad out back. It's only 'bout half an hour from the centre of London, sometimes only twenty minutes.'

'What does he do in London?'

'Oh, something boring in the civil service. You really don't want to know, believe me. But I suppose Westminster's a handy place to work.'

There was silence for a while. Martin was frowning and gazing into the distance, looking as if he might break out into a whistle any moment. Eve felt she should make conversation again fast.

'And...and your mother writes books.'

'What? Oh, yes.'

'I...I don't think I've heard of her. What's her first name?'

'Oh, she doesn't use her real name. Her *real* first name is Katherine, but her pseudonym is her middle name and single surname - Seraphina Hussey, if you must know.'

'Oh!' cried Eve. 'Oh, I love her! I've read all of hers - *Hangman at Holly Cottage, Murder at Marsh End, Knives at Nightingale Nook*! Doesn't she base them all on real places? I'm sure I read an article that said that.'

Martin pursed his lips and nodded. 'Yes. I wonder what she'd call our little murder? I must think of a title. Yes, it would no doubt be "Murder in Michaelmas", since it's Michaelmas Term. She goes for alliteration in a big way - unfortunately.'

'Doesn't she buy a new place with the proceeds of each book and improve it and have it as a hotel?'

'Yes. Interior design is her thing really.'

'Oh yes, I read that too. So people can stay at the places she uses for each book and play murder games there. That's a good idea.' It then occurred to Eve: 'Oh, so when you said your mother wanted *this* place, you meant she wanted to buy this for one of her stories and base a murder here? Wow! But Jean-Luc beat her to it.'

'It was too big anyway, and too expensive, with not enough rooms. To make ends meet, it really has to be small but with a lot of rooms to pack 'em in - a difficult combination.'

'I think I saw an article of her at home....' Eve then fell silent. Perhaps she shouldn't go on. She could remember the recent article, which had made a big impression on her as she was contemplating her move to England. A large spread in a women's magazine. The stunning country home of the successful author, - Lakeland Massey in the English Cheshire countryside. An amazing eighteenth century mansion with its own lake and woodlands in acres and acres. The successful authoress, Lady Katherine - successful in everything except love, separated from a husband who lives and works in London - Sir Gerard. Two children at university - what was it... Xanthe? And of course...

Martin had taken out his soiled notebook and was frowning. He was now writing a list.

'We need to find out who knew Feral well,' he said as if Eve had never spoken of his mother. 'Who were her friends? I can question her tutor, and we need to know if she had a boyfriend - or girlfriend, I suppose, if she was that way inclined. What societies was she in? Where did she hang out? Who had a motive for her murder?'

'But...but the police will do all that,' said Eve lamely.

'Why should they have all the fun? Anyway, you can be useful in that respect. You can pump your uncle for information to help us...'

'I am not pumping my uncle!'

'It's a new rap song, didn't you know?' Martin broke out in a hip-hop beat, singing 'pump your uncle' over and over again with electronic backing.

'Anyway, he's not my uncle,' protested Eve. 'It would drive him crazy to have us interfering. The police hate amateurs getting involved. Don't even think about it.'

'But we can do so much they can't! People will open up to us in a way they won't with the police, especially as we found the body...'

'Oh, don't,' said Eve, holding her stomach.

At that moment their food was brought to the table. Martin tucked into his straight away. Eve just looked at hers. They didn't speak until Martin had finished.

'Thank God,' he said. 'I needed that. Think yourself lucky you didn't throw up earlier. At least you don't have a completely empty stomach. Don't you want that?'

'I don't know. I feel incredibly hungry - ravenous. But the thought of actually eating food makes me feel sick.'

'I know. I feel like that every time I see a college meal. But it doesn't stop me eating. Come on. You've got to have something inside you. I'm not carrying you home.'

Eve began reluctantly to spoon up her soup.

'Come on,' urged Martin. 'I can't have my next course until you finish. Oh, damn it, I'll break with convention and have my main course now, since you're abstaining.'

He motioned for a waiter to bring his next course. They continued in silence - Eve trying to chew the bread rolls and swallow the wildly expensive soup in front of her and Martin sucking on his pen and jotting down notes in between mouthfuls of staggeringly expensive fish. Every so often he would throw back his hair and Eve would cringe. But she did reflect on the fact that Martin now seemed relatively normal to her now. He must have been... *exaggerating* himself when they first met earlier on in the day, trying to make an impression, living up to Charlie's introduction of him as the great actor. Huh - Charlie! What a waste of space he'd turned out to be. Just when Eve needed him most, he'd beetled back to his college at the slightest excuse! Although he had been very good at getting the police quickly. Maybe he was very tired after that second punt in such extreme conditions. She shouldn't be too hard on him. Although it was mean, leaving her in the tender clutches of his eccentric friend.

Another attempt on Martin's part to persuade her to play amateur detective failed and the two students ordered dessert. Martin had *Feuillantines Caramélisées aux Pommes, Crème aux Gousses de Vanille* (Leaves of caramelized Craquelin and acidulated Apples served with Vanilla Custard) and Eve manfully finished off a *Fruit Défendu* (Forbidden Fruit - a poached white Peach set on an Iced Parfait, imprisoned in a Cage of Blonde Caramel).

There was a ruminative silence until Martin called for the bill. He doesn't have to worry about using a credit card, of course, thought Eve maliciously - thinks he can do anything he wants, just 'cos he's rich. And living in a gorgeous place like Lakeland Massey! That's too lucky for words. There's no justice in the world.

On the way home in the car, Eve closed her sore eyes, pretending she was asleep. She really couldn't talk any more. And she had no intention of answering any more questions about her 'uncle' and certainly not her father. Martin had already come dangerously close to asking about... well, she didn't even want to think about it. It had already been a hell of a day.

They arrived at St Frideswide's. Eve looked at her watch. It was only four o'clock in the afternoon. She could hardly believe so much had happened since her arrival at the same place that morning. It seemed so long ago already.

She said a curt 'Thanks' to Martin as she undid her safety belt and tried to open the car door. But Martin caught her arm and said:

'I've been thinking about this for hours. I must read it before you go.'

And he took out of his jacket pocket the copy of Tennyson he had read from on the river only a few hours ago. He now read from 'In Memoriam', Tennyson mourning for his dead friend Arthur Hallam:

> 'Oh yet we trust that somehow good
> Will be the final goal of ill,
> To pangs of nature, sins of will,
> Defects of doubt, and taints of blood;
>
> That nothing walks with aimless feet;
> That not one life shall be destroyed,
> Or cast as rubbish to the void,
> When God hath made the pile complete;
>
> That not a worm is cloven in vain;
> That not a moth with vain desire
> Is shrivelled in a fruitless fire,
> Or but subserves another's gain.
>
> Behold, we know not anything;
> I can but trust that good shall fall
> At last - far off - at last, to all,
> And every winter change to spring.
>
> So runs my dream: but what am I?
> An infant crying in the night:
> An infant crying for the light:
> And with no language but a cry.'

'Makes you think, doesn't it,' he ended quietly.

'Mmmm. Yes.' Eve's voice sounded distant. 'Thanks.'

Eve struggled with the car door handle. Martin had to lean over and help her. She drew herself out of the car with an effort, feeling like an old woman. With a slight wave of his hand Martin pulled away. Eve did not look round but wearily trudged to the main door of St Frideswide's, but this time she had her own key to open the door.

But before Martin's car had left the college grounds, he stopped and wound down the window.

'Here,' he cried, 'you'd better have these!'

He threw a bouquet of flowers through the air. Eve automatically caught it. They were the flowers Martin had meant, for some reason, to throw to the ducks. She waved them as Martin pulled away.

As she trailed through the corridors up to her room again, Eve ignored all attempts by people there she'd never met before to say hello. She just wanted to crash on her bed and pretend the day had never happened.

As she let herself into her room, there was music pouring from the room next door. Someone was playing Rod Stewart singing 'The First Cut is the Deepest'.

CHAPTER EIGHT

"'Sir, if hit please you, woll ye go wyth me hereby into a chapel, that we may gyff lovynge to God?'"

[Sir Thomas Malory, *Le Morte Darthur*, 1485]

"There is a mystery about this which stimulates the imagination; where there is no imagination there is no horror."

[Arthur Conan Doyle, *A Study in Scarlet*, 1887]

Good morning,' said the smiling woman at the front of St Frideswide's Chapel, 'and welcome to our first official service of the year - Morning Prayer. For our liturgy we will be using Common Worship and for our hymns *Songs and Hymns of Fellowship* or the words will be on the overhead screen. We will begin by singing....'

Eve was sitting in a pew near the back of the chapel. She wondered how many of those around her were also first years. At least the instructions were clear so she didn't have to look like a newcomer. The woman at the front was dressed in a black cassock and a long pleated white surplice but wasn't yet wearing a clerical collar. She was probably an Anglican ordinand. She looked very friendly and Eve wondered what her name was. So far Eve had studiously avoided meeting anybody. She had spent all of yesterday - Sunday - literally locked in her room, apart from a foray to see if any local shops were open for food. She could not face college meals and the inevitable questions that would be asked by anyone she had to converse with. Anyway, she had just wanted to sleep, sleep, sleep, and sleep. That, and try and get over a return of the dreaded 'flu.

Eve looked around her as they were singing. There were about a hundred people filling the wooden pews of the small chapel, a surprising number. Where had they all come from? Perhaps many of them were married ordinands who didn't live in college but came in for meals, lectures, and services. Some looked as if they could be members of staff, although with the students being so much older than the average here, it made it hard to tell. Virtually everyone was dressed very casually in jeans and sweaters, with a few in more flamboyant ethnic clothing - perhaps a last bid to express their personalities before being subsumed under the official black and white vestments of office. They were all singing with gusto as befitted the professional faithful.

The sun was shining through one of the stained glass windows and causing a pattern of splodgy rainbow colours on the white wall opposite like an abstract painting. Now the hymn had finished and another ordinand at the front was leading them through the liturgy:

> 'Almighty God, our heavenly Father,
> we have sinned against you and against our fellow
> men,
> in thought and word and deed,
> through negligence, through weakness,
> through our own deliberate fault.
> We are truly sorry
> and repent of all our sins.
> For the sake of your Son Jesus Christ,
> who died for us,
> forgive us all that is past;
> and grant that we may serve you in newness of life
> to the glory of your name. Amen.'

Most of the community were obviously used to reciting things together. There was a common rhythm - the same intonation, the same length of pause for breath - that reminded Eve of a convent she had visited once. There the voices in unison had reminded her of a science fiction film, of an alien's voice that was many voices sounding like one, as if a person's voice had been recorded and then duplicated fifty times and all fifty recordings played at once. It had been an eerie experience. At St Frideswide's the voices were not that well co-ordinated as yet, and of course the mix of male and female would mean it could never be as unified as the same sex all speaking with one voice. If only the church as a whole could do that, Eve thought - speak with one voice to the whole world. Imagine how much time and worship together that would take!

But now it was time for the reading of Scripture. Even though individual students read the Old and New Testament readings from the front at a brass eagle lectern, most of the students in the pews also found the readings in the pew bibles to follow as it was read. Some were tracking the text using small blue Greek New Testaments. Eve even saw one using a larger black Hebrew Old Testament. Phew! She would really have to get up to speed on her biblical languages soon. The bit of Greek she'd managed to cram in the last few weeks wouldn't last her very long here.

They were now reading the Psalm together. It was Psalm Ninety One:

> 'He who dwells in the shelter of the Most High
> will rest in the shadow of the Almighty.
> I will say of the Lord, "He is my refuge and my fortress,
> my God, in whom I trust."
> Surely he will save you from the fowler's snare
> and from the deadly pestilence.
> He will cover you with his feathers,
> and under his wings you will find refuge;
> his faithfulness will be your shield and rampart.
> You will not fear the terror of night,

> nor the arrow that flies by day,
> nor the pestilence that stalks in the darkness,
> nor the plague that destroys at midday.
> A thousand may fall at your side,
> ten thousand at your right hand,
> but it will not come near you.
> You will only observe with your eyes
> and see the punishment of the wicked.'

Eve suddenly remembered a dream. It must have been one she'd had last night. Or perhaps it was during one of the many bouts of sleep and half-sleep she had lived through yesterday. But the image came back to her now, along with the fear.

She was in a wood by the water. She was being stalked. She never saw what it was that was waiting for her, following her, but she knew it was there. She could almost hear it breathing. It was dark but she could see every tree around her as if it was floodlit from a weird angle that highlighted the outline of each leaf without illuminating the ground. Intuitively, she knew what the thing looked like that was following her. It was like a tall wooden bird but in the shape of a man. It was definitely made of wood but come to life and very stiff. She had turned around quickly thinking it was at the side of her, but it wasn't - it had retreated in an instant behind the trees again. But now she knew that it had a beak - a long cruel wooden beak that was trying to peck her, to peck her neck, and that alone would kill her. She didn't want to die! She looked around to see if there was a way of escape, but all she could see in the mud were the footprints of the monster - long thin wedge shapes in the mud, like a bird's claws with wooden boots on.

In the chapel, everyone was now reciting the obligatory ending to the Psalm:

> 'Glory to the Father and to the Son
> And to the Holy Spirit,
> As it was in the beginning
> Is now, and ever shall be,
> World without end, Amen.'

Eve returned to the present. There was actually sweat on her forehead. She wiped it off and tried to focus on the people around her. As the woman at the front announced the next hymn, someone opened the door at the back of the chapel. The iron handle gave a metallic grating sound even though the woman who entered was trying to be quiet. People involuntarily looked round. The woman, who looked like one of the secretaries, found the Principal on the back pew and whispered something to him. He frowned and got up and left the chapel.

The service had finished. Since it was usually the Principal who would now stand up to end the service officially with announcements and notices for the week before giving the final Blessing, there was something of an awkward silence. However, the Vice-Principal now rose and walked slowly to the front. He was a tall stooping elderly man whose face gave the impression of someone who had suffered a lot but whose faith had managed to pull him through to final triumph. Eve had automatically liked him when she had read about him. He was famous for his work with the poor in the East End of London after the last war and had gone on to champion the cause of the deprived at every level of the church until he was now near a belated retirement. He now spoke to the congregation in a surprisingly strong voice:

'Since our Principal is obviously detained, it therefore falls to me to give you the blessing. The no-doubt fascinating and earth-shattering weekly notices you'll just have to wait for. I believe we are all due to meet in a quarter of an hour in the main lounge to begin Induction Week. So now let us say together the final Collect:

'Almighty and everlasting Father,
we thank you that you have brought us safely
to the beginning of this day.
Keep us from falling into sin
or running into danger;
order us in all our doings;
and guide us to do always
what is right in your eyes;
through Jesus Christ our Lord. Amen.'

Everyone echoed 'Amen', some crossing themselves, and began to stand up to file out while others remained bent in prayer. Yes, His peace, thought Eve - that's what I need at this moment, in shovelfuls.

But as they filed out of the chapel, the Principal was waiting outside. He was obviously looking for someone.

It was her.

'Ah, Eve,' he beckoned to her. 'Can I see you in my office for a moment? There are reporters outside asking for you. I think you'd better tell me what's going on.'

The enormous modern Dining Room at King Henry Hall was packed with students, all talking at once. Instead of the usual early morning introductory session for Freshers, the whole college had been called together, meaning that hundreds more students than usual had had to be shoehorned into the available space. Meals in the dining room were usually served in two sittings and so it was a very rare occasion indeed when all the 'King's Men' (and now King's Women too) were in the same place at once. The huge wooden tables positioned lengthways down the room did not help the cramped situation.

Martin was seated with some friends from last year and was catching up on news when the main doors opened and the Principal of King's walked in. He was a tall good-looking suntanned middle-aged man wearing academic dress and was flanked by the Bursar, the Student Advisor, the Hall Nurse and the Chaplain wearing their respective uniforms of office. The clamour of voices grew softer as if someone had suddenly turned the volume down in a wave that washed across the whole room. The Principal led his colleagues to the far end of the room, up the steps of the dais and behind the High Table where he turned to face the student body. Voices now had sunk to a murmur. The Principal lifted a small gavel on the table and banged it on a wooden block with a series of deafening cracks. Everyone, after flinching, stopped talking.

'Thank you. Allow me to welcome you all here today,' said the Principal, in an American accent, 'particularly those of you who are attending King Henry Hall for the very first time. A particularly warm welcome to you.'

'What does he think this is?' whispered Martin to a friend. 'A quiz show?' His friends dutifully sniggered.

'I won't keep you all for long. This should only last about ten minutes, then the second and third years can leave and we will progress with our normal timetable of welcoming the Freshers.'

'Note he didn't use the Latin salutation,' whispered another friend to Martin.

'Americanus est,' said Martin. *' Toti Americani barbari sunt.'*

'Have you heard what Winston Churchill said about Americans?' whispered another friend. 'That America is the only country that has leapt from Barbarism to Decadence with no intervening period of Civilisation!'

Martin snorted and then hid behind the person in front of him as everyone looked round.

The maligned Principal continued.

'The unusual circumstances that have called for this special meeting are as follows. It is my sad duty to inform you....,' and here he gave a tantalising pause before continuing, '...that a student from this Hall has been found in tragic and suspicious circumstances over the weekend. The deceased student's name is Fern Harrison, apparently known to you all as Feral Harrison. She was to be a second-year student...'

The murmurs around the hall that had begun with the word 'deceased' had now grown so loud that the Principal was forced to use the hammer again to call for quiet.

'She was a second-year student... thank you... she was about to begin her second year studying French. We have with us Detective Inspector Andrews from St Aldate's police station who will now tell us how we can be of help.'

The Principal motioned to someone at the front of the crowd and sat down. Martin held his breath as DI Andrews suddenly emerged from nowhere to walk up to the dais. He must have been sitting at the front amongst the students without anyone noticing. There was complete silence as he began:

'Yes, I'm sorry to be taking up your time at the beginning of a new year when you want to be getting on with other things, but this can't wait. It would seem that this is a murder investigation.'

(More murmurs). 'Obviously we are taking every measure that is usual in these tragic circumstances. This includes the necessity to question all of those who knew the deceased. We will therefore be interviewing all second and third years and postgraduates in a systematic fashion over this week. However, if there are any of you - *any* of you - who know *anything* relevant to the investigation, it is absolutely *vital* that you tell us *immediately.* We have set up an Incident Room in the Morris Room in Dryden Quad. There will be police on hand there at all times to receive any evidence or information that you can give us. We are currently estimating the time of death at between seven and seven thirty on Saturday morning. This means the victim probably left this college by boat some time before seven o'clock - that's around dawn. If *any* of you saw anything suspicious around that time, you *must* come and tell us, as soon as this meeting is over. Everything you tell us will be in the strictest confidence. Obviously we want to catch the perpetrator of this crime as quickly as possible. Meanwhile I would like to warn all students, particularly female ones, to be extremely vigilant about their security - the security of their rooms and their persons, particularly at night. Thank you. I know I can count on your co-operation. There is no reason why we can't have made substantial progress by the end of the week and be able to put this all behind us. Thank you for your time.'

Andrews nodded to the Principal and sat down again. The Principal indicated to the Chaplain that it was now his turn. The murmuring reached a crescendo and then fell as the Chaplain rose to speak.

'For those of you who don't know me, my name is Charles Hargreaves and I am a priest in the Church of England and Hall Chaplain.'

'Charlie Chaplain!' one of Martin's friends sniggered in his ear.

'I wish to add my hope to that of the Detective Inspector that this business will be over with quickly. However there may be those of you who find yourselves affected by this sudden shock very deeply. You may have lost a friend...' (the students surreptitiously surveyed each other - who were Fern's friends?) 'or this loss may remind you of another painful trauma. I wish to say that I am always available for you to speak to, again in strictest confidence, as is the University Counselling service and telephone helpline. We are also circulating other useful telephone numbers that will be displayed on noticeboards around the college. There is to be a special time of prayer at lunchtime every day this week and the chapel is to be open at all times for private reflection and to be an oasis of peace that I would urge you to take advantage of. Thank you, Principal.'

The Principal stood up.

'That is all we have to say on this sad matter at the current time. In a moment the second and third years may leave and the Vice-Principal will be hosting the Freshers' Introductory Forum. I now wish to see the JCR President and...' the Principal frowned and donned bifocals, '...Crispin de Beauchamp-Massey in my office immediately. Thank you.'

The eruption of noise now was total as everyone talked at once about the amazing news as the second and third years battled their way out of the dining hall. The Principal himself was caught up in the scrum as Martin was mobbed by people asking him in what inventive and creative way he'd been a naughty boy this time.

CHAPTER NINE

"Armour is not what you learn about all at once. It takes a very long time to find out about it. My own armour in early days was of a very inefficient kind."

[Edward Burne-Jones speaking to Thomas Rooke, 1896]

The office of the Principal of King Henry Hall was situated in the oldest and most beautiful part of the college. Two rooms had been connected by a door in the last century to provide an office for the Principal's secretary to be next to her master. This was where Guy Fastness, the Junior Common Room President, and Martin were now standing, waiting to see the Principal. Guy was running his fingers through his crinkly blond hair, his open pleasant face unusually creased with worry.

'So, what are you up for?' Martin asked jokingly. 'Been stealing the college silver again?'

'Oh God, Martin,' said Guy, 'you don't want to know. Honestly, it's horrible. I can't believe I've landed myself in this right at the beginning of term. It's like a nightmare!'

At that moment a phone rang on the Secretary's desk, she answered it and said with a grin: 'Mr Fastness, you can go in now.'

Guy looked up to heaven and crossed his fingers and said to Martin: 'Think of me when I'm gone.'

'That bad, eh?'

Guy knocked on the Principal's door. The Principal called out: 'Enter!' and Guy grimly went in to discover his fate.

'Come away from there!' said the secretary to Martin as he tried to listen at the door. She smiled at him as he protested; he was one of her favourites.

'Gillian, you've got to help me! I need to know what's going on. What's the new guy like?' he said, referring to the Principal.

'He seems pleasant enough,' Gillian demurred. 'Very efficient. That's probably why he's so pee-ed off at everything going wrong right at the start of the year.'

'Everything? Why what else has happened - I mean, as well as the murder.'

'Yes! How are you, you poor thing?' said Gillian in her motherly way, even though she was only in her twenties. 'I heard you were one of the ones who found the body. How awful! The poor girl! And we've had reporters phoning up today about it, you know. It's going to be on the news.'

'Really? Oh dear. Oh well, I suppose that was inevitable.'

'Yes. Anyway, the other crisis is the Chichele armour - it's been stolen!'

Martin was silent for a few seconds as he goggled at the secretary.

'What? The... the... bits in Guy's room - that we were all looking at on - when was it? - Friday night?'

'You saw them? Yes, that's it,' Gillian nodded. 'But they weren't all taken. Just the helmet, the glove things, and the feet and shin bits - I think. They've got such funny names, I can't remember.'

'But it was all in big black cases, all padded...'

'Oh, the cases weren't taken, just the armour. That's why,' her voice sank to a whisper, 'poor Guy thought it was all there when he went back to his room, you know, after the fire drill. But it wasn't. Someone had nicked the armour and left the cases standing there as if nothing had happened.'

Martin whistled softly. 'Poor Guy. No wonder he's being carpeted. I bet the Principal's ballistic!'

Gillian nodded, wide-eyed.

'But where was the Principal this weekend? Why wasn't he here?' Martin asked.

'Oh, he was in some Arab countries raising funds for the Hall, and giving legal advice to private clients at the same time.'

'Raising his private funds...'

'Sssssshhhhhh! It's all part of the job. He's still a practising lawyer, you know.'

'Hmmmm,' Martin murmured, then, as the Principal's door opened and Guy emerged, 'Oooops. My turn now.'

As Guy walked past them, he put one hand round his throat and pretended to pull on a rope with the other, mimicking being hung, his eyes rolling and his tongue sticking out with a choking sound. The two students then hit each other's hands in a 'high five' as they passed and Martin said: 'Wait for me, I shouldn't be long. Chat up Gillian for a while.'

'OK.'

Gillian tutted and giggled as Martin walked into the Principal's office and shut the door.

'Ah,' said the Principal looking up over his bifocals, 'please take a seat. I won't be a moment - a ridiculous phrase that of course means "I'm going to be several".'

Martin sat down and surveyed the new Principal's office. It had been moved around and changed a bit since last year. The text books on the shelves looked newer. The last Principal, a Classics man, had stacks of ancient tomes that looked as if they had had one careful owner around the time of Julius Caesar. But Smithfield Henderson was a much more recent model and looked a lot more successful. It was easy to see why he had been chosen to manage a college gearing itself up for the rigours of the twenty first century, particularly with all the fund-raising that it now entailed. It was just a pity that the new Principal's first weekend on the job had entailed him being on the other side of the world while one of his students was murdered and a priceless college treasure was stolen.

'You are Crispin de Beauchamp-Massey?' the Principal was now saying, closing a book of papers and regarding Martin.

'It's pronounced "Beecham" actually - one of our quaint old English ways. Don't want it sounding too French. Oh, and I tend to be called Martin.'

The Principal paused, then said:

'Any particular reason?'

'It's my name.'

Silence again.

'My middle name,' said Martin, 'well, one of them. People tend to just call me Martin Massey - it's a lot easier. I wouldn't want you thinking I was two different people. That would confuse things.'

'Fine,' said the Principal with an edge of impatience. 'Now I assume it was you, Martin Massey, who used my parking space as if it were your own over the weekend and are therefore to be fined and reprimanded - or was it your friend and double Crispin de *Beecham*-Massey?'

'Oh! So that's what this is about! Oh, phew, I thought it was about, well, you know, the *other thing*...'

'The *other thing*...?'

'You know,' said Martin conspiratorially, 'the *murder*.'

The Principal let out an enormous sigh.

'We'll talk about that later. At the moment there are reporters wanting to speak to us about it, but I advise you not to do so.'

'Of course,' said Martin, making a mental note to do as he jolly well liked.

'Anyway, the fine for the parking offence will be added onto your Battels for this term by the Bursar, unless you wish to pay separately, of course.'

'Oh no, add it to my account,' said Martin breezily.

'I believe you were one of the last people to see the armour on Friday night.'

'To see it alive? Yes, it sounds as though I was.'

'Well, the police will want to see you about that too. I believe you have already made a statement about the murder.'

'Yes.'

Martin suddenly felt deflated. The first proper day of term and here he was, the last to see some stolen goods and the first to see a murdered girl. He had now been fingered for a petty parking violation. His record was not looking good. And why hadn't the Principal just left it up to his minions to deal with this? Why was he getting special treatment?

'That's all...' said the Principal.

'Oh good,' said Martin getting up.

'...for now.'

'Ah. Er, thanks. Good bye.'

Martin walked towards the door. The Principal seemed engrossed again in his papers. Martin couldn't resist turning round to say 'Have a nice day!' before he closed the door behind him. He grimaced at Guy who was now sitting on Gillian's desk, taking Martin's advice to the letter.

'We need to talk - pronto,' said Martin to Guy, then in a fake American accent, 'Hey Guy, get that butt of your's over to the Buttery.'

'You say the nicest things,' said Guy. 'Take me, I'm yours. Bye, Gillian. Thanks for the biccie.'

'You gave *him* a biscuit!' said Martin in mock outrage. 'I take exception to that.'

'You weren't here,' said Gillian, waving them goodbye and answering the phone.

'That's no excuse to be unfaithful to me,' said Martin as the two students left. 'My pride is most definitely wounded.'

'Don't worry,' said Guy, 'that's just the effect of the Principal's bollocking.'

'As bollockings go, it wasn't too bad.'

'*Mine* was,' protested Guy. 'I'm in a real shit-hole over this armour thing.'

'Well, I'm in a shit-hole too.'

'No, you're not! I'm in a much worse shit-hole than you are.'

'Now you're getting all shit-holier-than-thou!' said Martin, very pleased with himself over the pun.

'Oh, ha-bloody-ha. Look the Buttery's completely full...'

'Absolutely 'jammed', you might say...'

'Oh, give it a rest, Crisp. This is serious. Let's go to my room.'

'Best offer I've had this week.'

The two men fled the packed cafeteria that was full of students either having a late breakfast or early elevenses and jogged the short distance to Guy's rooms. He was at the top of a staircase in large rooms reserved each year for the Junior Common Room

President, the idea being they were large enough to do a lot of obligatory entertaining.

'Shit!' said Guy as they entered. He kicked aside his gown that had fallen off the back of the door. 'This is the last thing I need at the start of the year. I can't believe I was so stupid! Fancy leaving them unattended while I fart about at that bloody fire drill! I didn't know *what* I was doing...'

'*That* was obvious...'

'And while I was out of the room, some bastard must have nipped in here and nicked them! And now my rear end is being fried and it's not even my fault. I didn't ask for a wretched fire drill on the first night...'

'Who did?'

'What? Oh, no one seems to know. It looks as if it was just a prank.'

'Oh great.'

'I know. Bloody marvellous, isn't it. All the second and third years are back in Hall and most of the first years have arrived, we're all sorting out our rooms and luggage, everyone's in the middle of unpacking and milling around, and some idiot lets off the fire alarm! Of course, I hadn't had a chance to study the new routine yet, so even though I'm Fire Officer I was completely clueless, as you saw. I think I'm going to propose that we separate the roles of JCR Pres. and Fire Officer. JCR President has enough to do without pansying about playing Fire Officer as well.'

'Absolutely. Oh, mine's white, two sugars,' said Martin as Guy looked at him quizzically as he poured out the coffee.

'I've even got the porter into trouble as well,' Guy continued. 'He should never have let me have the armour unguarded in my own room. It was asking for it.'

'Oh, you're being too hard on yourself, as they say in American sitcoms. How were you to know someone would filch the armour. It was a great idea to do something with it at the Freshers' Ball. They'd all have been crapping themselves. Much more interesting than having Sir Eddie just sitting there while the Freshers file past.'

Martin was referring to the custom at King Henry Hall of the Freshers' Ball at the end of Noughth Week. It was traditional - at least from around 1840 - to have the Sir Edward Chichele armour, that normally stood in a cabinet in the Old Entrance Hall, on show at the party. The suit of armour would be seated at High Table in the Dining Hall in the Principal's chair and the Freshers would have to file past, kneel and kiss one of his gauntlets and swear allegiance to the College and their fellow students. Guy's brilliant idea, so he had thought at the time, was for him to actually be inside the suit of armour and magically 'come alive' at the end of the ceremony.

'I was really looking forward to frightening them all to death,' complained Guy. Then, 'Oh gosh, perhaps I shouldn't have said that - what with this murder and everything.'

'Yes,' said Martin thoughtfully. 'Did you know I found the body?'

'*What?! No!!*'

'Yes. I was out punting with some friends Saturday morning, and lo and behold, we found her down a side stream just past the boathouses. Freaky.'

'Wow!'

Of course Guy made Martin tell him all about it. Only then did Guy return to the issue uppermost in his mind:

'Hey, you know all those old stories about Sir Eddie - getting up to all sorts of stuff.'

'You mean the suit of armour coming to life, going round on its own?'

'Yes, it's like zombies or mummies or the Night of the Living Dead stuff. All those old stories about Sir Eddie's armour suddenly coming to life at certain times of the year, getting up to all sorts. Well, bit of a coincidence, eh? The armour goes missing one night and the next thing we know someone in college has been killed! Makes you think, eh? Perhaps it's old Eddie come to life, up to his tricks again!'

Martin finished his coffee and said drily, 'Or perhaps it's your brain liquifying.'

CHAPTER TEN

"'O, MAN OF EVYLLE FEYTH AND POURE BYLEVE! WHEREFORE TRUSTIST THOU MORE ON THY HARNEYSE THAN IN THY MAKER? FOR HE MYGHT MORE AVAYLE THEE THAN THYNE ARMOUR, IN WHAT SERVYSE THAT THOU ARTE SETTE IN.'"

[SIR THOMAS MALORY, *LE MORTE DARTHUR*, 1485]

Anyway, turn that fire on, can you?' continued Martin. 'It's getting chilly up here.'

'I know. These rooms hardly get the sun at all,' said Guy turning on the ancient gas fire on one wall. 'I don't suppose Hall will turn the heat on for another couple of weeks, with all the cutbacks.'

'They obviously want us to feel like gen-u-wine aristocrats in our breezy stately homes, having to chip ice off the soap in the morning. Have you got any biscuits? Another coffee wouldn't go amiss either. That was good stuff.'

Guy switched the kettle on again as Martin took out a notebook.

'This is all serious do-do,' Martin said. 'We need to go over precisely what happened.'

'Oh, I've done that with the police. Yesterday morning when I discovered it was missing. Of course the place was crawling with police already 'cos of the murder, although I didn't know that at the time. It makes me look so stupid! How on earth can I expect the Freshers to take me seriously now?'

'But it's not your fault if some miscreant chose to nick it when you weren't there.'

'But I should have been there! Or I shouldn't have left the armour alone! You should have seen the policeman's expression when I confessed to having left a priceless treasure in my rooms. I could tell he thought I was a complete fool.'

'Well, he was right there, of course,' said Martin blithely. 'But that's not the point. The fact that some blighter came in afterwards and filched a few case loads of the heavy metal stuff is not your fault. The important thing now,' said Martin getting a pen out of his pocket, 'is to establish exactly what happened and who could have stolen it.'

'Huh. You sound like the police,' said Guy, pouring out their second cup of coffee.

'Oh good, that's the whole idea. Now, let's get the timetable straight. When were we all in here? You invited me over for about nine thirty on Friday night, if I remember rightly.'

'Yes, that's it. There was you here, and Minty, of course.'

Martin wrote down 'Araminta Douglas (2nd year English, Guy's girlfriend)' under his own and Guy's name.

'Then Rory and Angela dropped by...'

'So Rory Ablett - he's third year Electrical Engineering, isn't he?' asked Martin.

'Does it matter?'

'Probably not. I'm just trying to be efficient. What's Angela? Angela White, isn't it?'

'Well, she's a stunning blonde for a start. But apart from that, I think she's second year French.'

Martin was writing this down when he suddenly stopped and sucked his pen meditatively.

'Mmm. Second year French. Feral Harrison was Second year French.'

'So?'

'It's just that... well, they may well have known each other quite well - same college, same course. Didn't they hang around a lot together at the beginning of the First Year?'

'Er, you could be right,' said Guy vaguely. 'I seem to remember wondering what a gorgeous blonde like her was doing with a... well, let's say, not so gorgeous woman like, well... *her.* Of course, some women do it to make themselves look even better in comparison...'

'Casting my mind back to the distant memories of last year, I seem to remember that once Rory and Angela started dating, Angela didn't hang out much with Feral or Fern, what ever her name is - was - anymore.'

'That's hardly surprising,' said Guy. 'I don't think Minty's seen that much of her friends since we started dating. It's just one of those things. It takes quite an effort to keep up with everyone.'

'Mmmm, one of the ways of the world, the way of all flesh. Anyway, it might be significant. We have to cover every angle at this stage.'

'Are you trying to get a link between the armour going missing and this girl's death?' said Guy suspiciously.

Martin sighed and said: 'You really have had too many blows on the head playing rugby, haven't you. I can sense the brain damage from here. Come on, let's think who else saw the armour at the vital moment.'

Guy now sighed as well.

'It's hard to say. I had my door wedged open - remember? So as soon as I started to open up the cases with the armour in, and you all started oohing and aahing, the room filled up pretty quickly. It was as if the armour was like a magnet, drawing people into the room...'

'Oh, how poetic!'

Guy ignored Martin's interruption.

'... Pretty soon my room was jammed. I didn't really take any notice of who else was here. It was just a sea of faces.'

'And I was too busy looking at the armour,' said Martin, 'to see who was standing behind me.' He thought for a moment. 'Who else knew that you were going to have the armour in your room overnight? I wonder if the porter told anybody. Which porter was it on duty that evening?'

'It was Jackson. That's the only reason I was allowed to see the armour. He's a great chap. If it had been one of the other porters, there's no way they would have let me try the armour on. But I wanted to make sure it would fit before the Freshers' Ball to see if the joke would work, to see if I could actually move around in it.'

'And could you?'

'I never got the chance! Half of it was nicked before I could try it on. I only found out on the Saturday. All the cases were still here, looking perfectly normal, and I'd... well, had a bit too much to drink on Friday night to bother checking it was all there. It never occurred to me that some of it was missing from the cases, honestly!'

Martin insisted, 'But it was possible that someone saw Jackson bring the stuff up to your rooms. How the hell did he get it over here in the first place? It's usually locked up in that glass show case in the Old Entrance Hall.'

'Yes, where no one ever sees it. It's a real shame - it's so beautiful. Anyway, let me think. Jackson had got the whole lot in its packing cases 'cos it was going to be taken to be cleaned somewhere, professionally. I wouldn't have had the chance to try it on before the big day unless I tried it for size before it left. So Jackson - very naughtily as it turns out - brought it up here for me. It was supposed to just be for a few hours, but the fire alarm disturbed everything. Then we - you, me and Minty - went out for a drink, and by the time I was back here, Jackson was off duty and I thought I may as well keep the armour till the next day and try it on on the Saturday morning. I slept rather late, but when I got up, before I went to the loo or had a coffee or anything, I thought I'd take a look at some of the armour - I'd had a weird dream about it, if you must know. I think it was all those weird stories about it coming alive and the fact that I'd had to sleep in the same room with it over night. Anyway,' Guy cleared his throat, 'I carefully opened the first case on the right - the smallest one that should have been the gauntlets - and lo and behold! There they were, gone! I couldn't believe it! So then I checked the rest and was practically shitting myself, I can tell you...'

'I can imagine,' Martin interrupted. 'But you still haven't said how Jackson got the armour up here, so we don't know who could have seen him.'

'Oh, it was on one of those wooden trolley-things the porters use for carrying trunks - you know, one of the upright, fork-lift thingies. All the separate black cases were loaded up on that,

Jackson wheeled them over here to the bottom of the staircase and then we carried them up by hand, two at a time. Or rather, he did. I stayed guard over the remaining cases at the bottom.'

'Oh, you did the hard bit. So all people would have seen would have been these mysterious black cases. They wouldn't necessarily have known what was in them?'

'Of course not,' said Guy huffily. 'It was the day when we were all moving back into hall. Everyone was having cases moved around. They didn't have bright neon signs on them saying "Priceless Antique Armour in Here - Please Steal"!'

'But at that time of night most people would be moved in. It must have looked unusual at nine at night.'

'Yes, I suppose so,' said Guy reluctantly.

'And you being the incredibly popular JCR President and social hub of King Henry Hall - you would have attracted attention.'

'Possibly.'

'And there were a lot of people milling round at that time of the evening, as evidenced by the fact that a minute after you'd opened up the armour, your room was clogged with voyeurs. How on earth did you expect to keep your trick for the Freshers' Ball a secret when you're flashing the armour around to all and sundry?'

'I was not flashing it around to all and sundry, as you put it! I was only intending to show it to you two when Rory and Angela turn up and then half of Hall!' Guy said angrily.

'OK, OK, don't get defensive. I'm sure it could have happened to anyone - anyone with the IQ of the average flea, of course. So there were God knows how many people crammed in here looking at the armour. Can you remember *any* of them?'

'Now you really *are* sounding like the police. No, I didn't really look up at them, I was too busy looking at the armour. They were all just a sea of faces. I didn't take them in. I think there were some geeky ones in specs...'

'Well, that could be half of King Henry Hall for a start...'

'But names... I'm terrible with names...'

'And you're JCR Pres! You didn't put that on your manifesto last year: "Please vote for me, and I promise I'll never remember your name..."!'

At that moment there was a knock at the door. Someone flung it open without being asked to come in.

'Guy, you're on in five minutes! The Principal's waiting. You'd better come down,' said the student who looked round the door and then disappeared again.

'Oh shit,' groaned Guy. 'It's this wretched Freshers talk. I've got to do my bit. I haven't worked out anything to say. My name's probably mud already.'

Guy began to hurl himself around the room frantically as if he was looking for something.

'I've just been jotting down a timetable for Friday night,' said Martin casually as if nothing was happening. 'Tell me if this is right. Nine thirty-ish. We are all ogling the armour in your room. Nine thirty five-ish. The fire alarm goes off. You start to fasten up the cases while we all mosey out. Now, Guy, were you the last person out of your room? You weren't stupid enough to leave anybody in here with the armour?'

'What? Oh no, of course not. I was definitely the last person out.'

'And presumably you locked your door.'

'Er, well, er, not exactly. Damn, where are my notes?'

'*You mean you didn't lock your door?!* Bloody hell, man, what were you thinking of?'

'Oh shit, I know. It sounds incredibly stupid. The police looked at me as if I was deranged or something. But it was the fire alarm and I was responsible and all I could think about was finding the bloody list of names to check everybody off as they assembled in the quad. And if I hung around searching for my key I'd keep everybody waiting outside in the rain. It was raining, remember.'

'I *do* remember.'

'Of course, I couldn't find the list of names *either* so I dashed down with everyone else who were pouring out into the quad. I tried to find somebody official who might have a list of the names of everyone at college, but there was no one! It was all up to me! So I tore back up here, managed to find the list that time - in a really obvious place, of course - and went back down to the quad. There was no one up here. I thought if my door just looked closed people would think it was locked. No one would come up here - they were all supposed to be lining up outside to be checked off.'

'Well, *someone* came back.'

'Anyway, then it was a complete nightmare down there, with people slow-handclapping me and yelling at me. It wasn't *my* fault. There wasn't supposed to be a fire alarm that night. Some idiot must have set it off as a joke.'

'Oh, really? How convenient.'

'Damn it, where are my blasted notes? I can't get up there in front of two hundred Freshers without notes!'

'I'm amazed you were prepared enough to make any in advance,' said Martin mercilessly. 'So when you finally did check people off on your list, who was missing?'

'Oh practically everybody!' said Guy, looking as if he was going to tear his hair out any moment. 'There were about a hundred missing. Nobody took the alarm seriously. A lot of the first years didn't arrive till Saturday anyway. And people were just wandering around college as if nothing was happening. You know how people are about fire alarms - everyone assumes it's a joke unless the flames are actually licking their backsides. The whole thing was a fiasco!'

'Oh, thank you, that really narrows it down. That means there are about a hundred people who could've nicked the armour!'

'Well, quite a few had already gone out to the pub or whatever that evening anyway, so *they* weren't there...'

'Could I have a copy of the list anyway? It might help eliminate a few later on.'

'Do what you want,' said Guy bad-temperedly. 'I'm already down the toilet without a paddle. You'd better piss off now. I've got to go.'

'Do make sure you lock your room, won't you,' said Martin in a soft feminine voice, oozing with sarcasm, his hand on Guy's shoulder.

'Oh, piss off! Anyway, I *did* lock my room on Friday night. After the fire drill. When we all came back afterwards.'

'Ah, yes! Before we went out to the pub. Well, that does make a difference.'

'Yes, I found my key in my gown pocket, saw that the cases were still there - never guessing some bastard had nicked some of the bits out of them - locked my door, and off we went. Oh, my gown!'

Guy grabbed his gown off the floor hurriedly put it on. He then felt in the pockets. He drew out two small cards triumphantly.

'My speech!'

The two students then hurried out of the room, Guy locked the door and ran down the stairs without a word, leaving Martin alone in the small corridor.

Martin looked around him for a few moments. There were no other rooms on that floor. The only other door had been sealed up aeons ago to provide the extra room for the JCR President. There was a small cubby-hole opposite, quite deep into the stone wall, and loaded up with dusty old furniture - a desk, a couple of chairs, an old lamp, all covered over with a white sheet that was half hanging off. Martin spent a few minutes eagerly peering into the gloomy hole. But there were obviously no bits of extremely expensive armour lurking in the shadows. The police must have already looked, judging from the fresh marks made in the dust here and there.

On second thoughts, Martin wrote a question on his notepad, ripped it out and slipped it under Guy's door.

CHAPTER ELEVEN

"She thought she had never seen such a strange-looking soldier in all her life. He was dressed in tin armour, which seemed to fit him very badly."

[Lewis Carroll, *Through the Looking Glass, and what Alice Found There*, 1871]

Eve was feeling very pleased with herself but very nervous. She had organized her first tea party. It was to be at four o'clock on Monday afternoon - a time when nobody in their right mind would be working but when any mere mortal would want to give up on whatever turgid tome they were supposed to be studying and let their thoughts wander to the refreshment of the body. There was even an official pot of tea - two huge stainless steel ones, in fact - waiting for anyone who cared for them in St Frideswide's Common Room at that time of day. Several students made that, and a read of the newspapers, part of their daily routine. But most students preferred the casual privacy of a neighbour's room, particularly as one's neighbours tended to have the addition of a ready supply of biscuits.

At lunchtime in the dining hall that day, Eve had taken her courage in both hands and invited those who were sitting around her to tea in her room that afternoon. A couple of them had looked surprised but all of them looked pleased. Eve had then not done any work the rest of the afternoon but had gone panic-shopping for interesting tea and food for her guests. There were going to be six of them! Eve had not intended there to be so many, but it was difficult not to invite all the people within earshot.

She had already found a delicatessen in the centre of town. Here she bought Lapsang Souchong and Earl Grey tea (she had inherited a *penchant* for tea from her English mother), Scottish shortbread biscuits (even though she didn't like them), and a German kiwi fruit cake completely covered in chocolate. The layer of chocolate looked so thin she hoped it didn't all break off before she managed to get it home. (Home! Wow, she'd called her room at Frideswide's 'home'!) Would that be enough? She already had milk and coffee, in case anyone was perverse enough to want coffee at tea-time. She also had to buy three more mugs as she only had four. She bought three William Morris ones from Arcadia on St Michael Street, plus a print of old Oxford she hadn't intended to buy (surprisingly enough a view of St Aldate's, heavily featuring Christ Church, with King Henry Hall in the distant background). It wasn't a view she intended to put on her wall just yet.

But by five past four no one had arrived. Eve had boiled the kettle a quarter of an hour ago and so had to switch it on again. Would there be enough water for seven of them anyway? She had never had to use the kettle for so many people before. It didn't have an indicator on the outside. Perhaps she should boil some more water in the little kitchen on the landing. She was just about to leave the room to do this when her first guest arrived.

It was Lincoln Grace, a handsome black guy from Virginia who was paying his own way to study in Oxford. He was shorter than Eve but made of pure muscle. He had the thick neck of a football player and dressed with an exquisite smart casualness. He wore several chunky gold rings and had a dazzling smile. Every time he had looked Eve in the eyes so far she had felt as if she was melting.

'Oh, hi,' she said as she was about to walk out of the door, 'I was just going to boil up some more water just in case. You're early, well, not early, just earlier than anyone else. I mean, all the others are late.'

'Ah, that's Oxford time for you. Always at least ten minutes late for everything.' Lincoln presented her with a packet of Oreo

Cookies. 'I just had a shipment from the States. I know you can buy them here, but this feels more authentic. I'm doing my bit to educate the Brits about our cookies.'

'Oh, thank you! Please come in and sit down. Perhaps I don't need more water after all.' There was something about the open friendliness and chunkiness of Lincoln that made Eve relax and feel everything was alright and under control.

'You're looking very lovely today, if I may say so,' said Lincoln, oozing charm.

'Oh, um, thank you,' said Eve, blushing, 'would you like tea or coffee? Or cookies or cake? Oh, there's someone else at the door...'

'I'll get it.'

Lincoln opened the door to two other guests who were chattering enthusiastically. One was Dominic Brock, a somewhat effeminate Anglo-Catholic with whom Eve had already had a stimulating political discussion and enjoyable lambast of the sins of the government. The other was Marion Gateshead, a friendly motherly-type in her thirties with whom Eve had felt an instant affection. Dominic was in his normal gossip mode.

'I'm telling you, that's why they call him the *Vice*-Principal!'

'Oh, don't be ridiculous,' Marion was laughing.

'What's that?' asked Lincoln, smiling.

'Oh, Dominic is spreading the dirt as usual,' said Marion. 'About our Vice-Principal's supposedly sordid past during his early ministry - with prostitutes! Hello, Eve, how are you, you poor thing? Did you get a nap this afternoon as you promised?'

'Actually, no...'

'I hope you haven't been chasing around all day to impress us,' said Dominic with frightening accuracy. 'I was going to bring a cake as my contribution, but I ate it.'

'Oink, oink,' said Marion. 'Who else is coming?'

'Did Frank say he was coming?'

'Oh God, keep him away from me,' cried Dominic, crossing himself. 'We had the most awful row about transubstantiation last night.'

'Don't tell me they let you into one of their late-night cocoa sessions,' said Marion.

'Yes!' said Dominic striking the arm of the sofa in triumph. 'I penetrated the stronghold!'

'What's this?' said Eve.

Marion answered.

'The Hot Prots - that's Conservative Evangelicals, to you -,' said Dominic, 'have cocoa together every evening at about ten o'clock! It's a highly secret organisation!'

'It's to stop them doing anything more naughty,' added Marion, 'at that time of night.'

'And they have terribly earnest discussions on important doctrines...'

'Hey, why haven't I been invited to this yet?' asked Lincoln.

'Oh, you're black!' said Dominic.

'Dominic!' said Marion. 'That's not the reason. No, you're just new. You haven't shown sufficient evidence of theological soundness yet to be trusted with such an honour.'

'Why aren't these guys at Wycliffe?' asked Lincoln. 'Or isn't it sound enough for them?'

'Oh, they're infiltrating,' said Dominic. 'They see it as their mission to divide and conquer our ecumenical establishment.'

'Dominic, you do exaggerate...' protested Marion.

'What tea do you all want?' asked Eve breathlessly. 'It's Earl Grey or Lapsang Souchong. And there's cake too, and cookies, er, biscuits.'

After some arguing, they decided on Lapsang Souchong. Eve busied herself with the tea while they all helped themselves to food which Eve had laid out on borrowed plates on the coffee table in the centre of the room. But as there was another knock at the door, Eve realised that there were not enough chairs. Any newcomers would have to sit on the bed or the floor.

The next guest was the already-defamed Frank. He was tall and good-looking with brown hair and what seemed to be a permanent smile. He was wearing jeans and a navy sweater with a subdued pattern. For some reason his open friendliness made Eve feel on edge. Maybe underneath he was as nervous as she was.

'Good afternoon, Eve,' he said. 'Ah, Dominic! Have you seen the light yet?' he smiled as a joke.

'He's trying to convert me,' Dominic explained to everyone.

'But there's a long way to go,' said Frank. 'The Church of England is certainly a broad church.'

'It has to be to let in Polly!' said Dominic, referring to a rather large and overweight member of college.

For this he earned a slap from Marion. But he continued unabated and said to Frank:

'Is it true your friends call me Damien - after the possessed guy in *The Exorcist*?'

Frank looked sufficiently astounded to prove that this was true. Fortunately two more people knocked on the door and entered the room as Eve was still pouring the tea. But someone followed them in. Eve almost dropped the kettle when she heard the familiar voice.

'Hello, I seem to have stumbled across a party! I had no idea you lived it up so much at St Frigid's!'

It was Martin.

Eve turned round, still holding the kettle.

'Um, we're all having tea. Would you like some? I'm afraid it's only Lapsang Souchong.' (Oh no, why had she said 'only'?)

Martin smiled.

'Oh, I shall feel in the Lap-sang Souchong of Luxury!'

This earned him groans and applause from the others.

'I'm so sorry to gatecrash your little tea party, Eve,' said Martin. ('No you're not,' thought Eve, 'and don't patronise me!') 'Aren't you going to introduce me to everyone?'

Eve sighed and did this reluctantly. She still couldn't remember Martin's full name, so Martin Massey would have to do. He didn't seem to mind. As Eve poured his tea and then added the milk, Martin exclaimed:

'Oh, the foul American habit of adding the milk last! I'm telling you, the Yanks are taking over.' Everyone looked from Eve to Lincoln, who grinned. Eve thought, 'Oh great, he's going to systematically insult everyone in the room.'

But then Marion shrieked: 'Oh, you're *Martin! That* Martin. The one who...' She indicated Eve, '...with Eve, the two of you...'

'Oh, is this an *affaire du coeur*?' asked Dominic. 'Do dish the dirt.'

'No,' said Marion in belated hushed tones, 'they're the ones who - you know - *found the body!*'

Several people had not read the papers and did not even know there had been a murder. Eve was cringing, not wanting to talk about it at all. She dreaded her first impression at college as being 'The One Who Found The Body'. But Martin was now giving everyone a masterly summing up of the events of Saturday morning in a way that Eve had to admit was discretion itself. By this time everyone had drunk their tea - or let it go cold - and eaten most of the cake and biscuits on the plates.

'Anyway, that's why I'm here,' Martin finished. He waved a folder he had brought with him in the air. 'We need to discuss the case.'

'Oh, well, we can leave,' said Marion, taking the hint.

As did everyone else. Eve was appalled to see the room empty, everyone wishing her all the best and thanking her for the tea and cake, but leaving her alone with Martin in moments, in spite of her protests 'But you don't need to go...!'

As the door closed behind them, Eve surveyed the empty cups and plates strewn around and Martin now in the only comfortable chair.

'Well, you certainly know how to clear a room,' she said.

'Yes, people are funny about murder,' said Martin casually. 'Anyway,' he said, speeding up and taking a sheaf of papers out of the folder, 'I have stuff in here to make your hair curl. Oh it already has. Well, perhaps it will straighten it and make it stand on end. I think I've found some vital leads.'

Eve could hardly believe her ears.

'You've *what?*'

Martin ignored the note of menace in her voice.

'Take a look at this,' he said, holding out some photocopied sheets of paper.

'Good God!' said Eve. 'What is it? Yuk! Why are you showing me that? Put them away, it's horrible! I hate things like that.'

'This,' said Martin majestically, 'is the Sir Edward Chichele suit of armour, known to more irreverent students as "Eddie".'

'It's vile!'

'Oh, I don't know. I think it's rather beautiful.'

'What, with all those spiky bits? It looks horrible, like a big insect!'

'Tut! Women do have a thing about insects. As exoskeletons go, this is extremely clever. It's like a beautifully tailored suit of clothes but in metal. Look at the fit! The way it goes in sharply at the waist, the way the separate bits of plate are moulded together around the shape of the man and articulated for full movement. I'm telling you, by the time this was made - in the 1460s - armour-making had reached such a peak of perfection that it never really got any better. I've been reading about it in King's library this afternoon.'

'Really,' said Eve drily. 'And what has this got to do with anything?'

'Everything! The armour's been stolen - *this* suit of armour. Well, some of it anyway. And I think it was by our murderer!'

Eve was silent for a few seconds as she tried to take in this astonishing claim. All she could say was:

'What on earth are you talking about? And don't say *our* murderer.'

'Look. Some of this armour was stolen on Friday night. It was in packing cases in my friend Guy's room - he's JCR President and he was going to try it on to play some sort of trick on the Freshers later on in the week. The armour's normally kept in a big locked glass cabinet in the Old Entrance Hall where no one ever goes to look at it because we don't use that old entrance anymore - anyway, that's not the point. The point is that while the armour was all in separate bits in packing cases in Guy's room, there was a fire alarm. This was on Friday night. Can you remember me telling you about it on Saturday, about what a rotten night I'd had?'

'I think you told *Charlie* about it,' said Eve pointedly.

'Whatever. Anyway, it was about nine thirty and there were quite a few of us in Guy's room looking at this when the fire alarm goes off and we all dash out. Guy leaves the room unlocked like a complete imbecile for about half an hour while we're all standing outside in the rain freezing to death. Anyway, the next day when Guy checks the armour in its cases, some bits of it are missing!

The helmet - a visored bascinet, to be precise - the gauntlets, the greaves and the sabatons. That's the gloves, the shin and foot bits, to you.'

'Thanks. So... what are you saying?'

'That the murderer nicked the armour on the Friday night - or somehow found it or got hold of it after it was nicked - and used the vital bits to conceal his (or her) identity for the murder on the Saturday morning!'

Eve rubbed her hands over her face and grimaced. All this was going rather fast.

'What on earth...,' she began, 'why on earth would...? Why would anyone want to go to the trouble of stealing armour, for goodness' sake? Murders have been successfully committed for centuries without it!'

'Ah! But don't you see? Look at the precise parts that were stolen. The bascinet - that would stop anyone seeing his face (I'll say "he" for the time being, if you'll excuse me being sexist). The gauntlets - that would stop any fingerprints...'

'Eeeuuuurrrrh!' cried Eve all of a sudden. 'I've just thought... oh God, you don't think... do you mean she was strangled by... by *those things?!*'

Martin nodded with a sigh.

'It would be consistent with the injuries. You remember the cuts on her neck? Oh no, of course, you didn't see them. But I did. And I think they could easily have been made by the edges of these gauntlets - look how spiky they are. And there were other odd markings that would match...'

'But there isn't an underside to these gloves, these gauntlet things,' Eve interrupted. 'Would it have been his bare hands underneath?'

'No, he would've worn gloves. They used to wear leather gloves under the gauntlets even in the middle ages. The metal part only protects the top of the hand and the thumb, like articulated fingers - to protect you from sword cuts. But the sides of the metal fingers would've sliced into her throat, and on this sort of gothic armour you've got all sorts of additional spikes and sticking-out bits for added effect. No wonder she had cuts on her hands too - defending herself.'

'Yuk,' said Eve again. Then, frowning: 'How can armour be gothic? I thought that was buildings.'

'It is, but it's also the style of Sir Edward's armour. Let's see, where's my notes. Ah yes. 'Late fifteenth-century German armour... differed from the previous popular Italian styles... decorated with the fluting or ridging of surfaces - to help deflect sword blows, of course - piercing and fretting of the overlapping plates... the style became known as "Gothic" because of its resemblance to the later Gothic forms in the other arts, particularly ecclesiastical architecture'. What he means is, it's very pointy. Spikes and pointed bits everywhere.'

'Good God!' exclaimed Eve. 'I've just thought...!'

'That'll be a first...'

'The feet! The... the... oh, what are they called?'

'The sabatons,' said Martin with a grin.

'Those, yes! The footprints in the wood... in the mud!'

'I wondered when you'd get to that,' said Martin with a superior air. 'I'd been waiting patiently for the old cogs to clank round. Absolutely. You take a close look at these pictures - which I slaved away all afternoon in the library to find. This is the only close-up of the armour available and it's only a nineteenth-century drawing. The college hadn't even got it insured properly with photos and everything, so this is all we've got to go on. No wonder the Principal's furious. Anyway, look at the shape of those feet.'

Eve stared at the photocopy in silence. She had not wanted to look at the armour close-to. She'd always hated armour, robots, insects, even when she was a kid. There was something really creepy about something covered in protective plating, often of aggressive design. The feet of the suit of armour were weird and long and curved. They must have been at least twice the length of a normal foot, possibly three times as long. And they were so thin. Like a bird's claw or talon. The part where the man's foot would have fitted was in lots of little sections all joined together, or 'articulated' as Martin kept saying. But the rest of the sabaton then shot out in a long pointed talon, curving downwards like a felon's claw.

'How on earth would you walk in those things? Wouldn't this pointy bit at the end keep digging into the ground?' she said.

'Exactly. It did. But it was never made for walking in. This is for a "chevalier", for someone on horseback. If you were in battle and someone's raining blows on you, particularly if they're on the ground, you need foot protection that will ward off the blows. This design isn't for fancy ornament, it's utterly practical. Instead of getting your foot hacked off, the sword should just slide off it.'

Eve looked dubious.

'Surely people then were pretty small. I mean, this armour looks very slim and tight. Wouldn't we be looking for someone about five foot tall?'

'Not Sir Eddie,' said Martin. 'He was a giant for his day. About my height.'

'Which is?'

'Five ten.'

'Ah. So the feet wouldn't be ludicrously small.'

'No, sorry, the murderer wasn't a midget. The armour is adjustable in places anyway. It's all tied on by leather straps where its not actually fitted. So there is some room for adjustment.'

'Oh great.'

There was silence for a while.

'So the marks in the mud,' Eve began, 'were consistent with these weird feet thingies.'

'Yes,' said Martin eagerly, 'the deep heel marks, the elongated shape and the long thin marks at the end...'

'But how on earth would anyone walk in these in mud. Wouldn't the pointy bit at the front really stick in? You said yourself they weren't designed for walking, only horseback.'

'You've obviously never been scuba-diving!'

'What? What's that got to do with it?'

Martin stood up and demonstrated.

'He walked *backwards*. Just as you do wearing flippers when you're walking into the sea. Look. The heel goes back into the sand really deeply, the rest just drags along. That's why we saw very deep heel prints and only a faint line for the front bit being dragged along. It makes perfect sense. *The Murderer Walked Backwards!* What a great name for a murder mystery - I must tell my mother...'

'How horrible,' said Eve. The thought of someone dressed up in these peculiar metal bits walking backwards through a wood was very unnerving. 'I suppose we'll have to tell the police.'

'I already have!' said Martin. 'At lunchtime. I think we can be a great asset to them.'

'Oh, don't start interfering. The police hate amateurs fooling around.'

'You sound like my mother sometimes. I have no intention of "fooling around" as you so indelicately put it. I intend to put the reserves of my mighty brain power at their disposal, that's all. What a blast it would be the solve the case before they do!'

'Don't even think about it. You don't know what you're doing.'

'I've done pretty well so far. I've just given them their most valuable lead yet. Don't you want to join me?'

'What...what are you, a megalomaniac? I'm not going to join you or anybody. The police can manage perfectly well without us. Don't meddle with things that don't concern you...'

'There it goes, my mother again! I shall do what I jolly well want! It's you that'll be missing out. I can't believe that you of all people can rest with the case unsolved - with your history...'

'What history?' said Eve sharply.

'You know... your father, being a policeman...'

'Get out!'

There was silence. Eve's voice had suddenly changed - it was deeper, more authoritative, hardly like her voice at all. Martin frowned at her. He got up quietly and walked slowly out of the room.

Eve sat on the bed.

She mustn't begin to shake. She mustn't cry.

She must just breathe deeply and calm down. Why could he set her off like that? It was all so stupid...

There was a knock at the door. Eve caught her breath. Was it Martin?

'Eve! Phone call!' someone yelled through the door and left.

Eve walked slowly to the door and out into the hall, feeling as though her limbs were made of lead. The phone for her stairway was in a kiosk on the next floor down. The call was from Detective

Inspector Andy Andrews, asking Eve to meet him at the Incident Room at King Henry Hall on Wednesday. Of course he had asked Martin to be there as well. That young man had seemed very helpful. Perhaps they could both be of use. And when was she getting a mobile phone, so he could be in touch more easily?

Eve went back to her room. There was washing up to be done. But there on the bed was another picture of the Chichele armour. Martin must have left it. It was a sideways cross-section of the bascinet. Eve breathed in sharply. For the helmet had a metal beak, like a bird.

CHAPTER TWELVE

"When I had gone through my schools at Oxford, I who had been originally intended for the Church!!! made up my mind to take to art in some form...."

[William Morris writing to Andreas Sheu, 5 Sept 1883]

'There's something almost vampirish about young flesh,' Detective Sergeant Gavin Woolston was saying as he was leaving the room that Eve was entering. 'I don't think we should rule out an older bloke. Who says it's got to be a student? I think, look for a kinky older bloke.'

A policewoman was disagreeing with him. They were too absorbed to notice Eve. Their voices now disappeared down the corridor.

Eve looked around the Morris Room at King Henry Hall. It was not difficult to see why it was called the Morris Room, in spite of police attempts to turn it into open-plan offices. It was a late nineteenth century room with large oblong windows almost to the floor, decorated with small additions of Arts and Crafts stained glass. The curtains were huge expanses of William Morris' 'Strawberry Thief' design that Eve had just bought on a mug. These looked like original material that was more like a thick tapestry than modern-day curtains. The wallpaper also looked like the original Victorian - a complex design of beige and white flowers and birds that blended beautifully with the pale oak half-panelling of the lower walls. Eve was staring up at the ceiling with her mouth open when Martin's voice called her over.

'Ah, here she is! Eve, we're in here.'

Oh no, Martin was there already. Eve hoped he wasn't going to embarrass her in front of her godfather. She walked over to where Martin was standing. He was next to one of the white dividing screens that had been erected in the room to divide them up into small offices, each with their own phone line, desk, and computer.

Detective Inspector Andrews was sitting at a desk in one of these small 'offices'. He indicated to the only chair that wasn't occupied for Eve to sit down, with Martin on the other side. There was already an enormous collection of files and papers on his desk and he was ignoring the phone ringing.

'Thanks for coming, Eve,' he smiled. 'How are you?'

'Um, fine, fine,' Eve gurgled and then coughed, sounding anything but.

'Oh dear. Anyway, I've asked you to come here today to be filled in on a few details so you can be of more help to us, if that doesn't sound too mercenary...'

'Oh, are we going to be your snouts?' Martin interrupted.

Eve could have kicked him.

'If you want to put it that way,' said DI Andrews with a cold smile. 'Eyes and ears might be a better phrase. We're not asking you to play at detectives, of course...'

'Oh, of *course!*' Martin said eagerly.

'...but since you are students and you are the ones who found the body, other students might open up to you or pass on information that will be useful to us. It will also be easier for you to mingle with other students in certain settings more easily than my officers, young geniuses though they all may be. In view of this, and the help you've been already,' Andrews said, looking at Martin with a slight nod, 'I've decided to brief you on a few more of our findings that might help you know what to look out for. Alright?'

Both the students nodded, Martin enthusiastically, Eve doubtfully. Eve couldn't help wondering just how much of this was really for the reasons her 'uncle' was giving.

DI Andrews pulled a pile of papers on his desk a bit closer and continued speaking, now mainly looking at the papers rather than the students.

'We have now positively identified the victim and she is indeed Fern Harrison, known to most as "Feral" - a nickname she adopted at school and carried with her to university. She was nineteen, in common with most second year students who have not taken a year off to go and do something more enjoyable.'

Eve noticed Martin's mouth twitch slightly at this. How old was he? Had he taken a gap year?

'She was born and brought up in Brighton. Single-parent family. We've seen the mother. She came up to identify the body yesterday. Liz, our Family Liaison Officer, is working with her. Unfortunately the mother is too upset to answer questions particularly coherently at present, which is understandable but not much help to us. Suffice to say, she is completely at a loss as to who could have done this and why. There are no siblings. Ms Harrison is returning to Brighton to make arrangements for the funeral, although we are not quite sure when the body will be released.'

'How awful for her!' Eve exclaimed. 'And to have no one else.'

The two men nodded silently.

'That brings me to the cause of death,' said Andrews, turning over another sheet in his file. 'We should have the final pathologist's report soon, but meanwhile we have quite a lot to go on. As you know, the estimate of the time of death is between seven and seven thirty on Saturday morning. Dawn was at 7.12 am that day, so it makes sense that it was when it was starting to get light. We have other reasons to believe that the dawn was a significant time - I'll say why in a moment.'

'Martin's idea of the Chichele armour being used by the murderer is looking a distinct possibility, if not probability. We have yet to recover the relevant pieces of armour and so cannot match them exactly with the injuries to the body - all we have are the pictures from the Library from nineteenth century plates, which I believe you've seen, Eve.'

'Yes.'

'One of the main problems with this is that the pictures do not show the undersides of the gauntlets and, er, feet things...'

'Sabatons,' said Martin helpfully.

'...thank you, so we can't make an exact comparison as yet. We're making the finding of the missing armour a top priority as a result.'

'Interesting choice of murder weapon,' said Eve.

'In other words, are we looking for a real nutter?' Andrews smirked at her an imitation of a smile. 'Not necessarily, of course. It doesn't look sexually-motivated, at any rate. There's been no molestation in that respect.'

'Well, that's something,' said Eve.

'Although someone who prances about in medieval armour in the woods at the dead of night - I wouldn't like to bet on him being sexually normal,' said Martin.

'You could be right,' said Andrews in his reserved way. 'But at least we know that sex wasn't the main motivation for the attack.'

'Is it ever?' asked Eve. 'Don't we tend to believe now that even sexual attacks aren't really about sex, but about power?'

'That's the politically-correct view now, yes,' Andrews sighed.

'Don't you believe it?' asked Martin.

'It doesn't matter what I *believe*,' said the Detective Inspector. 'It's the evidence that's important.'

Eve felt as if they'd had their wrists slapped. Her 'uncle' continued:

'Cause of death - strangulation - at first possibly with some sort of thin strap or belt which didn't do the job. Then the use of hands in the usual manner, but we are guessing in leather gloves covered by the stolen gauntlets. This makes any leads on the stolen armour absolutely essential.'

'But,' said Martin hesitantly, 'it might not be the same person who stole the armour who did the murder. I checked with Guy - Guy Fastness - on Monday - I left him a note - about whether he had any plastic bags or carrier bags or whatever lying around his room, you know, bin bags perhaps. We'd all only just moved back into our rooms that day at the start of the year and so everyone had tons of bags kicking around. Well, why couldn't the thief take the armour out of the packing cases in Guy's room on Friday night, shove the relevant bits into some bags Guy had lying around and waltz out of the room and then hide them?'

'No reason why not,' said DI Andrews, 'as long as the bags were strong enough to carry the armour.'

'Well, Guy thinks he might have had some strong enough. You know those Blackwell's plastic bags, and other book shops that have to sell mega-reinforced ones to cope with heavy tomes. Well, Guy thinks he may have some bags missing from his room, and I think they were hidden in that cubby-hole opposite his room for a while. The dust...'

'Meaning someone else could have found them and nicked them,' Andrews finished the conclusion for him. 'Yes, you're right. But we still need to know who took the armour in the first place. The more pieces of the picture we can fill in, the better. Now let me show you something.'

DI Andrews reached inside a large manilla envelope and took out some photos. Eve automatically recoiled in her chair. She didn't want to see photos of the body.

'Does this mean anything to you?'

It was a photograph of a black marking on the inside of someone's wrist, presumably the dead girl's. It looked like a stylised picture of a sun rising above the sea. There was a black sun with wavy rays shooting out from it into the sky above the waves of the ocean.

'Is it a tattoo?' asked Eve.

'That's right,' said Andrews, 'but we don't yet know where from. It may be of no significance, of course. It was on her left wrist.'

'Oh,' said Martin, 'I didn't see that because of her hands crossed over her chest.'

Andrews replaced the photo in the envelope as suddenly as he had taken it out, with no further explanation, and continued:

'Apart from that, there's not much to go on as far as the body's concerned. You know the eyelids were removed...'

The two students nodded soberly.

'... no sign of them yet. Obviously we're dragging that part of the river, doing a fingertip search, etc. People we've spoken to so far have confirmed that Feral had a penchant for extremely long and thick false eyelashes. We've found several pairs in her room...'

'I've been wondering...' Martin interrupted eagerly.

'Yes?'

'...if perhaps the murderer didn't mean to remove the eyelids. I mean, we now know he was wearing the gauntlets. Perhaps he just meant to pull off the false eyelashes, but the gauntlets made him clumsy.'

'Entirely possible, didn't know his own strength perhaps,' said Andrews drily. 'At the moment it doesn't really matter one way or the other. I suppose deliberately removing the eyelids might take the killer a few more notches up the loony scale, or it might have some symbolic significance. But at the moment I just want to catch the bastard, I'll leave the psychological profile to our shrink.'

Eve felt the psychological equivalent of slapped wrists again.

'What about, um, Feral's friends here?' she asked to change the subject. 'Do you want us to get to know them, or what? I'm not part of this college, so it would be difficult for me.'

'You can always come here as my guest,' said Martin. 'Come to as many meals and things as you want.'

'That would be one way of doing it,' agreed Andrews, 'although of course nothing too obvious. There's really only one friend that we want to keep an eye on, as it were, at the moment, and that's Angela White. Do you know her?' he asked Martin.

'I know her a bit. She goes out with Rory Ablett. I know him better. I do know that she was great friends with Feral at the beginning of last year, but then there was a distinct cooling-off, about the time when Angela started dating Rory probably.'

DI Andrews nodded. He then reached into another envelope and pulled out two plastic bags.

'Have a look at these.'

He passed the plastic bags over the desk to them. Eve had a bag containing an envelope. It was made of thick pale green paper which looked very good quality. The edge of the envelope looked ruffled as if it had been badly cut - like handmade paper - and there was a silver wax seal on the flap, a fancy mock-medieval depiction of the letter 'L'.

Martin was now reading out loud the letter that had come inside the envelope that had been handed to him. His reading was slow and halting, as if he was translating it as he went along:

'To my Derest Ladye,

From her most loyale and obedient subject and bondslave:

'Thou knowest that thou art my one trewe Love. Why tormentest thou me in such fashion? I beg thee to allowe me to proove that love one more tyme. Mete mee at the clering nown as the Waste Foreyste at sun rise tomorrow morn and I will shew thee the trewe stayte of mine hearte and the regard in wyche I hold thee, my onlye Ladye and Sovrayne.'

There was silence as the two students digested the impact of the letter.

'Found on her desk,' said DI Andrews.

'The letter that lured her to her death,' said Martin, as if reading a newspaper headline.

'Who is "L"?' said Eve frowning.

'That's what we want to know,' said her uncle. 'Is it "L" who stole the armour? All this medieval stuff... seems to be quite a theme.'

'The letter's in gothic script,' said Martin, holding it up to the light. 'And beautiful calligraphy. Whoever wrote this was very good. Oh! And it's Churston Deckle notepaper! Wow, I thought I recognised it.'

'You recognise it?' said DI Andrews mildly.

'Yes, my mother's got tons of the stuff. I think they stopped manufacturing it in the early eighties, but she bought a lot of the last sets. It's some of the most beautiful paper ever made - I'd kill for more of it, but they've stopped manufacture... oh, forget I said that! Of course, I wouldn't... Anyway, someone else must have got hold of some.'

'So it would appear,' said Andrews.

There was an awkward silence for a while, as Eve now looked at the letter.

'It's all in old-fashioned spelling,' she said, 'like Chaucer, or something.'

'Was there anything else of importance in her room?' asked Martin.

'Oh, there's a lot to sort through. The poor girl had hardly had chance to unpack, so a lot was still in bags and boxes. We're still going through it. The only other immediate lead is the fact that Feral was in the University French Society, but seeing as that has about five hundred members it might take us a while to ferret through it. Anyway, you two can help by just keeping all this in mind and keeping your eyes and ears open. As I said, people may well be willing to let things drop in conversation with you that they wouldn't if they thought the police were in the vicinity. Anything that strikes you as odd or unusual - anything at all, you let us know. I've told DS Woolston to look after you - Gavin. He'll be your contact.'

Eve felt her heart sink. She then rebuked herself for being so silly as to think her 'uncle' would make an exception for her and keep in touch with them personally. Perhaps he really did just want to use them because they found the body, not because of her special link with him. 'Special link' - huh! Who was she kidding? She'd hardly seen 'Uncle Andy' over the last few years - although he did make it to her Dad's funeral. Eve started to feel angry. What right had he got to try and involve her in a murder inquiry? He should be protecting her from all this, not throwing her further in it - especially in view of... what had happened to her father.

Martin was standing up, taking the Inspector's last statement as a cue to leave. The phone rang and Andrews picked it up. Eve stood up too, ready to go.

'Great, great,' Andrews was saying, 'I'll be right over. See you.'

He looked up with a cross between a grin and a grimace.

'Well, we've found the boat - the boat the murderer used to get to the scene, we *think*. It's a college boat, with "кнн" burnt into the hull. You'll be familiar with that,' Andrews said to Martin.

'Yes, one of King Henry Hall's. Where was it found?' Martin frowned.

'Near an old abandoned boat house on the other side of the woods - nearer the Donnington Bridge end. Must have left it there and come back another way. Mmmmm.'

'Does that mean it's more likely to be a student from King's?' Eve asked.

'No,' said Martin defensively. 'Anyone can pick the locks on the boats - I mean, anyone who knows how to pick locks. The padlocks on the boat chains are accessible to anyone at the back of college where all the boats and punts are lined up - you saw them. Anyone with a college key or copy of one could do it as well of course.'

'I think that will be all,' said DI Andrews. 'Thank you for your time. I must be off now.'

He shooed them out ahead of him, out of the Morris Room and into the corridor where he said a curt goodbye. When he had disappeared around the corner, Martin hissed:

'Wow, I thought he was going to have me nailed for the murder any moment!'

'Huh. I'm surprised he didn't suspect me,' said Eve, still stung by her 'uncle's' attitude. 'Pretty soon I'll have to produce my bus ticket to prove I was travelling from London when it happened.'

'Guilty until proven innocent,' Martin announced melodramatically. 'Do you fancy a cuppa? My room's nearby. Let's collapse over a cup of the black stuff and recover from our ordeal.'

'Oh, I don't know...' Eve looked at her watch. 'I think I've got a lecture soon. Or have I already missed it? Oh no, I think I'm late for it already.'

'In that case, you may as well be even later and miss it altogether,' said Martin happily, leading her down the corridor towards Sanderson Quad. He pointed out Feral's room as they walked past.

'Of course, the police have got it all taped off,' he said. 'I looked yesterday. Got a very gruff rebuke from the officer on duty as if I was a very naughty boy for wanting to look inside. It was 'more than his job was worth' to let me have a peek, of course.'

'I should think so!' Eve exclaimed. 'Curiosity killed the cat!'

'Particularly if they're of the feral variety,' riposted Martin.

'Hmmm.' Eve could not think of a suitable reply.

And she also could not restrain her curiosity from wanting a 'peek' at the room of Crispin Martin Alexander de Beauchamp-Massey.

CHAPTER THIRTEEN

"Each little fault of temper and each social defect
In my erring fellow creatures, I endeavour to correct...
I love my fellow creatures - I do all the good I can -
Yet everybody says I'm such a disagreeable man!
And I can't think why!"

[Gilbert and Sullivan, *Princess Ida*, 1884]

Martin and Eve approached the stairway marked 'H' in the Sanderson Quad. As they clattered up the wooden stairs, loud insistent thumping music began on the first landing. A threatening guitar thrash made it even louder and Martin cried out in an agony of exasperation.

'I'm going to kill that bastard!' he yelled as he ran into the first floor corridor and hammered on one of the doors. Even the old stone walls seemed to be resonating with the sound.

'Baker, you shithead!' Martin was yelling and peering through a gap at the side of the door. 'I can see you're in there! Turn that bloody awful stuff off!'

There was a slight pause and then the music lessened in volume.

'Is that OK?' a voice from the room cried resentfully. 'I thought you were out.'

'I was. But I'm back. Why don't you put headphones on, you bastard?' said Martin. 'I've got a guest. We don't want to hear

Metal Slime and the Demonic Dickheads! We want to be able to hear our conversation.'

There was another pause. Then the music disappeared altogether. The culprit must have donned his headphones.

Martin glared at the closed door for a few more seconds to make sure, then turned back to where Eve had been standing. Martin ran his hands through his hair and looked genuinely astonished.

'Anti-social shit!' he exclaimed in disbelief. 'How can anyone think that's acceptable behaviour?'

'At least he thought you were out,' said Eve.

'That's no excuse. There are other people who'd be able to hear it. Anyway,' Martin sighed and flung his hair back, 'I'm up on the next floor. Let's see if we can recover some peace and sanity before my homicidal desires get the better of me.'

They reached the next floor. Martin's room was number eight, the first of three rooms on that landing. Martin took out a bunch of keys and opened it up, 'Open sesame seed!' followed by 'Oh God, I hope it's not too much of a mess.' He turned round to Eve before she could enter. 'How sensitive a flower are you? Will the sight of male underwear drying on a radiator give you the vapours?'

'Depends what kind of vapours they're giving off!' said Eve.

Martin responded with 'Arf, arf' and let her in.

He had to switch the light on as the curtains were already drawn. Apparently he had been out all day and had never opened them. This gave rise to Martin re-telling the old joke:

'Why don't students open their curtains in the morning? Answer: Because it gives them something to do in the afternoon!'

Now it was Eve's turn to feign laughter. But really she was much more interested in taking in as much as possible of Martin's room without him noticing her doing so.

It was a breath-taking combination of beauty and clutter, of mess and elegance. The room itself was obviously very old with a low beamed ceiling. The walls were white and the beams were painted black. The wardrobe and desk, chairs and cupboard, were all old mahogany, carved and warped into interesting shapes. The walls were covered in old pictures and silly posters - a landscape painted in oil in a gilt frame, a poster of a cartoon character called

'Mr Happy', a soppy Victorian print of a spaniel greeting its owner, a black-and-white poster of Brigitte Bardot wearing very little, another oil painting of someone who looked suspiciously like an ancestor, and an advertisement for a University Drama production of *Hamlet* - with none other than Martin in black doublet and hose looking striking and soulful in the lead role. His long swept-back hair, instead of annoying, looked perfect.

But it was rather hard to see anything else as virtually every surface was covered with something - rolled up socks, inside-out sweaters, muddy trainers, mugs, bottles of wine, bottles of after-shave, a computer and printer, CDs in and out of their covers, and books and paper everywhere, and more books and paper.

'Wow,' was all Eve could say as Martin cleared away a slurry of books and odds and ends from one of the chairs (onto the floor) for her to sit down. Now she recognised the smell. It *was* Martin's after-shave. She must have smelt it on him before and not taken any notice. But here in his room it was overpowering, as if she was in the eye of a storm, at the centre of some huge fragrant emanation that Martin absorbed and carried with him where ever he went. What was it's name? She couldn't see an obvious bottle lying around. It was surprisingly pleasant. Anyway, thought Eve, looking at the underwear Martin was scooping off the radiator and the many socks lying around, it could have been a worse smell.

'Have you really only been in here for...' Eve calculated, '... six days? How could you make it so messy in so short a time?'

'This isn't mess,' said Martin brightly, 'this is evidence of my creative genius - at least, that's what I tell my mother. The trouble is,' he added more gloomily, 'she can lay claim to creative genius, and she is immensely, if not neurotically, tidy and enhances any room she goes near. So that one definitely doesn't wash with her.'

'Hmmm.' Then Eve suddenly exclaimed: 'Oh my God, you've got a piano in here!'

'You've only just noticed? Ten out of ten for observation. Anyway, if you'll look more closely, you'll see it isn't a piano at all.'

Eve sprang out of her seat and went to where Martin was flipping up the lid on what she had wrongly identified as a piano.

It too had so many envelopes and items of clothing on it that it was hardly surprising Eve had at first glance assumed it was a large desk.

'Oh, wow,' breathed Eve as Martin sat at the keyboard and ran his hand up and down a few scales, 'it's a harpsichord!'

'A virginal was so-called because it was played by virgins,' said Martin playing grand portentous chords. 'A harpsichord should therefore be played by harpies. Can I tempt you to try?'

Eve pretended to hit him. Martin ducked and laughed. He smiled up at her radiant face and broke into some frantic Mozart - the 'Turkish Rondo'.

'Oh, please,' cried Eve teasingly. 'Everyone knows that one!'

'Well, how about this?' Martin broke off and began to do a Noel Coward impersonation that turned into 'A Room with a View'.

'That doesn't sound right on that instrument,' complained Eve. 'Play something more appropriate.'

Martin thought for a moment. He then began to sing in Italian. Eve looked away, trying to remember what it was. She knew it instinctively, it was one of her favourites. Ah, of course. It was 'Amaryllis', a baroque love song that her Aunt Barbara had on an old record sung by Dame Janet Baker. It was beautiful. Too beautiful. She had played it a lot last year...

'Alright,' she said hastily, 'that's a good one. What else do you know?'

'What is this?' said Martin frowning, 'a competition? The woman won't let me finish anything.'

'You have a very good voice,' said Eve, wanting to make up for her rudeness. 'Um, very strong and clear - a good tenor.'

'Oh,' said Martin in a high voice, 'and here was me hoping I had a sweet soprano!'

'Was *Hamlet* the musical version?' said Eve in revenge, nodding towards the poster.

'Oooh, bitch! Now let's see what you can do. Tinkle those old ivories. And they *are* old ivory, too.'

Martin stood up for Eve to take her place at the keyboard.

She said 'Wow' again, and licked her lips, trying to think of something appropriate to play. The only one she could think of offhand was a John Danyel song, written in 1606. It was originally for the lute but she had simplified and adapted it for piano a couple of years before. That should do. She lifted up her head and sang:

> 'He whose desires are still,
> are still abroad, I see,
> hath never any peace at home the while.
> And therefore now come back,
> come back my heart to me.
> It is but for superfluous things we toil.
> Rest alone, rest alone, with thyself -
> Be all within,
> For what without thou gainst, thou dost not win.
> Honour, wealth,
> Honour, wealth, glory, fame,
> are no such things,
> but that which from imagination springs!
> My wretched heart that seems to overgrow,
> doth creep but on the earth,
> lies base and low!'

'Mmmmm,' said Martin after a long pause when Eve was sitting with her hands quietly in her lap, 'an uplifting little ditty. They were certainly into Life as a Vale of Tears in those days, weren't they? Well, you do have a magnificent voice. Pure and lovely. One of the clearest and cleanest sopranos I've ever heard...'

'Oh, thank you!'

'But...' and Martin paused tantalisingly.

Eve didn't know whether to ask him or not. What was he going to say?

'But..?' she said defensively.

'Hmmm. I can't tell you now. You'll go all huffy.'

'No, I will not!'

'You are already! Oh, OK, OK, I'll say it.'

Martin went over to the armchair he had cleared for Eve earlier and sat down. He flicked his hair back (it was annoying this time) and sat with his hands clasped, sucking two of his fingers.

'I don't know whether I know you well enough to say this.' He glanced at her. 'Oh well, here goes. Your voice is stunning. One of the loveliest I've ever heard. But... but there is something... something in the background, on the edge of it. I think it's pain. Yes, there's an edge of pain in some of the higher notes that's... painful to listen to. It's sounds like a broken heart - I know that sounds corny, but...'

But Eve had already knocked over the piano stool in her hurry to cross the room, grab her coat, and leave.

As the door sighed to behind her, Martin leant back in his chair.

'Oh shit,' he said. 'Open mouth, insert foot. Find sore point, press hard.'

It was obvious he shouldn't follow her. Anyway, at that point there was a knock at the door and a friendly face surmounted by a turban looked round the door.

'Was that tornado from your room? Have you been breaking female hearts again?'

'Occupational hazard, Al,' smiled Martin at Albert Singh. 'Come in, mate.'

'I'm only here to ask if you would grace us with your many talents in the Gilbert and Sullivan Society this year. I'm President, as you know.'

'Fanatic, more like.'

'How would you like a change from the tragedy of Shakespeare to the comedy of G and S? It's not going to be amateurish at all.'

'That will make a change.'

'It's *Princess Ida*. We'll be performing in the Debating Chamber of the Union in Eighth Week. We have wonderful costumes - lots of velvet and tights and even suits of armour! I have you in my mind's eye in the male lead - the tenor - Prince Hilarion. All we need now is to find your Princess, your Ida, whom you have been destined to marry since you were betrothed as mere babes! Do you know any good sopranos this year?'

Eve inevitably came to Martin's mind - she hadn't really left it - along with a very large bouquet of flowers that might well be in order.

CHAPTER FOURTEEN

"We'll storm their bowers
With scent and showers
Of fairest flowers that we can buy!"

[Gilbert and Sullivan, *Princess Ida*, 1884]

Eve was trying to sleep in, even though it was a Friday and she was supposed to be at Chapel. She rolled over and squinted at the digital display on her clock radio. Good grief, it was only seven thirty! Exactly the time when she was normally wakened by the alarm! Did her body clock have to be quite that efficient and become a clone of the real thing? My brain must be like a computer, Eve thought, there's a darned clock ticking away in there all the time.

Eve felt she had a right to be grumpy. She needed more sleep. It had been a crazy week. Why, it was only six days ago that..., well, she didn't want to go into that, but for an Induction Week at College, it had been somewhat unusual. And although Eve now had shaken off the sore throat and runny nose side of the 'flu, she still felt deeply weary, right down in her muscles. Oh, please God, don't let it be some awful long-term post-viral thing, she half-thought, half-prayed. It can take people years to get over that. I just need more sleep.

So Eve lay for another useless half-hour in bed - too awake to go to sleep, too tired to get up. Perhaps I'm just a hypochondriac, she thought, that's what Martin said. Oh forget Martin, said another part of her. And so she argued with herself for a while. At least it passed the time.

When she finally got up, she went to the sink in her room to wash. Ow! What was that? She looked down. There was a big cut on her left hand, as if she'd sliced it down something very sharp. The cut was not bleeding but was red and sore, her skin at the side feeling tight and puffy, the industrial-strength soap making it sting terribly. She had no idea how she'd done it.

Eve immediately thought of Feral. She had had cuts on her hands. The armour had been very sharp - so many sharp jutting out edges, and spikes on the gloves. Bare flesh pushing against that to fend the killer off had no chance. How much had she felt? Did she notice her hands being ripped to shreds if she was being throttled? Do you get such a rush of adrenalin in a life-threatening situation that you don't feel much of the pain? Or is the panic itself enough?

'Stop it, stop it, stop it!' Eve suddenly said out loud. She looked up at herself in the mirror. Her eyes looked wide and wild, as if she'd really frightened herself. I mustn't do that again, she thought. She remembered how the thought of how her father had died had kept her awake on so many nights a year ago - the horrible graphic, physical detail that would parade through her mind against her will, imagining what he had suffered when the bullet had gone into his chest and another into his arm. Which had hurt the most? What had it felt like? It had taken him a while to die - no one would tell her how long. Did the pain get better or worse? Did he know what was happening when he was taken to hospital? Did he know what they were doing to him there, as he lay cold and dying on a trolley, surrounded by people he didn't know?

Oh God! Eve put her hands over her face. She mustn't let it come back. She mustn't let the death of this person she didn't even know bring to mind that of the one she loved most in the whole world. Eve had been amazed at the appalling clinical detail about death that could trot through her mind at three in the morning and have her pacing up and down the room, trying to tire herself enough to go back to sleep. The pills had helped for a while, but sometimes with them she had felt she was even less in control of her mind if she did wake up, and her imagination would have an added edge of nastiness that hadn't been there before, as if the chemicals had added an extra kick. It was then that she really began to believe, not just in theory, in a personal force of evil that tempts and torments human beings, that kicks them when they're down. It felt really evil that she was being teased with such thoughts at her most vulnerable moments.

So, it was happening again. She would just have to pray for protection.

Eve hurriedly brushed her hair (into a complete fuzz) and put on jeans and a large sloppy sweater. She ran down to breakfast, looking forward to human company for a change.

As she entered the Dining Room there were about thirty ministerial students already seated at the large tables. When they saw her, they all began to yell and whistle:

'Here she is!'

'Whoa!'

'Who's the lucky man?!'

Eve stopped in her tracks and looked behind her to see if anyone else had come in. No, they must mean her.

'What on earth are they talking about?' she asked the person nearest her.

They all laughed and Marion shouted:

'Haven't you looked at your post yet?'

'No, I came straight here...'

'Well, I'd advise you to go down to the pigeon holes and see what's waiting there for you.'

Eve hesitated for a few seconds, then said, 'Oh, alright,' reluctantly and left the room, to the sound of more laughter.

It was not surprising that they were laughing, really. For waiting for Eve by the pigeonholes was the most enormous toy rabbit sitting amongst a basket of flowers. It was holding one paw up to its eyes as if it was crying and was wearing a bib with 'I'M SORRY!' embroidered on it in pink.

It had to be Martin. Eve didn't even need to read the card that was stuck to the polythene. She lifted it up grimly and went back to her room. There was no way she was appearing in the dining room with it.

In her room again, she slipped on a coat, took up her bag and ran down the stairs again to leave St Frideswide's by a side door.

Outside the air was fresh and cool after rain during the night. Eve trotted happily over to Little Clarendon Street and went into 'Le Café Rouge' for a breakfast of *pains au chocolat* and strong *café au lait* and a read of the French newspapers kept in racks there. At least they wouldn't have any news of the murder in them. Eve hadn't dared look at the English newspapers all week.

Although, to be fair, even if she had, she would not have known the main development in the case that there had been that week. It had not been given to the media.

For, in response to some of the leaflets circulated by the police asking for information, a woman had come forward.

Anne Macready had been walking her dog just before dawn on the morning of the murder. The dog had been restless and, as they were walking down by the river near Donnington Bridge, the dog had run off towards the woods. Mrs Macready had been obliged to follow, but soon the path was too muddy and Mrs Macready was becoming too scared to go much further amongst the trees all on her own. She was now near the part of the woods where the old Boat House stood, a fairly small one built in the Edwardian heyday of the river, but now no longer used since the river had silted up so much in that area. It was slightly misty, so the view was far from perfect amongst the trees, but Mrs Macready was suddenly shocked to see something emerge from the Boathouse. The door had creaked quite loudly as if it hadn't been used for a long time.

But it had been all Mrs Macready could do not to scream when she saw the strange figure that emerged. It was a suit of armour! Walking all on its own! Well, she supposed there must have been someone in it, but it was such a shock to see it that she didn't think of that at first. It was walking rather awkwardly, as if it hadn't been used for a long time either. When it turned round she'd almost screamed - the face was frightening, with like a bird's beak in metal. She could see a breastplate too, and - what's it called - chain mail over the upper part of the arms. She couldn't really see his lower half because of the trees. What then amazed her was the thing started to walk backwards through the woods behind it, as if it was a video being played backwards in slow motion. It almost fell over at one point but righted itself by grabbing at a tree. Yes, it was wearing metal gloves too. Did it have a sword? Yes, she thought it might have had one.

The police were both pleased and annoyed. It was superb confirmation of the use of the armour by the murderer, as well as the use of the Old Boathouse, which had already been checked by the police forensic team. The police had merely asked the public if they had seen anything 'suspicious' around that time on the Saturday morning, not mentioning the armour at all. This alone made Anne Macready's evidence convincing. What *was* a problem, however, was her seeming embellishment of the details. She had mentioned a breastplate. But the Chichele breastplate had not been one of the items stolen (perhaps not surprising, as it weighed around fifteen pounds). Had the murderer acquired a breastplate from elsewhere? Or was Mrs Macready's imagination running away with her - all alone in the woods in the dark and the mist? The police had then tested her by asking if the man was carrying a sword. The fact that Anne Macready said he might have been again threw doubt on the accuracy of her memory.

Then another witness had come forward later on in the week. Or perhaps 'come forward' is the wrong way to describe the fact that an elderly drunk in one of the police cells overnight started rambling on about having seen a medieval knight. The drunk was singing away and laughing and yelling out. But then the sergeant on duty heard him making jokes about 'night' and 'knight' - seeing a medieval knight in the woods at night, or perhaps it was morning. The sergeant had the man questioned and it turned out that the man had seen something relevant in the woods near Donnington Bridge (the drunk had been wondering about sleeping in the Old Boathouse). The drunk also described the knight as wearing full armour, although he could not remember a sword. But a notorious drunk who had been known to have hallucinations - how reliable a witness was that?

But it still left the police with the problem - *if* the murderer was wearing *full* armour, where on earth did he get the rest?

CHAPTER FIFTEEN

"THIS HELMET, I SUPPOSE,
WAS MEANT TO WARD OFF BLOWS,
IT'S VERY HOT, AND WEIGHS A LOT,
AS MANY A GUARDSMAN KNOWS,
SO OFF, SO OFF THAT HELMET GOES."

[GILBERT AND SULLIVAN, *PRINCESS IDA*, 1884]

Eve felt revitalised after her indulgent breakfast. She should now do something useful. It was the second day of the Freshers Fair at the Examinations Schools building on the High Street. She should go there and see what university societies were being offered that she could perhaps join. It would be good to be part of something in the wider university, rather than just sticking to Frideswide's.

She paid for her meal (in French, which didn't impress the English waiter) and began the walk down St Giles to Cornmarket and the High Street. The streets were lively with traffic and the detritus of autumn littered the pavement, mainly wet leaves in treacherous clumps, slippery and soggy underfoot. But for the first time since she had arrived in Oxford, Eve was feeling glad to be alive. St John's College and then Balliol on the left and the Randolph Hotel ahead of her managed to look even more beautiful than usual, their Cotswold sandstone made darker and more dramatic by the rain. There was a refreshing tang in the air, a clean feeling of a new beginning. The other students who passed by her on the pavement seemed fresh-faced and optimistic - laughing, smoking, in urgent discussion, and generally looking 'cool'. By the time Eve had reached the Examination Schools building, she felt ready for anything.

There seemed to be a lot of people hanging around the tall imposing building. Eve fought her way through the marble lobby seething with other students all making a noise and entered the first of the many rooms given over to the Freshers Fair. The high-ceilinged hall was full of stalls surmounted by banners proclaiming the name of the Society they represented. Each room had a theme - Political, Religious and Charitable, Sporting, Social, Literary, etc, etc. Eve could hardly believe her eyes. Each stall was manned by students who were passionately advocating their society and urging people to sign up.

How could so many eighteen- and nineteen-year-olds have developed such determined and eccentric personalities so young? They all seemed set on carrying their obsessions to the ultimate limit. Eve soon began to feel that when she was a five year old playing with dolls, all these strange characters around her must have already mastered the violin and irregular Latin verbs. They all seemed well-defined before their time. Eve couldn't help but compare them to many eighteen year olds she had left behind in her home town, now just drifting, or worse - systematically destroying themselves.

Eve's teenage rebellion had taken the form of becoming religious. She had gone along to a local church youth club and become transfixed by the concept of God. She had begun to read Theology books on the sly. Mmmm. Maybe she was weird too. That had been her eccentricity, the individuating passion that had already defined her.

By the time she had fought her way through the first three rooms, she had already signed up for the Oxford Union Society, the C S Lewis Society, the William Morris Society, and the Oxford Inter-Collegiate Christian Union. What with her already existing membership of Amnesty International and Greenpeace, how was she ever going to get any work done?!

Just before leaving she decided to pop into the last room and see what was in there. There seemed to be a lot of people in costumes. There was the Dark Ages Society - two young men were standing behind that stall dressed in chain mail and breastplates with short pointed helmets. Eve might have felt scared at the sight of armour again but the two young men looked so anaemic and weedy instead of butch warriors that it was all Eve could manage not to laugh. Next to them was the Tolkien Society - the students appeared to be dressed as Hobbits. Oh, and here was someone in a grey cloak with a long white false beard coming over - Gandalf, presumably. Next to them was the OU Fantasy Society - a monster with two heads and a woman in tight black leather studded with spikes manned that stall. Eve hardly dared imagine what they got up to. Their neighbouring stall was the Retrotech Society - people in exaggerated 80s clothes and makeup with huge mobile phones and computers on display. Next to them was the Launcelot and Guinevere Society, presumably devoted to Arthurian legend. The woman there was dressed as a medieval maiden with a laced bodice and a tall pointed hat with a flowing chiffon scarf hanging down the back.

On the other side of the room was the OU Psychodrama Society. Eve decided to wander over and find out what it was about.

'Hi!' she said to the earnest girl in glasses behind the stall. 'Can you tell me about your club?'

'Oh, certainly! We form quite a tight-knit little group. If we get a lot more members this time we'll divide into more groups - it's good not to have more than seven per group. Anyway, then we get to know each other and do exercises together to build up our level of trust.'

'Exercises?'

'Both physical and psychological, mainly centring on forms of meditation. We're then ready after a couple of weeks to do the main exercises together, that are aimed at accessing our subconscious material. We are given a certain situation as a group - different roles to play - and then we act out those roles, eg. Parent/Child conflict, Sibling Rivalry, problems with an Authority Figure, etc. And through the specific concrete situations we get in touch with what's really inside us. If you have a problem with your mother or father, for example, you can act it out with one of your group and let all your repressed emotion out. It's very healing. There can be lots of tears,' the girl smiled.

'I think I'm doing that every day at the moment,' Eve smiled back, 'I don't need to join a group! Thanks anyway.'

The two of them laughed and Eve moved on to the next stall.

It was the OU New Age Society. The stall was covered in jewellery and scarves with astrological signs, incense, a pack of tarot cards were laid out in a display, and a brass model of the moon and the sun was hanging above their sign.

'Are you interested in this sort of thing?' asked the pretty girl behind the stall.

'Oh, no,' Eve smiled 'I'm a Christian.'

'You can be a Christian and interested in this. Lots of my friends are.'

'I don't think so...'

'We're all on the same path really, it's just that we call things by different names.'

'Well, if you want to believe that, I can't stop you!' Eve smiled.

'So we can't get you to sign up then? You could come to our first open evening - there's lots of food and drink. And we've got the best spiritualist in town to come and do a session for us - it'll be very entertaining!'

'Um, no,' Eve frowned, 'spiritualism is forbidden in the Bible. We're not supposed to try and get in touch with the dead.'

'But don't you have a loved one you'd like to get in touch with who's gone...'

'Um, no, no,' said Eve hurriedly, 'thank you, no.'

Eve marched off as quickly as possible without wanting to look unfriendly. The room was a blur. Who the heck were all these people anyway? Tons of them milling about, all completely crazy! She ought to get out, get some fresh air, get something to eat.

But just before she left the hall, a thought occurred to her, or rather an image came into her mind. Frowning and reluctant she traced her steps back to the New Age stall.

'Oh, it's you again!' said the girl. 'Had second thoughts?'

'No, well, in a way, yes,' said Eve uncertainly. 'If I said to you... if you saw someone with a tattoo - a black sun rising over the sea - would that mean anything to you? I mean, is it symbolic of anything you've ever heard of?'

The girl looked interested and thought for a while.

'Hmmm, a black sun... rising over the sea... hmmm, could it be Egyptian? There was a strong solar cult on and off for centuries in Egypt - you know, Akenaten and all that. Of course, the Greeks also had a thing about the sun - Apollo. Are you sure the sun was rising? Could it be sinking? In which case that would mean nightfall rather than dawn.'

'Wow, I don't know. There weren't any arrows on it to show which way it was going!'

'Can't you ask the person concerned? Or is it a secret?'

'Um, it's a secret.'

'Well, sorry I can't be of more help. But you could probably look it up in the library. My bet is it's Egyptian.'

'It didn't *look* particularly Egyptian... oh well.'

'It could be important whether it was rising or setting,' said the girl seriously, 'as to whether it represents Life - rising - or Death - sinking down to the Underworld of the dead.'

'Well, thank you, I'll have to give it more thought.'

'It's probably easiest just to ask the person concerned!'

'Um, yeah, thanks. Bye.'

Yes, and I bet you'd like me to ask her via a spiritualist at your next session, thought Eve grimly. Of course, the police had been known to use so-called psychics to get leads on murder inquiries. But somehow Eve couldn't imagine her 'uncle' going along with that. Not unless he got really desperate. Eve hoped it wouldn't come to that. It wasn't exactly good publicity for the police if they couldn't solve a crime on their own and it also gave credence to some of the worst forms of dabbling in the supernatural. Eve could imagine Martin giving short-shrift to the whole thing too. Not that she cared about what Martin thought about anything.

On the way out Eve couldn't resist going over to the weedy guys in armour at the Dark Ages Society.

'Come to our Celtic Rave!' one of them called out to her. 'Saturday night - unlimited beer!'

'What sort of thing do you normally do?'

'Oh, re-enactments, mostly. And eating and drinking!'

'We re-enact great battles of the Dark Ages,' said the other guy, his glasses looking ill-at-ease under his helmet. 'Then we drink too much around an open fire...'

'With wenches serving our every need!' said the first guy. 'Would you like to be one of our wenches?'

'I don't think so!' Eve laughed. 'Where do you do all this - what is it, re-enacting?'

'Oh, there are plenty of fields and open clearings in woods around here...'

'Good God,' said Eve quietly, her thoughts elsewhere.

The two guys looked at each other.

'It's not that bad,' said one of them.

'And where do you get your armour from?' Eve asked.

'Oh, a local blacksmith makes it for us. Some people try and make their own, but you need specialist tools really...'

'And a furnace!'

'...so mostly we go to this local chap. 'Course some people already have their own set when they come up here.'

'Yes, lots of school kids are into re-enactments at an early age - what with fantasy films and computer games - you know, Sword and Sorcery stuff.'

'And graphic novels too.'

'Oh, right,' said Eve, 'thank you.'

'Here, take an invitation to the Celtic Rave. Come in costume. It's amazing what you can make with a few old sheets.'

'We had one guy at the last party wearing Paddington Bear sheets! It wasn't exactly authentic!'

Eve took the invitation and waved goodbye. She really did need some fresh air... and some sane people.

It was strange, she reflected on the walk home, how innocent it all looked on the surface - just students having fun, undergraduate high spirits, and all that. But she'd just met some people who represented whole groups dedicated to delving into areas of the subconscious and the spirit that they probably shouldn't be touching with a ten foot pole.

She walked back via the University Park. There were still some flowers out and Eve enjoyed drinking in the sight of such a huge expanse of grass. There was a cricket pavilion in the distance and the gentle sight of the occasional person walking a dog, students kicking a ball around, and the sound of the quacking of ducks on a unseen pond. A sudden gust of wind pelted her with dead rose petals.

Over coffee and biscuits in her room, she went through the bag of stuff she'd been given at the Fair. It had a National Union of Students logo on the side, sponsored by a national newspaper which was offering cheap annual subscription to students. Eve didn't need that as they had the main newspapers in St Frideswide's Common Room each day. Of course, you couldn't always get to read them on the day they came out because of the demand. Perhaps she should order the *Guardian* or the *Independent*, or whatever, if they were doing good deals.

Other special offers that spilled out of the plastic bag were for cheaper travel, music to download, winning your year's rent in a competition, 'BOLD' washing powder welcomes you to University' with a £1 voucher, a huge Radio One schedule in a cool red and black format for your wall, OXFAM offers, a free sample of 'Witch Doctor' antiseptic astringent to 'SOOTHE SKIN IRRITATION' (a polite way of saying adolescent zits), a list of city centre coffee shops, a large yellow cut-out mobile from the Oxford Community Church ('JESUS CHRIST AT A CINEMA NEAR YOU' and a quote from Nietzsche: 'Don't trust a God who can't dance'). There was an advisory leaflet on Sex from the Student Union, saying that your first sexual encounter as a student would probably be under the influence of drink or drugs, so always carry condoms as you wouldn't be in a fit state to procure them when the need arose.

As if to emphasise the point, a small purple and yellow card containing a Durex 'extra safe' condom fell out of the bag onto Eve's lap. It had a British Safety sign on it and the words 'Love Carefully - the HIV virus can lead to AIDS'. Eve sighed and put it back in the bag. She pulled out another sheaf of leaflets - the

OU Cave Club (potholing), the OU Underwater Exploration Group (with a picture of a dolphin), the Rambling and Hillwalking Club, the Lesbians Bisexuals and Gay Men Society (plus 'Queer Rights'), and the Hang Gliding Club ('the cheapest way to fly'). Or Eve could spend her time at Oxford canoeing, wine-tasting, learning Korean martial arts, or helping the homeless or rape victims.

She put it all on one side and held her coffee mug meditatively. She needed to clear her mind. So much to do, so little time...

But perhaps she had already been given her mission for her time at Oxford. For the foreseeable future, at any rate. Pity it involved her with an 'uncle' she was basically scared of, a guy she'd been crazy about but who didn't seem to care whether she existed or not, and another male undergraduate she never wanted to set eyes on again. Certainly nothing was shaping up to a situation where the small gift in the purple and yellow card would come in handy, even if she had wanted.

CHAPTER SIXTEEN

"THE ACTS OF THE SINFUL NATURE ARE OBVIOUS: SEXUAL IMMORALITY, IMPURITY AND DEBAUCHERY; IDOLATRY AND WITCHCRAFT; HATRED, DISCORD, JEALOUSY, FITS OF RAGE, SELFISH AMBITION, DISSENSIONS, FACTIONS AND ENVY; DRUNKENNESS, ORGIES, AND THE LIKE. I WARN YOU, AS I DID BEFORE, THAT THOSE WHO LIVE LIKE THIS WILL NOT INHERIT THE KINGDOM OF GOD."

[ST PAUL, *LETTER TO THE GALATIANS*]

"FOR THE PURPOSES OF OUR DRAWING WE NEEDED ARMOUR, AND OF A DATE AND DESIGN SO REMOTE THAT NO EXAMPLES EXISTED FOR OUR USE. THEREFORE MORRIS SET TO WORK TO MAKE DESIGNS FOR AN ANCIENT KIND OF HELMET CALLED A BASINET, AND FOR A SURCOAT OF RINGED MAIL AND A HOOD OF MAIL AND SKIRT COMING BELOW THE KNEES. THEY WERE MADE FOR HIM BY A STOUT LITTLE SMITH WHO HAD A FORGE NEAR THE CASTLE."

[EDWARD BURNE-JONES WRITING TO JAMES THURSFIELD, 1869]

It was Friday night at St Frideswide's and everyone was supposed to be out having fun. The maternal Marion had invited Eve to come to the pub with a crowd of other ordinands, to meet at nine o'clock in the Common Room. Eve was so pleased to have the chance to socialise with Frideswide people after her foray into the Freshers Fair in the morning. At least her colleagues were older and more mature and more in agreement with her own world view. Although that did leave the lurking suspicion - is this what it's going to be like all year, torn between those my own age I don't agree with or those I do agree with who are much older than me and have different interests and social lives? That was the price of being the 'baby' of the college that Allie the housekeeper had warned her about. The Lady Frances Fairfax Scholar was doomed to fall perpetually between two stools.

So Eve's expectations were high as she swept into the Common Room, admittedly five minutes late. But no one was there. They were all supposed to be meeting at the snooker table - but the room was dark at that end instead. Eve could see the snooker cue lying uselessly on the baize, the balls scattered. On her left a lone Indian student was watching TV by the light of a 1960s standard lamp.

Eve felt instantly furious and upset. Why couldn't they have waited five minutes, a measly five minutes?! Marion knew she intended to go with them. Everyone in Oxford was at least ten minutes late for everything! Eve stalked over to the snooker table as if expecting to find evidence that the others had been there. Had she got the time wrong, the day wrong? No.

Eve felt as if she had been ambushed. The familiar pit that was always inside her had claimed her again. Emptiness. Her mother's death when she was eight. Deep feelings of rejection. The counsellor had explained it all to her last year. It sounded so corny and clichéd, and Eve knew it and understood it, but the rush of fury that she felt now was so overwhelming that she could have picked up the snooker cue and hurled it through one of the windows like a javelin.

Good God, Eve, calm down, she told herself. This is what they told you would happen at one of those introductory sessions earlier on in the week - that it's easy to feel rejected in a communal environment. If you live on your own, you don't know what everyone else is doing and you feel fine, but in College you know that everyone else has gone out and left you behind. Every tiny social letdown is magnified.

Eve wondered if she should redeem the situation by talking to the Indian guy in front of the TV. No, perhaps he'd take it the wrong way. Anyway, she couldn't remember his name. No, she was darn well going to go round every pub in Oxford if she had to till she found them.

Eve ran down the steps from the Common Room, almost tripping over the belt of her coat, and heaved open the main door. She stepped out into the night.

She was about to breathe in gratefully the sharp clear air when she saw a figure sitting on the wall at the end of the driveway. He was smoking. She could see his outline, hunched up in a heavy coat, and the red glow of the tip of his cigarette briefly as he rested his hand on the wall.

Damn. She would have to walk past him to leave the grounds. Even though he had his back to her, she didn't like the idea of going anywhere near him in case it was a loony. Who knows how many of them were hanging around the streets in Oxford. Equally she didn't want to go back inside and suffer the sense of anticlimax again. She would just have to brave it and walk the gauntlet. As her shoes crunched on the gravel giving away her presence, she couldn't resist thinking: Men! Women can't even have a walk out at night without being scared. It should be a basic human right for us to walk down the street any time we want, and instead we're intimidated.

Her memory suddenly brought up a dark alley back home. She had been all alone and had suddenly found herself at night walking down a road she didn't recognise. The street lights had been wrecked and she was walking down the middle of the road between two enormous apartment blocks that looked deserted, like huge grey cliffs. She had become aware of the darker shadows, and the noises, as if she was a small animal with its senses suddenly hyper-alert for the attack. That feeling of threat was with her now - the cold sweating skin, the pounding heart, the feeling of paralysis in her muscles, that she couldn't get away if she tried.

By sheer force of will, she shook off the fear and began to make a run for it down the driveway. As she did so the man on the wall cried out:

'Eve, is that you?'
'*Martin?!*'

'I was just popping by for a visit. Do you want to come to a party?'

'Why... why... why are you smoking?'

'*Why?* Do I have to have a reason?'

'I just... didn't realise you did.'

'What's the matter with you? You don't know everything about me, you know. I have all sorts of awful little habits you know nothing of. Do you want to come to this party or not?'

'Oh, alright.'

Martin stood up and the two of them began to walk towards the centre of town.

'*Are* you alright?' Martin asked. 'You look a bit breathless. Of course I have been known to have that effect on women, but I wouldn't have thought you were one of them.'

'I've... I've just been a bit silly, that's all. My imagination was working overtime.'

Now all Eve's feelings of self-pity and anger and despair looked like one huge over-reaction. She really mustn't be so neurotic. Maybe it was Marion that had done it - feeling rejected by motherly Marion... yes, that was it. Eve dragged her mind back to concentrate on Martin.

'The party's at Guy's,' Martin was saying. 'Guy Fastness. He's the JCR President. I'll give you the low-down on the people we're going to meet. There'll be a huge crowd of King's people there. I'm hoping we'll find ourselves hob-nobbing with the murderer.'

'You're joking!'

'You're there as my bait. With three of us who found the body there, we're bound to get people talking to us about it.'

'Three? You mean Charlie's coming too?'

'Of course.'

'Oh.'

The evening for Eve was getting better already.

'So what I want you to do,' Martin continued, 'is to chat to some prime suspects. So you can be the Watson to my Holmes, the Hastings to my Poirot.'

'Huh. Your Peter Wimsey to my Harriet Vane,' said Eve, meaning to have a go at Martin's wealthy background and to bring in the name of a female sleuth. But Martin didn't get the point.

'Didn't they end up getting married? Is this a proposal?' he exclaimed.

'No, it is not. I just... Oh, never mind.'

'Oh, and another thing. Have you heard the latest about the armour?'

'What latest?' she said suspiciously.

'Well, I've been greasing up to good old Gavin - that's Detective Sergeant Woolston to you - and it appears that some witnesses have come forward, saying that they spotted the murderer on Saturday morning, wearing - wait for it - full armour. Not just the itsie-bitsies stolen from Guy's room, but chainmail, breastplate, the whole works. So that means he...'

'...must have got it from somewhere else.'

'Brilliant as ever. Anyway, I've been phoning up blacksmiths and trailing around fancy dress hire shops to find out how easy it is to get a suit of armour around here. I even rang up the British Plate Armour Society.'

'I didn't know there was one,' said Eve as they crossed over The High and walked down St Aldates.

'Why would you? Anyway,' said Martin with a sigh, 'the police had usually been there before me, which was very annoying. I really wanted to get an advance on them. Of course, someone could make a breastplate in a factory or in their own backyard, if they had the right equipment. But it does add a very interesting angle. I had been wondering what the killer would've worn with the bits of the armour he actually stole. Apparently the police haven't heard of any armour being stolen anywhere else, apart from some ages ago in Newcastle-upon-Tyne that was black with silver etchings, which doesn't sound right. Anyway, that was ages ago.'

'I suppose one thing to find out this evening might be to ask who was in Guy's room on the Friday night and saw the armour before it was stolen.'

'Right. Another thing is to try and talk to friends of Feral - that is, if she had any. From the stonewalling I've been getting so far,

I'm beginning to wonder. Either that, or everyone has something to hide.'

As they made their way through King Henry Hall to Guy's staircase, they could already hear the music and laughter. Since it was the JCR President's Bash, as many people as possible were crammed into his rooms and were lining and filing up and down the stairs, like a medieval painting of the divorce between heaven and hell. Eve began to feel rather nervous, which wasn't helped by Martin whispering loudly in her ear as they began the ascent:

'Just remember that anyone you speak to may be the murderer!'

CHAPTER SEVENTEEN

"Then jump for joy and gaily bound,
The truth is found - the truth is found!...
Which is most creditable to
Your powers of observation, O!"

[Gilbert and Sullivan, *Princess Ida*, 1884]

'Oh, you're back!' Guy cried out to Martin as they entered the heaving mass of students. 'Did you bring any more wine?'

'No,' yelled Martin, 'something even better,' and pointed to Eve.

Guy smiled and nodded as if in recognition. Eve was mystified. How did Guy know who she was? Don't say Martin had told people she was the girl who found the body. Oh no, not here as well. Although, Guy was rather good-looking. He was about the same height as Martin, dark blond hair that would have been curly if not cut so short, suntan, an open pleasant face radiating good health. Yes, very good-looking.

Then again, so was his girlfriend. Eve was introduced to 'Minty', Araminta Douglas. She was tall and slim with straight ash blonde hair that flowed down over her shoulders. She wasn't wearing much makeup but didn't need to. She was very pretty in an understated way and was wearing the sort of simple casual dress that probably cost a fortune. Guy was obviously very proud of her and a bit possessive. He kept touching her, putting his hand on her shoulder as if protecting her from something. Each touch proclaimed 'This is mine!'

Minty smiled at Eve.

'So you're the famous Eve Merry - or should I say infamous! Martin has been going on about you all week!'

'No, I have not!' protested Martin.

'Well, more than any other woman for a long time,' grinned Guy. 'We've been thinking this must be the real thing!'

'Oh stop it,' said Minty, 'we're making her blush. No, it's really been about the... you-know-what. Guy's the idiot who lost the armour so we're rather involved...'

'I didn't *lose* it,' interrupted Guy, 'someone stole it. There is a difference.'

'Ends up as the same thing,' said Minty mercilessly. 'So it's in our interest to find it.'

'Clear my name,' Guy smiled ironically. 'Minty's people couldn't have her marrying a complete fool, now, could they.'

Eve smiled weakly, not sure whether this was serious or not. Minty's people - what had Martin just told her about them? That her father had been a government minister but had had to resign over getting his secretary pregnant? Something like that. Wow.

But Martin was now trying to drag Eve away.

'Come on, meet Rory and Angela.'

Was everyone in couples, Eve wondered?

If Guy had been good-looking in a sporty-hearty sort of way, then Rory was good-looking in a pop star sort of way. In fact he looked like the lead singer of a group that had just had a Number One in the Charts. He had dark blond hair that fell to just below his ears. He had to keep flicking this back out of his face as the hair at the front was as long as the hair at the back and he didn't have a fringe. For some reason, Rory flinging his hair back didn't automatically annoy Eve the way it did when Martin did it. Perhaps this had something to do with the fact that Rory had piercing blue eyes, as if he had enhanced them with tinted contact lenses. They could stop a girl's heart from the other side of the room. His skin was very pale. As he stood up, he was obviously very tall - perhaps six feet four? Broad shoulders and very fashionable clothes completed the effect.

Eve was introduced by Martin and the two of them shook hands, Eve hoping that her face wasn't pink. Then again, it was hot in the room.

It was only then that she noticed Angela, Rory's girlfriend. Angela White was tiny compared to her boyfriend, perhaps only five feet one. And slim too. She looked like a porcelain doll next to an enormous bear. Her skin was even more pale than his and her hair was also blonde, although cut with a fringe. She was wearing a tight ribbed T-shirt in burgundy and dark blue jeans and had a flowered chiffon scarf wrapped several times around her neck, tied in a tight little knot. As she reached out shyly to shake Eve's hand her wrist clattered with an assortment of bracelets.

'So you're the famous Eve,' Angela said as well.

Eve was beginning to think Martin couldn't keep his mouth shut if he tried.

They were now joined by some other students who had overheard Eve's name. She was introduced to a Linda (long brown hair and dreamy eyes); Simon (tall and earnest in glasses, looked super-brainy but also clueless); Wyn (a smiling Welsh chap with loose brown curls and crooked teeth - Eve tried not to stereotype him as a Dylan Thomas drunk, but it wasn't easy); Anthony (thin, repressed public school, silent small nods); and Al (ebullient Asian in a turban, a huge smile, slightly tubby).

'So I hear you have a beautiful voice,' Al was saying, 'so Martin tells me. I am the President of the Gilbert and Sullivan Society and...'

But he was silenced by Martin putting his hand over Albert's mouth.

'Er, can we change the subject?' said Martin smiling. 'Have you all been quizzed by the police yet?'

Everyone nodded. They had all had their five minute 'quickie' interview in the Morris Room.

'What did you cough up?'

'Well, I didn't know the girl,' said Wyn, 'didn't know her from Adam - or should I say, Eve,' he said with a smile at Eve. 'But I do think she was creepy. I told the police that. She used to collect bits of people and keep them in her room.'

'Yes,' said the half-asleep Linda, 'she had little plastic boxes with bits of fingernail in, and stuff like that. Hair clippings and bits of material.'

'I caught her trying to cut some of the fringing off one of my scarves once,' said Simon earnestly, adjusting his glasses. 'Very odd.'

'She stole some of my notes,' said Anthony quietly. 'I thought she wanted them just to catch up with Baudelaire, but then I saw she'd been copying my handwriting. So I told her where to go in no uncertain terms.'

'Oh, she liked to pretend she was a witch,' said Linda. 'Or perhaps she really was, I don't know.'

Eve thought of the badge 'WITCH BITCH FROM HELL!'. Was it perhaps one that belonged to Feral herself? She asked those around her. Yes, Feral had been seen wearing it before - once at a fancy dress party, for example, where she had actually come as a witch - probably last Halloween.

'She could really look the part,' said Wyn. 'Lots of white makeup, wearing black. It's rather sad really, looking back. Perhaps she took it all a bit seriously.'

'Yes,' said Linda, suddenly livening up, 'but the question is, who would want to kill her?'

'Perhaps she cast a spell on someone,' said Simon eagerly, 'and they didn't like it. That's what I suggested to the police,' he added modestly.

'Was there anyone who particularly disliked her?' Eve asked.

She noticed out of the corner of her eye, Rory and Angela glance at each other, then look at the floor.

'Oh!' exclaimed Linda. 'Sarah. Sarah Zorginsky. She couldn't stand her, although she had good reason. Where is she? Oh, *Sarah!*' She called to a tall young woman with shoulder-length brown hair. Linda waved her over and Sarah obediently came, carrying a drink that she managed to spill on someone en route. While it was being wiped up, Eve noticed a nervousness in Sarah's manner. Although she was tall and 'rangy' (one could easily imagine her in a basketball defence lineup), she looked physically timid and hunched up. Perhaps she had got into the habit of trying to disguise her height.

Sarah eventually made it over to the group with an apologetic smile.

'You called?'

'Sarah,' Linda began, 'you didn't like Feral, did you? We're just talking about her.'

'Oh.' Sarah's face dropped.

'Oh, it's alright,' said Linda brightly, 'we're not trying to grill you. I don't think any of us would've liked her if she'd done to us what she did to you.'

'Thanks,' said Sarah drily, her eyes flickering nervously around the room as if looking for a way of escape.

'It was last year,' Linda was telling Eve. 'Sarah's mother died and Feral said she could get in touch with her - you know, from beyond the grave. Well, Sarah was furious, of course. Weren't you?' she said, addressing Sarah again.

Sarah nodded briefly, grimaced and looked away.

'I can imagine,' said Eve in wide-eyed sympathy. If anyone had done that to her in the last year... But would it be enough to kill someone for?

'She nearly had a breakdown over it,' Linda whispered to Eve, meaning Sarah.

Eve nodded in understanding. She decided to change the subject for poor Sarah's sake.

'Was Feral in any Society in particular?' Eve asked everyone. 'Like, perhaps the Dark Ages Society, or the Launcelot and Guinevere Society?'

There was the equivalent of silence in the group, despite the loud music.

Simon piped up: 'Angela, weren't you in the Launcelot and Guinevere Society?'

Angela looked up and said hurriedly:

'Yes, er, yes, I was in that for a while. But not for long.'

'Wasn't there some sort of rumpus?' Simon continued. 'Didn't you get Feral thrown out?'

Angela flushed very pink and stammered: 'Er, yes, but it wasn't just me. There were a few of us. It was the whole committee really.'

'Why?' said Martin. 'What happened?'

'Oh, Feral had got carried away with this witch thing,' said Angela hurriedly, as if it was no big deal. 'Kept saying she was casting spells on people, and of course they didn't like it. It...er... it got very complicated. It was best just to get her expelled from the Society.'

'Ex-spelled! Arf. Get it? Oh well, never mind,' said Martin. 'But wouldn't that make her even more mad - getting expelled? Wouldn't she just cast even more spells on you in revenge?'

Rory suddenly took over for the quailing Angela:

'Oh, they didn't take the spell thing that seriously. It was just an anti-social way to behave and she got expelled for it - pure and simple. The same thing would happen if you'd been drunk and disruptive at a meeting or something like that...'

'Oh, you'd know all about drunk and disruptive wouldn't you, Rory,' said the quiet Sarah who looked at the floor again immediately afterwards as if she hadn't said anything.

'Oh, like last Friday night!' exclaimed Linda. 'You'd put away a few then!'

'Come on,' said Rory, getting up and pulling up Angela behind him. 'We don't have to put up with this.' And he pushed roughly through the circle towards the door.

'Yes,' Wyn shouted after him, 'didn't you threaten to kill Feral last Friday night, Rory?!' Wyn then laughed, enjoying his moment of power while the others shushed him and Martin and Eve looked at each other in amazement.

'What was that?' said Martin. 'Why didn't anybody tell me?'

'Oh, it was nothing, really,' gurgled Wyn. 'Just Rory drinking too much as usual and getting aggressive. It was in the JCR.'

'Yes, I was there,' said Sarah. 'F...F...Feral was sitting talking to me and all of a sudden Rory barges in and starts yelling at her. Saying something like 'I'm warning you, if you start this up again I'll kill you!' I've no idea what it was about, and Feral said she didn't either. She just shrugged her shoulders and smiled.' Sarah's voice trailed off and she looked extremely sad.

'Wow,' said Wyn. 'I wonder what it was about. Someone should ask Rory. I wonder if the police know.'

'I...I didn't tell them,' mumbled Sarah. She looked up wide-eyed as if she was appealing for help.

'Well, you'll have to,' said Martin, as kindly as possible.

'Oh, I've just remembered,' Simon burst out, 'there is someone else who didn't like Feral. 'You remember Tony Greer? He was a first year here last year. He had a bit of a persecution complex about her. Had a sort of breakdown during his exams and left. I think he's working at a pub now, although I don't know which one.'

'It's 'The King's Arms', on the corner of Holywell Street,' said Wyn.

'He wouldn't hurt a fly, though,' said Linda. 'Wasn't he gay?'

Some of the men sniggered.

'If he wasn't,' said Anthony, 'he did a good impersonation.'

'The police asked me,' said Linda, 'if I knew about some ex-boyfriend of Feral's who was supposed to be up here last weekend. I didn't know anything about him, though. But perhaps it means it is an outsider who did it and not one of us at all, which would be great.'

'I'm just going to get a drink,' Eve mouthed to Martin who nodded.

Eve's throat was so dry with the heat and the smoke that she felt as if she was crawling through the desert as she tried to fight her way to the drinks table. Fortunately there was still some orange juice and lemonade left, that is after she had tried several cartons that had turned out to be empty. As she was gratefully pouring herself some orange juice she noticed a young man hovering just out of her view. She looked round. It was some geek with spots and specs who smiled broadly at her and approached. Oh no, she thought, this is all I need.

'So, you're the one who found the body,' the geek said.

'Um, yes, that's right.'

'What did she look like?'

'What?!'

'I mean, when she was dead? I've never seen a real dead body.'

'Well, think yourself lucky!' Eve tried to back away but he was edging closer to her all the time. He smelled of sweat and onions, a stale kebab van sort of smell. There were stains on his un-ironed shirt.

'I heard her eyelids were ripped off,' he said smiling, his eyes magnified and goggling behind his glasses, 'is that true?'

'Where did you hear that?' Eve demanded.

'Oh, here and there. I have my sources,' he said with a stupid grin that looked like a leer to Eve.

'Excuse me, I really have to be going,' said Eve, and turned and pushed her way back to Martin.

She put down the orange juice, it felt somehow tainted, and said to Martin:

'I'm leaving now. I've had enough.'

'Oh, let me walk you home,' said Martin getting up to follow her.

Eve didn't care whether he escorted her or not. But then she thought of the creep near the drinks again and thought it might be a good idea to not be wandering around on her own at night. As they waved goodbye to Guy and Minty, Eve said to Martin:

'There was this awful creepy guy near the drinks asking me awful questions about Feral. Wanting to know about her body and...yuk! Can you tell me who he is?'

'Point him out.'

But of course the geek was no where to be seen. When Eve described him, Martin just said it could be half the college and that was that.

'But if you see him again,' said Martin as they ran down the stairs, 'do tell me. Perhaps you should come to a meal here and point him out.'

Eve shuddered and said 'Yuk!' again.

It was a great relief to be out in the cool night air. Martin made Eve wait while he got his bike so he would be able to ride back to King's. Apparently he too had been on orange juice in order to be alert for clues from the conversation that evening.

'I do take my hat off to you over the Lancelot and Guinevere Society thing,' he was saying earnestly. 'What on earth led you onto that?'

'Oh, it was at the Freshers' Fair this morning. I saw some students at the stalls dressed in armour - the Dark Ages Society.

And then there was the Launcelot and Guinevere Society with a girl dressed in medieval clothes. Well, Feral was found in medieval style clothes, she was killed by someone wearing armour, and Launcelot begins with "L" - like the letter that was sent to Feral telling her where to meet up that morning. It just went *ching-ching-ching* in my mind and I put two and two together.'

'Well, I hope I'm there next time your brain goes *ching-ching-ching*! Of course, I should have made the connection with Launcelot - damn! It's all in the 'Lady of Shalott' - remember I was reading it on the punt? Well, it's Launcelot that she's obsessed with. She kills herself for him, in fact, or dies for love of him, or something. Although that would make it suicide, which it most definitely wasn't in Feral's case...'

'Anyway, I don't want to think about it anymore,' interrupted Eve. 'That dork gave me the creeps.'

'But this is the best lead we've had! We've got to follow it up with these people. What do you say we split them up according to gender - or is that too sexist for you? I'll do the paranoid Tony Greer, now at 'The King's Arms', I'll tackle the ferocious Rory Ablett, and track down this mysterious ex-boyfriend who was supposed to be lurking around last weekend. That means you do the blushing Angela and the neurotic Sarah.'

'Oh whoopee.'

'Oh, could you go to the Launcelot and Guinevere Society too? You're the Fresher - you can go along to their Freshers' Bash.'

'Oh no! I have work to do, you know!'

'But you came up with the lead, it's your fault! Oh, and there's something else for you to do as well...'

By this time they were outside St Frideswide's. Martin took a CD out of his jacket.

'It's a recording of *Princess Ida* by Gilbert and Sullivan. See if you can do the lead soprano. The lyrics are in there. I've told Albert Singh how good you are and he's expecting wonders...'

'What!'

'Well, if you won't be Hastings to my Poirot, or Watson to my Holmes, you can at least be Princess Ida to my Prince Hilarion!'

He slotted the CD into her coat pocket.

'I'm never second fiddle, only first violin!' said Eve.

Martin snorted with derision and left laughing at her. Eve could have kicked herself for making such a pathetic, weak and haughty joke. With someone like him! She really shouldn't try and play him at his own game. He'd managed to beat her even when she'd had the last word.

CHAPTER EIGHTEEN

"The sun came dazzling through the leaves,
And flamed upon the brazen greaves
Of bold Sir Lancelot."

[Tennyson, *The Lady of Shalott*, 1832]

Martin strolled back to his room from the bathroom at ten o'clock on the Saturday morning, feeling as though his eyelids were glued together and someone had syphoned off most of his blood supply during the night. He really shouldn't have gone back to the party and drunk so much. And what on earth was he doing up so early? Oh yes. There was that reading to do on Linguistic Theory he hadn't managed earlier on in the week. Of course he'd scheduled it for Saturday morning before he'd known he was going to have a hangover then.

Back in his room, he rummaged around in a few drawers and on the floor and managed to find a matching pair of socks, a semi-ironed white shirt, and a mustard sweater. His black jeans were still thrown over a chair from last night, or rather, this morning. He combed his hair back, looking in the free-standing mirror on the chest of drawers. Thank goodness his hair was now more brown than red. Being teased at school over red hair had been the pits. Then again, if it hadn't been that, it would have been something else. Kids were such bastards.

Martin was just wondering whether to go out for some breakfast on his own or invite Rory out for some, when there was a knock at the door. It was Rory. He shambled in looking defiant and sheepish, and as if he was also deficient in oxygen to the brain.

'Hello, mate.'

'Hello', said Martin. 'What was all that about last night?'

'Ohhh.' Rory groaned and flopped down into a chair. 'I can't believe it's coming back to haunt me.' Rory's slight Yorkshire accent could be heard, which was unusual. 'It was some silly business last year between Angela and Feral or Fern or whatever her name was. She could be such a bitch. Made Angela's life hell sometimes. Anyway, I wasn't going to have it starting up again.'

'What starting up again?'

'Oh, the notes, the persecution. Stupid threats. And to cap it all...' Rory paused and breathed deeply, exhaling sharply through his nostrils in disgust, 'Feral used to say she would take me away from Angela! It was ridiculous, of course. There was no way that could be true!'

'I should think not. You're not blind,' said Martin, amazed. 'There's no comparison between Angela and Feral.'

'Exactly!' exclaimed Rory. 'That's what I kept saying to Angela. But you know what women are like. I think Feral made Angela feel insecure.' Rory frowned. 'I often wondered if she had some sort of power over Angela, as if there was something secret I didn't know anything about. Anyway, Angela didn't tell me. But what happened last Friday made me think the whole stupid business was starting again. Angela had received an anonymous note - on bright pink paper, the sort that Feral used to use. And it was in her writing. It was threatening to use magic to get me away from her, from Angela!'

'Wow! So you flipped.'

'I certainly did. Poor Angela was incredibly upset. I think she believes in this magic stuff, as if Feral could do something to hurt us. But I told her it was all nonsense. She'd threatened the same thing last year and nothing had happened.'

'So you barged into the JCR and started yelling at her.'

'Yes,' Rory sighed. 'I'd already had a bit to drink I suppose. And I wanted to show her we weren't afraid of her.' Rory yawned loudly. 'She could cast as many spells as she wanted, I wasn't going to let her intimidate us!'

'Quite right,' said Martin. 'Do you want to get some breakfast, or have you eaten?'

'Oh, I've had quite a lot already this morning. I woke up feeling like shit. Could hardly move. But when I'd eaten I felt a lot better. I didn't drink much last night, in fact, hardly anything. Angela's got me sworn off it. Says it makes me violent.'

'I think I'll have to nip up the road for something. Do you want to come?'

'OK.'

Martin grabbed a coat and the two of them left college and made their way up St Aldates. It was already busy with Saturday shoppers.

'So,' said Martin casually, 'what were you doing between the hours of six and eight o'clock on Saturday morning last?'

Rory yawned again.

'I was in bed, of course. Wasn't everybody? Well, apart from the murderer, of course.'

'And Feral.'

'Yes, and her. Personally, I didn't get up till about eleven o'clock. I really felt like shit. That's one of the things that's persuaded me not to drink so much. I was lying in bed feeling as though I'd died! I couldn't move! God, I've never had such a bad hangover.'

'And can anyone corroborate your story?' said Martin with mock formality.

'No, I'm afraid I wasn't with anyone at the time. Angela had gone off in a huff at me being drunk.' Rory sighed. 'Can't blame her, I suppose.'

They chose a sandwich shop and entered. Martin ordered chicken sandwiches, a luxurious chocolate brownie and a mango drink. He continued with his questions while the shop assistant took his money.

'If I said "spotty creepy geek in specs" to you, who would it remind you of? In King's, I mean.'

Rory thought for a moment.

'Huh. There are so many sad bastards at King's, it's hard to know where to begin! Let me see. Well, there's Jeremy East for a start...'

'Oh yes!'

'He's got terminal acne, poor sod, and appalling bottom-of-a-milk-bottle glasses and his hair always looks greasy.'

'Yes, he'd do. What's his subject?'

'Electrical Engineering, I think. Yes. Second Year.'

'Anyone else?'

'There's his friend, Robert Baker.'

'Oh! Don't mention his name! He lives downstairs from me - complete prat! Plays appalling heavy metal music at all hours.'

'That's what playing these computer games does for you. He's probably soft in the head and thinks it's Mozart.'

'But he's not that spotty or creepy. Well, perhaps creepy in a different way. No, what I'm wanting is a dork of the first order.'

Rory thought for a while again as they left the shop and headed back.

'Richard Fairweather looked a real dork last year, but he's got contact lenses this year and looks almost human.'

'Yes. Was he at Guy's room on the Friday night when we were all looking at the armour?'

Rory shrugged.

'Dunno. Didn't take much notice. I was more interested in seeing the armour close to. I thought it was magnificent. I hope they find the missing bits. Of course,' Rory added, 'Robert Baker could have taken the armour.'

'What?'

'Yes, he was there in Guy's room on the Friday night. And he double-backed during the fire drill, saying he'd forgotten something. I saw him in the corridor. I thought he looked a bit furtive, although perhaps he always does.'

'You're probably right,' mused Martin. 'But he's no good for our murderer. He's got the perfect alibi.'

'Oh?'

'Me! I had to charge downstairs to tell him to turn down his music at the relevant time on the Saturday morning. We had a yelling match through his door. I could see the bastard through a crack at the side of his door where it's practically hanging off its hinges.'

'You should've given him a crack in his head.'

'Absolutely. I think Delia Rose had to go down to complain as well and he did the same to her. He was sitting at his desk playing with his computer like a complete prick. I can't believe people can be so inconsiderate about noise.'

'Mmmm. Noise pollution. Although I've probably been responsible for quite a bit myself,' laughed Rory. 'Anyway, are we saying that the person who stole the armour did the murder? Is that what the police think?'

'Don't ask me,' scowled Martin. 'I have a love-hate relationship with the police at the moment.'

'Poor Guy made a complete prat of himself over the fire drill, that's for sure.'

Rory then stopped in his tracks as if something had just occurred to him.

'But who set off the fire alarm?' he said frowning. 'If the person who stole the armour was in the room with it when the alarm went off, then he (or she) couldn't have set off the alarm. But if the person who stole it wasn't in the room with the armour, then we have no idea who it was. It could be anybody.'

'Hmmm,' said Martin glumly. 'Of course, the alarm going off at that moment could have been completely fortuitous. The thief may have just taken his chance on the spur of the moment. Or it may have been someone who already knew the armour was in Guy's room who set off the alarm outside and waited for the room to clear so he could steal the stuff.'

'How many people knew the armour was going to be in Guy's room?' asked Rory.

'Officially only the porter on duty knew. It was a bit hush-hush, 'cos the porter wasn't supposed to let the armour out of his sight, really. He may well get the push for this, poor chap. You know Jackson?'

'Oh yes. Oh no! So he might get the sack?'

'If our new Principal has his way, it wouldn't surprise me.'

After a pause while they both tutted over this, Rory suddenly said:

'What if Jackson's the murderer! What if he wanted to steal the armour but wanted to put the blame on someone else, so he made sure that Guy had the armour in his room when it went missing, rather than in the Porter's Lodge. That way Guy looks suspicious rather than Jackson!'

'Good grief, what a twisted mind you have,' said Martin, as they walked through the gateway of King Henry Hall and past the Porter's Lodge. 'In a college setting, having the Porter as the suspect is like saying "the Butler did it"!'

As the two students parted and Martin returned to his room to ruminate over Post-Structuralism and Deconstructionism, he automatically noted down the main points of his conversation with Rory as if taking down lecture notes. But what was really interesting, he thought, as the essays of Derrida lay unopened on his desk (and after he'd tried to think of a joke to begin his essay about 'deriding Derrida'), was that Rory had no alibi. And Rory had threatened to kill Feral the night before she died. And Rory had been in Guy's room and seen the armour. And if he had seen Robert Baker wandering back through the corridors looking furtive on the Friday night during the fire alarm, what on earth was Rory doing wandering around in the same corridor?

But what Martin didn't know was that the stolen armour had been found that morning. It was the inevitable woman walking her dog who had come across the missing Chichele pieces under a pile of rotting vegetation in a field near Donnington Bridge. It had been just out of the radius of the police search so far. The newly-found bascinet, gauntlets, greaves and sabatons were now being tested by the police forensic team. They had been in strong plastic carrier bags. Attached to one of the metal gauntlets was a silver bracelet with the word 'ANGEL' engraved upon it.

CHAPTER NINETEEN

"I BIND UNTO MYSELF THIS DAY THE STRONG NAME OF THE TRINITY...AGAINST ALL SATAN'S SPELLS AND WILES, AGAINST FALSE WORDS OF HERESY, AGAINST THE KNOWLEDGE THAT DEFILES, AGAINST THE HEART'S IDOLATRY, AGAINST THE WIZARD'S EVIL CRAFT, AGAINST THE DEATH-WOUND AND THE BURNING, THE CHOKING WAVE AND POISONED SHAFT, PROTECT ME, CHRIST, TILL THY RETURNING."
[ST PATRICK'S BREASTPLATE]

The police had also found Feral's ex-boyfriend, the one who had been mooching around on the weekend of her death. Apparently he had followed her up to Oxford from Brighton, intending to plead for the resumption of their relationship. He was nineteen and unemployed. He had greasy black hair, spots and glasses. He had got to know Feral at school and the two had dated for a while, but once she had gone to university she had only seen him intermittently. Yes, he had felt 'used' on occasions. But there was no way he would kill her! He loved her, the police had got to understand that! Did they have sex together? Harborough looked aghast and then had burst into violent sobs and refused to say any more. The police had let him go but intended to keep an eye on him. He was ordered to stay in Oxford for the foreseeable future in case he was wanted for more questioning.

This was mainly because John Harborough had no real alibi. He claimed to have been out jogging at the time of the murder.

DS Woolston, who had been questioning him, had displayed surprise that John had been jogging around Oxford at dawn. What possessed him? Were there any witnesses who could testify to having seen him at this unearthly hour? And wasn't it a bit of a coincidence that he'd been jogging along Donnington Bridge?

But John had insisted that, since he was staying in a bed and breakfast nearby on Iffley Road, it was the most natural thing in the world to run down to the river and along the bank a little way. But it had been very muddy and he hadn't wanted to go very far. At one point he almost fell in the water, it was so slippery. John could give the police his running shoes to prove he's been there, if they wanted. DS Woolston had shaken his head in disbelief. Didn't the poor sap realise that mud from the river bank only made him look more guilty? Woolston had written Harborough off as virtually mentally retarded from this point, or certainly somewhat intellectually challenged. No wonder the bright Oxford undergraduate Feral had wanted to ditch this loser from her old comprehensive in Brighton.

DI Andrews, when he too had seen the suspect, was dubious as to whether Harborough had the brains to carry out such an elaborate and well-planned murder. Where would he have obtained the armour, for a start? Admittedly, Harborough had been hanging around King Henry Hall on the Friday night, hoping to meet up with Feral. He could have followed the crowd to see the armour in Guy's room before the fire alarm, and then gone back to steal it when chaos had erupted after the alarm. But this seemed a bit ambitious for the pathetic specimen John Harborough appeared to be. Although, Andrews had warned his team, they could not write him off. His pathetic looks could be an act. He was a loner, and he was obsessive enough to follow Feral up to Oxford and virtually stalk her for the last night she was alive. They must not make the mistake of under-estimating a possible killer.

But Martin did not know about this, even by Saturday night. He had kept his promise to himself to do some work - had even fought off the temptation by two other students of playing squash or fencing - and so had been holed up in his room all day. If he got a lot done today it would leave more time during the week for investigating.

But what should he do in the evening? It was unthinkable to stay in on a Saturday night. He did toy with the idea of turning up at St Frideswide's and knocking at Eve's door smoking a pipe and wearing a deer-stalker, but he restrained himself. Instead he decided to wander up the High Street and down Catte Street, the short walk from King's to *The King's Arms*.

The pub was lively enough inside. Martin clumped along the wooden floor and sat down on a wooden seat at the bar. Martin had been wondering whether he would recognise Tony Greer when he saw him. Like Feral, Tony had been one of the many new faces last year that Martin had never got to know. In some ways, that was one of the disadvantages of having a lot of old Dragonshead people up at Hall. It had meant Martin had already had a social circle at King's without the effort of having to get to know new people.

But as soon as Martin saw the slight anaemic guy with the shaven head behind the bar, he knew it was Tony. Martin congratulated himself on his visual memory. He then thought that since Tony had been the only obviously gay man amongst the first years last year, it was perhaps not surprising that Martin should remember. One didn't need the well-developed public school antenna for such things to be able to tell which way Tony was leaning.

Tony Greer looked happy enough as he served some customers. He was wearing a grey jersey sweater tucked into black shiny PVC trousers and the inevitable earring. As Martin positioned himself on the stool at the end of the bar, Tony looked round and saw him. His face fell. He chewed on his lips and fiddled with a bottle and some glasses unnecessarily before he deigned to come over to serve him.

'Oh, it's you,' Tony said ungraciously.

Martin looked theatrically around him and said in surprise: 'I think you're right! I'll have a pint of your best, please.'

Tony turned round with a heavy sigh and, still sucking his lips, pulled a pint of beer for Martin. When he brought it over, Martin said:

'I hope you're not this enthusiastic with all your customers. You might bowl them over.'

'Oh, I'm not. Only people from King's.'

'Not exactly your favourite place?' said Martin, handing over his money.

'Huh. Understatement of the year.'

'Is there somewhere we could go and talk?'

Tony looked at Martin in mild surprise, as if appraising whether this was a come-on.

'No,' he said firmly and turned his back to serve someone else.

Now it was Martin's turn to sigh heavily. But he was determined to carry on sitting there and get some answers. Tony Greer may well have some vital evidence about Feral's character, if nothing else. And if he was supposed to have had some grudge against her, then he might be a suspect for the murder itself.

After half an hour of staring into a half-empty glass and eating a small packet of peanuts, Martin felt about ready to go home. Tony was still steadfastly ignoring him, making a point of serving people at the other end of the bar. Oh well. He'd just have to sit there all evening until Tony left work, if that's what it was going to take.

But it wasn't quite that long. After about an hour, Tony's boss told him to take a break and Tony was forced to come out from behind the bar, looking very sulky it must be said. He headed straight for the men's toilet. Martin shot off his seat and followed him, thinking, 'I can't believe I'm about to accost a gay man in a toilet.'

'You ought to be careful,' said Tony maliciously once they were inside. 'You can get a reputation for this sort of thing. I know several people who were convinced you were queer last year.'

'The burdens we actors have to bear,' said Martin. 'I can't help it if I look so good in tights.'

'Huh. You didn't look *that* good.'

Tony disappeared into one of the booths.

'I'll just stay here,' said Martin, 'to make sure you don't escape out of a tiny window.'

'Oh, piss off! I can't *do* anything with you listening!'

'Spot of anal retention there? Must be an occupational hazard.'

'Oh, ha-bloody-ha. Think you're so fuckin' clever.'

'Well, you can't be exactly thick or you wouldn't have been at Oxford at all.'

'What, even though I flunked my first year exams, you mean? Well, it is possible, Oh shit, this is no good,' Tony said, flushing the loo angrily.

As Tony came out to wash his hands, Martin decided to try the direct approach.

'You know I found Feral's body, don't you?'

There was a pause while Tony dried his hands.

'I'd heard that,' he said quietly.

'You knew her quite well, didn't you?'

'Huh. You sound like the police. I've already had them in here harassing me.'

'And what did you tell them?'

'What's it got to do with you?'

They walked out of the Men's together.

'Can I get you a drink?' said Martin.

'Alright. White wine.'

When Martin returned, Tony was seated at a side table, arms and legs crossed. His blasé 'I don't care' attitude was only on the surface. Underneath it seemed to Martin there was a definite nervousness.

'So,' began Martin, 'did you know Feral well?'

Tony shrugged.

'In so far as anyone did. She was deep... complex. You never knew quite where you were with her. She could be nice one minute, nasty the next. Or at least, you might not realise she was being nasty at the time, but afterwards you'd think it over and think "Bitch! That was horrible!"'

'Can you give me an example?'

Tony looked defensive.

'Often it was supposed to be a joke. I mean, we'd be ribbing each other about something, and then she'd go too far and say something really hurtful. At the time you accepted it, but afterwards you thought "Wow, she really had her knife into me then!"'

'Like...?'

Tony sniffed.

'Like once when we were joking about... well, us both liking the same man, at one point. And she... she made a joke about me being impotent, or if I wasn't then I soon would be.'

'Meaning?'

Tony sucked on his lips again.

'*Meaning* that she would cast a spell on me to that effect. She was a witch, you know.'

'So she really meant it?'

'Oh *yes*. I don't think the police believed me when I said it. But she was quite effective, in her own way. She had all sorts of books on it that she let me have a look at once, and she kept bits of people - like nail clippings, stuff like that - to use in her spells. You often need something belonging to the person. Anyway, I was interested in New Age stuff, so we often chatted about it. But she was actually *practising*. I never really did it for real. And she was... No, I'd better not say that.'

There was a pause. Martin held his breath.

'What?' he burst out.

'Oh God, I've been in enough trouble,' Tony moaned, suddenly looking seriously worried. 'I don't want it to start again. Please... I can't...'

'What to start again?' said Martin in his best sympathetic voice.

Tony looked close to tears.

'I can't... I can't.... That's why I had to give up during the exams. It all got too much. It's time for me to start work again,' Tony said standing up and walking towards the bar.

This is too good to miss, thought Martin. He decided to wait till Tony finished work. He ordered a pub meal and made himself at home for the next hour and a half. The pub then emptied at last and Martin was left alone with the bar staff who paid no attention to him - he was a friend of Tony's.

'Where do you live?' Martin yelled to Tony as he spotted Tony putting his coat on and walking briskly out of the pub. 'Hold on, wait for me!'

To Martin's amazement, Tony did wait. Martin felt suddenly sorry for Tony who was looking shrunken and exhausted. Martin was sure it wasn't just from his night's work in the bar. It was an utter weariness of the soul, a look of total despair. Was there anyone waiting for him at home? Did he even have a dog or a cat for company? Martin thought, if we pass a bridge, he'll be throwing himself off it at this rate.

They began to walk down Broad Street together.

'Why are you still in Oxford if you hate it so much?' Martin asked, hoping this was a more neutral subject.

'Oh, my boyfriend's here,' Tony sighed. 'And I'm waiting for Brookes to accept me on a course. At least it's called a university now. It doesn't sound as bad as going to the old Polytechnic.'

'Oh, that's good.' After a pause, Martin said, 'So are the police giving you a hard time?'

'No, not really. Not yet. But they might. I suppose they'll be examining my alibi.'

'Which is...?'

'I was with my boyfriend. We were at his flat when the ... murder took place,' Tony said mechanically.

'So you're alright then!'

'If he doesn't lie about it, just to get me into trouble, the lying bastard!' said Tony with real bitterness.

'Wow,' said Martin. 'That would be rough. How are you going to prove it?'

'Dunno.'

'You'll have to.'

'S'ppose so.'

Tony didn't sound as if he had much interest in life, as if the future wasn't really his concern. Was he suicidal again? That had been the reason for him dropping out of college in the first place.

'What,' began Martin carefully, 'what was the thing you couldn't tell me in the pub, if you don't mind me asking. You see, it could be really important. And if we can nail the real culprit, then you're off the hook.'

'Oh, I wouldn't say that,' said Tony, sounding sarcastic.

'Why not?'

Tony paused as if thinking of a diplomatic reply.

'You don't think someone involved in magic would let anyone get away with something like that, would you?'

'You mean,' said Martin slowly, 'that if you tell me about this person, he or she might get revenge on you.'

'Oh, there's more than one of them!'

'Can't you give me some clue as to their identity?'

'Huh, I could if I knew. But even I don't know who they are. They were... they were some group Feral met with, that's all I know. All women. Men couldn't join.' Tony sounded infinitely weary again. 'Feral used to joke about me being almost eligible for membership, 'cos I was almost an honorary woman. But she said they wouldn't have me.'

'What was it,' Martin scowled, 'a sort of feminist group? And they were into witchcraft as well?'

Tony yawned.

'That's about it. But you mustn't tell anyone I told you,' he said, speeding up again, 'or I'm done for. I couldn't stand it happening again. Nearly bloody killed me last time. Did my head in.'

'What did?'

'Oh, letters, whispers, persecution. Knowing she'd put a hex on me, you know the sort of thing. It's sounds so bloody stupid, but it's terrifying when it happens to you. Perhaps that's what's happening to me now. Perhaps that's why the police suspect me. She's having her way.'

'Oh, don't be so stupid,' said Martin impatiently, mainly because he was starting to feel out of his depth. 'Of course she isn't. Just 'cos they're all bloody loony, it doesn't mean you've got to join them! Get a grip. It's just like bullying in the play ground. You've got to show them you don't care.'

'Oh really? I'll tell you about bullying...'

And Tony lifted up his jacket and sweater. There were two ugly scars on his stomach.

'That's when two fascist bastards jumped me for being gay. So don't you tell me about persecution. I know what it feels like, and I'm not going to have it again!'

And with that, Tony ran down the road away from Martin, disappearing into the late-night crowd on George Street.

Martin wondered whether to follow. But if Tony was already paranoid, being physically pursued wouldn't exactly help. But what if Tony kills himself tonight? a voice inside Martin's head said as he walked home. If he does, it will all be your fault. No, it won't, Martin argued back, No, it won't. But as he unlocked the door of his room, and sat alone with only the grey light of the moon through the window, he found it wasn't easy to contemplate going to bed and trying to sleep.

CHAPTER TWENTY

"Yet she was false, for she was one of the damesels of Morgan le Fay."
[Sir Thomas Malory, Le Morte Darthur, 1485]

It was Tuesday morning and Eve had just cycled back madly from a lecture in the centre of town to be at another one at St Frideswide's. Her new bike was giving her a bit of trouble but she didn't know who to ask to have a look at it. As she walked out onto the landing at the top of Red Lodge where her room was situated, she was taken aback by the sight of someone sitting on the floor outside her room, obviously waiting for her. It was a small blonde girl in jeans and a thick check jacket that was far too big for her.

'Oh, Eve, I've been waiting for you,' she said, getting up. 'I hope you don't mind. But they told me you'd be back soon.'

'Oh! Angela, isn't it? Didn't I see you at Guy's party?'

'That's right.' Angela smiled, but then frowned, 'We had to leave in rather a hurry.'

'Yes, you were with Rory,' said Eve, unlocking her door. 'Come in and take a seat. Would you like a coffee?'

Eve gave up on the idea of going to her next lecture. She could copy the notes later. Martin had been nagging her to see Angela and Sarah and she had been resisting. Now at least she could claim to have seen one of them, with very little trouble to herself.

Eve took off her coat, switched on the kettle and her music. Oh good, it was Prokofiev's *Romeo and Juliet*. That should provide a nice atmosphere.

But as she turned round again to offer Angela a biscuit, she saw that Angela had begun to cry - small snuffling tears, like an animal in distress. Perhaps *Romeo an Juliet* hadn't been the right music.

'I'm s..s..sorry,' Angela gasped, 'I'm sorry.'

She was hugging herself inside the enormous jacket. Was it Rory's? Eve grabbed some tissues and went over to sit with Angela on the hard little sofa in the far corner of the room, the one covered with the ugly red candlewick bedspread. Should she put her arm round Angela to comfort her? Eve hadn't done the counselling course at St Frideswide's yet, and suddenly, instead of doing what would come to her naturally, she felt an anxiety to do the 'right thing' professionally.

Angela was now blowing her nose and looked ready to spill the beans regardless.

'It's... it's Rory. The police have taken him... have taken him in for questioning again! I think they think he did it! Oh, what am I going to do? I thought... I thought, well, that you knew the police - isn't he your uncle, or something? Couldn't you see him and tell them it wasn't Rory?'

Eve exhaled sharply in amazement.

'Oh, I'm sorry, I'm sorry,' gabbled Angela. 'I know I shouldn't ask you something like that, but I'm desperate. He's all I've got. I don't know what I'll do if anything happens to him!'

And she began to cry again.

But what if he did the murder, thought Eve? Isn't it better that justice is done? Suddenly Eve wondered how much of Angela's grief was for Rory and how much was just self-pity and concern for her own well-being.

'I can't really help,' said Eve, tempted to say that she could in order to get more information out of Angela. 'Why are the police coming down so hard on Rory anyway?' Eve secretly thought Angela was probably over-reacting to something quite routine. 'I know about him threatening Feral the night before the murder, that he could have stolen the armour and that he has no alibi for the... uh, for the Saturday morning. Do the police have something more on him?'

'Isn't that enough?!' Angela shrieked. 'He was only trying to protect me from Feral! He wouldn't really have hurt her. He just didn't want... didn't want anything starting again between us,' she ended lamely.

'Starting again?'

'Feral could be very vindictive.'

'In what way? Oh, you tell me, while I make the coffee.'

Angela sighed heavily and began her story as Eve got up.

'You know how everyone says that when you come up to university and become huge friends with someone on your first day, you then spend the rest of the year trying to get rid of them?'

Eve didn't, but couldn't help thinking of Martin.

'Well, "Feral", as she called herself, was my big mistake. I suppose I should have guessed from the name that there was something wrong with her. But I thought it was her real name - you know, spelt "Ferrell", something like that. Lots of people have unusual names, perhaps a surname used as a first name, or something. Anyway,' Angela sighed, 'that was mistake number one. We were on the same staircase and I suppose in that very first week we were sort of thrown together. I think I felt sorry for her - ha! It's hard to imagine now. But she did seem a bit of an outsider. I think I felt that way too and so I latched onto her. Perhaps I wanted to be with someone who seemed even more insecure than me. And she had a slight limp, you know. She had one leg slightly longer than the other - I think it was from an accident at her birth. She used to joke that the resurrection of platform shoes was a real gift to her, 'cos she could wear her built-up shoe without it looking too obvious. Although she usually used to hide it with long clothes.'

'Yes, we saw that,' said Eve, handing Angela her coffee and sitting in the armchair to listen. Angela grimaced slightly at this reminder that Eve had seen Feral's dead body, then she continued:

'I think she'd been tormented quite a bit at school about it. Of course she couldn't do games properly and got left out a lot. She used to sit and read in the library on her own when it was games lessons. I think that's how she got into Oxford, because she was from quite a poor family - just her mother, you know. And it wasn't a particularly good school. So that made things even worse - she started to be a lot cleverer than everyone too - it was a disastrous combination. So you can understand why I felt sorry for her.'

'Oh, absolutely,' Eve agreed, feeling a slight uncomfortable identification with the dead girl. She knew the syndrome of the Bright Outcast a bit too well from her own history.

'She could be very funny as well though,' Angela added. 'Although it was usually funny in a mean sort of way, looking back on it, particularly about men. Oh, she was very good at finding someone's Achilles' heel almost instantly and exploiting it. It was as if she could see people's weak spots with sort-of X-Ray eyes. She said it was their auras that gave them away and she could read them like a book.'

'And what do you think?'

'Oh, I don't know about auras. *I* could never see anything like that. But she was usually right about people's characters - their dark side, as it were. She...she particularly had a thing about...'

Eve waited for a moment before prompting her. 'Yes?'

'...about Rory,' Angela sighed, clutching her mug of coffee as if she needed the warmth. 'She was crackers about him, actually. She could sense all the... power and energy that there is underneath the surface with him. He has a very powerful personality.'

He's also staggeringly good-looking, thought Eve, but said nothing.

'Anyway, Feral was very jealous when Rory chose me instead of her.'

'Was there ever a competition?' said Eve in amazement, in spite of herself.

'Not as far as Rory was concerned. But Feral seemed to like to think there was. At first Rory couldn't see me without Feral hanging around. Remember she was supposed to be my best friend at this point - this was in the first term last year. Anyway, then Rory moved in for... oh, gosh, I almost said "the kill"! Oh no, I mean he began to really get serious just before Christmas, before we were all due to go home. Of course there were tons of parties and Rory and I... well, we got together then. It was wonderful!'

'But Feral was furious?'

Angela nodded contemplatively. Eve wondered how much she was enjoying the relating of her conquest.

'At first it wasn't obvious because it was the Christmas vacation anyway. Unfortunately I put off seeing her in favour of seeing Rory - which she found out about later, although I thought I'd lied quite well.'

'So not only did you get the gorgeous Rory - if you don't mind me saying - you also spurned her friendship and went back on your word.'

'Well...' Angela obviously wasn't too keen on this description of her actions. 'My arrangements with Feral had never been that firm. And she'd been very iffy about whether there'd actually be room at her mother's house for me to visit. I think she was ashamed of how poor they were compared to my family - both my parents are doctors and we have a lovely house and all that. Anyway, it wasn't a problem over the Christmas vac, but then when we got back...'

'What happened?'

'Notes. Letters. All done on lovely paper in beautiful calligraphy. But it was really weird. They weren't signed by Feral as herself, but as Morgan! You know, Morgan le Fay!'

Eve looked mystified.

'I'm sorry, you've lost me,' she apologised.

'You know,' said Angela eagerly, 'like in Arthurian legend. The Launcelot and Guinevere Society! Oh, I assumed you knew all about it when you mentioned it at the party the other night.'

'No, no, I don't know a thing. I was just putting two and two together.'

'Well, Morgan was King Arthur's half-sister - well, she was a lot of things, but I won't go into that now. Anyway, the key thing is that she was a witch. And Feral really identified with her and sort-of adopted her as her identity. This was at the beginning of the second term. She always denied it was her sending the letters. But then it started with other people in the society as well and we all got really riled. She was saying horrible things. She said she was going to split me up from Rory and that it was only her love potions that got him interested in me in the first place, so I owed her a massive favour.'

'A love potion!'

'Oh yes. I think it was bats' wings and mice. It was an authentic medieval one, I looked it up.'

'Good Lord!'

'Oh, everyone's very into Authenticity in the L and G Soc. It's the 'A' word. They go on about it all the time. So last year, at the end of the second term, we found out that there were several of us in the Society that she'd been plaguing. And so we called a special meeting and had her expelled. *That* didn't go down very well.'

'Wow, I can imagine. What did she do?'

'She went quiet for a while. But then the letters and spells and things got worse. I started to get really scared. There was one lad who virtually had a breakdown and had to leave college.'

'Didn't the college - King's - have anything to say about it?'

'I don't think they were told. It's not the sort of thing you say to your tutor. They'd just think you were being silly. I don't think they believe in the existence of Satan, somehow.'

'Is that what she was threatening you with?'

'She certainly implied that something very nasty was going to happen to us, probably supernatural in origin,' said Angela stiffly.

'Wow.'

Eve felt out of her depth. If there was a course in Exorcism at St Frideswide's, she thought ironically, it wasn't advertised in the prospectus.

'So you can see,' Angela hurried on, 'why Rory was so furious with her on our first night back - our first night back! And she was starting all over again. We'd had a bit of a break over the summer - Rory and I had had a wonderful time, we were even talking about marriage - and then as soon as we come back she's up to her old tricks again. So Rory wanted to show her it wasn't going to work. We didn't owe her anything. And she'd better leave us alone!'

'Yes,' said Eve meditatively. 'But can you think of anyone else who hated her - hated her enough to actually kill her, I mean? Like the other people that she threatened in the, um, L and G Soc.?'

Angela went strangely silent and looked away from Eve.

'Mmmm, em, yes, I think there were two other guys, but I can't remember their names... No, it's gone!' she ended cheerfully. 'Can't remember. Oh, is that the time? I'm sorry, I've taken up so much of your time. How selfish of me. I must be getting back. Thanks for the coffee.'

Eve was surprised by this sudden turn.

'But.. but... what about you?' Eve said following Angela to the door.

'Oh, don't worry, I'll be alright...'

'Oh no, actually, I meant...' Eve now felt embarrassed. Was she being callous? Oh well, Angela probably deserved it... 'What were you doing between the hours of seven and eight on the morning of the murder?'

'*Me?!* You're asking *me?* Em, I was in bed. Yes, I was in bed.'

'Can you prove it?'

'I can as a matter of fact,' said Angela haughtily for her height. 'I had a phone call at seven thirty in the morning. It was a friend from abroad. Someone came and knocked on my door and I got up to answer the phone.'

'Oh, so you're alright then,' said Eve smiling. 'Bye.'

'Goodbye,' said Angela frowning.

Eve closed the door and thought: Wow, I can't believe I was that nasty. Why don't I like her? I couldn't resist moving in for the kill either - in questions, at any rate. Perhaps it's in the genes. Then again, she was trying to use me, to get her darling Rory off the hook with the police. Perhaps Feral wasn't the only one who could be manipulative where a man was concerned.

CHAPTER TWENTY ONE

"THE WORLD IS BUT A BROKEN TOY,
ITS PLEASURES HOLLOW, FALSE ITS JOY.
UNREAL ITS LOVELIEST HUE, ALAS!
ITS PAINS ALONE ARE TRUE, ALAS!."

[GILBERT AND SULLIVAN, *PRINCESS IDA*, 1884]

Later on the Tuesday afternoon of First Week, Martin cycled down the Cowley Road. He was in search of Quest Avenue. In his survey of friends at King's as to who sprang to mind when the phrase 'spotty nerd in glasses' was mentioned, one student had risen to the surface like scum every time. Jeremy East. Jeremy was not the sort of person Martin would be seen dead hanging out with and so he decided to visit him in his digs.

Martin enjoyed the eclectic mix of the Cowley Road, with its semi-trendy bars, Indian, Caribbean, Chinese and Italian restaurants, second hand clothes shops, 'Everything for a pound' shops, arty-crafty jewellery and clothes, and health food shops. Unfortunately the immensely shabby 'Anarchist Tea Rooms' of legend had closed a while ago.

Quest Avenue was about half way down on the left, just past Tesco, and fortunately was one-way in the direction Martin required. Number forty three. Yes, it was the most dilapidated of a whole row of abandoned-looking houses. Some had been livened up with graffiti and paintings on the outside that were supposed to be art (clouds and dolphins seemed to be a favourite theme). The front garden of Jeremy's house was hardly worthy of the name. It was an abandoned wilderness-cum-trash heap. It was certainly a rare student who would interrupt important working or drinking time to wield a lawnmower or pair of hedge clippers. What it needed was a willing parent with a pair of secateurs - no, make that a flame thrower.

Martin got off his bike and picked his way down the front path over the litter (there was no lid on the trashcan and the local dogs and cats had obviously discovered its delights). Martin wondered if his bike would be safe left outside, even if it was locked. If anything could persuade him further that it had been a good decision to stay in college rooms for his second year, this was it. (It didn't occur to him that not everyone might be able to afford to.)

Instead of a door bell there was a homemade intercom system. Martin pressed this impatiently and, when he had persuaded Jeremy that it *was* really him, and yes, he *did* want to see Jeremy East, Martin was buzzed.

This rigmarole hardly seemed necessary as Jeremy seemed to have been standing at the other side of the door anyway. He gawped at Martin as if unable to believe that one of the coolest people at King's (if not *the* coolest) was deigning to pay him a visit. This probably added to his usual state of nervousness.

'What are you doing here?' Jeremy asked Martin, backing down the hallway and tripping over a pile of bottles.

'I just want to ask a few questions,' said Martin, wishing he didn't sound like the police. He sniffed the air. Yuk? Was that house mould or human sweat, or both?

'What questions?' said Jeremy scowling.

'Well, if you let me come in, I'll tell you.'

'Oh. This is my room.'

Jeremy indicated the door on the right. Martin hesitated but it would seem Jeremy was waiting for him to go in first. As he did, he wished he had a peg for his nose. Wow, he'd been in some smelly men's rooms in his time but this was the worst. Definitely 'eau de socks' or jock-strap, although Jeremy was hardly a jock.

'Have a seat,' said Jeremy in a neutral voice.

Martin stepped over the things littering the floor to reach a high-backed wooden chair near the wardrobe. As he moved the chair his hand touched the wardrobe handle.

'OW! Shit! What the hell was that?!' Martin exclaimed as what felt like an electric shock shot through his hand.

Jeremy giggled maniacally.

'Just my little security system,' he guffawed. 'Oh, you should have seen your face!'

Yes, and you'll be seeing your face with this chair wrapped round it, thought Martin, but decided politeness was the best policy.

'Oh, what a good idea,' Martin said manfully, rubbing his hand, 'I suppose it protects your possessions from intruders.'

'That's right,' said Jeremy cheerfully. 'And it's a good trick to play on friends.'

'I'm surprised you have any,' Martin grimaced.

'Oh, they all like that sort of thing. We all do it to each other. Of course the wardrobe one is very basic,' said Jeremy earnestly. 'I've been doing that for years, to stop my little brother nicking my things. But I've got the whole room wired up to this remote - look!'

And Jeremy picked up a remote control from the coffee table (made of empty coke cans stuck together in a table-shape) and began to press the switches. The light went on and off, the gas fire lit itself and then went out several times, the radio came on and a very loud alarm went off. Jeremy left it on for longer than was strictly necessary, grinning, before he switched it off.

'Great burglar alarm,' he said.

Martin wondered why any burglar would be mad enough to think there was anything worth stealing in a house like this. Then again, students were renowned for having a lot of computer and audio equipment and tended to be prime targets. Student insurance was outrageously expensive.

'Oh, do you want a coffee?' said Jeremy dubiously.

Martin glanced down at the furry cultures of mould he could see in the only two coffee mugs in sight, and declined graciously.

'Biscuit?' said Jeremy.

He lifted a plate off the table from under a pile of papers and held it in front of Martin. It appeared to be Winnie the Pooh and Peter Rabbit biscuits with their heads missing.

'I break the heads off first,' said Jeremy grinning.

'Oh, em, thank you, I think I'll let the torsos rest in peace.'

'Oh good, that's what everybody says. All the more for me,' said Jeremy, tucking into one of his little victims with relish.

Oh God, let me out of here, Martin groaned inwardly. How am I going to have a sensible conversation with this nutter? Oxford seemed to encourage eccentricity in students who seemed to think it was a sign of genius to be as weird as possible.

'So you found the body,' said Jeremy, suddenly solving all Martin's problems by bringing up the subject himself.

'Oh! Oh, yes, I did, with some others.'

'I met one of them, at Guy's party. She seemed very nice. A bit nervous though.'

So it *was* you, thought Martin with satisfaction.

'Yes,' said Martin, 'she mentioned you.'

'Really?!' Jeremy blushed.

Martin was giggling inside. Suddenly he could feel the power in this encounter starting to flow his way.

'Wow! But she didn't know who I was!'

'You must make an impression on some people.'

'I suppose so.'

Jeremy sat down and looked at the floor frowning.

'So, you've come about the murder,' he said after a pause. His voice sounded like somebody about to give themselves up.

'I know it can't be Robert Baker!' Jeremy suddenly burst out, looking up earnestly at Martin. 'I'm sure it must be Rory! Isn't he the one the police suspect?'

Martin blinked a few times, feeling the conversation several light years out of control again.

'Robert Baker? Why on earth are you bringing him up? And yes, the police do seem to be going for Rory at the moment. No one's suggesting it's Robert Baker!'

'Oh good,' Jeremy sighed with relief.

'Why would they be?'

'Oh, no reason. I'm just glad they're not. The murder was about seven o'clock on the Saturday morning, wasn't it?

'That's right,' said Martin cautiously.

'Oh, good.'

'Why good?'

'Well, I was at King's visiting Rob Baker then. We'd agreed to meet at his room. But when I got there he was busy on some work and told me to sod off. He was playing really loud music,' Jeremy snickered. 'Must have been really annoying people.'

Martin felt the same annoyance rise up in him now.

'So Baker can provide you with an alibi for that time.'

'*An alibi! Me! Why would I need an alibi?!*' cried Jeremy.

'I don't know. You tell me. Did you know Feral?'

'Of course.'

'Were you in the Launcelot and Guinevere Society last year?'

Jeremy hesitated then said:

'Yes, I'm not ashamed of it.'

'Why would you be?'

'No reason.'

'Was Rob Baker in the Launcelot and Guinevere Society?'

'No. He wouldn't *join* anything,' said Jeremy as if that were somehow beneath the dignity of his friend.

'What on earth were you and Baker supposed to be doing at that time on a Saturday morning?'

'He didn't say.'

'So you just turned up on the off chance? Do you always do what Baker tells you to do?'

'Of course not! Well, usually. It's usually good. But, as I said, that morning he was busy. So, yes, he can give me an alibi, if I need one. But I don't.'

'Did Feral used to write to you?'

'What?' Jeremy's facial colour alternated between white (and spotty) and pink (and spotty) rapidly several times.

'Why would she write to me?' he mumbled, looking at the carpet. 'We weren't anything special. She didn't fancy *me*.'

'Then who did she fancy?'

Jeremy shrugged and looked out of the window. He sniffed. He obviously wasn't going to say any more.

In the silence, Martin noticed that he couldn't smell the room any more. His nostrils must have become acclimatised. Presumably that's how Jeremy's nose functioned all the time.

'So,' said Martin, getting up to leave, 'you don't mind if I check your alibi with your friend Baker?'

Jeremy looked up at him, a look of such vulnerability on his face that Martin felt almost alarmed. Had he pushed him too far? He felt almost sorry for this twit with the huge blue magnified eyes staring up at him, mouth hanging open.

Jeremy seemed incapable of speech.

'Alright, I'll let myself out then,' said Martin, 'as long as there aren't any more booby traps awaiting me, of course.'

He picked his way across the room, knocking over a half-empty can of cold baked beans. Fortunately there was a stale slab of pizza on a plate next to it to catch them.

'Bye then,' said Martin as cheerily as possible, when it was obvious Jeremy was not going to budge to see him to the door. 'Thanks for the...em...' There hadn't been a coffee. Martin could hardly thank him for the electric shock. 'Anyway, be seeing you, Jeremy.'

Martin closed the door behind him and unlocked his bike, fortunately still there. Perhaps he should ask Jeremy to design a bike chain that would electrocute any thief that tampered with it. Would probably make him a fortune.

As Martin cycled away, he looked behind him. Behind the grimy window and the lace curtain, he could see the silhouette of Jeremy East, waiting for him to leave.

That night was the auditions for the Gilbert and Sullivan Society. They were being held in the main debating hall of the Union building - a beautiful and ornate piece of Victorian neo-gothic right in the heart of Oxford. Martin was thrilled to see that Eve had decided to come after all and audition for the role of Princess Ida. He led a round of applause and whooping for her after she had sung Ida's first solo, 'Minerva! Minerva, oh, hear me!', beautifully. Eve gave Martin a curt curtsey.

'No pain in my voice that time?' she said to him sarcastically as they all piled into the bar afterwards.

'Not a drop,' smiled Martin, 'although a touch would be useful for "The world is but a broken toy" that you have the pleasure of singing with me. Ow! No need to thump me. Anyway, tonight you were superb. I think you're a cert for my leading lady.'

'Oh well, you can't have everything in life. I guess we'll just have to put up with each other.'

'What do you mean, "put up with each other"? I thought we were getting on very well. Oh, I have some more news to pass on. I found out who the geek in specs was who grilled you at Guy's party. His name is Jeremy East and he's decidedly shifty. I'm going to check out his alibi as soon as I can, although it depends on a friend of his who might lie, I suppose. Oh well.'

Martin then told Eve about his meeting with Tony Greer on the Saturday night.

'Do I have news for you too!' said Eve impatiently, and told him all about her encounter with Angela earlier on that day.

'To say she's trying to get Rory off the hook,' said Martin, 'she's not doing a very good job. Anyway, have you heard that the police have confirmed that there were particles of Feral's blood and skin on the Chichele gauntlets?'

'Hardly surprising.'

'*And*, Ms Smartypants, fibres of grey cotton found on the seat of the boat used by the murderer - probably from a tracksuit. So there.'

'How do you know all this?'

'I've been cosying up to DS Woolton. He can't stand me but is very flattered when I plead ignorance and want his help. It's a class thing. We rich boys have that effect on people sometimes,' he said grinning at Eve.

'You mean you're being utterly manipulative.'

'Something like that.'

'I wonder,' said Eve, trying to change the flow of the conversation, 'if Rory has a grey tracksuit.'

'Or John Harborough. Or Tony Greer.'

'Or Jeremy East.'

'Or Angela, for that matter,' said Martin.

'Oh, no way!' exclaimed Eve. 'I can't see the tiny Angela heaving herself around in the Chichele armour.'

'Hate makes people do funny things,' said Martin. 'They can often show tremendous physical strength.'

'Only on a once-in-a-lifetime surge of adrenalin.'

'Hmmm, you're right I'm sure. But don't forget the armour was adjustable to some extent. There are leather straps and lacings that could alter the size. And the main tailored parts weren't stolen. Anyone could wear the bascinet, gauntlets, greaves and sabatons.'

'You like saying that, don't you,' grinned Eve. 'Do you want another drink?'

'Em, no, I won't on this occasion, thank you. I could get some work done if I go back in the near future.'

Martin got up to leave.

'Do you need walking home?' he asked Eve.

'No, there's someone going up to Keble College that I can go back with,' she replied. 'Thanks.'

'OK. Oh, that reminds me. There was one weird thing I found out today that I can't make sense of.'

'Oh?'

'On the first Friday we all came back at the beginning of term, several people at King's had empty envelopes left in their pigeon holes. They were large brown envelopes with their names printed on, but nothing inside them. I wouldn't have thought twice about it if it hadn't been for the fact that three of the people were sitting on the same table at lunch time today and all chimed in about it. Just seemed an odd coincidence.'

Eve shrugged.

'I can't make anything of it.'

'Oh, and another nail in the coffin for poor Rory. Someone at lunch said they saw Rory on the vital Saturday morning at about eleven in the morning looking terrible. She said he looked as if he'd been up all night, not having a sound ten hours' kip. She was worried she may have got him into more trouble by telling the police.'

'She probably did,' said Eve callously.

'Well, happy hunting. It makes you wonder what the police are finding out while we're all dozing peacefully in our beds. All sorts of exciting things could be developing we know nothing of.'

'I think I can cope without any more developments for the time being,' said Eve. 'Bye.'

But something was developing that the police knew nothing about. That afternoon a woman had taken a roll of film into Boots on Cornmarket. She wanted to know if any photos would come out properly, as her son had found it in an old camera half-submerged in the river when he was out fishing. The assistant behind the counter smiled and said they would do their best.

CHAPTER TWENTY TWO

"What do you think I and two friends of mine are doing here? Painting pictures nine feet high with life-size figures, on the walls of the Union Society's new room here... The work goes very fast, and is the finest fun possible. Our pictures are from the *Morte d'Arthur*."

[Dante Gabriel Rossetti writing to Charles Eliot Norton, July 1858]

"If we needed models, we sat to each other, and Morris had a head always fit for Lancelot..."

[Edward Burne-Jones writing to James Thursfield, 1869]

'It's Wednesday - it must be the Launcelot and Guinevere Society,' thought Eve wearily, as she trudged through the rain to the Oxford Union building again.

It was the Wednesday night of First Week. She had agreed to meet Martin at the L and G Soc after arguing with him and refusing to go on her own. He had said he would hold her hand in case she was afraid of meeting any murderers. Eve had predictably said she would rather meet a murderer than hold Martin's hand any day and he had pretended to go off in a huff. But the arrangement still stood for them to meet up.

Writing an essay on the dates of the Synoptic Gospels instead had suddenly looked very attractive to Eve. Why on earth was she having to mix with these loonies who liked dressing up like characters from medieval legend? What she could remember of the story of King Arthur was minimal, mainly from Walt Disney's cartoon *The Sword in the Stone*. She knew that had been based on T H White's book *The Once and Future King* and that it was mainly about Arthur's boyhood. But Launcelot and Guinevere hadn't featured in the cartoon at all. Guinevere had been unfaithful to Arthur with Launcelot, Eve knew that, but the rest was a blank. Oh well, perhaps she'd learn some more tonight.

Eve showed her Union card and entered the huge neo-gothic building. The Society was meeting in the Reading Room. The place was full of students talking and laughing and drinking, but it wasn't difficult to find the right place. Eve just had to follow the women in the tall pointed hats. Oh no, costumes, thought Eve. I wonder if Martin will be wrapped in a sheet. Somehow she couldn't imagine it.

No, there he was, already in conversation with someone (a girl in a lace-up bodice that pushed her breasts together and upwards). He was wearing black jeans and a white shirt and a heavy black leather jacket. His hair seemed to be slicked back with some sort of gel. It looked surprisingly alright. Honestly, his hair looked different every time she saw him. Eve suddenly felt very ordinary. She should have worn something more interesting. She suddenly hated her boring beige raincoat and the fact that she was wearing her glasses instead of contact lenses. Because she hadn't wanted to come out tonight, she hadn't made an effort with her appearance in protest, and now she was regretting it. She turned round and walked out.

But Martin had spotted her. When she was half way down the hall, caught up in a crowd of boozy rugby players, she felt a squeeze on her shoulder.

'Ha! Don't think you can escape that easily, little girl,' said an old crone's voice, aka Martin Massey. 'I saw you trying to get away.'

'You saw right,' said Eve resentfully. 'I see you were already making headway with the investigation. Did she *reveal* anything useful?'

'Oh no,' said Martin cheerfully. 'No, I was just chatting her up, oozing the old charm, you know.' Martin was steering Eve back to the Reading Room.

'I was just thinking how little I knew about King Arthur and all this stuff,' Eve complained.

'Don't worry, I've read Malory - well, some of him. We shall survive! Oh, have a look at the ceiling in here. It was painted by Rossetti and William Morris and Edward Burne-Jones - you know, the Pre-Raphaelites, all that lot. One of their first commissions. And it's a wonder it wasn't their last because they knew fu-, em, nothing much about it and the paintings only survived a few years. They had to be completely restored.'

'You can't see them very well now,' said Eve, squinting up at the sloping ceiling above the many bookshelves. The whole room looked like a Victorian gentleman's club with old leather armchairs, dark wood tables and a huge fire place that had a real fire with enormous logs.

'William Morris had armour made especially for the models. Of course he used to have his own as a little boy, riding around on horseback in the woods pretending to be a knight. There's King Arthur there,' said Martin pointing up at the ceiling. 'Can you see him with Guinevere? Oh, and there's Launcelot. There's our man.'

But Eve was looking across the room at a young man wearing armour standing by the fireplace. The armour shone and was reflecting the flames. He had shoulder length brown hair and a beautiful face. Eve shivered.

Eve pointed this out to Martin.

'I know,' said Martin, 'there are a few in armour here. Look - one there in the corner, another over there...'

At this point they were interrupted by another buxom maiden who offered them a cup of warm spiced mead from a tray. Eve and Martin accepted with a smile.

'Can you tell me which one is the President of the Society?' Martin asked her.

'Oh, that's William. Er, where is he? Oh, there, look. With the gold circlet on his head. He's King Arthur, of course. Doesn't he look great?'

'I'll go and talk to William,' said Martin, indicating to Eve that she should stay and talk to the serving wench.

'Um, how long have you been in the society?' said Eve, suddenly finding she was having to follow this girl around as she served more drinks.

'Oh, I joined as a Fresher last year. It's great fun! You can choose which character from King Arthur's time you want to be. Of course *everyone* wants to be Launcelot or Guinevere so there's a limit on numbers for that. Usually only finalists are allowed to do that. As a first year you tend to be one of the lesser characters.'

'Oh, I see. And who are you?'

'I'm just a serving maid tonight - one of King Arthur's court. But this year I'm hoping to be Elaine the White.'

'And who's she?'

The girl looked surprised that Eve didn't know.

'She's Launcelot's great love! Or rather, he didn't love her but she loved him. She *died* for love of him.'

'Oh, is this the Lady of Shalott?'

'That's right,' beamed the girl. 'I'm trying to grow my hair really long so I'll look more authentic. She was the daughter of Bernard of Astolat and Launcelot wore her sleeve as a love token during a joust as a sort of disguise so no one would know it was him, because everyone *knew* he was supposed to be in love with Guinevere.'

'So she died in the end. And she was found lying dead in a boat.'

'That's right.'

'Did you know Feral Harrison?'

The girl offered drinks to some more people before replying.

'What? Oh yes, Feral. Yes, I knew her, vaguely. She was kicked out of the Society half way through Hilary Term last year.'

'She'd been pretending to be Morgan le Fay, I'm told. That's a witch, isn't it?'

The girl sighed.

'Yes, there are some who like to pretend to be the witches. I don't understand it, not when you can pretend to be some beautiful heroine. Why pretend to be a horrible witch? You don't even get to wear such nice clothes. But some women are into feminine power in a different way. I think it's nicer for women to control men with their beauty, don't you?'

'Uh, well, um...'

'I mean, look at this bodice! The men love seeing you dressed like this. My boyfriend - he's Sir Galahad, even though that's Elaine's son in another story, a different Elaine - he thinks it's fantastic. It's when men were men and women were women - that's the whole fun of it!'

'Who's this other Elaine?'

'Oh, she was the daughter of Pelles, I think it was. She was crackers about Launcelot as well - basically, all women were - and she managed to trick him into sleeping with her, fooling Launcelot that she was Guinevere. He was furious when he woke up and nearly killed her!'

'Wow,' said Eve in genuine amazement. 'I never thought of Launcelot killing a woman. I thought he was supposed to be the essence of chivalry.'

'Oh, he was. And normally he is riding around defending women left right and centre. But I suppose where Guinevere was concerned he was rather sensitive. Anyway, it all worked out for the best because *this* Elaine had Galahad from him - his baby - which had been prophesied anyway so I suppose they didn't have much choice. It was probably destined. Of course, that was all done with the help of a witch, so I suppose they had their uses.'

'What was done?'

'Elaine being able to fool Launcelot about who she was. They were always doing it. Arthur himself was only born because Merlin cast a spell to make Uther Pendragon look like Igraine's husband.'

Eve sighed, 'You've lost me.'

'Well, Igraine was a faithful woman, you see,' the wench explained patiently, 'and she wouldn't have slept with anyone other than her husband, so Uther needed to look like her husband in order to sleep with her - simple!'

'Oh, I see,' said Eve, thinking it all sounded rather complex.

'It's like a medieval soap opera!' said the girl. 'Everybody sleeps with everybody else! And with the help of magic, it's all so much easier to be deceptive about your appearance and who you really are. Anyway, do excuse me, I must get some more mead for the masses.'

'Thanks. And you are?'

'Just call me Elaine,' the girl grinned.

Oh great, thought Eve. Even if I do get evidence out of somebody, I'm not going to know their real identity. I can't see Uncle Andy being very keen on calling Elaine the White to the witness box.

Meanwhile Martin had been talking to William, or King Arthur as he preferred to be known.

'So you have a membership list for last year,' Martin was saying.

'Yes, the Secretary has it. In fact he should have it on him now. Hey, Merlin!'

Several people looked round, who were all dressed as versions of Merlin. But it was one in particular that the 'king' required on this occasion and he did indeed have the membership book in a black leather bag. It was a smart leather-bound book with names of members and the minutes of each meeting written in beautiful calligraphy.

'That must take a while to write out in full,' said Martin.

'Oh, I don't do it,' said 'Merlin'. 'I have a novice do that for me. I have several novices, several adepts in the black arts. Oh course, this one just does handwriting,' he ended lamely.

'And who's that? I'm sure it's a friend of mine...'

'Well, here he's called Goon...'

Martin roared with laughter. 'That figures!'

'That's a good Dark Ages name,' said 'Merlin' huffily.

'Did Goon do it last year?'

'No, I don't think so. No, it was... oh, who was it?'

Merlin flicked through the front pages of the book.

'It was some twit who wanted to be Mordred, but we wouldn't let him - too senior a role. Oh here we are. His real name was Jeremy East. Is that who you were thinking of?'

'Oh yes, that'll do nicely,' Martin grinned and admired Jeremy's masterly calligraphy. 'My, what a lovely gothic script.

Obviously hides his light under a bushel. Could I have a copy of that membership list for last year?'

'That's a lovely outfit,' said Eve to a girl dressed in a long burgundy velvet dress with a low sweeping neckline edged in thick white fur. 'It's looks quite Christmassy. Who are you supposed to be?'

'I'm Brusen, or Brisen, depending on which version you read,' the girl smiled. She had bronze coloured hair wrapped in coils around her ears. 'I'm a witch.'

'Oh! Oh, I would never have guessed. You don't look... I mean, I would never have guessed...'

'I know. I'm not in black and purple, or anything corny. But witches don't have to be ugly, you know, with hooked noses and warts! I copied my costume from a nineteenth century painting by William Russell Flint. He did wonderfully pervy renditions of Arthurian legend and he did this picture of Brisen casting a spell on Launcelot so he'd sleep with Elaine.'

'Oh, I was just talking to an Elaine about that. That was so Launcelot would mistake her identity and think... Oh wow.' Eve's face suddenly fell and her eyes stared into space.

'What?' said 'Brisen'. 'What's the matter?'

Eve blinked rapidly and tried to recover. Just the phrase 'mistaken identity' was enough to throw her.

'Oh, nothing, nothing. Something just hit me, that's all. Um, tell me more about, um, who was it? Brisen?'

'There's nothing more to tell. Are you sure you're alright? You look a funny colour.'

'It's just the drink probably.' Eve scowled and decided to go for the jugular. 'Did you know Feral Harrison?'

'Oh, her! Poor girl, isn't it terrible? Yes, she was a witch - in reality as well, by the sounds of it. Stupid girl. She shouldn't have messed around with it.' 'Brisen' got closer and whispered to Eve, 'They say she began to think she really *was* Morgan le Fay. Went potty!'

'Really?' said Eve in a similarly hushed voice. 'Poor girl.'

'Yes. She was chucked out of the Society. Started casting spells on people. Of course, no one would stand for that. It's alright as a joke, but...' 'Brisen' frowned. 'She took the whole re-incarnation thing a bit far. I mean, it's one thing to say you've been Nefertiti in a previous life - at least she really existed. But it's another to say you were a mythical figure. There are enough crackpots in Cornwall who think they're King Arthur as it is.'

'Really?'

'Oh, the place is crawling with them. There's probably a few like that here,' said 'Brisen' scanning the crowd with her eyes. 'But it seems to be worse with some of the characters than others. Everyone wants to be Arthur or Launcelot, of course. Usually you don't get people advertising themselves as the shadier characters.'

'But Feral did.'

'Yes, and look where it's landed her. Although at least she can come back in another form and do it right next time.'

There was a pause before Eve said, 'Huh? What do you mean?'

'You know,' said 'Brisen', 'her next life. Since she was murdered she'll probably have quite a good time next round to make up for it. I'm only sorry I won't have any more. But my Guide says I'm going to be so successful in this life that I won't need any more.' 'Brisen' sighed. 'It's rather a shame really. Perhaps I shouldn't enjoy myself so much.'

'What guide?'

'My Spirit Guide, of course!'

'And this says you're a success. How do you define success?' said Eve in amazement.

'I'm happy,' said 'Brisen'.

'What if you're happy, but hideously wrong?' said Eve stubbornly.

'How can I be wrong if I'm happy?' 'Brisen' replied, looking at Eve as if she was mad.

It was not difficult for Eve to conclude that 'Brisen' had gone beyond the place where rational opposition would have any further point.

But they were now interrupted by someone blowing a trumpet for them all to be quiet. A large screen was being erected at one end of the Reading Room and they were told to arrange chairs so they could see the screen. There was going to be a showing of

'Camelot' (wild cheers). Everyone was invited to sing, get up and dance, and generally join in any way they wanted. Many of the older members knew it off by heart, so it was going to be done like *The Rocky Horror Show* with the characters from the screen acting out the parts in front. Eve noticed that the beautiful young man in armour she had noticed earlier was to be Launcelot. The President of the Society predictably was to be King Arthur.

Martin had slipped into the seat beside Eve and murmured:

'So it looks like we're going to be prostituting our vocal talents for yet another night.'

Eve gave a cross between a grin and a grimace looking, for once, remarkably like her 'uncle' Andy.

CHAPTER TWENTY THREE

"And Lancelot answered nothing, but he went,
And at the inrunning of a little brook
Sat by the river in a cove,
And watched the high reed wave, and lifted up his eyes
And saw the barge that brought her moving down,
Far-off, a blot upon the stream..."

[Tennyson, *Idylls of the King*, 1859]

Eve walked into town on the Saturday afternoon of First Week. She needed to catch a bus to take her to Iffley where her honorary uncle and aunt lived. 'Aunt' Maggie had deigned to ask Eve over for a meal. Eve felt very anxious. She had never felt that Maggie liked her that much but she had no idea why that might be. Admittedly, Uncle Andy wasn't exactly warm either, or rather he could switch any warmth he had on and off very rapidly so you never knew where you were. Perhaps if he'd been doing that to Maggie over the years, she'd just frozen up in response. But no, that couldn't be it. Eve could distinctly remember on one family occasion years ago being the only person ignored by Maggie while she made a fuss over everyone else.

Oh, for goodness' sake, Eve told herself as she walked down Cornmarket, don't be so juvenile. Oh, should I take a present, chocolates, or something? The Covered Market was probably the best place to find something nice, but would that make her late in getting to Iffley? Eve had no idea when the buses ran from Queen Street. But as she walked down Cornmarket in indecision she began looking in shop windows for alternative ideas. But the first window was covered with little black cut-out witches on broom sticks, white ghosts and skeletons, all covered in fake cobwebs. Eve inhaled sharply in surprise, then it dawned on her that it was only a week or so to Halloween.

But as virtually every shop she passed displayed the same sort of items regardless of whether they were selling greetings cards or insurance, Eve began to feel indignant. Didn't they know it was supposed to be a Christian festival, All Hallows' Eve - the celebration of all the believers who had gone to be with God? It should be all the Saints they were celebrating - saints who had lived their lives to help others and do good - not giving publicity to weirdos who cast spells and try to do harm. How much better to have the shop windows with pictures of St Francis, or St Damian the Leper, or Julian of Norwich! Life-enhancing people who had given their lives to help the poor and the sick, or received revelations from God that had inspired millions! But no, here instead was a juvenile glorying in the dark side - pretending it was all a joke in order to make money out of it, of course. Eve shook her head in amazement at the combination of Materialism and Magic.

She was still none the wiser as to what present to take to her aunt's. Would they be expecting one at all? Eve now saw the bus to Rose Hill she was to catch. Too late now. She leapt on the bus as it was about to leave and tried to explain to the driver where she wanted to go, lurching and swaying as the bus stop-started out of the busy junction at Carfax.

Her uncle had told her that it was a five minute walk to his house from the bus stop. It was more like fifteen. Fortunately it wasn't raining but it was becoming quite cold. And dark too. Eve had to walk past rows of allotments on her right, a park on her left and then down a grove of overhanging trees where there was no sign of civilisation at all. Her heart was beating too fast and she began to run. Where were the street signs? She felt as if she had left Oxford behind and was in another part of the country altogether. Iffley Village really was a village in its own right.

It was almost four thirty when Eve finally arrived at DI Andrews house. It was a modern bungalow that didn't fit in with the more elderly houses of the rest of the village. Uncle Andy greeted her at the door, putting his coat on.

'Let's go for a walk while Maggie's making the meal,' he said. 'She doesn't like to be disturbed. And I can show you the village. Pretty, isn't it? Even in the dark. Would you like to see the old church? It goes back to the ninth century.'

Eve didn't seem to have much choice, even though she would have preferred being inside a warm house. The wind was blowing the leafless trees, their discarded leaves wet underfoot. Eve wondered why people always assumed, just because they thought she was 'religious', that she liked being dragged around draughty old churches. It hadn't been the architecture that had attracted her in the first place.

Her uncle was pointing out the old schoolhouse and the way to the river. The village itself did have pretty little cottages and well-kept gardens and window boxes, Eve could tell even in the fading light. The church seemed to be in the centre of the village behind an old low stone wall. All was quiet. Eve could see her breath curling out in front of her as they walked up the slight hill and into the church yard.

'I wonder if there'll be frost tonight,' said Andrews, pushing his hands further into his pockets.

'It does feel very cold,' said Eve.

'Come round to the front of the church and have a look at the old doorway. It's Romanesque, a very old zig-zag design. Beautiful and simple. I don't know why they can't design things like that now. How's your grandma, by the way? Is she still, er, alive? Your Mum's mum?'

'Yes, although she's not that well. I'm going to have to visit her at some point soon. I don't think she's well enough to come here.'

'Isn't she up north somewhere now?'

'Yes, she moved up to a little village in Lancashire.'

'Ah. Well, give her my regards when you do see her. And Patricia and Gordon and the boys?'

'Aunt Pat and Uncle Gordon are in Shanghai...'

'Blimey!'

'Yeah, it's Uncle Gordon's job that's taken them out there, but Aunt Pat is teaching English too. David and Simon are learning Mandarin! But hopefully they'll be back in London soon and I can visit them.'

'Ah, that'll be nice.'

There was a silence. Eve felt a bit weird about the fact that DI Andrews knew some of her family from years ago and so began to admire the church's arched stone doorway. To make conversation, Andrews tried the door but it was locked.

'Shame. There's a lovely John Piper window in there I would have liked you to have seen. His widow donated it. I wonder if the Rector's in. I could get the keys off him.'

Andrews looked round at the house in the church grounds, a low and ancient looking building, obviously medieval. But there were no lights on.

'Oh well, some other time.'

A distant dog barked and howled. The sinking sun had left a pattern of deep orange and red in the distance behind the bare branches of the trees all around them. The branches formed an intricate pattern, like the thin veins on the back of the eye. Eve was just about to comment on an old grave with an unusual name carved on it, when Andrews suddenly said:

'How well do you know Martin?'

Eve stood up suddenly and looked at her godfather in surprise. She couldn't even think of anything to say at first.

'Sorry, I interrupted your thoughts...' he began.

'Oh, no, it's OK! I just... well, it's a hard one to answer,' Eve blustered. 'I suppose it's all relative. How well do I know him compared to what?'

'I know you knew Charles Boscombe before you came up to University, for example, so you could tell me a bit about him, if I asked...'

'Why would you ask?' said Eve sharply.

'Oh, no reason. We like to know the reliability of our witnesses. Of course, I can vouch for *you*.'

'Oh thanks,' said Eve ironically.

'It's a simple question. Would you say Martin Massey was a friend of yours?'

Eve was speechless again, groping for words.

'Why am I being interrogated in a graveyard?!' she burst out. 'What's going on?'

'Oh, Eve, I'm sorry, I didn't mean it to seem like that. Oh, I'm sorry, love, my job must be getting the better of me. No wonder Maggie won't let me talk about police stuff in the house...'

'Won't she?'

'No. I think I probably bored her with it too much in the early years. She's old enough now to put her foot down,' Andrews smiled bleakly. 'Anyway, all I wanted to know was, can you remember - on the day when you were punting down the river and one of you saw the abandoned boat that contained the body - who was it that saw it first? See if you can cast your mind back.'

'Phew!' Eve sighed with the effort. It wasn't something she wanted to remember. 'Well, let's see, it was whoever had the binoculars at the time. Oh, Charlie was doing the punting and so it must have been Martin. Yes, he was fooling around with them, even though they belonged to Charlie.'

'So Martin was the first one to alert you all to the presence of the abandoned boat.'

'Um, yes, I think so. And then he said we should take a closer look.'

'It was definitely his initiative?'

'Oh yes, the rest of us - I mean Charlie and me - we weren't keen on having to do a detour, especially since it was raining.'

'Would you have noticed the boat - think carefully now - would you have noticed the boat down this obscure side stream, if Martin hadn't pointed it out?'

'Well,' said Eve awkwardly, 'we might have seen the boat in the distance as just a thing stuck amongst the trees. But I might not even have been able to tell it was a boat, not to mention what was in it, without someone using binoculars. You couldn't see much with the naked eye. And we certainly weren't planning to punt near that part of the river.'

'So it was Martin that saw the body and persuaded you to go down the side stream for a closer look?'

'Um, well gee, I can't remember, it's possible. It's all so confused...'

'And who was the one who identified the body?'

'Oh, well, Martin thought he recognised her and then he checked it later with the porter at King's...'

'So Martin knew who she was. Who estimated her time of death - you or him?'

'Well, him of course! He was the one... he could feel the *rigor* had just begun, so it was easy for him...' Eve finished lamely.

'So Martin accurately estimated the time of death. According to our forensic report, he couldn't have been more accurate if he had actually been there and seen it done with a bloody stopwatch in his hand.'

There was silence. Eve felt as if she couldn't breathe. She couldn't look at her uncle.

'And who was it who guessed the Chichele armour had been used in the attack?' he continued. 'And who saw it in Guy's room and had the chance to steal it? And who knew where the murderer's footprints were in the woods?'

'But that... that was an accident! He was sick!'

'And who knew the brand of notepaper that the murderer used and was one of the few people who could get hold of some of that discontinued line?'

'But... but if he *was*... if he was the murderer, he wouldn't tell you all this!'

'Wouldn't he?' said DI Andrews. 'Wouldn't he? Do you want me to tell you how many murderers have helped in the investigation of their own crime? Do you know how many killers are the first to supposedly 'find' the bodies of their victims?'

'I know that's what the police often assume...'

'And for bloody good reason!' exclaimed Andrews. Then his voice softened. 'I'm sorry, Eve, I don't want to be hard on *you*, I just want you to be *careful*, that's all. You know how it is when a case is going...well, I won't say *badly*, it's not that far yet, but it is proving bloody difficult. We have several suspects, any one of which could have done it. We have plenty of evidence, but nothing that conclusively pins down any one of 'em. It's bloody frustrating. And of course, we want to get an early result. We're going to have to go national soon, although I think that'll only complicate things more. I'm sure it's a local job. I'm sorry. I didn't want to frighten you. I just... I just want you to be on your guard, that's all. And if you notice anything that makes you at all suspicious, you must tell me immediately - OK?'

'OK.'

The two of them walked back to the bungalow, Eve feeling as if her mind had been blown apart. How on earth was she going to relate to Martin now? Should she tell him he was a suspect? Or had he already figured that out? Was that why he was so keen to solve the case? Or did he have more insidious reasons to be involved - perhaps to throw up as many other suspects as possible?

Oh, this was all too much. Having a godfather who was a detective didn't help matters at all. And his wife seemed barely able to manage a show of politeness to Eve during the meal. Why didn't Maggie like her? Oh well, Maggie didn't seem to like her husband much either.

At the same time Eve was having her meal, Martin was having an early supper at King Henry Hall. He had deliberately positioned himself near Robert Baker, otherwise known as 'the Prat Downstairs' who treated Martin to the kind of music he abhorred on a regular basis.

'Oi, Baker, pass the salt,' said Martin as he broke up a bread roll for his soup.

Baker did as he was requested, barely looking up from the book he was reading.

'What are you reading - *War and Peace*?' said Martin, knowing he was being annoying.

Baker merely lifted up the book so Martin could read the cover, and carried on. It was *The Magic of Mordern* by someone called

Maurice Abbotts. Martin had never heard of it, but judging from the cover it was an adventure fantasy on another planet peopled by men and women with ridiculously large muscles and very few clothes.

'Sorry to disturb your serious reading,' said Martin, his mouth full of soggy bread, 'but I need to know something about a friend of yours.'

Rob's eyes slid to one side and examined the table for a few seconds.

'Oh?' he said, his eyes returning to his book.

'Yes, Jeremy East. I paid him a visit the other day.'

Rob blinked rapidly a few times but didn't show any interest. He dunked his bread in his soup.

Martin sighed inwardly. This was going to be hard work. He studied Baker for a moment. Baker had short brown curly hair, large tortoiseshell glasses, and seemed fairly neat and tidy. He had an anonymous but not unpleasant face. Martin would have to ask Eve sometime to say whether he was attractive to women or not. Martin suspected that at a party he would fade into the woodwork, assuming he bothered to turn up at all. He didn't seem to mind advertising his isolation by reading at mealtimes, which was a big social no-no. He certainly wasn't repellent like his friend Jeremy, at any rate.

'You know the morning of the murder...' Martin said innocently.

Baker took a sharp intake of breath and began to cough on some crumbs that had gone down his windpipe.

'Oh, sorry, didn't mean to startle you,' said Martin. 'I suppose it's not exactly pleasant mealtime conversation. Anyway, I was just wondering... You alright now? Good. OK, so did Jeremy East come to your room at about seven o'clock that morning?'

Baker coughed again and nodded, his eyes watering slightly.

'Weren't the two of you supposed to be doing something together? I mean, Jeremy claims that you'd asked him to come to your room and you were supposed to be off doing something together. But you didn't.'

'Yeah, that's right,' Rob croaked and coughed again. 'I was doing something on my computer as it turned out, so I didn't go.'

'Do you often work that early in the morning? I mean, term hadn't even started.'

Rob scowled at Martin in incomprehension.

'I often get inspired,' he said. 'It can be at any time of the day or night.'

'Wow, must be tough, being a genius!'

Rob looked at Martin in disdain.

'If you like,' he said and looked down at his book again.

But Martin continued remorselessly.

'Can you confirm it was actually Jeremy at your door at that time?'

'Of course!'

'But you didn't actually see him?'

Rob grimaced in impatience.

'Of course not, I can't see through doors. But I recognised his voice.'

'So he could see you through the crack in the side of your door...'

'Yes, I'm going to get that rehung, it's a bloody nuisance...'

'But you couldn't see him.'

'Yes! God, you're being a pain today!'

'So you could have been mistaken about his voice! You see, I'm just trying to establish that Jeremy actually has an alibi for the time of the murder. I'm trying to do your friend a favour!'

This really caught Rob's attention. He looked up in genuine amazement.

'You're not saying... you don't think...!'

And with that, Rob burst out laughing.

'You think Jeremy could've done it! Bloody hell, and I thought you were supposed to be clever! Ha, ha, ha!'

'Alright, don't rub it in. I must admit, I can't see him doing it either. But if the police think it, he'd better make sure his alibi is in order.'

'Huh, I suppose you're right.' Rob looked meditative.

'Oh, thanks for turning your music down a bit recently, although it can still make my floor vibrate sometimes,' said Martin as he got up to leave. 'I'm telling you, if it gets too loud again, I'm going to come in and smash whatever's the source of that unholy row!'

Martin had meant this as a joke, but he wasn't prepared for the look on Rob's face. It was the same fear and vulnerability that he had seen in Jeremy's face - and the same hint of threat.

CHAPTER TWENTY FOUR

"WORRY - VB. 1.A. TRANS. TO KILL (A PERSON OR ANIMAL) BY COMPRESSING THE THROAT; TO STRANGLE."

[COMPACT OXFORD ENGLISH DICTIONARY, 1989]

"DO BOYS STILL READ MALORY? DO THEY LIE ON THEIR STOMACHS IN ORCHARDS WITH THAT BOOK PROPPED UP BEFORE THEM IN THE GRASS? DO THEY FORGET TO GO HOME FOR FOOD AND LIE ON TILL THE HARVEST BUGS SET ABOUT THEM AND THE DUSK FALLS, READING THAT WILD GALLANTRY?"

[H V MORTON, *In Search of England*, 1927]

It was two weeks since Eve had last seen Martin. In terms of an Oxford University term of only eight weeks, that was a lifetime. It would be wrong to say she had forgotten him. Whatever she was doing, whatever she was supposed to be thinking - whether she was in chapel or in a lecture, with friends or alone in her room - her mind kept being dragged back to Martin like a dog on a leash. What was she supposed to think about him? Should she get in touch with him? Should she warn him he was a suspect, or would that destroy the whole point? Each time she decided not to be silly and to see him as if nothing had happened, she found herself not returning his phone calls, or answering his messages, and one afternoon even pretending she wasn't in when he knocked on her door and called out her name.

On the surface, Eve's life was as it should have been. She was getting to know people better at Frid's and was getting to know other people on her course at the University. She seemed to be impressing her tutors, who had no idea at what time of night or early hours of the morning she had been forced to work because she had spent the day seeking distraction and the nights too disturbed by dreams to go back to sleep.

There had been a dream about Martin. At least she thought it was about him. She had been in a graveyard, probably the one at Iffley, or one like it. It was very old and there was a mist swirling in the air like a cliché from an old-fashioned movie. Then she saw a little boy. He had bright orange hair and looked mischievous and innocent at the same time. She knew from his face that he was old for his years, as if he had seen a lot of suffering. Eve automatically knew there was some danger around, there was something she needed to warn the little boy about, but she didn't even try to speak because she knew she couldn't.

The urge to get in touch with Martin in real life after that dream had been immense and had driven her all the same day, but that evening, at the reasonable time to call to catch him in, her nerve had failed her. She certainly couldn't tell him about the dream, he would think she was stupid. And she certainly couldn't tell him anything else, so what was there to say? Eve had the ludicrous vision of herself phoning him and as soon as he said 'Hello', her hanging up.

She had even managed not to see him at the rehearsals for *Princess Ida*. The first week, Eve had claimed a sore throat (sort-of true) as her excuse not to go, and the second week she had found out in advance that Martin wasn't even going to be there, so it was safe. Apparently he had gone home for a few days since it was his birthday, on St Crispin's Day, his namesake. His mother was throwing him a big party at Lakeland Massey.

His birthday! Eve felt awful that she hadn't known. Maybe his visit to her room had been to say he was going away - or maybe even to invite her to his party! Eve had a vision of herself drifting down a huge staircase in a floaty ball gown at his parents' country house. But how ridiculous! It would never be like that. It was a good thing she didn't have to bother saying no, she couldn't go.

At least that's what one half of her told the other half.

But when a few days after that, Eve received a gold-edged invitation from Martin, her curiosity was aroused. It was only to tea and crumpets in his rooms ('a *feast*') but the formal invitation did imply there would be other people there and so she could ease herself back into his society in a less pressured way. It was to be at 4pm on Friday of Third Week, November the First.

Of course, Eve was wrong. As she stuck her head around Martin's door and said shyly: 'Oh, am I the first?' Martin replied: 'The first what?'

'The first guest.'

'You're the only guest, as far as I know, unless I have Multiple Personality Disorder and one of my many other selves invited a few more I don't know anything about. Come in and sit down!' Martin beamed. 'I've even cleared a chair for you. Look at this - a real gen-u-wine toasting fork. The only way to do crumpets!'

Martin was obviously pleased with himself as he sat cross-legged in front of the elderly gas fire, a pile of Sainsbury's crumpets lying in their open packet next to him.

'I hope they don't feel any pain. I wonder how it felt for Cranmer and his lot on Broad Street when they were being burnt? Oh, what's this, a card?'

'Um, your birthday,' murmured Eve. 'I'm sorry, I didn't know.'

'How could you? You're never in.'

Martin put the envelope down next to him unopened.

'Is it funny or a rude one? Oh no, you wouldn't send one like that. I bet it's very tasteful and quaint.'

It was. Eve didn't trust herself with humour and Martin at the moment.

'There you are,' he said triumphantly, handing her a crumpet, 'the first one's for you. There's butter and honey, jam, marmalade, Marmite, everything - paté - it's all on the table. Help yourself.'

'Thank you. It looks great.'

'I'm so glad you came to my Arthurfest,' said Martin cryptically as he started to toast a crumpet for himself.

'Your what?'

'Arthurfest! You know, festival of King Arthur. I've been going mad reading Malory for the past two weeks - all seven hundred bloody pages! Well, almost read - I suppose I skim-read a lot of it. Serves me right for not doing it properly last year when it was on my syllabus. Anyway, I'm very proud of my copy of *Morte Darthur* etc, etc - it was only 30p second hand from a bookshop in Witney. Are you ready for a bit of Olde English?'

'I don't know,' Eve replied. 'Is it difficult? I did some Chaucer at school.'

'Oh well, you're an old hand then. I must stop being patronising about the American educational system. Especially as I went to a lowly comprehensive school myself.'

'You didn't!' exclaimed Eve, in spite of herself. 'You went to Dragonshead with Charlie – a smart private school!'

'Only for a while. It was my finishing school, you might say. Before then, Mum and Dad had been playing tug-of-war with my sister and I, and we'd been sent all over the place, including the good old local Comp for a while. Short for Compost Heap, of course.'

Eve's mind was boggling. She couldn't imagine Martin with ordinary mortals at...well...how?....what?...

'How did you cope?' she finally burst out.

'Oh, by being utterly miserable and suicidal. Dad had me sent to a prep school when he was in the ascendant, and my mother reluctantly agreed (she's supposed to be a Socialist - or was then). Then in my early teens - when my hair was at its reddest and my skin its most scrofulous - my mother was in the ascendant and had me and Xanthe packed off down the road to Lakeland Massey Comp. The fact that our names were the same as the school didn't help. So, after three years of torment, when I managed to fail every exam known to man, woman and child, and after a... well, a rather unfortunate episode with a friend, my father came into his own again and insisted we were sent private. Thus Dragonshead, and friendship with Charlie, Guy, etc.'

'Wow!' Eve was silent for a while, but then couldn't help herself. 'What... "unfortunate episode with a friend", if you don't mind me asking?'

'Oh...' Martin fiddled with the toasting fork and burnt his fingers. 'Ow! You don't want to know. It was all very silly. I didn't know what I was doing. Another crumpet? I think this one's ready.'

So, Martin was determined to remain a man of mystery. Eve tried not to let her imagination run riot in the next few minutes. Could it have been something that would link in with the murder? What had he done with this 'friend' he referred to?

'So. Malory,' announced Martin, 'or Sir Thomas Malleoré, as it is in the original. I do think we should be as Authentic as possible, don't you, in view of the circumstances?'

'Oh yes,' said Eve shivering involuntarily. Even the word 'authentic' was tainted for her now.

'I bet you don't know what a character Malory was. He wasn't some effete writer at court, you know. Oh, his dates, by the way, are circa 1410 to 1471, so well within our gothic period.'

'What gothic period?'

'Oh, this building is gothic, the Chichele armour is gothic, the handwriting on the letter to Feral was in gothic script. Haven't you caught on to the theme yet?'

'Doesn't look like it,' mumbled Eve.

Martin sighed as if dealing with a recalcitrant pupil.

'As I was saying, Malory was a bit of a wild one. He came from a well-off family, was a Member of Parliament for a while, but of course we're talking the Wars of the Roses at this point, and so he had to trot up and down the country in various armies constantly. He seems to have taken the rape and pillage bit rather seriously - he ambushed and tried to murder the Duke of Buckingham, he stole money and treasure from an abbot, he "forced" the wife of one Hugh Smyth, he did cattle-raids, muggings, murder and escaped from prison twice!'

'Yuk!'

'Oh, but he was a great chap! When you read him, you'll forgive him anything. He really knows what he's talking about when it comes to the blood and guts side of fighting, and it sounds as if he knew quite a lot about romance too.'

'Huh!'

'You're obviously not convinced yet. I'll have to convince you. Of course, Malory isn't the earliest source for the Arthur stories. There's a mention by Aneurin in the "Gododdin" in the sixth century, but scholars say the line may be a later addition.'

'Huh! Sounds like Biblical Criticism.'

'It probably is. Most of these scholars should be fiction writers themselves. Then there's a monk called Nennius in the ninth century, who says that Arthur was just a soldier who came to the aid of local rulers when the British were trying to kick out the Anglo-Saxon invaders after the Romans had bailed out - blah, blah. Then we leap to the twelfth century and Geoffrey of Monmouth. Now he actually goes to town on the story of Arthur, saying he was one of the early kings of Britain in his *Historia Regum Brittaniae*. He tells us that Arthur was the son of Uther who gained a huge empire for himself by conquering both the barbarian invaders and the Romans.'

'The Romans as well? Wow,' said Eve inadequately.

'Of course, meanwhile all was not well on the home front. While the cat's away, and all that. Mordred, his nasty nephew, or whatever he was, had grabbed Guinevere and was calling himself king. This leads up to the final battle and Arthur's fatal wound. Anyway, then the story of Arthur gets wings and travels to the continent where the French take to it like... well, nothing before or since, probably, and they embroider and embellish it until we come to our man Malleoré. He gets hold of the French versions of the story and translates them into English, or "reduces" them as he calls it. In other words, he does a lot of heavy editing and actually makes them readable.'

'How come the French liked a story about one of the British kings so much? I thought you two countries didn't like each other.'

'Ah, well, this is the period of courtly romance, which just happens to have been invented in France.'

'Oh, I remember this. The chivalric code. All those knights going around falling in love with married women.'

'You've got it. I suppose everyone was married off very young and divorce was non-existent and so the only way you could get your kicks was by longing after married women. I suppose a sort of idealised adultery was a way of channelling the young men's passions until they settled down. And if it meant they were inspired to kill a few more hundred of the enemy in order to impress some broad, all the better.'

'Tut! You're sounding very cynical about one of the greatest romances of all time!'

'What - Launcelot and Guinevere? I'm telling you, Malory has to walk a fine line sometimes when he's trying to present Launcelot as the hero of the hour when he's actually screwing his master's wife on the side and betraying his king. The story of Tristan and Iseult is in here as well - very similar. Tristan does the dirty on King Mark of Cornwall by seducing his intended. And this was supposed to be a Christian era!'

Eve chose to ignore the jibe and asked instead for a cup of tea.

'So Launcelot du Lac is French, of course,' she said. 'Perhaps that's why he's so rampant.'

'Oh, but he isn't - rampant, I mean. Or only with Guinevere. No, he's faithful to his queen, if not his king.'

'How did Guinevere get to marry Arthur in the first place?'

'He rescued her father's kingdom for him. There's an awful lot of that early on in Arthur's reign. Local rulers won't accept the boy King Arthur, even after he's so spectacularly pulled the sword out from the stone and fulfilled the ancient prophecy. These local chieftains keep rebelling until Arthur defeats them. That's essentially the early part of Malory's book. Guinevere's father is so grateful at being rescued that he gives his daughter to Arthur and the Round Table as a wedding gift.'

'Oh, the Round Table! Isn't that supposed to be in Winchester?'

'Have you seen it? No? Well, it's worth a trip. We'll have to go. Of course, it's not the real one, but it's enormous and hung up on a wall in the old palace there. It is genuinely medieval at any rate. Henry the Seventh made a big thing of it. His right to the throne was so tenuous that he wanted to claim his lineage all the way back to Arthur.'

'Oh, he called his first son Arthur, didn't he,' Eve exclaimed. 'The one who died after marrying Catherine of Aragon. Then Henry the Eighth married her.'

'Yep. Then the divorce and the rather convenient Reformation.'

'Wow, I'd never thought of them being at all concerned with Arthur. That fits into the time scale too, doesn't it. Wasn't King Henry Hall named after Henry the Seventh?'

'Mmm. It was being built when Malory was gallivanting round the country with Edward the Fourth in the Wars of the Roses. Then it's Henry Tudor beating Richard the Third at Bosworth in 1485 and grabbing the throne.'

'So claiming he was descended from the great King Arthur would be pretty useful. What an awful time to live! It must have been terrifying...'

But before Eve could finish her sentence, Martin's door was thrown open and four men in black balaclavas burst in waving guns and yelling:

'Alright, where are they?!'

CHAPTER TWENTY FIVE

"And I thought... that most of us have belonged to that Round Table – so many of us, in fact, that if Arthur came back to give us youth again and called us out to joyous adventures he would have an army great enough to ride from Camelot to the conquest of the earth."

[H V Morton, *In Search of England*, 1927]

Eve cried out as two of the men held Martin down in his seat and a gun to his head, while one who appeared to be female began turning over his room.

'They're on the chest of drawers, for God's sake,' said Martin impatiently. 'In that tin. There's no need to wreck the place.'

The woman in black lifted up the tin and opened it. She cried 'Aha!' in triumph and the three terrorists ran out of the room with the tin. Martin pursued them to the door.

'And bring the bloody tin back!' he yelled after them. 'Bastards! Children!' He turned back into the room and looked at the terrified Eve.

'Are you alright?' she gasped. 'What's going on?'

'Oh it's just the Biscuit Brigade,' Martin sighed, sitting down again. 'They're a self-appointed terrorist group here. If you're found guilty of serving up bad biscuits, they come and kidnap them and hold them to ransom. You have to promise to provide decent biscuits in future, or the same thing will happen again. I think in my case it was some soggy Bourbons last week that were the last straw.'

'Wow!'

'Sorry if they scared you. It's OK if you know what's going on, I suppose. It was quite a good joke to start off with, but it's going to get pretty lame very soon. I suppose I'll have to buy something elaborate and foreign with chocolate on. Although some plain British biccies are approved - there's a list of Cool and Uncool cookies.'

'How fascist!'

'Yes, I suppose it is. Anyway, where were we?' Martin sighed. 'Oh, I thought we should start with what we know, I mean, what we know for sure. We know that Feral thought she was Morgan le Fay. So I've marked in Malory every place where she's mentioned to see if it gives us any clues. The next thing is Launcelot. Now we're not so sure about him...'

'Oh, you're right! We've just been assuming that that's what the 'L' on the letter stands for, but we don't know for sure. Oh dear.' Eve looked crestfallen. 'This could get very complicated.'

'You're telling me. Here's a sample of a few of the other possible "L"s in the legends - Ladis, Ladon, Lahelin, Lailoken, Lambor, Lamorak, Launcelot's grandfather who was also called Launcelot...'

'Oh no...'

'... Lanceor, Laris, Lascoyt, Lavaine, Leodegrance, Levander...'

'Oh, please,' exclaimed Eve, 'I think I've had enough! Surely our Launcelot is the best bet - isn't he?'

'I've marked the relevant bits about Launcelot in here anyway. I think he is our best shot. We know the murderer was wearing armour, we know he used a name that begins with "L", he's linked with a woman being found dead in a boat, he writes a love letter to his lady - all of those things point to Launcelot,' Martin summarised, but there was doubt in his voice.

'I suppose so. But the woman in the boat was Elaine, wasn't she? The Lady of Shalott? How is Launcelot linked to Morgan?'

'Ah! Patience, my child. All will be revealed.'

Martin lifted up a dark navy book that had 'Malory: WORKS' in gold on the spine and the crest of Oxford University stamped into its cover. There were an alarming number of little bits of paper stuck into it as bookmarks.

'You're not going to read the whole thing out loud!' exclaimed Eve.

'Of course not,' said Martin resentfully. 'I've already been through all seven hundred pages. I've told you, I'm just going to read out the relevant bits.'

'Thank heaven for small mercies. It doesn't look like seven hundred pages.'

'It's on very thin paper - look. Like a Bible. Not very nice really because you can see the print from the other side. Anyway...'

Martin turned to one of the many marked places in the text. Eve noticed the little bit of torn paper had an 'M' on it.

'If we're starting with what we know for sure, that means beginning with Morgan herself. I've checked with the Launcelot and Guinevere Society and Malory is the definitive text they use for their re-enactments.'

'So... if Feral and the person we know as "L" had intended to do a re-enactment that morning, it would be one of these scenes they would be using.'

'Exactly. Of course, we're not sure Morgan was herself that morning. I mean, she could have been playing another character...'

'Oh, don't confuse things, just get on with it!'

'Ja, mein Kapitän! OK, first reference I've noted on page thirty. Arthur has sent for his mother, Queen Igrayne, in order to sort out the mystery of his birth. She comes and brings her daughter with her, Morgan le Fay, *"that was a fayre lady as ony might be".*'

'Oh,' said Eve, sounding surprised and disappointed. 'So Morgan was beautiful. I wasn't expecting that. I'd been assuming, 'cos she was a witch, that she'd be ugly. But I suppose that's a stereotype. I suppose that also explains why people in this Society don't mind being a witch character. She wasn't using supernatural power over men to make up for being ugly.'

'No. In fact there's plenty of very good-looking women who cast spells over men in Malory in order to get their own way. If a man won't sleep with them - bingo! Women are always doing that to Launcelot, as you'll see in a bit.'

'That sheds an interesting light on our case. Remember what Angela said about Feral and Rory. Feral fancied Rory like mad - said it was only because of one of her love potions that Angela had got together with him.'

'But that's magic after the event,' protested Martin. 'If Feral fancied Rory, why wouldn't Feral use a potion to get him to love *her*? She's hardly likely to use her magic to get the man she loves off with her best friend!'

'True,' agreed Eve. 'But we do only have Angela and Rory's word for all this. Obviously Feral can't speak for herself.'

'Thank God for that. The last thing we need is a witch coming back from the grave to point an accusing finger...'

'Oh, don't!' Eve shivered. 'Get on with your quotes.'

'OK. Now, I hope you noticed the important fact we have so far - Morgan is Arthur's half-sister. They have the same mother, Igrayne.'

'Is that important?'

'Perhaps not for us. But it was for them. Morgan felt rejected by Arthur and continually tried to destroy him - for example she sets up a battle between him and another knight and then gives Arthur a counterfeit Excalibur to fight with. She has a court of other "false damsels" who do her dirty work for her. Someone called Accalon of Gaul says here,' (Martin turned to the next marker) '"*They were fendis and no women*" - fiends, in other words, whom he accuses of casting enchantments upon men. Morgan also has a dwarf who does her bidding and carries messages for her. Bit of a giveaway, really - only the baddies in these stories have companion dwarves.'

'So what happens to Arthur?'

'Oh, I think he's injured by this Accalon chappie, but then Accalon realises who he is and relents. Arthur swears revenge on Morgan for her "*false craftis*" and "*false lustes*" and all Christendom shall speak of it. He's particularly bitter because he trusted her more than any one else in his family, even his wife.'

'Well, he was right there,' added Eve. 'He couldn't exactly trust his wife.'

'I think he could at this point. It's fairly early on in the story - only page eighty eight. We don't hear much more about Morgan for a while. The next point I've marked is page three hundred and sixty seven. Arthur has tried to buy off Morgan by giving her a castle on the outskirts of Camelot - big mistake. It means she's got a stronghold inside his realm from which to make all kinds of trouble for him. It says here: *"And as ever she myght she made warre on kynge Arthure, and all daungerous knyghtes she wytholdyth wyth her for to dystroy all thos knyghtes that kynge Arthur lovyth"*. So any knight from Arthur's court who goes past her castle has to joust to the death with the thugs and mercenaries she's collected around her.'

'But that doesn't necessarily link her to Launcelot.'

'Oh, give her time,' Martin grinned. 'She'll get round to him. Who does Arthur love and trust most of all his knights? Launcelot. And who's the most fanciable man on earth, that has women panting to rip off his *fauld* and *tassets*?'

'His *what?!*'

'The relevant bits of armour. The *mail fauld* is the codpiece.'

'Oh.'

'Anyway, it's Launcelot, of course. He even has stunningly gorgeous women, who are normally beating men off with a stave, resorting to magic to...'

'Get into his *mail fauld*. Yes, you've said that already.'

'Sex and the supernatural!' Martin exclaimed, doing an impersonation of a nuclear explosion. 'Even when Morgan seems to be doing a man some good, she's really got devious motives. Ah, here we are. There's this chap sir Alysaundir - Alexander - he's wounded - with sixteen great wounds - and Morgan offers to heal him in her castle.'

'Oops.'

'Quite. First of all she puts ointment on his wounds that gives him even more pain so he's in agony all night, then when he complains in the morning, she puts more ointment on that takes away the pain.'

'So she tortures a wounded man! What a bitch!' cried Eve. 'Talk about hitting a man when he's down.'

'It reminds me of a kid I used to know at school - I mean, when I was really young - about five or six. He would put his cat on a lead and swing it round and round a room so that it's feet actually left the ground and it would be bashing into things...'

'Oh, the poor thing!'

'...and we'd be there killing ourselves laughing...'

'Brute!'

'But then he would cuddle and comfort it. The poor thing was terrified, of course - it's ears flattened back, its eyes wide, clinging to this kid's sweater. He'd stroke it and calm it down, then start all over again, swinging it round! The cat never seemed to learn. It would still cling to him for comfort each time...'

'That's terrible!'

'Yes, but little kids are like that.'

'I wasn't!' protested Eve.

'Well, you were probably a saint. But most of the boys I knew... well, I won't go into detail. But aren't you in Amnesty International? You must have read about how many people are still being tortured in the world. And that's adults. And a lot of them are supposed to enjoy it. Wasn't there some experiment done in the sixties about how easy it is to get just some person off the street to administer electric shocks to someone they don't know? We're all potential torturers.'

'Speak for yourself. No, I have heard of that research - I think it was someone called Milgram who did it years ago. And it's just been done as an experiment with people in a game show setting - some celebrity tells people to cause some stranger pain and about eighty per cent of those taking part torture someone with no questions asked, even when the victim is screaming for them to stop. But isn't this interesting in regard to Feral. Her chosen name is a cat's name for a start - a wild cat.'

'A cat that's wild, out of anyone's control, independent, doing it's own thing,' said Martin meditatively. 'I suppose that's how she liked to see herself, even back in schooldays.'

'Wasn't she supposed to have been tortured there?' asked Eve.

'Well, tormented psychologically - persecuted. I suppose you could call it verbal abuse. We don't know if she was physically abused too, or bullied.'

'I wouldn't mind a bet on it. Anyway, back to Sir Alysaundir. Morgan made him promise to stay in her castle for a year in return for making him well. He thinks this is a good bargain, but of course, as soon as he is well, he wants to get away. A woman who is Morgan's cousin comes along and tells him: "*quene Morgan kepyth you here for none other entente but for to do hir plesure whan hit lykyth hir*". To which he understandably replies: "*A, Jesu defende me frome suche plesure!*" I'm sure I don't need to explain what the pleasure was.'

'Wow,' sighed Eve. 'Morgan's a real control freak, isn't she? She wants this man completely in her power and she'll use her magic to keep him there. She'll pretend to do him good when she's really doing him harm,' Eve continued slowly, putting two and two together. 'She's utterly manipulative. She doesn't seem to be able to love a man, she only knows how to control one for her own ends. She probably can't allow herself to be vulnerable because of past hurt and a deep sense of rejection. So gaining power over men and controlling them is her only option.'

Martin broke out in applause.

'Well, that's Feral on the couch!' he said. 'I think that's a pretty fair summary of what we know so far.'

'No wonder she chose Morgan as her "persona". It fits everything we know about Fern Harrison's background.'

'I wonder if she was allowed to be such a senior character in the L and G Soc?' Martin wondered. 'Surely as a Fresher last year, she should have been a more minor character.'

'Sounds as though she wouldn't let something like that stop her. Perhaps it gave the L and G Soc more of a reason to expel her. She'd disobeyed their protocol.'

'Hmmm. Could be,' mused Martin. 'Although it sounds as if she'd freaked them out so much in general that they wouldn't need an excuse. But getting back to Morgan herself. Next she's torturing a woman by having her half in fire and half in ice until she's rescued by a knight - charming. But the last reference to Morgan in Malory is when King Arthur has been gravely wounded in his last battle with Mordred. There's the famous scene of Arthur being taken away on a ship to Avalon to be healed of his wound.'

'So Arthur never actually dies?' interrupted Eve. 'Isn't there a myth about him coming back one day when England is in its hour of greatest need?'

'That's right. Malory emphasises that in all the authoritative manuscripts he's consulted for his story, none of them give any hard evidence of Arthur actually dying. This is it - page seven hundred and seventeen:

> *"Yet som men say in many partys of Inglonde that kynge Arthure ys nat dede, but had by the wyll of oure Lorde Jesu into another place; and men say that he shall com agayne, and he shall wynne the Holy Crosse. Yet I woll nat say that hit shall be so, but rather I wolde sey: here in thys worlde he chaunged hys lyff. And many men say that there ys wrytten upon the tumbe thys:*
>
> HIC IACET ARTHURUS, REX QUONDAM REXQUE FUTURUS."'

Eve interrupted excitedly:

'So that's "Here lies Arthur, the once and future king." Is the tomb the one at Glastonbury?'

'Yes, or "Glassyngbyry" as it's written here,' replied Martin. 'But the important thing for us is that Morgan is one of the women in the ship accompanying Arthur to Avalon.'

'No!' exclaimed Eve. 'I think if I was dying of a mortal wound, she's the last person I'd want on board.'

'Ah, but she is sort of supernatural, isn't she. She's a suitable person to take someone on to another world...'

'Oh, like a psychopomp,' said Eve.

'A whattie?'

'A psychopomp,' said Eve, as if it was obvious.

'I thought you said 'cycle pump'.'

'No,' said Eve scornfully. 'You obviously haven't read much psychology. A psychopomp is an archetype - a link between the conscious and subconscious mind. It's a figure that crops up in mythology a lot, and literature. Like Virgil who leads Dante through hell and purgatory. It can be a guide to the underworld.

It's a figure who can link this world and the next, both human and supernatural at the same time...'

'OK, OK, so Morgan is one of these cycle pumps. She's one of the three queens who escort Arthur to the next world. I only mentioned it because it's the only connection between Morgan and a boat.' Martin sounded resentful. Was he annoyed at Eve knowing something he didn't?

'Hardly likely to be the re-enactment in question though, is it?' said Eve, trying not to sound superior. 'It's Arthur who's the body in the boat, not Morgan.'

'Alright,' said Martin, still sounding bad-tempered. 'I agree it's probably not the re-enactment we're looking for. There are much more promising ones, as I shall reveal - if you give me the chance.'

'I'm not stopping you!'

'Good. I vote we move on to Launcelot.'

'Fine by me.'

'Good. So, Launcelot and Guinevere - one of the great love stories of all time - a bit like us really...'

'Huh!'

'Oh, but a man and a woman studying this story together can be dangerous. You must have heard of Paolo and Francesca - another of the great "forbidden love" stories. Paolo was supposed to be escorting Francesca to marry someone else, but then they started reading the story of Launcelot and Guinevere together and...' Martin slid onto the arm of the chair where Eve was sitting and put his arm around her and breathed into her ear, 'it says, "then they read no more"...'

Before Eve could respond, there was a banging at the door and Albert Singh walked in. Eve shot out of her seat and greeted him with such blushing enthusiasm that Al was convinced she had a crush on him for the rest of that term.

CHAPTER TWENTY SIX

"For when was Launcelot wanderingly lewd?"

[Tennyson, *Idylls of the King*, 1859]

I'm glad I've found you two together,' said Albert in his clipped voice. 'I wanted to tell you that we need to book a fitting for you - for your costumes for *Ida*. We're trying to get hold of some armour that will look authentic. Pity we can't borrow the Chichele pieces, but that might be a bit, well, unfortunate in the current climate.'

Martin and Eve looked at each other.

'It hadn't occurred to me that... that we'd be wearing armour,' said Eve hesitantly.

'Only for the end of Act Two and the beginning of the next. It's when Ida is defending her university from the hideous male onslaught. They wore armour in the video production. Haven't you seen the DVD yet? Martin, you said you were going to show it to her!'

'Sorry,' said Martin, 'but she's been rather hard to get hold of recently. I wanted to show her a film at the Ultimate Picture Palace too but she's been very elusive.'

'What film?' said Eve, in spite of herself.

'It was called *Alexander Nevsky* - a 1930s Russian one, anti-Nazi propaganda. But it's about a Russian prince who's like their version of King Arthur and there are stunning scenes of thousands of men in armour - admittedly the wrong period for us. It was more like Crusaders with metal buckets on their heads.'

Eve's heart sank. So when Martin had been hammering on her door and ringing her, it wasn't to invite her to a posh birthday party but rotten Russian propaganda.

'I think I can live without seeing any more armour, thank you,' she said.

'Well, don't leave it too long,' said Albert, thinking she was talking to him. 'We don't want all the best armour hired out so we're landed with the dregs.'

'Oh, don't worry about it,' said Martin, 'we'll get kitted out.'

'Perhaps I'd better bring some possible ones next week to rehearsal,' said Albert dubiously.

'Albert, don't you trust us?' exclaimed Martin.

'Of course not. Anyway, I'll see you then.'

'Oh, Albert, please stay for a crumpet!' said Eve.

'Now there's an offer you don't get everyday,' smiled Martin.

'Er, no, thank you, Eve, it's nearly supper,' said Albert, backing away towards the door. 'I'll see you, Martin. Bye, Eve.'

'Bye.'

There was a short silence after Albert had closed the door behind him.

'Armour,' said Martin. 'I hadn't thought of that. Oh well, it will probably be plastic and very fake. Don't get anxious about it.'

Eve sighed and sat down on the floor.

'A cup of strong coffee wouldn't go amiss at this point,' she said.

'Absolutely,' said Martin, trotting over to his kettle and switching it on. 'You could come in to supper with me, if you want. It's in another ten minutes. Come on, and I'll point out the rest of the suspects to you. If you're really lucky, I'll get you a seat next to Jeremy East, that well-known lady-killer - in the metaphorical sense, of course.'

Eve groaned and gave in. At least she wouldn't be on her own with Martin.

But the only 'suspects' as such at supper were Rory and Angela. Jeremy East was nowhere to be seen, much to Eve's relief. Martin threatened to take her to the *King's Arms* that evening to see Tony Greer but Eve refused outright. She had work to do. Yes, even on a Friday night. She was shown Robert Baker, seated two tables away. Did Eve think he was good-looking? Perhaps without his glasses - why? No reason. But why would he be friends with Jeremy East, a complete geek? Perhaps Robert had been a geek at an earlier age and grown out of it, Eve suggested. Possibly. Martin then suggested they should track down John Harborough, Fern's ex-boyfriend. Eve was adamant - there was no way she was spending her Friday evening doing that. Anyway, they hadn't finished going through Malory. What about all the stuff on Launcelot? Martin grinned then laughed out loud. Eve was suddenly furious to realise that Martin had got her to do what he wanted to do all along - for them to spend the evening ploughing through the rest of Malory.

'Now,' said Martin with great satisfaction as they were seated back in his room with the kettle on again, 'now for the Noble Tale of Sir Launcelot du Lake.'

'Shouldn't it be "du Lac"?' said Eve.

'Not in Malory. But his spelling's all over the place and he mixes English and French up quite a lot. This is before dictionaries, remember.'

'I know that!' snapped Eve.

But Martin was impervious to her bad mood.

'Launcelot is introduced as a super-hero straightaway. He's probably Malory's alter-ego, what Malory wanted to be:

> "*in all turnementes, justys* (that's jousts), *and dedys of armys, both for lyff and deth, he passed all other knyghtes, and at no tyme was he ovircom but yf hit were by treson other inchauntement.*"'

'So,' Martin continued, 'Launcelot's physical prowess knows no bounds. His only vulnerabilities are through betrayal and sorcery.'

'I suppose,' said Eve morosely, 'that any woman who wanted to get the better of him had to manipulate and trick him, or resort to witchcraft.'

'Exactly. And that's precisely what happens two pages later. Morgan...'

'Huh! Didn't take her long to turn up!'

'Less of the heckling, please. As I was saying - don't throw raw crumpets at me - Morgan and three other queens just happen to ride by while Launcelot is asleep under an apple tree.'

'Oh, so he does take some time off from saving the world.'

'Yes, even the mighty Launcelot needed his kip. And as soon as these babes see his face, they all swear they're going to have him - literally. So Morgan says, let's not fight, I'll cast a spell on him so he doesn't wake up for seven hours, we'll take him back to my place, and then he can choose which of us *"he woll have unto peramour"*.'

'They didn't mess about in those days. And this was before women's liberation.'

'Oh, the women are as rampant as the men in these stories.'

'Malory's wishful thinking,' said Eve.

'I wouldn't be so sure. I saw how you looked at Albert. Anyway, when Launcelot wakes up in a strange bedroom - not for the last time - the four queens greet him and say they know he's committed to Queen Guinevere, but he can forget about her right now, 'cos he's got to choose one of them or die!'

'Wow!' said Eve, forgetting her bad mood. 'So what does he do?'

'He says he'd rather die, which is a pretty brave thing to say to Morgan le Fay. He also says they're slandering Guinevere who's really true to her husband, which is a bit rich. Anyway, there's some serving damsel who helps him escape, as usual, if he'll joust on behalf of her father. This happens practically every time Launcelot's in a tight spot...'

'Launcelot uses his lance a lot!'

'Hmm. Anyway, about twenty pages later on, Launcelot has just killed some poor sap who dared to challenge him, and a damsel says to him:

> *"hit is noysed that ye love quene Gwenyvere, and that she hath ordeyned by enchauntemente that ye shall never love none other but hir..."'*

'Guinevere!' burst out Eve. 'By enchantment! Her as well!'

'I told you,' said Martin, 'they're all at it, even the kosher ones. Anyway, Launcelot has a great reply for her:

> *"Fayre damsell," seyde sir Launcelot, "I may nat warne peple to speke of me what hit pleasyth hem. But for to be a weddyd man, I thynke hit nat, for than I muste couche with hir and leve armys and turnamentis, batellys and adventures. And as for to sey to take my pleasaunce with peramours, that woll I refuse: in principall for drede of God"...'*

'He then says,' Martin continued, 'that if you sleep around you can be beaten by knights who aren't as good as you; you lose your edge, as it were. And if you take a paramour you become unhappy and make everyone around you unhappy.'

'Gee,' said Eve. 'He sounds like a born again James Bond.'

Martin laughed.

'You're absolutely right! So this poor tart he's talking to hasn't got a hope. She complains there are many, of high and low estate throughout the land, that *"make gret sorow"* because of Launcelot's celibacy.'

'Are you trying to say our murderer could be in this position?' said Eve. 'One minute it's looking as if Feral and "L" are probably having a wild affair, and now you're saying that Launcelot is strictly look-but-don't-touch. It's very confusing.'

'Just wait till you hear about the next fair damsel. Page one eight six. Launcelot the chick-magnet is in another encounter. As usual, she recognises that because of Guinevere, she hasn't got a hope. But she's a bit more resourceful. She says:

> *"I have loved the this seven yere, but there may no woman have thy love but quene Gwenyver; and sytthen*

> *I myght nat rejoyse the nother thy body on lyve, I had kepte no more joy in this worlde but to have thy body dede. Than woll I have bawmed hit and sered hit, and so to have kepte hit my lyve dayes; and dayly I sholde have clypped the and kyssed the, dispyte of quene Gwenyvere."'*

'What on earth does that mean?' said Eve impatiently.

'Aren't you following this?' said Martin, also impatiently. 'I'm reading it phonetically, you ought to have a clue.' He sighed and explained, 'She's called Hallewes the Sorceress and she's been in love with Launcelot for seven years. But 'cos she can't have him alive, she wants him dead - to have him dried and embalmed so she can embrace and kiss his body for the rest of her life.'

'Oh, yuk!' cried Eve. 'How revolting! That's... that's necrophilia!'

'I suppose so. Anyway, Launcelot says *"Jesu preserve me* (ha ha) *frome your subtyle crauftys"*, gets his horse and rides off. The sorceress meanwhile dies of sorrow within a fortnight.'

'Is this Morgan?' said Eve sharply. 'Oh no, you've already said it isn't. So what has this got to do with our case?'

'It's a sorceress threatening Launcelot. Do we know that Feral always played Morgan? What if she pretended to be other sorceresses sometimes?'

'Do we need any more complications?' said Eve, sounding tired.

'Probably not. But I think we can assume that there was a history of threats between Feral and "L", don't you? We know Feral liked to write nasty letters to people. I think we can safely assume that she'd been writing threatening letters to our 'L' for some time, perhaps most of last year, and even during the summer vac. What if she liked to be authentic? What if she liked to use threats from 'Morte Darthur'? I think if someone threatened to have me dried and embalmed so they could have power over me forever, I wouldn't be very pleased.'

'That's a huge assumption,' Eve frowned. 'That would mean Feral was actually threatening to kill someone - "L".'

Martin returned her gaze.

'What better motive for killing someone - to kill them before they kill you?' he said slowly.

'That is a *huge* assumption, Martin. I can't go along with it.'

'OK, OK. Let the evidence mount up.'

Martin turned to the next marker in Malory, marked 'L'.

> *'But, as the Freynshe booke seyde, quene Morgan loved sir Launcelot beste, and ever she desired hym, and he wolde never love her nor do nothynge at her rekeyste, and therefore she hylde many knyghtes togydir to have takyn hym by strengthe. And bycause she demed that sir Launcelot loved quene Gwenyver paramour and she hym agayne, therefore dame Morgan ordayned that shylde to put sir Launcelot to a rebuke, to that entente, that kynge Arthure myght undirstonde the love betwene them.'*

'Did you follow that?' Martin asked with an edge of sarcasm.

'Yes. Sounds like our Rory, Angela and Feral threesome. Morgan loves Launcelot, can't have him 'cos he loves Guinevere, so Morgan swears revenge on Launcelot, arranging it so Arthur can see what a louse Launcelot really is. Except we don't have an equivalent of Arthur in our case. It's just Feral's unrequited love for Rory and jealousy of Angela.'

'Well, Morgan certainly gets her wish - that Arthur will find out about the affair between Launcelot and Guinevere. And of course, that's what drives the whole story and brings about the debacle at the end. But one of the early signs of the impending doom is when Launcelot gets caught up with Elaine, daughter of King Pelles.'

'Is this the Lady of Shalott?'

'No, that's another Elaine - Elaine the White, I think. There's a prophecy that if this Elaine sleeps with Launcelot, he will beget Sir Galahad upon her, as Malory puts it...'

'Very graphic!'

'But it's dame Brusen the witch that's responsible. She gives Launcelot a doctored cup of wine so that he'll think Elaine is really Guinevere. So he stumbles into bed, thinks it's his one true love and - whahay! Of course when he finds out in the morning, he's none too pleased and is about to kill her with his sword when she begs for mercy. He sees how *"lusty and yonge"* she is, as she just happens to be kneeling before him naked, and he understandably forgives her. He then says he'll kill Brusen instead for her *"wycchecrauftys"*, for deceiving him. Elaine says don't blame Brusen - they were only trying to fulfil the old prophecy, and anyway, Elaine has lost more than he has, 'cos she'll never get her maidenhood back again.'

'What a mess!' exclaimed Eve. 'Huh, it must have been very handy in those days for a man to be able to claim that every time he slept with a woman it was because she'd enchanted him!'

'You women don't realise your power over men,' said Martin, teasing her, knowing how much she'd hate him saying it. 'Anyway, the main point is that Launcelot is threatening to kill a witch, even if it is Brusen rather than Morgan. It's closer to our scenario than anything else so far.'

'There's also him threatening to kill Elaine who tricked him into sleeping with her,' added Eve. 'Hmmm. Mistaken identity. I've been wondering if that's a factor in our murder.'

'You mean,' said Martin slowly, 'what if Feral thought the person in the armour who met her on that morning was somebody else?'

'No, I don't mean that,' Eve frowned. 'What do I mean? Perhaps I don't mean mistaken identity in the traditional sense. What I'm trying to get at is more like *switched* identities, I suppose. What if Feral thought she was playing one character in a re-enactment - she obviously thought it was one where she'd be safe or she wouldn't have turned up - but the person she's meeting chooses to treat her as another character instead, one he can kill. What do you think of that?'

'Yes, I can see that,' said Martin, also frowning. 'But it makes things a hell of a lot more complicated. It certainly makes one feel a lot more sorry for Feral. She turns up at the set time in all innocence - if one can apply the word innocent to her - thinking she's meeting a lover, and instead he switches the story on her, pretends it's a different re-enactment to the one she's expecting, and she's killed.'

'*She thinks she's meeting a lover,*' Eve repeated. 'That's got to be the key. So if it's a lover of Launcelot, that leaves us with - who? Elaine or Guinevere.'

Martin was silent for a while, flicking through Malory to his various bookmarks.

'Well, Elaine isn't killed,' he said. 'She has Launcelot's child - Sir Galahad. Of course, when Arthur's court hears that Launcelot has been naughty there's uproar. Guinevere goes off in a huff, but when Launcelot explains that it was all a mistake because of an enchantment - she looked just like you, darling - Guinevere forgives him.'

'Puh!'

'Then Elaine turns up at court...'

'Really? Oh dear.'

'Launcelot is too ashamed to speak to her...'

'I'm not surprised!'

'So she's heartbroken. But Brusen the witch is on hand again. Guinevere tells Launcelot that he'd jolly well better go into her that night or else. But Brusen instead leads Launcelot to Elaine's room. He has such a good time and talks so loudly in his sleep about how much he loves Guinevere that Guinevere hears him through the wall and there's hell to pay. She calls him a false traitor, he faints and then leaps out of the window in his night shirt and is on the run for two years, stark staring mad.'

'Launcelot goes mad?' frowned Eve. 'I didn't know that.'

'*"Clene oute of hys mynde"* is how Malory describes him.'

'Hmmm. Our murderer was probably clean out of his mind as well.'

'Yes,' said Martin, 'but not for the same reason surely. Oh, I don't know though. The love of his life has found him sleeping with someone else. The shame of that knowledge and her rejection of him drives him crackers. Hmmmm. I'm not convinced for our chappie. It's rather sweet in Malory, actually. When people meet Launcelot who is obviously unbalanced at this point, they assume he has gone mad because of some great sorrow of his heart. Let's see, where is it? Ah yes, *"...doute ye nat he hath bene a man of grete worshyp, and for som hartely sorow that he hath takyn he ys fallyn madde"*. It's a much nicer way of looking at madness than in our society.'

'Hey, you're right,' said Eve. 'That is very charitable. Yes, I'm sure if you knew the story of all the people we write off as mad, you probably would find some great sorrow at the root of it.'

Martin was silent for a while and then said:

'Is that what we're looking for with our "L"? Is it someone who has gone mad from some great sorrow of the heart?'

Eve and Martin remained silent for a while, their imaginations caught up with this new theme. What could the great sorrow have been to drive a man to madness - and then to murder?

CHAPTER TWENTY SEVEN

"'Launcelot's very hard to get right. But when I've tingled it up with brighter points of light, and buzzed about it and given it atmosphere I'll get it right at last. Hard to get colour into it because of the night - or the knight.' (Laughing)."

[Edward Burne-Jones in conversation with Thomas Rooke, 1896]

'I think I'd better go now,' said Eve slowly, 'and get some work done. Wow, yes, is that the time? Thanks for the meal and, uh, crumpets.'

'But you can't go yet,' Martin protested. 'Launcelot's still mad. You've got to see him cured. You'll like it - he gets religion. The only thing that can cure him is the Sankgreal - that's the Holy Grail, to you - and he has visions, repents of all his misdeeds... Of course then he gets back with Guinevere again - hotter than before, in Malory's words. Then there's the episode of the fair maid of Astolat - the Lady of Shalott, who dies of unrequited love for Launcelot. She's found in a boat on the Thames, not unlike a certain other person...'

'I really must go,' said Eve getting up and reaching for her coat.

'Then Launcelot,' Martin continued unabated, 'gets shot in the butt by a huntress! You really can't miss this.'

'Oh yes I can. I'm sure you know enough about it for both of us.'

'Oh.' Martin half-closed Malory in sudden disappointment. 'I suppose it is a lot in one go.' Then, 'I was going to read you the bit we saw in *Camelot*, where Launcelot comes to Guinevere at night when Arthur's away - you remember, when he kills lots of soldiers in his escape and Guinevere is condemned to the stake! But of course she's rescued at the last moment and Launcelot carries her off to his castle.'

'Oh. He has his own castle?' said Eve in spite of herself, her coat half on.

'Yip. It's called "Joyous Garde". That is until Arthur returns and nicks Guinevere back again - then Launcelot renames his castle "Dolorous Garde" and never lives in it again.'

'Huh, they certainly liked to do things by extremes. Anyway...'

'They were extreme times!' Martin stood up to theoretically help Eve on with her coat, but still had the navy book in his hand and continued talking. 'It's terribly sad that they don't end up together, but it would hardly be one of the world's great love stories if they did. After the final battle between Arthur and Mordred, when Mordred's killed and Arthur's fatally wounded, Guinevere becomes a nun and Launcelot a monk. He tries to see her again but arrives half an hour after her death - tragic, wonderful! It's all in this last section: *"The Dolorous Death and Departing out of this world of Sir Launcelot and Queen Guinevere"* - sounds like one of my mother's murder mysteries: *The Dolorous Death and Departing.* She'd love all that alliteration...'

Eve interrupted: 'I wouldn't mind doing some departing of my own right now.'

'Oh, you modern girls have no soul! You'd leave Launcelot weeping in a wood and scrabbling in the earth on her grave, like a dog...!'

'Yuk! Sounds like Heathcliff. An obsessive.' Eve sighed. 'Martin, *I really do have to go!*'

Martin closed Malory with a snap and turned his back on her. 'OK.'

'It's very interesting an' all,' said Eve reassuringly, taking her chance to make for the door, 'but I think my head will explode if I have to take in any more.' She looked down at the unopened birthday card Martin had left on the floor. 'I hope you had a happy birthday. I guess I'll see you at the next *Ida*.'

'Great. Plastic armour,' said Martin morosely without looking at her.

'Bye then.'

Martin didn't reply but just raised one hand as Eve left the room, chewing his lips meditatively.

Eve was relieved to be outside again. She collected her bike from where she had left it locked in the courtyard next to Martin's quad and walked out of King Henry Hall. St Aldates was a one way street, going the other way. She decided to walk with her bike past Christ Church. She then remembered that virtually all the roads leading north up to St Fridewide's were either pedestrianised or One Way - the wrong way. So it was either walking with her bike, or taking a huge detour down the High and up Long Wall Street. She sighed and decided to walk.

Her thoughts were in a muddle. She had been given so much new information this evening, it was hard to sift through it all. Probably the thing that amazed her the most was the way she had been able to be normal with Martin again, even after DI Andrews had hinted at him being a suspect. It had been no problem at all to forget that and just relate to him as she had done before. But was that a good thing? It meant that, even if there had been clues as to his guilt, she could have missed them entirely. She frowned as it began to rain quite heavily. Had she missed something?

Eve was now walking past Christ Church. She automatically sighed and thought of Charlie. That bleep-bleep-bleep hadn't been in touch with her at all since that first awful morning at the beginning of term. Just her luck to have the man of her dreams associate her with a grisly murder and never want to see her again. Of course, Eve had never thought of Charlie as a murder suspect.

Eve found herself parking her bike and walking inexorably through the gates of Christ Church and towards the quad where

Charles Boscombe lived. With any luck Charlie wouldn't be in anyway. It was a Friday night. Charlie would be out, Eve reassured herself. She didn't have to see him.

Charlie was in. His light was on. Eve took a deep breath and began to mount the stairs up to his room.

But as she approached his landing, there were screams and cries for help. Eve ran onto the landing and burst into the little kitchenette opposite Charlie's room.

Charlie was grappling with a woman on the floor who was doing the screaming. She was crying: 'No, No, please don't!' in between gasps and Charlie was panting and laughing. The girl on the floor tried to point at Eve but only after a few more tussles did Charlie catch on to the fact that they were not alone. He looked round and greeted Eve without embarrassment.

'Oh Eve! She was trying to say she wasn't ticklish. I think I've just disproved that!'

He got up off the floor and helped the woman up from underneath him. Eve was aware her expression had changed from wide-eyed astonishment and was now trying to stop her mouth looking as if she'd been sucking a lemon but her facial muscles seemed to have a mind of their own. Fortunately Charlie seemed oblivious to any hint of disapproval.

'Are you ticklish, Eve?' asked Charlie, making a lunge towards her that would have made a rugby player quail.

'Uh, no, uh, yes, uh, yes!' cried Eve, backing out of the kitchen, practically falling over in her attempt to escape.

'Is he a friend of your's?' said the (very attractive) girl who had now managed to upright herself and was smoothing her hair.

'I think so,' said Eve.

'Of course I am,' cried Charlie. 'Eve, can I get you a drink?'

'No thanks, I've just had several. Can we talk?' said Eve, sounding a lot more serious than she meant to, but she just wanted to extricate herself from the situation.

'See ya later, Charlie-warlie,' said the girl in the kitchen.

'See you. Eve, you know which is my room?'

'I think so.'

'That's funny. You haven't been here before, have you?'

'Um, I think Martin pointed out which one it was, when we were passing once.'

'Oh, so you and Martin have been seeing each other,' said Charlie knowingly.

'Just as friends,' said Eve hastily.

They were now in Charlie's room. It was spartan in the extreme. Apart from the obviously college furniture, there was very little sign of Charlie's character imposed on the room. A few framed photos of rugby and rowing teams, featuring Charlie, hung on the wall, plus an enormous oar - heavily varnished and painted with the names of other Oxford colleges.

'Wow, where did you get that?' Eve asked. 'It's very impressive.'

'If you're in a winning team you can bid for it,' said Charlie modestly. 'It cost me sixty quid for the blade and ten quid for the pole. We won it last year by winning Bumps.'

'Bumps?'

'When all the college boats race and try to bump the boat in front. The more you catch up with and manage to bump, you overtake and end up as the head of the river. Anyway,' said Charlie, 'you want to talk about Martin. Why? Is he giving you a hard time?'

'Why would he be giving me a hard time?' said Eve defensively.

'I don't know,' said Charlie, throwing himself down in a chair. 'You tell me.'

'I'm not having a hard time,' Eve said nervously. 'I just... I just thought it would be interesting to know things from your perspective.'

'You haven't fallen in love with him, have you!' Charlie suddenly exclaimed.

Eve was so taken aback she couldn't speak, seeming to confirm Charlie's suspicion. To have her recent crush think she was in love with someone else was too ironic for words.

'You really mustn't fall in love with Martin,' Charlie was saying earnestly. 'You do know..., oh dear, perhaps I shouldn't tell you this... perhaps it's confidential...'

'What?!' Eve cried out.

'Well...' Charlie hesitated. 'Martin will kill me if he knows I've told you.... but I should tell you for your own good. Oh no, what a dilemma!'

'Tell me!'

Charlie sighed and stared at the curtains, his blue eyes troubled, obviously tussling now with his conscience. Then he said apologetically, assuming that Eve was head over heels for his friend:

'Martin... Martin's in love with someone else. He has been for years. It's not done him any good. It goes way back to school days. They had a sort of pact... it got them into a terrible mess.'

'Oh!' Light was dawning for Eve. 'He mentioned something silly he'd got up to with a friend. Is this it? Is it... this person?'

'Probably.' Charlie sighed and rubbed his blond hair as if trying to erase something. 'They both tried to commit suicide. They were both miserable at their schools - I think when they were about fourteen. It was before I knew Crisp- er, Martin. Anyway, they'd agreed to do it on the same day at the same time, even though they were in different places. But when it came to it Martin didn't really follow through on it properly, but Henri did. So when Henri was taken to hospital and nearly died, Martin felt really guilty, as if it was his fault...'

'HENRY!!' Eve exploded. *'This is a guy?! So Martin is gay!'*

Charlie frowned in incomprehension.

'Henrietta's a girl,' he said, as if Eve were somehow being stupid in misunderstanding him. 'It's only Henri for short - with an "i" like the French, except it's pronounced "Henry". She's Henrietta Garrett-Brown. You must have heard of her. She's always in the gossip columns. Goes skiing with royalty. Had an affair with that MP - what was his name?'

'I don't read gossip columns,' said Eve harshly.

'No, I suppose not,' said Charlie, as if he was only just remembering that Eve was in the room. 'Anyway,' he sighed, 'that's it. Martin's torturing himself with unrequited love... and guilt... while she's partying her way around the world's capitals. He does see her about twice a term, but it's not enough for him.

I suppose they may spend Christmas together. I've told him not to keep torturing himself, but I suppose it's... it's...' (Charlie was lost for words) 'oh, one of those grand passion things. It seems to have spoilt him for anyone else, which is a shame. Perhaps he'll get over it eventually. Although she is incredibly beautiful, of course. It's easy to see why anyone could be hooked. She has this naked painting of herself in her flat. Martin showed me once when she was away. Anyway,' Charlie recovered himself, 'I just thought I'd better warn you. For God's sake, don't tell Martin I've told you - he'd kill me. Although I'm sure it's common knowledge. I just thought *you* might not know, not mixing in the same circles an' all that.'

'No,' said Eve guardedly. 'You're right, I don't. Thank you.'

If she was confirming Charlie's suspicions about her feelings for Martin it was just too bad. Eve stood up and walked towards the door, feeling again as thought her brain was on overload. Now hardly seemed the moment to try to subtly quiz Charlie as to whether Martin was capable of murder.

She said a quiet goodbye to Charlie, who looked as troubled as if he had just kicked an already injured small animal. Part of Eve's brain, the part that wasn't feeling completely blown away, was finding the proceedings almost amusing. Imagine Charlie thinking she was in love with Martin! Perhaps she should blow Charlie away by saying: 'Well, actually, Charlie, it's *you* I've been in love with for the past year.' But then the part of Eve's brain that was still functioning questioned whether that was still true. Charlie was kind of an idiot...

Eve walked out of Christ Church and retrieved her bike. She felt in a daze. So Martin was in love. In love with someone who didn't love him. Wow. This was Martin in a whole new light, as if a painting of Martin before Eve's eyes was having new washes of colour spilt over it, new details blackened in, an outline of deformities added, that made Martin more sympathetic, more pathetic. Poor Martin. And for him to feel responsible for this girl's suicide attempt! The guilt pursuing him for the rest of his life, uneraseable. Martin as a victim of unrequited love. Martin as a victim - full stop. Eve had never thought of him like that before.

She was still walking. She was walking down past King Henry Hall towards the river. This wasn't the direction she was meant to be going. She had no intention of seeing Martin. She hurried past the doorway of King's hoping Martin wouldn't suddenly emerge. He didn't. Eve continued past the *Head of the River* pub and over Folly Bridge. Perhaps she could avoid the centre of town altogether and cycle down Abingdon Road, left down Donnington Bridge Road and then go back into North Oxford via Marston. She needed air. She needed to think.

Eve was now walking past ordinary houses in the residential district of Grand Pont, as it was known locally. It was a relief to see everything so normal, away from the medieval grandiosity of the centre of town. It could almost be the town where her mother came from. Eve sighed away some of the tension that had built up inside her and imagined herself walking down the street to her mother's old home.

That was a mistake. 'Home'. All of a sudden, just that word was too much. Eve's eyes began to fill with tears as she continued down this ordinary but unfamiliar street. What on earth was she doing hanging out with the likes of Crispin Martin de Beauchamp-Massey and Charlie Boscombe. She must be crazy. It wouldn't do her any good.

Why couldn't she just press a button and be home? Where on earth was Donnington Bridge Road anyway? It looked much closer on the map she had studied earlier in the day. Eve had now passed several shops and pubs and yet more houses, but still the road she wanted had not appeared on the left.

She should think of something else instead of letting herself get homesick (and self-pitying). What about the case? Had she really learnt anything from all Martin's rambling on about Malory?

The description of Launcelot had been interesting. A 'born-again James Bond'. A celibate with high ideals, but who had one Achilles' heel - a woman. His passion for one woman had been his undoing. (Could Fern Harrison have inspired a man with such a passion?) He was a man who couldn't be overcome except by betrayal and sorcery. And if he was betrayed by a witch, his first instinct was to kill her. (Feral had been a witch - but whom had she betrayed and why?)

Suddenly two small demons jumped out at Eve from behind a wall. They had evil faces with horns, flapping capes, and began to jab her with tridents. Eve shrieked as they cried 'Die! Die!' in falsetto voices.

Perhaps because of her genuine alarm, the two little boys stopped almost immediately and one removed his mask.

'It was Trick or Treat last night,' he lisped in his high voice. 'We got lots of sweeties.'

The other boy held out a paper bag, either offering her some candy or in proof of his friend's statement.

Halloween. So that was it. She should have remembered.

'Uh, no, thank you,' said Eve in a low, shaken voice, trying to recover some dignity. She put her bike on the road and cycled at full speed without further comment towards Donnington Bridge Road, ignoring the yelling of the driver who had been forced to swerve as she had pushed out into his path.

But during that day a somewhat larger boy had been in to the photographic department of Boots on Cornmarket to finally pick up the photos his mother had left to be printed. He was the one who had discovered the half-submerged camera in the river while out fishing.

He had looked at the photos handed to him by the assistant straight away. She apologised that there were only two that it had been possible to develop because of water damage.

But the two developed ones were brilliant! It looked like a medieval knight in front of some trees. They were a bit blurred and foggy, but that made them look even more creepy! The boy asked if they could be made into posters from the negatives. They looked just like a character from one of his 'sword and sorcery' computer games. But he wouldn't tell his mum. She didn't like him being interested in that sort of thing. Said it encouraged violence in 'young males'. Huh! What did she know? Perhaps he wouldn't even tell her the photos had come out.

CHAPTER TWENTY EIGHT

"I HEARD A STRANGE BELLOWING IN THE BUILDING, AND TURNING ROUND TO FIND THE CAUSE, SAW AN UNWONTED SIGHT. THE BASINET WAS BEING TRIED ON, BUT THE VISOR, FOR SOME REASON, WOULD NOT LIFT, AND I SAW MORRIS EMBEDDED IN IRON, DANCING WITH RAGE AND ROARING INSIDE."

[EDWARD BURNE-JONES WRITING TO JAMES THURSFIELD, 1869]

Another week passed. Eve only saw Martin at the *Princess Ida* rehearsal where he had become even more adept at playing the smart and superior Prince Hilarion who is intent on rescuing Ida from a 'bluestocking' existence of serious study and a life without men. Eve had to try twice as hard to stay in character while her mind was still boggling over Charlie's revelations about Martin and Henrietta Garrett-Brown. Charlie really shouldn't have told her. It was confidential. Then again, perhaps it was important that she should know. It was certainly an antidote to... well, certain *illusions* she might have been tempted to entertain each time Martin sang of his love for her.

Eve and Martin had swapped news of the investigation over the usual drink after rehearsal. Apparently Tony Greer was in deep trouble with the police. He had lied about his alibi for the time of the murder. He had not been with his boyfriend at the vital moment, but with another guy he'd picked up in a club the night before. When his boyfriend had found out the real reason Tony had wanted him to lie, the boyfriend had told the police the truth and split up acrimoniously with Tony. But since the new man in Tony's life could now vouch for him instead, there was still no more evidence to put Tony Greer on the spot.

Martin had still not been able to find a link between Guy Fastness and Feral, nor had he been able to break Jeremy East's alibi. Eve still did not tell Martin about any police interest in his direction, simply that her uncle had given her some of Feral's books to have a look at. They were about magic and all sorts of New Age stuff that Eve didn't want to touch with a ten foot pole. She had felt rather affronted that DI Andrews would assume she would be interested just because they were on the 'supernatural'. The police had their own experts to consult on such matters, of course. Martin had finally been given the old membership list for the Launcelot and Guinevere Society, but it wasn't much use. Angela White and Jeremy East's names were there as members. Feral's name had been whited out. But since anyone in the university could go along to any meeting they wanted for a pound a time without ever joining or having their name taken, the benefits of the membership list were somewhat limited.

Admittedly 'Merlin', who had delivered the list to Martin, had hinted at an unofficial re-enactment taking place after Trinity Term last year that could be relevant. But since he didn't know who had been involved and no one else seemed to either, that too was of limited use. Apparently some students - at least two - had re-enacted the love scene between Launcelot and Guinevere, where they are discovered and Launcelot is forced to escape for his life. 'Merlin' insisted that Feral had played Queen Guinevere, even though it was out of her normal character of Morgan le Fay. Since she was no longer a member of the Society she could do anything she wanted. But who played her Launcelot? That Merlin did not know. It had taken place one summer evening at King Henry Hall when there were hardly any students still around. Whoever the poor sap playing Launcelot had been, he had actually put a ladder up to one of the second floor windows and climbed in to his Guinevere, just like in Malory - and the film 'Camelot'.

'But that's got to be it!' Eve burst out when Martin told her over their drink in the Union bar.

'I know,' sighed Martin. 'But we have nothing to go on. The only person who knows who Launcelot was is dead, or if there was any one else there, they're certainly not saying.'

'But that's really dangerous,' said Eve frowning.

'What is?'

'If there was someone else there! If someone else knows the identity of Launcelot! If we're right about the murderer being Launcelot, then anyone else who was there for this re-enactment must know who he was. This is the only link we have between Feral and a Launcelot.'

'But it might not be the same Launcelot,' said Martin stubbornly. 'This could be some other poor sap Feral had in her clutches. Anyway, the whole thing is only hearsay at the moment. We don't have any proof it actually happened at all. I only have this weirdo who likes to think he's Merlin giving me the information.'

'Well then, you need to check up on it!' said Eve, who then thought in the next moment: And I've only got Martin's word that any of this happened at all.

'Have you told the police?' she asked.

'Oh, Merlin has apparently.'

'Good.' But again Eve wondered if Martin was telling her the truth. Perhaps she should check the whole thing with her uncle.

'Oh, and another interesting thing,' Martin said. 'Apparently Launcelot did the whole stunt in a suit of armour. He had his own.'

Eve gaped.

'This is it!' she cried. 'He's our man!'

'Yes, but we don't know who the hell he is,' Martin smiled. 'And assuming the whole thing isn't a fabrication by someone in the L and G Soc who want to distract us. Feral playing Guinevere just doesn't sound right to me. Anyway, whoever this Launcelot was, *if* he existed, I hope his armour was better than the plastic crap we had to try on tonight, or he wouldn't manage to seduce anybody.'

Eve was still feeling excited about this new development the next morning as she walked up the Banbury Road to register with a doctor. All new students had been nagged at the beginning of term to do this, but at the beginning of term it had hardly seemed like a priority. She had finally managed to shake off 'flu symptoms, but still felt very vulnerable physically. There was always someone sick with something at college and the thing spread in waves. Students must be some of the best spreaders of disease on the planet. So Eve thought it wise to walk for what felt like miles up the Banbury Road to her local doctor's office.

As usual she had to wait a considerable length of time before being seen. The magazines in the waiting room were more expensive than ones she would normally read. She flicked through 'Country Life', 'Tatler' and 'Vanity Fair', finding little to interest her, thinking 'So this is Martin's world'. There was a Diary section in 'Vanity Fair' and Eve inwardly grimaced at the photographs of society balls and parties and weddings. Everyone seemed impossibly beautiful and suntanned and wealthy and well-dressed. Even relatively ugly people seemed to carry it off with a certain glow of *hauteur* and superiority. A woman that you wouldn't look twice at in ordinary clothes with a perm in the average street, seemed transformed by the photographer just because she had sleek straight hair, a suntan and a stunning necklace.

Eve was just wondering about her own sallow skin and stooping posture when she turned the page and saw Martin. Yes, it was him! It was his birthday party at Lakeland Massey. There he was in a dinner jacket and bow tie with his mother 'the best selling novelist, hotelier and interior designer 'Seraphina Hussey''. His father Sir Gerard de Beauchamp-Massey could not attend. Eve quickly scanned the pictures of stunning beauties in tight-fitting party dresses. Ah, there she was. Miss Henrietta Garrett-Brown. Good heavens. Yes, she was absolutely gorgeous - perfect bone structure, delicate, ethereal. Pale skin, long dark hair. Huge eyes, looking a bit startled, the only one in the group not smiling, as if she knew that a solemn expression was the best to show off her beauty and make her stand out from the crowd.

Eve was called in to see the doctor at that moment. She only just managed to answer the detailed question about her health and history of childhood illnesses with a semblance of coherence.

Before she left the surgery she had to look at the magazine again and read the account of the party. The guests had feasted on smoked salmon and venison, game pie, intriguing salads, and delicious sorbets. The highlight had been the blowing out of the candles on the enormous cake, preceded as always by Crispin de Beauchamp-Massey's recital of the famous speech from 'Henry the Fifth' rallying the English at Agincourt on St Crispin's Day. Crispin was a well-known thespian at Oxford University where he was reading English Literature. (Huh! More like reading beer bottle labels! thought Eve.) In past years Crispin had usually worn a suit of armour for the speech, handed down through his mother's side of the family, but decided this year it was getting too small.

Eve put the magazine down and walked out of the health centre. She walked at top speed to North Parade and into the newsagent's. They still had a copy of the November 'Vanity Fair'. She bought it and raced back down to St Frideswide's. Uncle Andrew had to be told about this.

Eve then slowed down her frantic pace. What if he already knew? What if the police had already questioned Martin's family? She had no way of knowing. Martin presumably wouldn't tell her, even if he knew himself. Eve held her forehead and said all the swear words she could think of. She then remembered to pray.

Eve was still praying for everyone connected with the case as she entered St Frideswide's and swept into the entrance lobby. She was suddenly greeted by a gaggle of men all greedily enthusing about some large box waiting for her near the pigeon holes. A respectable married man hailed her with: 'I'm longing to get my hands on your equipment!'

This was soon explained when Eve saw the box. For her aunt had sent her the latest in computers and now every technophiliac in Frid's was her friend. Eve should have been thrilled with such a useful present, but in her present mood could only think: Oh no, another impossible thing to figure out.

CHAPTER TWENTY NINE

"O SILENT WOOD, I ENTER THEE
WITH A HEART SO FULL OF MISERY
FOR ALL THE VOICES FROM THE TREES
AND THE FERNS THAT CLING ABOUT MY KNEES...
THERE I WILL ASK OF THEE A BOON,
THAT I MAY NOT FAINT OR DIE OR SWOON.
GAZING THROUGH THE GLOOM LIKE ONE
WHOSE LIFE AND HOPES ARE ALSO DONE,
FROZEN LIKE A THING OF STONE
I SIT IN THY SHADOW - BUT NOT ALONE.
CAN GOD BRING BACK THE DAY WHEN WE TWO STOOD
BENEATH THE CLINGING TREES IN THAT DARK WOOD?"

[ELIZABETH SIDDAL, *POEMS*, 1855-59]

Eve made her way back to the top floor of Red Lodge through the gauntlet of sudden admirers. But outside her room was what looked like a large bundle of washing propped up against the side of the door. A few seconds later it metamorphosed in front of Eve's eyes into Angela White, huddled up in baggy clothes with a hood over her head and half covering her face. As Eve approached she stood up and said melodramatically:

'Thank God you've come!'

Feeling rather alarmed, Eve took out her key and opened the door. Angela was wearing sunglasses even though it was a gloomy November day. What was going on?

As soon as they were inside Eve's room and Angela took off her glasses, it was easy to guess. She had the most enormous black eye, horribly purple and puffy, virtually closing her right eye completely.

'Oh my goodness, what happened?' Eve exclaimed.

Angela's lips began to tremble. She looked away and began to sniff. Eve was torn between hugging her and getting her a drink. She wasn't exactly in the mood for this, but it looked serious enough to warrant her full attention.

'Sit down, Angela, please,' said Eve, guiding her over to the uncomfortable sofa. 'I'll make us a drink. Or do you want something stronger...?'

'Tea will be fine,' snuffled Angela. 'Do you have any tissues?'

'I think so.'

Eve found some, put on some music (some jolly Mozart, not *Romeo and Juliet* this time) and waited for Angela to speak.

'It's very good of you to see me,' said Angela.

Did I have any choice? thought Eve.

'I'm flattered that you think I can be of help.' said Eve, wishing she could be more 'motherly' in situations like this. Then again, she didn't really have a role model. Marion would be great in a situation like this. 'Do you want to tell me what happened?' said Eve, handing Angela her tea.

'It was Rory, of course,' said Angela with a long sigh, trying to sound dignified. But just the mention of his name set her off crying again. 'I d...do l...love him,' she stammered, 'but he makes it s...so hard sometimes! I didn't want to split up with him, but I couldn't stand it any more!'

Angela looked up at Eve, who was now sitting opposite, as if she was expecting Eve to agree with her action.

'So,' said Eve, 'you two have split up.'

Angela nodded and seemed ready to pour out more. Eve felt rather pleased with herself. Marion had told her about a counselling technique called 'mirroring' - where you just repeat what a person has just told you in another way, to hold up a 'mirror' for them while they spill their guts. It seemed to be working.

'Yes,' sniffed Angela, running her fingers through her short blonde hair. 'He... he's getting out of control. When I split up with him - yesterday - he... well, got out of control and...' She pointed wordlessly to her black eye. Eve looked wide-eyed and sighed, not sure whether to repeat what Angela had just said or not. Angela seemed to have already repeated it herself. Eve then thought: why am I being so intellectual about this? Normally I'd be in tears by now if someone came to me who'd been beaten up. Don't I like Angela? Why don't I trust her?

'The reason I've come to you is because you're friends with the police,' Angela was continuing.

'Well, I don't know about that...'

'Oh, you are! Compared to the rest of us. There's your uncle. He's the one who's caused all this!'

'What!'

'By questioning Rory again and again and threatening to arrest him! Rory got so desperate he wanted me to provide him with an alibi for the time of the murder. Well, of course, I can't! I've already given the police my alibi - the truth! And Rory has already given an alibi too. But I think he got so scared that they were after him and wanted to nail him that he wanted me to lie for him. And... and when I said I wouldn't...' She pointed again to her terrible bruising.

'He hit you,' said Eve.

Angela nodded, looking down at the carpet, biting her lip.

'I can't say I was with him when I wasn't, can I?' she said, looking up at Eve pathetically. 'I can't say we spent the night together when we've already told the police we didn't. It's too late now. That's what I told him. Oh, but he was drunk - as usual! - and got terribly angry with me.' She looked as if she was about to cry again.

Eve was confused by her own reactions and thought again, Why don't I like her? Am I jealous of her having the gorgeous Rory? But the gorgeous Rory seemed to be an abusive drunk. Could he have done the murder? Eve hadn't thought of him for weeks.

'I think Rory's getting paranoid,' Angela continued, her voice wavering but urgent. 'Did you know he was called "Roar" at school for short - because he used to get roaring drunk and shout a lot? It's supposed to be a joke - huh! And, believe me, he hasn't changed. He's an embarrassment in public sometimes. I should have left him ages ago. I should never have gone out with him. The police know about the bracelet.'

There was a pause while Eve tried to catch up.

'Bracelet?' said Eve, not 'mirroring' but genuinely repeating what Angela had said in her confusion.

'With the Chichele armour - you know, when the police found the missing armour. There was a bracelet in one of the gauntlets with my name on. Well, "Angel" anyway. That's what Rory called me. We had matching bracelets made last year - huh!' Angela spat out the word. 'How pathetic! I can't believe I ever loved him, the bastard! Look, here's the other bracelet. It has "Rory" on it. Have you got a waste bin?'

'Um, yes, there.'

And to Eve's amazement, Angela got up and walked over to Eve's waste bin and dropped the silver bracelet into it.

'Thank you,' said Angela, suddenly a lot more calm. 'You've been a lot of help. I think I know what to do now. I think I should go away for a few days, get my head together.'

Angela threw up her hood again and put on her sunglasses.

'I'll see you when it's all over,' she said and walked towards the door.

'But... but...' was all Eve could manage before Angela disappeared.

Eve thought for a moment and then rummaged in her bin for the bracelet. She held it up and read Rory's name engraved in the silver. Was it evidence? Should she give it to the police? And then Eve thought - if it *is* evidence, what is it evidence of? That Rory did the murder and was foolish enough to wear an identity bracelet that he left with the murder weapon? That someone else took a bracelet known to be Rory's and deliberately planted it to be found with the armour? Or is this bracelet brand new, bought by Angela to get her own back on a man who's beaten her up? She could claim it was a matching bracelet and it would be her word against Rory's. (Local jewellers and engravers would have to be checked. But what if Angela had taken a train to anywhere that morning and in her dark glasses had the bracelet made? The police would have to check for miles.)

Could Angela have worn the Chichele armour? Yes. The fact that she's small wouldn't have made any difference. It would have been awkward, but possible. Couldn't Angela have left her own bracelet...?

Oh, this is ridiculous! Eve felt very impatient. She had gone from thinking Martin must be the murderer, to Rory, now to Angela, all in the space of a quarter of an hour. She needed to get a grip. Maybe she should just have it out with Martin once and for all and get it over with. She felt a sudden urge to see him.

There was a knock at the door. Eve yelled 'Come in', her heart beating wildly in case it was Angela again. But it was Marion.

'Oh, thank goodness it's you,' said Eve in relief.

'Who did you think it was?' said Marion in surprise. 'You looked scared stiff!'

'Do I? Oh well, I've just had a difficult encounter. I managed to do some of that "mirroring" you told me about, though, and it seemed to work.'

'Well, you'll be turning into St Frideswide's most popular counsellor soon!'

'I hope not. It's exhausting.'

'Oh, I've brought you your mail,' said Marion and handed over a handful of envelopes. 'That should cheer you up. I'm not being friendly, just nosey. I couldn't help noticing the one with the fancy writing. Beautiful calligraphy, even though it's only on a brown envelope. I'm hoping it's from some gorgeous man you haven't told me about yet.'

Eve took the letter and ripped open the large brown envelope. Out fell a smaller pale green envelope, also addressed with her name in beautiful gothic script. She slowly turned the envelope over. On the back was a silver wax seal with the letter 'L' stamped in it.

Eve put it down on the coffee table gingerly and put one hand on her chest. She was starting to hyperventilate. Already her chest was tight and she felt as if her eyesight was going funny.

'Good Lord,' cried Marion, 'is it bad news? What's the matter?'

Marion came over and began to rub Eve's back, saying 'Calm down, calm down' soothingly. Her hands then slid up to Eve's neck and began to massage her neck and shoulders. But Eve stood up, knocking her hands away.

'I've got to go! I'm sorry, Marion, I've got to go!'

Eve hadn't yet taken off her coat. She put the letter in her bag and ran out of the room, calling back to Marion:

'Make sure the door locks when you leave.'

Eve dashed to the bathroom and used her mobile to call St Aldate's police station. She found out that her uncle was interviewing at King Henry Hall, so she hurried out of St Frideswide's, got her bike, and began cycling at full speed with a dangerous lack of concentration down to King's.

But when Eve arrived at the main gate of King Henry Hall she had no idea what to do. She had a letter with her, probably from the murderer. She should take it to the police. But she had no idea what it said. She wanted to tell Martin about Angela's visit. She had the bracelet with her. That too should go to the police. But Eve's first instinct was also to go to Martin with it. Anyway, she told herself with a deep breath as she headed towards Sandy Quad, it would be interesting to see Martin's reaction first hand.

She ran up the stairs and knocked on his door. An angry voice yelled:

'COME IN!' as if it were the last straw.

Eve timidly looked round the door. Martin was sitting at his desk surrounded by open books and piles of papers, his hair sticking out at right angles.

'Oh, it's you,' he said in relief when he saw her. 'Come in and save me from myself. Make me a cup of coffee quick.'

'What's the matter?' said Eve, crossing the room to switch yet another kettle on. 'How are you?' She must sound calm.

'Put it this way,' Martin sighed. 'If I had a bumper sticker on my forehead, it would read: "I'd rather be unconscious". Oh God, I hate Linguistics! I just want to read novels all day. Have they no mercy in this place?'

'Oh, essay crisis,' said Eve with understanding.

Somehow it was easier to be sympathetic to Martin in his pseudo-crisis than it had been to be nice to Angela in her real one.

'Do you mind me interrupting you?' she asked, just to make sure.

'Hey, no, I'm grateful for the distraction. It's just a pity you haven't brought any cake with you. You haven't, have you?' he said hopefully.

'No, sorry.' Eve paused and poured out their drinks. 'But I have brought something else. Two things in fact.'

'Oh?'

She showed him the bracelet with 'Rory' engraved on it and told how she had acquired it. Martin seemed disgusted at the huge Rory hitting the tiny Angela. Eve worried again about her own reaction - she should have felt more like that herself. Wow, she really must have a thing against Angela White, for some reason.

Eve then took the green envelope carefully out of her bag. Martin's eyes grew wide.

'Where...?' he began. 'How...? Is it evidence, or is it a new one?'

'It's a new one,' said Eve as calmly as possible. 'It came for me at St Frideswide's today.'

'You don't think...'

'What?'

'... that Angela could have brought it with her?'

Eve was astounded. She couldn't speak for a few moments.

'Was it delivered by hand?' Martin asked.

'Yes. Yes, it was. It was in a brown envelope, with my name on in calligraphy and St Frideswide's. So it was either by hand or the university post. Why didn't it occur to me it could be Angela?'

'Only an idea - you're probably too nice to be suspicious,' Martin shrugged. 'But you haven't opened it yet.'

'I don't think I dare. Do you think I should take it to the police first?'

'I don't know.' Martin thought for a while, then said, 'Personally, I'm just dying to see what's inside. I have a paper knife here.'

'OK,' said Eve. She took the slim knife and slid it under the silver seal. She kept looking up at Martin for reassurance but also to see his reaction. She was beginning to feel very nervous again.

Inside was the familiar piece of pale green Churston Deckle writing paper with the wavy edge. Eve unfolded it. It was the same handwriting and in medieval English, just like Malory.

> *'To my lady Eve, from the knyghte "L", who has synned moste grevously. I beg you, do not come any closer. Do not make me synne agane. Have mercy, fayre lady, or my hand will be forced agaynst you. You will not see the light of the sunne agayne. I will be watching you.'*

Eve read this in a low quiet voice, managing to keep the shaking out of it until the end. But then she burst out:

'Oh God, Martin, he says he's watching me! Oh God, it's like a stalker! What am I going to do? And why me? Why now?'

Martin too looked shaken. He reached out for the paper, but then drew back his hand, saying:

'Oh, I'd better not touch it. You know what the police are like. I suppose it's alright with your fingerprints, but not... Anyway, yes, let's give it to the police. They'll have to decide if you need any protection. Although I see what you mean. Why you, and why now?'

'We're no closer to solving the case than we were, are we?' asked Eve in desperation. 'I don't see why he's suddenly got it in for me.'

'Mmm. Neither do I. Perhaps we've stumbled on something and we don't know it's value or meaning.'

'Have you been up to anything I should know about?' Eve asked.

'Not to my knowledge,' said Martin. 'I've actually been working hard for a change. It was either that or face a firing squad of tutors. Anyway, let's take this little beauty to the Morris Room and the strong arm of the law and go for some decent lunch. By that, I mean outside college, of course.'

Eve allowed herself to be escorted to the Morris Room where they dropped off the letter with suitable explanation. DI Andrews was no longer on the premises. Martin then took Eve next door to the *Head of the River* pub. They sat at a table on their own from which there was a good view of the river near Folly Bridge. Martin insisted that Eve eat something even though she said she didn't feel like it and distracted her by talking about a book he'd been reading on the history of Salter's boatyard that they could see opposite them on the river. The talk then somehow turned onto the ins and outs of Rory and Angela's alibis. Then Eve suddenly said:

'And what about your alibi, Martin?'

'Mine?!' Martin looked genuinely surprised and nearly spilt his drink.

'Yes,' Eve said with a deep breath, hardly daring to look him in the eyes. 'It must have occurred to you that you were a possibility - I mean, from the police point of view. Haven't they asked you about it?'

'Of course. They've asked everybody,' Martin said defensively. 'And they asked to search my room. I said they could. Needless to say, they didn't find anything.'

Eve felt very strange. A wave of nausea washed over her as the food was put in front of them - a fish chowder with hunks of granary bread.

'And my "alibi",' Martin was continuing, 'even though I don't need one, has been confirmed by Robert Baker. He had me banging on his door and shouting for him to turn his music down at the relevant time, if you remember...'

'How did he know it was you?' Eve said, trying to concentrate. 'I mean, he didn't actually see you, did he?'

'Charming! Do you doubt my word! Well, he couldn't see me, even though I could see him. I suppose he could have seen me if he had got closer to the crack at the side of his door and actually eyeballed me, but he didn't. He was otherwise engaged. But he says he thinks it was my voice...'

'He only *thinks...!*'

'Well, he didn't know me at the beginning of the year. He's heard me yelling enough times since though to recognise my dulcet tones a mile off...'

'But he wouldn't have known on that morning it was you for sure,' Eve said insistently, marvelling at how she could still speak coherently when her head felt as if it was swimming in the fish soup.

There was the sound of voices shouting outside. A crowd seemed to be gathering on Folly Bridge and down by the water.

'Eve, I don't *need* a bloody alibi!' Martin said impatiently. 'I didn't do it, believe it or not!'

But he was half-smiling at her, she couldn't tell why.

Two men rushed into the pub and up to the bar. It was impossible not to overhear them. They told the barman to ring for an ambulance and the police. A body had been found in the river.

Martin and Eve looked at each other in amazement and both stood up at the same time. They quickly followed the two men out of the pub, Eve putting on her coat and slinging her bag over her shoulder determinedly, like a first world war soldier told he's got to go over the top one more time.

They waited with the crowd on the bridge. People were shouting all sorts of contradictory things. But one thing became clear. The body in the river was in bits. So far a severed hand had been seen and part of the torso. Someone else yelled that someone had just seen the head. The crowd 'oohed' and gasped.

Martin managed to catch Eve unintentionally as she fell sideways on him in a faint.

CHAPTER THIRTY

"Never within a yard of my bright sleeves
Had Launcelot come before - and now, so nigh!...
'Just for one night.' Did he not come to me?
What thing could keep true Launcelot away
If I said, 'Come'? There was one less than three
In my quiet room that night..."

[William Morris, *The Defence of Guenevere, and Other Poems*, 1858]

Eve could tell she was lying down. It felt comfortable. She didn't want to wake up. She didn't want the dizziness to start again. She had heard some odd cheering and shouting but had taken no notice. Someone's hands were on her body, holding her shoulders... near her neck...

Eve's eyes flew open. Martin's face was above hers looking down. She began to cry out, but Martin put his hand over her mouth and said:

'Sssshhhh. I'm not going to hurt you. Gosh, your eyes do look like Oscar's.'

He took his hand away. Eve blinked rapidly a few times.

'Oscar?' she said, confused.

'My spaniel. At home. You look just like him. I'm tempted to throw you a stick but you probably wouldn't be up to fetching it at the moment. I hope you appreciate me carrying you back to my room - well, with a bit of help. I must say, it will have enhanced my reputation at college no end, being seen carrying a damsel in distress back to my lair. You should have heard the cheers.'

'I did.' Eve frowned and tried to raise herself up, but she felt so weak she fell back down again immediately.

'Whoa, steady on there,' said Martin, now as if she were a horse. 'Let me get you a drop of something.'

'A cup of tea would be nice,' Eve murmured. 'Tell me... tell me about the body...'

'What body? Oh, you mean the dummy! It wasn't a real body at all, only one of those shop mannequins. Probably some pathetic student's idea of a joke. Anyway, some poor soul saw some of the bits and thought it was real. Yelled up to some old gits on the bridge who panicked and drew a crowd. So of course people think an ambulance and the police are needed. All a storm in a tea cup.'

'Oh God.' Eve closed her eyes and groaned. She'd made a complete fool of herself for nothing. What on earth had she rushed down to King's for anyway? Martin must think her a complete... Oh well, there was no point lashing herself about it. It was over now... that is, if Martin could forgive her for asking about his alibi.

Martin was sitting on the bed again now. She could smell his aftershave or cologne. His presence felt warm and comforting. It was so nice of him to make her tea and look after her. Eve looked up at him again. He must have combed his hair. It didn't look so wild. He wasn't that bad looking really...

A knock at the door. Martin yelled: 'Come in.'

It was Rory Ablett. He bounced into the room looking radiant.

'Oh hi, I didn't know I was disturbing anything. Don't mind me, I can come some other time...,' Rory sniggered, looking at the two of them on the bed.

'Ha-bloody-ha,' said Martin bad-temperedly. 'And to what do we owe this pleasure?'

'I've got some good news.'

'What, that you've beaten up your girlfriend, a girl half your size,' said Martin sarcastically, moving off the bed and into an armchair.

'Oh, you heard.' Rory's face fell. 'But she gave me this first.'

He pointed to a long red mark down one cheek.

'She hit me with a book. Bloody painful. I know I shouldn't have hit her, but she was going nuts. I had to stop her.'

'You expect us to believe that,' said Martin scowling.

Rory looked surprised.

'Believe what you want.' He looked at Eve, who was now sitting up, as if wanting her support. 'Anyway, that's not what I came here for.' He waited to be asked what his purpose was, but neither Martin nor Eve spoke. 'OK. I realise I did the wrong thing and I'm sorry, but... what I came here to say explains everything.' Rory looked at Martin appealingly. 'I came here first to tell you because I thought you were my friend!'

'Tell me what?' asked Martin.

'Am I allowed to sit down?' said Rory ironically.

Martin motioned towards another chair piled high with books. Rory cleared it off and sat down, saying, 'Bloody hell, I feel as though I'm in court and you're both wearing black handkerchiefs on your heads.'

'Well, you must admit,' said Martin, 'you have behaved like an absolute shit, hitting a woman.'

'I know, I know! God, you won't let me get it out, will you? That's why I'm here. I wanted to tell you why it happened, and I suppose Eve may as well know too. I know Angela has been to see you.'

'That's right,' said Eve guardedly.

'Well,' said Rory, looking pleased with himself again, 'I know now why it happened, why I kept getting angry and losing my temper at certain times. It's all to do with my blood sugar levels...'

'What!' cried Martin, as if he couldn't believe Rory was being such a wuss.

'I know it sounds stupid,' said Rory defensively, 'but I've just had some tests and apparently I'm hypoglycaemic - in the extreme. That's why I feel as though I'm at death's door sometimes and I can hardly move - that's when I've got low blood sugar. And at other times, when I've got too much adrenalin in my system, I get really jumpy and edgy and feel completely homicidal! That's when I lose my temper and hit people.'

'How do you know this?' asked Eve.

'Blood tests at the hospital. I was sent to see a specialist. They gave me blood tests all morning after I'd eaten certain things to see how it affected me. I had really wild reactions. It's the opposite of diabetes, but apparently it can turn into it in later years. Anyway,' Rory sighed, 'the reason I wanted to tell you in the first place, Martin, was because it gives me a rock solid alibi for the time of the murder.'

'It does?'

'Yes. You see, on that Saturday morning, I was a complete waste case. In bed. Couldn't move - literally. I just wanted to die. Thought I'd never had a hangover like it. But it was because I'd had so much alcohol - sugar, you see - that it meant I'd used up all my adrenalin to process it, and I had none left - literally no energy. I only managed to crawl out of bed to the other side of the room at about eleven o'clock in the morning and drank some left over coffee that had sugar in it, and that gave me enough energy to go downstairs and get some orange juice and something to eat. Normally I'm supposed to avoid sugar, but when I'm that bad, I can have some.'

'Riveting,' said Martin, sounding bored.

'But don't you see?' said Rory eagerly. 'The police have got to believe me now! I've got a letter from the medical specialist outlining my condition. Now I'm supposed to keep a banana and some orange juice by my bed in case it happens again and I can't get up. Oh, and I'm to have a protein drink every morning. That'll get me going. No more booze though,' he added sadly.

Martin looked as if he could barely contain himself.

'What's to stop you scarfing a banana and drinking a whole carton of O.J. on the morning of the murder?' he said impatiently. 'Then your blood sugar levels would've been just fine and you would have had the energy to merrily murder all morning?'

'But... but...' Rory looked dumbfounded. 'But I didn't know about it then. I've only just found out. I didn't have a banana by my bed that morning...'

'Oh!' cried Martin, leaping to his feet. 'Ladies and gentlemen of the jury, I now call on all bananas on Staircase H to swear that they were not in the vicinity of Rory Ablett's bed on the morning of the crime!' Martin looked as if he could tear his hair out as he paced up and down. 'You idiot! How the hell can you prove you didn't wake up feeling fine? How can you prove your hypo-whatnot had affected you that morning or that you didn't already know how to compensate for it? Bloody hell, Rory! How did you squeeze into Oxford?'

Rory looked appalled.

'So... so I don't have an alibi after all? Shit!'

Martin sighed and slapped Rory on the back.

'Oh, I don't know. The real murderer wouldn't come up with anything so daft. If terminal stupidity is an alibi, you've got it in shovelfuls.'

'Thanks,' said Rory dubiously. 'I'll... I'll be off now.'

Eve felt rather sorry for him as the huge man walked slowly towards the door. Martin yelled after him to tell the police anyway, just in case and then closed the door after him.

Martin sat at his desk with a sigh and ran his fingers through his hair so it looked a mess again. He seemed to be preparing to re-enter work-crisis mode. Eve stood up, taking the hint to leave.

'At least,' she said, 'if Rory had been seen drinking a lot of alcohol the night before the murder, that is sugar, it would mean he would be ill the next morning. I suppose it is a sort of alibi, if he genuinely didn't know how to compensate for it.'

'I can see it all now,' said Martin. 'This case will be known as "The Case of the Missing Banana".'

'"The Case of the Missing Carton of Juice".'

'"The Case of the Missing Case of..." oh, never mind,' said Martin. 'Not a title my mother would go for, that's for sure. Although we do have definite proof of one thing.'

'What's that?'

'Rory's terminal stupidity.'

'You mean... thinking he had an alibi...'

'No.' Martin held up something silver with a grin. 'I mean missing his bracelet that was lying on my desk all the time. It even had the side with his name on lying facing upwards.'

'Perhaps he didn't see it,' said Eve slowly, trying to think of all the implications.

'Perhaps.'

'Or perhaps it never belonged to him.'

'What do you mean?' said Martin intrigued.

'Perhaps the other bracelet never belonged to him either. Perhaps they're both "blinds" or red herrings or what ever, to make it look as if Rory's involved.'

'You think Angela could be lying about the whole thing? But surely Rory's admitted the other bracelet had been his but he'd lost it.'

'Is that what he's been saying? Oh, I didn't know that. Perhaps he's lying for Angela...'

'Why would he do that?'

'Oh, I don't know!' Eve held her head. It was all too much.

'Are you alright?' asked Martin. 'Only I do have work to do. I suppose I might be able to concentrate if you lie on my bed again, but I doubt it. I'll get you a taxi home.'

'But it's still daylight...'

'No, I insist. I'll just phone for one. I'm not walking you home, that's for sure. Perhaps you should eat a banana - raise your blood sugar,' Martin said mischievously as he lifted the receiver on an old plastic 1980s phone on his desk.

Eve sighed and closed her eyes, murmuring, 'Wow, what an old phone - I'm surprised you're not in the Retrotech Society,' but she was thinking: What a confusing set of clues, if that's what they were. She'd better take the bracelet to the police, perhaps she couldn't trust Martin.

Or could she? It was very difficult to think badly of him at this moment, after he had been so chivalrous.

Eve then paused. 'Chivalrous' - the chivalric code, courtly love, Launcelot and Guinevere... oh, she didn't want to think about them any more. She'd had enough.

'Your taxi will be here in about ten minutes,' Martin said as he put the phone down. 'You can help me with my essay.'

'Oh, great.'

Eve looked at the mess on Martin's desk.

'Martin, have you opened your mail recently? Isn't that a pile of letters there - under those two books?'

'Oh, that's just bumpf - some rubbish in my pigeon hole. At least, I think so...'

He pushed aside the books and sorted through the various leaflets advertising pizza restaurants and curry houses and various envelopes. A blank brown envelope. He ripped it open.

'Oh joy, look what I've got,' he said in an ironic voice.

A green envelope, gothic writing, sealed with 'L' in silver. Martin opened that and read it silently. He then waved it over to Eve as if he was holding it with pincers.

'I don't suppose my fingerprints matter this time, and yours shouldn't.'

Eve then read silently too:

To C.M. de B-M, from your sworn enemy Sir L de L.

Make no mystake, I am watching you. If you come any closer I will strike to your eternal ruination. Do not tempt me further. I have synned once and I will synne again. Have mercy, if you have a soul.

'Oh no,' Eve breathed. 'What on earth have we done? Why is he picking on us now?'

'Beats me,' said Martin with fake jocularity. 'Things must be hotting up for him or he wouldn't bother, unless he gets a kick out of threatening people, which is possible. Anyway, the prose is complete crap. Not a patch on Malory. But at least we know for sure he's pretending to be Launcelot – "Sir L de L".'

'I suppose the chances are he'd enjoy intimidating people, trying to make us afraid...'

'Which the bastard's not going to do. Oh well, another little present for the police graphologist, much good may it do him.'

'You did say Launcelot went mad...'

'Yes, but he didn't start sending nasty letters to people. He just wandered around woods in his nightshirt on the whole and let women have their way with him. But what I want to know, as you say, is *why now?* What have we done to scare him? Are we closer than we realise?'

'The taxi will be here soon,' said Eve looking at her watch. 'Let's go down and drop off everything in the Morris Room.'

'Absolutely. I'll see you safely to the taxi.'

While Martin was putting on his jacket Eve glanced down at his desk, at the notes he'd been writing when she arrived. They weren't on computer, as she would have expected. They were handwritten with a fountain pen in beautiful italics.

That evening in the Common Room at St Frideswide's, Eve had her answer as to why 'Launcelot' might be worried. On the Six O'Clock News was a photograph of a medieval knight against a backdrop of trees. Apparently a boy had found an old camera in the mud near the River Isis and police believed that this was a photograph of the murderer of Fern Harrison. There were also diagrams shown of the pieces of armour that did not belong to the Chichele collection that the killer was wearing. If anyone could identify these pieces or knew of someone with similar, they should notify the police immediately. Everyone in the Common Room said how freakish and haunting the picture was.

Eve was on security duty at college that night. It was a rota system and they all took turns, but it meant she had to be the last person going around the darkened buildings, switching off lights and locking windows and doors. A torch was provided as many of the rooms had the light switches on the wrong side which meant one had to walk through the room in total darkness, trying to avoid banging into tables and chairs.

In the far corner of the deserted library, some idiot had left a window open. The curtain was flapping in the wind. Eve had to go over to close it. The computer next to the window was still switched on. Someone had left 'HA HA HA HA HA!' in big letters on the screen. How stupid.

Eve decided to leave her light and the radio on that night, just in case. She probably wouldn't sleep anyway. She certainly didn't want to dream.

CHAPTER THIRTY ONE

"HE PAUSING, ARTHUR ANSWERED, 'O MY KNIGHT,
IT WILL BE TO THY WORSHIP, AS MY KNIGHT,
AND MINE, AS HEAD OF ALL OUR TABLE ROUND,
TO SEE THAT SHE BE BURIED WORSHIPFULLY.'"

[TENNYSON, *IDYLLS OF THE KING*, 1859]

Although it was only the Wednesday of Fifth Week, Eve felt as if she had already spent several lifetimes in Oxford. More seemed to have happened to her in just a few weeks there than in a year back home. Admittedly the last year at home had been horribly eventful, with her father's murder... this very week, a year ago, to be precise...

How could she have been so stupid as to agree to go to Fern Harrison's funeral? Uncle Andy had said he would give her a lift to Brighton and that Fern's mother had expressed a desire to meet her and Martin. Eve looked at her wardrobe in despair. She couldn't face wearing the black suit she had worn to her father's funeral. Her usual dark navy trousers and cardigan would have to do. How could Uncle Andy be so inconsiderate as to ask her to go to this thing? Surely he knew what week it was. Or maybe he didn't. There wasn't the same reason why the date should be scarred on his memory as there was for Eve. Now Eve didn't know which she was dreading most - Fern's funeral and meeting her relations, seeing Martin again, battling with her own memories, or having to talk to DI Andrews for a three-hour drive.

She met DI Andrews in the car park outside St Frideswide's. He pulled up in his car and opened the passenger door for her to get in.

'Hello, luv, how are you?' he said. 'Seems like ages since you came round to dinner.'

'It does. But it isn't.'

'No, I suppose not. Oh, Maggie sends her love.'

Eve thanked him for the message but was dubious. She couldn't imagine Maggie sending her anything resembling love.

'Anyway,' said Eve, 'how are *you*? And how is the investigation going?'

'You mean they're one and the same,' said Andrews, smiling. 'Yes, I suppose I do tend to feel better when an investigation's going well - it's only natural. That means, of course, that currently I should feel bloody awful! Fortunately I don't feel quite that bad.'

'Oh, it's that bad, is it?'

'We've gone national, as I'm sure you've seen on TV. In my view that only makes things more complicated. It means you get hundreds of loonies phoning you up with wrong information instead of the usual ten that you already know and can automatically discount. Now we've got people from Land's End to John O'Groats telling us all sorts of wild things - aliens are the thing at the moment, of course.'

'What? An alien did it?!' exclaimed Eve.

'That's right. Of course an alien wouldn't need to steal armour - he could appear looking any way he wanted, so we're told.'

'Good grief!'

'I'm telling you, I wish more people would get abducted by aliens, then I wouldn't have them hassling me down here.'

They both laughed. But then Eve noticed that they seemed to be leaving Oxford itself already.

'Aren't we picking up Martin?' she asked.

'What? Oh no, work crisis apparently. Or perhaps he just doesn't like funerals. Not everyone can cope, understandably.'

What makes you think I can, thought Eve angrily. So that bleep-bleep Martin was escaping while she, like an idiot, was putting herself through purgatory for no reason. Typical! It also meant she was stuck on her own with her uncle for the whole journey.

'How are you...' Andrews was beginning haltingly, '...how are you feeling about this week? It was this week, wasn't it? Your dad?'

'Yes, that's right.' Eve was amazed at how strained her voice sounded just saying those few words. She coughed.

'I'm sorry to be taking you to another funeral this week,' her uncle said apologetically, 'but it shouldn't be as bad. Only at a crematorium, for a start. No graveside business.'

'I'll be alright,' Eve lied.

'It will be good for Fern's mum to meet you. I think she wants to feel some link with her daughter, and you were the last... well, she seemed to want to see you, I'm not quite sure why. Don't go describing the body to her though, will you? I know you're not daft and you're not likely to, but she might ask.'

'Oh, of course not. But didn't she identify the body anyway?'

'Yes, but we prettied her up a bit for that. She doesn't need to know anything else.'

'Does she... does she know about the, er, eyelids?'

'Yes.'

'Oh.'

There was silence for a while as DI Andrews negotiated the traffic islands that would get them out of Oxford and onto the main road south.

After a while, Eve ventured:

'So, you, um, don't feel any closer to a conclusion of the case.'

'I wouldn't say that,' said Andrews immediately. 'Obviously, we're *nearer* than when we began, but at the moment it's impossible to see how near. I'm very interested that both you and Martin received letters - we assume from the murderer. It implies we are getting closer.'

'That's what we thought, but we didn't see how. I was wondering if it was the release of that photo of the knight that was on the news that did it. I only saw it on the second day it was shown. But if the murderer saw it the day before...'

'I wish the press wouldn't keep calling this "The Lady of Shalott Murder",' said Andrews angrily. 'It can be very misleading, and it also dramatises the whole thing in a way that the killer's probably loving. I mean, if the killer had wanted to destroy the photos, he could have done. Fern must have taken them from the boat as she came near the shore for them to be at that angle. They were obviously taken from the water...'

'They? There was more than one?'

'Yes, but the other one was very similar and not such good quality so we haven't bothered releasing it. It doesn't show the rest of the armour any more clearly.'

'So some boy found Feral's... Fern's camera when he was out fishing. But you think the murderer doesn't mind us seeing the pictures, or he would have taken the film?'

'I suppose it's just possible that he didn't realise Fern had taken the photos, but it's unlikely. He must have been able to see her from where he was standing. He was looking straight at her. Even through that visor thing he would have been able to see, even though there was only a slit in the metal. No, I think he's bloody proud of it, the bastard! Shows how bloody clever he is. He hid the Chichele armour tantalisingly close to the scene of crime, knowing we'd find it. He plants a bracelet that we'll find out belonged to Rory Ablett via Angela White...'

'So you don't think Rory did it?' Eve broke in.

'Not unless Rory's brighter than he appears and it's a double bluff. We know Rory purchased the bracelets last Christmas back in his home town - it was when he and Angela started going out together. He bought them on a credit card and had them engraved at a small jewellers. He told us that from the word go.'

'Oh, I didn't know that.'

'But it doesn't necessarily mean anything. As I said, it could be a double bluff or a genuine mistake. But if the murderer wants to point the finger at Rory, that's very interesting. The murderer, we now know, also disposed of Fern's camera - knowing the film contained pictures of himself. The young lad who found it said it was only half submerged in water, stuck in the mud. If the murderer had wanted to get rid of the evidence, he'd've done it better than that. The same with the boat he used, although that would've been harder to get rid of. No, it's another bloody clue. He's proud of it. He's playing games with us, leaving clues littered about the place, just waiting for the plonking plodding police to stumble over them!'

'Like a computer game...'

'Oh? In what way?'

'Well, my aunt's just given me a new laptop...'

'Very nice of her.'

'And I've had practically all the guys in college in my room recently fooling around with it and showing me how to play their favourite computer games. In most of them, you're going on some sort of quest and you pick up things along the way that will be useful to you, help you solve riddles, and so on. It's like gathering clues. The way you described it, it sounded as if the murderer had deliberately left the clues along the route for you to pick up... But, sorry, I distracted you. Ignore me.'

'No, you could be right,' said Andrews dubiously. 'Anyway, it's a good job this young lad's mum was on the ball – the mum of the lad who found the camera. He was all for hiding the photos – and the poster he'd had made out of the best one. He said it was because his mum didn't like him mucking about with all these sword and sorcery sort of games you're talking about, but really it was because he'd got the money to make the poster from petty thieving. Anyway,' said Andrews with satisfaction, 'his good old mum finds the poster rolled up under his bed, no doubt under a pile of socks and revolting underwear and girlie magazines, and brings the boy and the poster to us.'

'I bet he was in trouble!'

'He is now,' said Andrews smiling grimly. 'By the way, if you want to stop for a quick drink or some sandwiches, do say. It is elevenses-time. I don't want you fainting from hunger in the service.'

Fainting? Had he heard about her fainting?

'No, I'm alright,' said Eve, 'I've got some chips – *crisps* – with me. Do you want some?'

'No thanks, you go ahead.'

While Eve munched, DI Andrews continued to think out loud.

'Since we released the photo of the knight in armour we've had even more responses from people saying they own armour or know some nutter who does. Do you realise how many re-enactment societies there are in Britain? It's unbelievable! Since this case started, I've begun to think that we really are a nation of eccentrics. Every weekend Britain must be full of people in fields prancing about in armour and fancy clothes pretending to be King Arthur or Oliver Cromwell!'

Eve laughed.

'There's the Sealed Knot - they're civil war re-enactments. There's... oh, all sorts. And as for the number of suits of armour that could go walk about at any given time, I think I've lost track. We must have checked up on every suit in the country - museums, stately homes, these weird societies, fancy dress shops - and the only one that's been nicked recently was from Tyneside but was nothing like what we're looking for - it was black with silver etching on it and from the wrong period.'

'But the picture does prove that the murderer had some armour of his own as well as the Chichele pieces, or at least he had access to some,' said Eve.

'That's right. A very plain breastplate and chainmail. The sort of thing someone could knock up in their garden shed if they had the right equipment.'

'What equipment would you need?'

'Metal cutters, a good fire, welding equipment perhaps. Or someone could make it at a factory, perhaps in their own time, without anyone necessarily noticing. People make armour for drama groups, amateur theatricals...'

'We've got to wear some in the Gilbert and Sullivan opera I'm in,' said Eve, 'but that's plastic.'

'No reason why the murderer's couldn't have been,' said Andrews gloomily.

There was a pause for a while. Eve wondered whether to tell him about Martin's family owning a suit of armour that he used to wear on his birthday each year. When she did, her uncle said they already knew. The police had a photograph of it. At least the photograph of the knight had helped them there - it obviously wasn't the same breastplate. It definitely had not been the de Beauchamp-Massey armour that the murderer had worn.

Eve was so relieved she couldn't speak. But she knew that it must be obvious to her uncle that she was partisan over this. He had given her a little sideways look as she had sighed and then yawned.

'Do you want to take a nap?' he asked. 'We're going to be another hour and a half.'

'No, it's OK,' Eve said, yawning again. 'I've just not been sleeping well.'

'Oh, why's that, do you think?'

Eve wished she hadn't said anything.

'Just starting in a new place, I suppose, coming to university, that sort of thing,' she bluffed.

'Mmm, I'm sure it's very stressful,' sympathised her godfather. 'And this nasty business doesn't help. I still can hardly believe it was you I saw when I answered that call on that Saturday. Couldn't believe my eyes. There was my Eve standing there by the river...'

DI Andrews carried on talking about the case, saying they'd interviewed over fifty students involved at all levels with the Launcelot and Guinevere Society but no one was giving away anything useful. He was feeling very frustrated, lots of leads, all leading nowhere...

Perhaps because Eve had been given permission to go to sleep, her eyes were drooping, her head was nodding sideways, and soon she was asleep. She only woke up when her uncle actually shook her gently when he had finally stopped the car. They were in the parking spaces at the crematorium.

Eve woke with a jump, her eyes blinking painfully. She had fallen asleep in her contact lenses and her eyes were sore. Her heart was beating wildly. She had no idea where she was until her uncle reminded her.

'Oh!' she wailed. 'Oh!' and put her hand up to her mouth. Her face began to crumple as if she was going to cry.

'What on earth's the matter?' her uncle asked in alarm. He looked at his watch. They'd be late if Eve chose to have a crisis.

There were already other cars there and some people walking in to the service.

'Nothing, nothing,' gasped Eve. 'Just a dream, that's all.'

'Are you sure? Are you alright to go in?'

'It's just... it's just...'

'Yes?'

Eve turned to look at her uncle face-to-face. He was taken aback at how open and vulnerable she looked, and how distressed.

'Uncle Andy,' she said, her throat tight with emotion, 'tell me about... Dad... when... it happened. Was he drunk?'

Andrews recoiled backwards as if his body had a mind of its own. He didn't know what to say.

'You... you don't need to know, love...'

'I do!' she cried. 'Please,' she tried to calm her voice down, 'please tell me. When he was shot at the garage robbery, was he... really b...b...brave or was he just...' And Eve burst into tears.

DI Andrews put his arm around her, hoping none of his men were around to see. At least someone crying at a funeral would look normal to everyone else.

'Hey, it's alright,' he said softly. 'If you're asking me whether your dad was brave or stupid... well, I'd have to say he was both - just like the rest of us. And even if he was... under the influence, he wouldn't be the first person to do a brave thing, er, in those conditions. We were all proud of him. When I heard what he'd done... well, it takes a lot of guts to put yourself in the way of a bullet, I don't care how many drinks you've had...'

'But how can I know?' Eve cried out. 'I want to know. Was there... did they... find out afterwards...'

Andrews took a deep breath and wondered whether to tell her the truth - that the post mortem had shown that Officer Merry was well over the limit when he had performed his heroic deed, in fact it was a wonder he'd been able to stand up never mind move so fast to protect a civilian. That there had been cruel jokes that he had only been shot because he had fallen over in the way of the bullet because he was so drunk off duty...

'Yes, he was drunk, Eve,' said Andrews. 'But that only makes him even more brave...'

'*No, it doesn't!*' Eve cried as if in physical pain. 'I j...just dreamt about him. Oh God, I can't bear it!'

And DI Andrews resigned himself to spending an indefinite length of time consoling the daughter of the man who had once been his good friend. If only he could tell Eve the truth about himself and her father... and her mother. No, he could never do that. It wouldn't be fair, not on any of them. And the dead couldn't defend themselves.

CHAPTER THIRTY TWO

"WHEN MEN TELL YOU TO CONSULT MEDIUMS AND SPIRITISTS, WHO WHISPER AND MUTTER, SHOULD NOT A PEOPLE ENQUIRE OF THEIR GOD? WHY CONSULT THE DEAD ON BEHALF OF THE LIVING? TO THE LAW AND TO THE TESTIMONY! IF THEY DO NOT SPEAK ACCORDING TO THIS WORD, THEY HAVE NO LIGHT OF DAWN."

[BOOK OF ISAIAH 8:19-20]

Andrews and Eve were late for the service. They sat at the back. Eve saw that DS Woolston was already there, plus perhaps another officer she didn't recognise. Perhaps it was Liz, the Family Liaison Officer, here to comfort the Harrisons. Eve comforted herself with the fact that her own red eyes couldn't be seen by anyone, although at a funeral it would hardly matter.

As Eve looked to the front it was a genuine shock to see the coffin. It was stupid. She knew she was going to a funeral, yet somehow, in that small chapel, she hadn't expected to be so near to Feral's body again. Just the physical proximity of it felt like a terrifying fact that she had been part of. A young girl, a bright and promising student at Oxford University, had been brutally murdered and she, Eve Merry, had been part of the finding out. She had been part of that horrible process of discovery that had ended with the girl's relatives and friends weeping and distraught, unable to bring back their loved one, no matter whom they called on or cursed.

Mrs Harrison was obvious on the front row, doubled over in despair, her daughter dead in a box. Poor woman. God have mercy on her, and all those gathered around her, in their new black suits and their new blank expressions. They were only just beginning to discover parts of themselves they didn't know existed - rage, and pain, anger again, and bargaining with a God they didn't believe in. And, of course, the desire for revenge.

As the congregation half-heartedly sang 'The King of love my Shepherd is', Eve was surprised that she didn't cry again. Usually it was the music that really got to her. But she must have cried herself out in the car. She felt strangely at rest and detached, as if she was looking down on the people from a peaceful cloud somewhere. Although perhaps 'peaceful' was too strong a word - 'numb' was more like it.

Now the vicar was giving his sermon, a summing up of Feral's life - the little there had been of it. Brought up by a loving mother in difficult circumstances (in other words, no father, Eve filled in), financially poor but rich in love and commitment between mother and daughter (really?), a tough time at school (bullied) where she managed to excel (stuck in the library), a promising future at Oxford University (being a pain in the neck to everyone) until her tragic death cut this short. The vicar encouraged the congregation to think of Jesus Christ, how he suffered a cruel death at the hands of murderers, but had risen to new life in the resurrection.

During the next hymn, Eve looked up at the stained glass window at the front of the chapel, directly above the coffin and the curtain behind it. It depicted Jesus in a white robe tied by a rope at the waist, like a monk's habit. He was carrying his cross, bending down beneath the weight of it. To Eve's eyes at this moment, it looked as if Jesus was reaching down, bending down, as if at any moment he would reach out to the poor girl in the coffin beneath him and lift her up to where he was. Eve felt her eyes filling with tears again, her cynical barrier blown away. She realised that she had been trying to protect herself during the music and the sermon from feeling any more pain. She began to pray for the foolish, twisted, persecuted and persecuting Fern Harrison. She wished she could have seen Fern alive and well and made friends with her. Maybe she could have helped her not to take that disastrous course in life...

But this was silly. Only God could help her now. Was there a chance for people after death, to change their ways and repent? Would God give another chance to someone who had perhaps never really heard the truth about Jesus the Saviour and Redeemer? The Bible didn't make it obvious. It mainly emphasised the importance of turning to God in this life while you had the chance and that Judgment awaits us after death. But what chance did Fern have to hear the truth in her short life? Eve sighed. It was a good thing it was up to God to judge people and not us. Only He could see the whole truth about someone's heart.

Eve's tradition did not encourage her to pray for the dead, but she did at that moment. She also prayed for the relatives and friends left behind. She even prayed for the murderer - that he (or she) would repent and be brought to justice. She prayed for her uncle and his colleagues...

Eve scanned the congregation as they were singing to see if she had missed out anyone. She then noticed some movement behind the glass doors to her left, the main inner doors of the crematorium. It was someone she recognised! Who was that girl? Tall, short dark hair - at Guy's party - Sarah - Sarah Something... Zorginsky!

Eve was so pleased with herself for remembering that she didn't at first think what Sarah's connection with Feral was. Now the hymn was on the last verse and the vicar must have pressed a button because the coffin was now moving slowly out of sight through the red curtains. There was a sudden wail from Fern's mother and other voices as she was comforted by those around her. Eve's guts felt as if they were being wrenched into knots. How awful! The poor woman - her only child.

But when the coffin had disappeared there was also a strange sense of relief, as if it was now all over. Some of the tension had gone with it.

Eve then noticed out of the corner of her eye that Sarah had disappeared too. Eve pondered for a moment then slipped out of her pew and out of the glass doors next to her. Sarah was not in the entrance lobby. Eve walked out of the crematorium. There was Sarah, heading at full speed down a path through the graveyard towards the main road.

Eve yelled:

'Sarah! Wait!'

Sarah looked round and then began to run. Eve had to run too. Fortunately she was wearing shoes with a good tread and began to catch up. Then Sarah left the path and began running through the graveyard itself, tripping over tombstones, jumping over others. Eve was amazed at her determination to escape.

'Sarah, hold on! I only want to... to find out how you are!' Eve gasped.

At last Eve caught up with her - Sarah was about to fall off a raised-up tomb as she tried to jump off it but had caught her foot. Eve had jumped up on the tomb and grabbed Sarah's arm just in time. For a moment Eve was the only thing stopping Sarah falling headlong onto the ground. Then Sarah righted herself and looked into Eve's eyes, furious. Eve still held on to her arm. She looked down. On Sarah's left wrist was a picture of a black sun rising over the sea. The tattoo was half-hidden by Sarah's watch strap, but as she looked up at Eve, it was obvious that Sarah knew Eve had seen it.

'Well?' panted Eve, still holding Sarah's arm.

Sarah looked up at the sky and sighed heavily, trying to catch her breath. She then looked back at the Crematorium. Nobody had emerged yet.

'I just wanted to make sure she was gone, alright?' Sarah snapped at Eve. 'Now let me go. I don't want to meet the family.'

'But...'

'I just wanted to see she was gone!'

'Why?' Eve burst out, unable to understand.

Sarah pulled her arm away from Eve's weakening grip.

'If I could go round the back and see her burn, I would!' she said, her voice trembling.

'Why?' said Eve again stupidly.

'After what she did to me? You heard.'

Eve tried to remember. Guy's party - Sarah being called over - her mother - Feral saying she could get in touch with her dead mother - Sarah having a breakdown. Ah.

Sarah had looked very nervous and jumpy then. She looked verging on the hysterical now.

'I've got to get away! I don't want to see any of them. There could be some of *them* there...'

'*Them?*' said Eve. 'Who?'

Sarah was trying to back away but had to keep looking behind her at the graves to make sure she didn't fall again.

'There are people the police should be speaking to, but they don't even know who they are...'

'Then tell me,' Eve said urgently. 'We've got to straighten this out.'

'I can't,' Sarah said, her huge eyes looking even larger. 'I can't. I promised I wouldn't. I'm bound by an oath.'

'And you haven't told the police?'

'No! They'd know it was me. They'd... they'd have revenge!'

'Who would? Look, what ever it is, we can help you. The police can protect you from anyone who's threatening you.'

Sarah laughed loudly and nervously.

'Ha! Not against them!'

'Tell me who they are?' Eve asked insistently.

Sarah pursed her lips and shook her head and began to walk away. Eve followed her, trying to keep up with the fast pace.

'Are they here now?' Eve asked.

Sarah shook her head.

'No.' Then after a pause, 'They'll come later. When everyone else has gone.'

'Why?'

'To make contact of course,' said Sarah bad-temperedly. 'And do the necessary rituals. You know what Feral was into.'

'I know she was interested in witchcraft...'

'*Interested!* She was more than interested. We all... I can't tell you any more, honestly. Please leave me alone.'

They were approaching the road now.

'Are "they" the people who killed her?'

Sarah actually stopped. She sighed and looked at Eve with a mixture of sadness and impatience.

'I've asked myself that. But I think they would have done it differently - if any of them had wanted to. Anyway, there was no need, at least none that I knew.'

'This is a group of witches, right? A coven?'

Sarah just looked away and began to walk again, but more slowly.

'None of them had a motive,' Sarah said as if to reassure herself. 'At least, none that I know of - but I don't know everything. I was only on the fringes, on the outskirts.'

'You have the tattoo, the mark.'

'Yes. I was accepted... at one point. Then it all went wrong. My mother died... I don't want to talk about it.'

'So,' said Eve insistently, 'you think that if one of this group had wanted to kill Fern... Feral... they would have done it differently? How?'

Sarah seemed to gulp and didn't look at Eve.

'I don't know.'

'Could they just put some sort of curse on her and that would do the trick?'

'It's possible. Look I really don't want to hang around...'

'If it *wasn't* one of them, would they seek revenge on her killer? Curse him, or whoever it was?'

'Of *course*. Look, I've really got to go...'

'We could give you a lift back.'

The mourners were now filing out of the crematorium. Sarah's face filled with fear. She ran off without a word, leaving Eve standing. Eve wondered whether to run after her again, but didn't want her uncle wondering where she was.

By the time Eve had reached her uncle's car, the rest of the mourners were already leaving.

'Are you alright?' DI Andrews asked her as he unlocked his car.

'Yes,' said Eve breathlessly. 'I saw Sarah Zorginsky standing outside during the service and followed her. Did you know she had a tattoo?' Eve lowered her voice as she got into the car, 'the same as Fern's?'

'On the left wrist. Yes. Won't tell us about it, though. Did she say anything to you?'

'Well, not really. It looks as though it's a sign that someone was accepted into their coven, the group of witches that Sarah and Feral were members of.'

DI Andrews sighed.

'It almost makes you wish you could torture people to get evidence out of them!'

Eve looked at him amazed.

'Oh, don't worry,' said Andrews, 'I'm not serious. It's just so frustrating to know of the existence of a group that no one will talk about. Sarah's our only link so far. They seem to have got her so scared she's not saying a word. We've questioned her several times, but she seems pretty fragile. We don't want to send her over the edge again. Apparently last time she had hallucinations - seeing all sorts of evil things attacking her. If she gets like that again, her evidence wouldn't stand up in court anyway. The Criminal Prosecution Service wouldn't accept her as a credible witness.'

There was a pause as Andrews turned the car down the drive to join the line of other cars out onto another road.

'Er, we're going to the Harrison's house - I hope that's alright with you. Mrs Harrison did want to meet you,' said Andrews as if he knew that Eve wouldn't want to go but she was going to have to regardless.

After a fifteen minute drive, they arrived at a stretch of 1930s terraced houses and pulled up behind the string of other cars. As Eve and Andrews walked towards the Harrison house, Eve noted that the front garden didn't look particularly well cared for. Mrs Harrison had already gone into the house, supported by a man who was her brother apparently and followed by his wife. They all took off their coats and left them in the hallway and went through to the living room where Mrs Harrison was seated. Other relatives were busying themselves in the kitchen, taking the clingfilm off the plates of sandwiches, making tea.

'We won't stay long,' Andrews whispered to Eve as they went in.

'Mrs Harrison, how are you? I see our Liz has been looking after you,' said Andrews in a kindly voice, striding across the room to where Mrs Harrison was seated next to a woman police officer and a young man. Andrews held out his hand to Mrs Harrison which she clasped gratefully. She was a plumpish woman in her forties, wearing a black suit and white blouse that was a bit too tight, as if it was an outfit she used to wear to an office a decade before. She had short dark hair that looked dyed, pale skin and large dark eyes that were half-closed. She looked like a middle-aged version of Feral. Eve was surprised at how alarming this was. She smiled nervously as she was introduced to her.

'Mrs Harrison,' said DI Andrews, 'this is Eve Merry. She was one of the ones who found... your daughter.'

Mrs Harrison took Eve's hand and stood up with a surprising amount of energy. She clasped Eve's hand in both of hers and looked deep into her eyes.

'Thank you,' she said in a low voice, 'thank you for coming.'

She was obviously on sedatives. Eve knew the look from this time last year when she herself had had to take them.

'How are you?' Mrs Harrison was asking, frowning. 'It must have been...' but she trailed off without finishing the sentence, her eyes flickering over to the mantelpiece where photographs of Fern were displayed. Fern as a baby, Fern sitting reading on her mother's knee as a small child, Fern in a party dress with a young man - the young man who was now sitting next to Mrs Harrison.

He too had stood up and now shook Eve's hand silently.

'This is John Harborough,' said Andrews. 'How are you?'

'Alright,' John said quietly. He kept his eyes down as if he didn't want to look at the Detective Inspector. He then sat down again.

'He's being like a son to me,' Mrs Harrison said to Andrews. 'I don't know what I'd have done without him. What with him and Jim, my brother, and his wife...'

Mrs Harrison shook her head as if she was basking in a pool of unaccustomed affection. Her sister-in-law brought in a tray of tea and began to circulate.

'We won't stop,' said Andrews, taking Eve's arm and beginning to propel her towards the door. He nodded in recognition to the sister-in-law and several others.

Eve suddenly felt desperate for a cup of tea. That was the result of five and a half weeks of constant imbibing in Oxford - she was an addict. Staying with Fern's relatives didn't seem half so bad if only she could have a cuppa.

Fern's mother called after them.

'Oh, wait a minute!' She seemed to be looking at Eve. 'You're at the University, aren't you?'

'Yes, that's right.'

'What was it?' Mrs Harrison frowned. 'Oh yes, a poem. Fern wrote a poem about me. It was published in a college magazine. I wonder... could you get it for me? She never showed it to me. It was last year. I wouldn't... I wouldn't want it... to be lost.'

'Certainly,' said Eve, looking at her uncle and wondering how she was going to find it.

But Mrs Harrison had suddenly crumpled. She was hunched next to John Harborough, clinging with both hands onto his arm, her face creased in a concentration of pain. Eve wondered if it was the word 'lost' that had done it. John Harborough, his hair and clothes smart for a change, looked at Andrews with a sullen vulnerability.

'I just...' wheezed Mrs Harrison, 'I just keep thinking... she'll be home for Christmas!'

Others gathered around Mrs Harrison making appropriate noises of condolence while others stared at Andrews and Eve as if it was all their fault.

'Come on, let's go,' Andrews whispered to Eve. Eve didn't know whether to smile or not at people on the way out.

When they were in the car again and driving home, Andrews said:

'That John Harborough - don't know what to make of him. He was certainly devoted. Do you know, he's been up to Oxford every week to put flowers near the spot where Fern was found?'

'Wow, how sad.'

But Eve was remembering the photograph of the flowers placed at the garage where her father was shot. None were from her.

Back in her college room, Eve rooted out a King Henry Hall student magazine that Martin had left for her what seemed weeks ago. There, on page five, was the poem by Fern Harrison. It was just called 'MOTHER':

> My Mother had a mechanical heart.
> No cosy soothing
> womb
> tomb
> gloom
> for embryonic me,
> for my mother had a mechanical heart
> that would tick and count the seconds go
> and hope that I'd be leaving soon.
> (I have)
>
> My mother had manipulative hands.
> No cosy cuddling
> warm
> dawn
> lawn
> for tiny baby me,
> for my mother had manipulative hands,
> steel claws with vulture grip
> to choke and make me obedient.
> (I'm not)

Eve felt a cold shudder stray across her back and she shut the magazine. Something told her she wouldn't be sending that to Fern's mother.

That night, when she couldn't get to sleep, that poem provided some of the many images of the day that haunted Eve. But the one that came to predominate was the stained glass Christ, carrying his cross, bent under the weight, reaching down to save. And her own arm reaching down to save Sarah Zorginsky from falling.

CHAPTER THIRTY THREE

"For thys dame Brusen was one of the grettyst enchaunters that was that tyme in the worlde."

[Sir Thomas Malory, *Le Morte Darthur*, 1485]

Why did it always rain in Oxford? Martin was asking himself this as he jogged through the gateway of King Henry Hall, feeling particularly hot and sweaty - in fact if he unzipped his track suit top there would probably be an eruption of steam. But it had felt good to exercise after a day and a night cooped up in his room with an essay. He really shouldn't leave them till the last minute, but he'd always worked like that. 'Pulling an all-nighter' was a well-recognised student pastime.

He jogged into the Porter's Lodge to check his mail and was hailed by an old schoolfriend.

'Hey, Crispie!'

'Oh hi, Giles, how are you?'

'In training for something?'

'No, just post-essay crisis masochism.'

'Did you just see Guy leave here?' Giles asked. 'Ran out of here like the proverbial bat out of hell. Nearly knocked me over. White as the proverbial sheet. Is it woman-trouble?'

'Not to my knowledge.'

'I think it was a letter upset him,' Giles rattled on as the two of them left the Lodge. 'He just stared at the envelope as if it was a terrible shock, ignored my salutations completely and practically knocked me down running out at top speed. I think Minty must have given him the push.'

Martin stopped. Up to this point he had only been half-listening.

'Did you say he just stared at the envelope?' Martin asked. 'You mean, he didn't even open it?'

'That's right! He must have known what was inside it without opening it. You know, one of those 'Dear John' letters.'

'Was this a pale green envelope inside a plain brown one?'

Giles looked at Martin as if he had gone mad, then laughed.

'All this sleuthing must have gone to your head! Is this a joke? How on earth could you guess the colour? Or have you taken up mind-reading?'

'Just tell me the bloody colour!'

'Well, it was pink, if you must know. A lurid bright revolting pink. That's what makes me think it's a woman.'

'Oh.' Martin frowned. 'Thanks.'

'My pleasure,' said Giles ironically.

Martin ran off in the direction of Guy's rooms. He knocked on the door. There was a distinct pause and the sound of a window opening and closing before Guy's voice said 'OK, come in!'

'Oh, it's you,' said Guy, sounding extremely relieved when he saw it was Martin.

There was a smell of burning.

'You've burnt it, haven't you!' Martin burst out. 'You've burnt the bloody letter!'

Martin rushed over to the desk where Guy was sitting and peered out of the window.

'And you've thrown it out of the window. You complete berk!'

'You are getting good,' said Guy in admiration tinged with apprehension. 'How did you know about it?'

'Giles saw you with it. I just met him.'

Martin then stopped and frowned.

'Hold on a minute,' he said, 'I don't even know what the letter was. Why am I getting so excited?'

'You're asking me?'

Martin flung himself down in a chair.

'You'd better tell me anyway,' he said in an officious voice. 'Giles thinks it's woman-trouble.'

Guy laughed grimly.

'You could say that.'

'Well? Come on, tell good old Crispies, your friendly local agony aunt.'

Guy smiled wanly then groaned and rubbed his face with his hands.

'Oh God, Martin, I don't know what's going on. I think someone's trying to frame me.'

'*Frame* you?'

'If I tell you,' said Guy earnestly, 'you must promise not to tell the police. Honestly, I can't face it. It's the last thing I need. And I don't know what it will do to Minty. She's had enough... scandal in her family recently without me succumbing as well. First the armour, now this. Someone must have it in for me.'

'Tell me what's going on, for Christ's sake!'

Guy was now pacing up and down the room, picking up items haphazardly and throwing them down angrily.

'I can't tell you if you'll tell the police. You must promise you won't.'

'Of course I can't promise,' protested Martin. 'You're being ridiculous. If it's to do with the murder, we'll have to tell the police. If you cover something up, it will only make it look worse later on, when they find out.'

'Oh God,' Guy moaned in genuine agony. 'It'll do a number on Minty. I can't bear it starting up again.'

Martin chose to stay silent and hope that Guy would spill his guts. Guy sat on the bed with his head in his hands. Martin tried not to worry about the burnt bits of letter getting wet and blown about down below in the Fellows garden.

But Martin was the first to crack.

'OK,' he sighed in exasperation, 'just tell me who the letter was from. For all I know it's your Dad telling you you're disinherited.'

'Well, that's the weird thing,' said Guy looking up at Martin with a worried face. 'It was from Feral Harrison.'

At about the same time that morning, Eve had a visitor. She opened the door of her room to find a woman standing there she had never seen before. In response to Eve's inquiring expression, the woman said:

'Hello, I'm sorry to bother you, but I saw you yesterday. We haven't met, but I saw you at the funeral.'

'Oh?' Eve was in the middle of some reading and didn't want to be interrupted. Who was this woman? Early thirties? Long dark hair. Open pleasant face. Long red wool coat with unusual fastenings and a hood.

'I'm sorry, I don't remember you,' Eve said politely, hoping the woman would go away.

'You didn't know Fern, did you,' the woman said. 'Oh, my name is Rowan Hunter. May I come in?'

'Oh, of course,' said Eve inwardly annoyed. 'I'm sorry, I don't have much time, I'm in the middle of something.'

'I won't be long. You didn't know Fern, did you?' Rowan repeated, taking a seat. 'But you know Sarah.'

'Sarah Zorginsky? Yes, sort of.'

Suddenly alarm bells were ringing in Eve's head. This woman wasn't interested in Fern. She was interested in Sarah.

'I saw you talking to Sarah at the funeral yesterday,' the woman continued. 'It was a shame she ran off so quickly. I would have liked to talk to her.'

Eve just smiled and raised her eyebrows in what she hoped was a friendly acknowledgement, but she felt as if her lips were glued together. What did this woman want?

'Aren't you going to offer me a coffee?' Rowan laughed.

Eve bit back the desire to just say 'No'. Instead she said:

'Oh, I would, I'm sorry, but I really am in the middle of something. I haven't really got much time, honestly. Just tell me what you want to know.'

Eve hadn't meant to end that abruptly but perhaps it was the only way of getting rid of this woman.

'Alright,' said Rowan pleasantly. She stood up and began moving about the room. 'I want to know what Sarah told you yesterday.'

'That's confidential,' Eve shot back.

'Did she tell you her name?'

Eve was confused.

'What do you mean? I know her name.'

'Ah, not her *other* name,' said Rowan with a smile. 'You know the way Fern was called Feral. Well, Sarah was called... do you want to know?'

Eve felt torn. She did want to know but she didn't want to play this woman's games. Also Rowan seemed to be moving her hands in a strange way over Eve's desk and some of her belongings. It was almost as if Rowan was 'reading' Eve's room with the palms of her hands.

'Stop it!' Eve suddenly cried out.

Rowan smiled at her in surprise and put her hands slowly into her pockets. Eve blinked rapidly, wondering if Rowan had put something into her pocket. Damn her contact lenses. Sometimes her sight felt so blurred. And her chest was feeling oddly constricted.

'I'll tell you Sarah's real name,' said Rowan still walking round the room, looking at Eve's pictures and photos. 'It was 'Starlight'. Isn't that beautiful?'

'I'm sure it is. Please put that photo down. Look, I don't have time to waste. Just say what you want and go...'

Eve then had to break off coughing. Her breath was feeling very wheezy as if her lungs had shrunk to half their size.

'Yes, you're tired,' said Rowan sympathetically, 'and ill. I can see that. But you are going to do very well here. I can see that you're very gifted.'

Eve wanted to retort 'Well, thank you, Mystic Rowan', but all she could do was cough again. It felt as if an iron band had been clamped around her chest and was being tightened, squeezing and constricting...

'I'll go now,' said Rowan, 'you don't look well. Perhaps I'll pop in and see Sarah. Oh, you have one of my books.'

Rowan lifted up a book from a pile on a chair. They were books that Andy Andrews had given her to read. She had only reluctantly agreed.

'*Runes and their Meaning*. Shall I sign it for you? Oh, there's already a name at the front. "Feral Harrison"! How interesting. So you have her books now.' Rowan's face suddenly became dark and cloudy. 'Great shame what happened to her. Terrible waste of young talent.' She put the book back on the pile and looked thoughtful. 'I'll leave you for now. Goodbye.'

Rowan left the room without looking at Eve.

As soon as she was gone, Eve felt her lungs expand and she could breath deeply again. She looked down, wondering why her finger was hurting. She had been clutching the silver cross around her neck so tightly it had caused a red mark.

Eve was in no doubt that Rowan was a witch. It would not have been a surprise if under the cuff on Rowan's left wrist there was a black sun rising.

Meanwhile, Martin was still questioning Guy Fastness.

'How on earth could the letter be from Feral? Wait a minute. What did it say?'

'I don't know,' said Guy, looking embarrassed, 'I just burnt it. As soon as I saw it was her writing.'

'You mean you didn't even open it?'

'Oh, I opened it, saw it was her writing, then burnt it. In my cereal dish. Hope I didn't drop ash and old cornflakes on anyone down below.'

'Assaulting a Fellow with low-flying cornflakes is the least of your problems right now,' said Martin impatiently. 'God, you idiot! I don't believe this! A vital piece of evidence, and you just trash it! Why the hell would Feral be writing to you anyway, especially from beyond the grave?!'

'Oh shit, Martin, you don't know the half of it.' Guy groaned and lay down on the bed with his arms over his face as if he wanted to block out the world. 'Last year. I kept getting these stupid letters from Feral. I think she had a crush on me. Well, I know she did. Don't tell anyone will you,' he said, peering out from under his arms, then covering his eyes again. 'I couldn't stand this being made public. And Minty...'

'Sod that!'

'Oh alright, I suppose I'd better come clean at last. Well, last year Feral, Fern, what ever her name was, started sending me these letters - all on this lurid pink paper. God knows where she got it from. Tasteless in the extreme. Anyway, at first it was just sort of flirting with me, saying she'd do anything for me, that sort of thing. And she started flirting with me in public - fluttering those awful eyelashes of hers at me - God, it was so embarrassing! Then she started coming to my room. Oh, and then there was this awful time when she came here, wrapped in this big overcoat, and then when I let her in she let it drop to the floor, and there she was starkers!'

'Bloody hell!'

'I'm telling you, it was not a pretty sight. And the strange thing is, I think she knew it too.' Guy turned round on the bed and leaned on one arm. 'I think she did it to tease me, but in a sort of.... Gosh, I don't know the word. It was as if the joke was against herself as well as me. It was as if she *knew* she wasn't very attractive and enjoyed forcing me to look at her. She said "Go on, Guy, take me now!" or something like that, and I knew that she was laughing at me. It was as if it was a test of my manhood, or something. I don't know what she'd have done if I'd have taken her up on the offer...'

'What an awful thought.'

'Looking back on it, it was actually tremendously sad. I mean, it was demeaning, wasn't it? What sort of mentality do you have to have to do something like that? Anyway, then the letters got nastier. More threatening. She said...' Guy paused and bit his lip.

'Yes?'

'She said she'd tell Araminta that we were having an affair - Feral and I, I mean. As if...! I'm sure Minty wouldn't have believed her, but it was right in the middle of all that mess about her father. And let's face it, the woman her father had an affair with was a bit of a dog, so it was possible that Minty might think I'd... well, do the same. God, what a mess! So you see why I don't want the police to know. They'll think I've got a motive for the murder. I got pretty annoyed at the time, but I wouldn't kill the poor girl. I just thought she was rather a sad case - when it came down to it, when I was looking at it in my right mind... Oh, that probably wasn't the best way to put it...'

'Too right,' said Martin. 'Phew, what a mess! But that still doesn't solve the problem of how on earth the letter could be from Feral, who is now deceased. As far as I know the Post Office hasn't started a delivery service from the Other Side yet. Or was it hand-delivered?'

'Em, it was posted in Oxford. I did look at that.'

'Recently?'

'Yesterday.'

'So it's not just the usual case of the Royal Mail taking six weeks to deliver something. So it's someone who doesn't want to risk being seen popping it into your pigeon hole. Was the writing on the envelope and on the letter the same?'

Guy sighed.

'As far as I could tell.'

'Pity you burnt the bloody thing. Anyway, you could tell it was her writing? It looked like the others you'd received?'

'Yes, I think so. The writing was a bit more wavy perhaps. A bit more uncertain.'

'Yes, it must be difficult when you're dead.'

'Oh God, you don't think it's from one of those seances, do you? You know, a spirit writing through somebody...'

'Automatic writing? Don't be stupid. It's much more likely to be someone imitating her writing. If it's the murderer, he probably has tons of examples of her writing to copy. He no doubt had quite a few of Feral's loving missives himself.'

'Oh, thank God for that,' said Guy, throwing himself back on the bed. 'The last thing I need is messages from her from beyond the grave.'

'But we should definitely tell the police. It looks as though the murderer is trying to cast suspicion on you. You've got to blow his cover.'

'Oh no, Martin, please, I...! Oh, I suppose you're right. Better they know now than later. If only Minty doesn't find out, I won't mind as much.'

'There's no need for her to know. Unless the police arrest you for the murder, of course.'

'Shit, Martin!'

Guy threw a cushion at his grinning friend and the two of them went down together to the Morris Room to tell the latest to the police officer on duty.

But there was no one there. The computer screens were on, a phone was ringing, but it was as deserted as the *Marie Céleste*.

'How odd,' said Guy. 'You wouldn't think they'd leave all this expensive equipment unattended. Should we just leave a note?'

But at that moment, they heard several people thundering past the room shouting, then several more. It sounded as if something was going on. Martin and Guy stepped out into the corridor.

'What's happening?' Martin asked the next person walking rapidly past.

'Someone's tried to kill themselves!'

'Who?'

The student shrugged. Martin and Guy followed him down the corridor. Outside in the quad a murmuring crowd was gathering at the bottom of one of the staircases. In response to Martin's questioning, he finally had the answer:

'In one of the bathrooms. Sarah Zorginsky's sliced her wrists. Apparently there's tons of blood!'

CHAPTER THIRTY FOUR

"More things are wrought by prayer
Than this world dreams of...
For what are men better than sheep or goats
That nourish a blind life within the brain,
If, knowing God, they lift not hands of prayer
Both for themselves and those who call them friend?"

[Tennyson, *Morte d'Arthur*, 1842]

Eve sat in a waiting room at the John Radcliffe Hospital in Headington later on the same evening. Apparently Sarah Zorginsky was conscious now although she still would not talk to the police. That was why DI Andrews had had Eve brought in. There was the continuity between Eve and Sarah from their talk at the funeral, to Rowan Hunter's visit to Eve, and then Rowan's threatened visit to Sarah. Is that what had precipitated Sarah's attempt to end her life?

Eve had already seen Andrews at the hospital, and now a woman police officer was beckoning for Eve to come into the room where Sarah was lying. Eve felt very unsure of herself. She had no idea what to say to someone who had just tried to cut their wrists. People sometimes say that if you have no words then just touching someone can be a help, to show your support. But Eve didn't even know whether you could hold the hand of someone with injured wrists or not. To make matters worse, the policewoman whispered to Eve at the door that Sarah would speak to her if no police were present, so she was on her own. The PC then left.

As soon as Sarah saw Eve she burst into tears and held out a bare arm with a bandaged wrist. It was easy for Eve to forget about herself and go to Sarah's bedside and hold the hand held out to her. Eve and Sarah looked into each other's eyes for a while, Eve feeling such a burst of compassion welling up inside her that it was hard not to cry too. She reached for a tissue to give to Sarah while still holding her hand. As Sarah blew her nose, Eve noticed that Sarah's right wrist was not bandaged. It was only her left wrist that was injured.

After a pause, Eve said quietly:

'You were trying to get rid of the mark, weren't you.'

Sarah inhaled sharply, then nodded and began to cry quietly again.

'I didn't mean... to cause so much trouble,' she gasped in between breaths. 'I just wanted to get rid of it. I thought... I thought I wouldn't cut very deep. It's only on the surface. But... the razor blade... Oh, I was so angry with myself! I hated myself so much! I didn't realise there'd be so much blood!'

Eve let her cry a while longer. It would be better when it was out of her system.

When Sarah seemed calmer, Eve said gently:

'Of course, I've seen it before. I was wondering what it stood for. I was wondering if the sun was supposed to be rising or going down.'

Eve then waited for the reply, hoping she hadn't pushed things too far too soon.

'It's - it's rising,' said Sarah with great effort. 'It's supposed to be dawn.' Sarah's voice faded away to a whisper. 'Black Dawn. That's the name of the group.'

Eve inwardly gave an almighty sigh of relief. At last she was getting somewhere. Although where it was leading, she had no idea.

'That's the group of women you were part of,' said Eve encouragingly. 'That Feral was part of... and Rowan.'

'Yes.'

Sarah looked away and Eve's heart sank. What on earth should she say now? Eve asked God for help. This was an unmissable opportunity for Sarah to confess everything she knew. Yes, that was it. Eve felt like a priest, waiting to hear someone's confession.

Sarah sighed again. Eve held her breath. Was it coming now?

'It's a group of six women,' said Sarah wearily. 'We... They're into exploring the Feminine - Feminine power. At first it was more like psychology - you know, discovering your true self. I got in touch with them after I'd been approached by Rowan. I don't know how she had my name - probably from Feral. No one knows who they are, they don't advertise or anything. You get picked by them, like joining a special club. I suppose,' Sarah sighed, 'that was part of the attraction. Makes you feel wanted, and special.'

Sounds like a cult, thought Eve.

'Anyway, the first couple of meetings seemed harmless enough,' Sarah continued, absentmindedly touching her wrist. 'We had talks from Rowan on the Inner Self and how various ancient cultures had known more than us about personal happiness and fulfilment.'

Hmm, I bet she didn't include ancient Christian cultures, thought Eve.

'It was all very interesting and convincing. I've never felt very happy with Materialism and Atheism and the horrible things modern science can do, so I found all this very attractive. It was emphasising something deeper than just visible reality - a deeper spiritual side to us that we can get in touch with.' Sarah sighed again. 'At least, that's how it seemed at first. Then we were given exercises to get in touch with our Higher Selves.'

Sarah seemed to have stopped and was thinking. Eve couldn't help asking:

'Did it work?'

Sarah frowned.

'I don't know. It got a bit scary. I don't know whether people were getting in touch with bits of their own subconscious or what. There was a lot of crying and yelling. Then one of the new girls started channelling a spirit. It was supposed to be a servant girl from the eighteenth century, I think it was, who'd been raped by her master and then murdered. She wanted us to get revenge for her. That freaked me out.'

'I can understand that,' said Eve, starting to feel freaked out herself.

'But the older ones in the group, like Rowan, just acted as if this was perfectly normal. It looked as if it was part of our initiation. I got so scared, I just pretended to do it one night. I pretended I was a soldier in Napoleon's army who died on the retreat from Moscow. They seemed to like that. I've no idea why I picked that. Anyway, that was when they accepted me into the group and I was allowed to...'

She lifted up her wrist from the bed wordlessly. The tattoo had obviously been the sign that she was a fully-fledged member of Black Dawn.

'But,' said Eve, 'what about the witchcraft part? What you've said so far sounds like what mediums and spiritualists do. Was there anything to do with magic?'

'We had some talks on it. Feral did one in fact.'

'Really?'

'Yes, she seemed very well-informed. She was into spells and curses, the whole lot. Of course, it was supposed to be White Magic, but I'm pretty sure Feral and one or two of the others were experimenting with... well, the other side of it.'

'Doing what?'

'Feral was a control freak. She liked to have power over people,' Sarah said in a dull voice. 'She liked to find your weak spot, then - pow! You wouldn't know what had hit you. She'd just go for you.'

'Why?'

'Oh, who knows? Deprived childhood - abuse - insecurity - just plain nastiness, who knows? You know,' Sarah said, looking up at Eve in a different way, 'it feels surprisingly good to talk about it. I don't think I've ever told anyone all this before.'

'That's good,' smiled Eve. 'Keep going, if you feel like it.'

'Well, what else is there? I feel sorry for... what happened to Feral. But I'm not surprised. If she pushed someone too far with all that stuff, and he - or she - was a bit unstable...'

'You think Feral could have sent someone over the edge?'

'Well, look what she did to me! I didn't want to be in her power. But I knew the spells could work, because I'd tried some myself.'

'You did?!'

'Oh yes,' said Sarah in a matter-of-fact voice. 'I was annoyed with one of my tutors because of some comments he'd made on one of my essays. So I cast a spell on him to make him sick, and it worked. He had to have the next two days off work.'

'It wasn't a coincidence?'

Sarah shrugged.

'You start to see so many "co-incidences" that you start to believe in your own power. That's the whole point. Anyway, I'd seen enough of women like Rowan and Feral in action not to doubt their power one bit. They called up spirit guides that told them things too, things they couldn't have naturally known. It was very impressive.'

'I can see why it was scary,' said Eve, feeling as though she needed someone to hold *her* hand now. 'And Feral saying she could get in touch with your mother - that was the last straw.'

'Yes, the bitch!' Sarah began to cry again and looked completely exhausted. Eve felt guilty about using up so much of her energy, but at least she'd found out what she needed to know.

'Am I allowed to tell this to the police?' Eve asked warily. 'They do need to know.'

'Oh God, I suppose I've already blown it by telling you. But I don't think any of them would have killed Feral. They were all on the same side. It was only me that left.'

'You'll have to give their names to the police, Sarah. There's no other way.'

'Oh God,' Sarah moaned. 'You don't know what they can do!'

'Then how do you know one of them didn't kill Feral?' said Eve, going for the jugular.

'Because they wouldn't have done it like that!'

'How would they have done it?'

Sarah went silent. Her face looked as if a shutter had come down over it. She then said:

'It wouldn't have been that physical.'

'But how do you know someone didn't curse Feral, or put a spell on her? I don't know much about it, but that has to be a possibility!'

Sarah closed her eyes, then opened them again slightly but wouldn't look at Eve. She obviously wasn't going to give anymore away. Eve felt very exasperated. What next?

'Can I pray with you?' Eve found herself asking.

Sarah looked away but then shrugged: 'If you want.'

Eve felt she hadn't got a clue what she was doing, but she would just have to trust God at this point. She took Sarah's hand again in hers and very gently laid her other hand on Sarah's shoulder. Eve closed her eyes, mainly because she didn't want to see Sarah looking at her.

'Oh Lord, heavenly Father,' Eve prayed out loud, 'please come and help us by Your Spirit. I really want to ask your help for Sarah. Please protect her from any evil. Oh, and heal her wrist. Please intervene in her life for good. I know you can do this by Your power.' At this point Sarah began to cry quietly again. Eve felt encouraged to go on. 'And please, Lord Jesus, I ask that by Your mighty name, You will deliver her from any evil that has got a grip on her life through all of this.'

Sarah cried out loudly as if in pain. There was then a few more seconds of sobbing, before she spoke:

'Oh God, please forgive me for the mess I've made! I don't want to go on like this. Please, God, help me!'

Eve murmured encouragement, and then gently prayed: 'Oh Lord, instead of all that mess, please fill Sarah with Your Spirit. In Jesus' name, amen.'

Sarah gave a long sigh. It almost seemed as if she had stopped breathing. Eve looked down at her in sudden anxiety about what was going on. But no, Sarah was breathing peacefully, almost as if she was asleep. Phew. Eve was very relieved. She suddenly felt very aware of the policewoman out in the corridor who might be wondering what was going on. But this was essentially a spiritual matter. Sarah had broken spiritual law and needed help to get on the right track again. Hopefully she was now finding the deeper side to life that she had so craved but looked for in the wrong place. As Eve sat holding Sarah's hand, she remembered the image of the Lord Jesus with His cross, bending down to save the likes of Sarah... and Eve too. What a terrible shame someone hadn't reached out to Feral before it was too late.

Sarah looked up at Eve dreamily as if she was on sedatives. She even managed a smile. There was something different about her face. Eve could now see how much anxiety there had been in it before. Now there was peace.

'There's something else,' murmured Sarah.

'Yes?'

'It's nothing to do with me, but it might help find who killed Fern. I think I'll call her Fern now. She had a stash of stuff hidden away. It was supposed to be a secret but I found out where it was. That was when I was scared she was doing a number on me, so I followed her one night. I can tell you where it is. It's where she kept stuff for her spells and things. If you write it down, I'll tell you.'

Eve took a pen and paper out of her bag and wrote down the directions from Sarah. It was quite complicated. A plastic toolbox hidden in a rotten tree in the woods behind King Henry Hall. Eve wondered how they were ever going to find it, particularly since it was now dark.

But she gave Sarah a hug and promised to visit her at King Henry Hall as soon as Sarah was released from hospital.

DI Andrews was talking to the PC outside Sarah's room. As Eve left the hospital with her uncle, she told him all the information Sarah had given about Black Dawn and Feral's secret hideaway. Eve didn't mention the bit about praying. She wasn't sure what her uncle would make of it. As far as she knew, he didn't have a religious bone in his body. He would probably think she was as weird as all these witches.

But he was very interested in what Feral might have collected on her victims.

'We've examined what was in her room,' he said excitedly for him, 'but this could be the stuff we're looking for. If she thought it was important enough to hide...'

DI Andrews looked so full of longing that Eve felt like suggesting that perhaps he should pray too.

It was several hours later when Eve was shaken awake to come to where DI Andrews was waiting for her. Eve had been slumped in front of the TV in the common room of St Aldates police station and now to be in the glare of neon lights in her uncle's office felt blinding. But the cache from Fern Harrison's hideaway now on Andrews's desk soon caught Eve's attention.

'Well, Eve, here it all is, for what it's worth,' said DI Andrews. 'We've already had a look at it. Don't worry about gloves, we're not expecting any prints other than Fern's on this.'

Eve looked at each item as her uncle pointed it out - the usual small plastic bags and boxes containing human hair, nail clippings, bits of material, all the sort of things they had already found in her room. Presumably these were back-up supplies or particularly precious ones. Or perhaps they were meant to be accessible for rituals in the woods.

'This is creepy,' said Andrews.

He pointed to four little dolls. They were cheap plastic things with plain faces. They had been dressed in crude medieval outfits - two were meant to be ladies and two were men. One of the men was wrapped in tinfoil armour.

'Do you think she stuck pins in them?' DS Woolston said laughing.

Andrews opened one of the plastic boxes and out fell long cruel pins. Woolston stopped laughing and swore instead.

'And perhaps most important of all,' said Andrews opening an envelope, 'photographs. Eve, see if you recognise any of the people on here.'

Most of the photographs seemed to be of men. Eve easily identified Guy Fastness and Rory Ablett on several of them. They had been taken around college and were utterly innocuous in themselves.

'Hardly blackmail material, most of them,' said Andrews. 'Here are some re-enactment ones with people from the Launcelot and Guinevere Society. Does that look like Jeremy East to you, Eve, the one in armour there? Interesting. But then it gets even more interesting.'

Andrews then showed them a photograph of Fern herself, in a long black dress with a purple shawl tied round her waist and a lot of jewellery - the same outfit she was wearing when she was found. She had flung two arms in the air over a bowl with flame coming out of it as if she was casting a spell. Eve shuddered.

'That's Feral as Morgan le Fay, I suppose,' Eve said. Then, 'Good Lord!' as Andrews showed her the next photo.

It was a naked Feral kneeling on a bed holding her arms out to a naked young man. It was a bit blurred and they were both sideways to the camera. Feral was smiling.

'Who is that?' said Eve.

It was hard to see the face clearly. He had short brown hair, pale skin and blurred innocuous features.

'At the moment we have no idea,' said Andrews. 'We're getting the picture enhanced as much as we can. But that looks more like blackmail potential to me. And what do you think that is shining in the corner there?'

Eve looked at the photo again.

'Armour!' she suddenly cried. 'He's taken off armour!'

'I think this is the re-enactment we've been looking for,' said Andrews in triumph. 'This could be our man.'

'But hold on,' said Eve, 'there must have been another person there, to take the photo. Who was that? They must know who the man is.'

Andrews held out the last photo. It was of a smiling blonde girl on her own in medieval dress, in the same setting as the previous photo.

'Angela White,' said Eve.

'Yes,' said Andrews. 'Pity she's gone walkabout. She's been missing for the last week.'

CHAPTER THIRTY FIVE

"There shall not be found among you anyone... that useth divination, or an observer of times, or an enchanter, or a witch. Or a charmer, or a consulter of familiar spirits, or a wizard, or a necromancer. For all these things are an abomination to the Lord."

[Book of Deuteronomy 18:10,11]

"Merrily ring the luncheon bell!... Feast we body and mind as well."

[Gilbert and Sullivan, *Princess Ida*, 1884]

Eve made the mistake of inviting Martin for lunch at St Frideswide's on the Friday of Seventh Week. He teased her mercilessly throughout the meal, asking impertinent questions about her to everyone seated around them, and generally being very loud. Eve felt herself trying to physically shrink as well as fighting the temptation to ram cutlery down his throat. To make matters worse, she had forgotten that Friday lunch at St Frideswide's was always just bread and soup (the money saved was given to charity). That didn't help either. Eve knew she wasn't going to be allowed to forget that for a long while. Thank goodness there were only two more weeks till the end of term.

Eve had spent the last week and a half going through Fern's books in her spare time (much to the surprise of the Principal who had come across her reading 'The Witches' Bible'). The police had been interviewing the other members of 'Black Dawn', the names finally given by Sarah. Sarah had now gone on holiday with her father to recuperate. Rory Ablett was off the hook a bit more as there was no way he was the man in the photograph with Fern. However, Angela White was still missing - the police had put out a nationwide alert. It now seemed she wasn't so much escaping a violent Rory but that she knew the real identity of the murderer, a murderer who could strike again. No wonder she had protested Rory's innocence so vehemently. Eve had been worrying now and again about Angela's safety and felt guilty about her dislike of the small blonde.

Meanwhile the police had enhanced the photograph found in Fern's hideaway and had shown it on nationwide television. But the face still looked anonymous in the extreme - still indistinct, pale, sideways on, short brown hair. And still DI Andrews did not want to commit himself to saying that was the murderer. There was no direct evidence linking the person in the photograph to the crime. Of the people who knew his identity for sure, one was dead, and the other was missing.

As Eve and Martin were leaving the dining hall and walking up to Eve's room, she said nervously:

'I've asked someone to join us, is that OK?'

'Need a chaperone, eh?' said Martin. 'That's understandable.'

'No,' Eve smiled. 'He was at your school...'

'Which school?'

'Dragonshead.'

'Oh, not an old boys' reunion,' Martin groaned.

'I haven't asked him 'cos of that, it's because of something else. Anyway, you two weren't contemporaries. He's about twelve years older than you, so he won't know the terrible truth about you.'

'Oh well, that's something.'

Eve unlocked the door of her room and they walked in.

'I see you haven't improved the place much,' said Martin, sitting with a wince on the hard sofa.

'Your manners haven't improved much either,' said Eve, switching on the kettle.

'She's talking to me about manners - the girl from the Colonies! Although, I suppose they do have manners there - "Here, hold my knife, old boy, while I just mug this old lady and steal her purse",' Martin said in a fake posh voice. 'Oh, and would you be so good as to hold my gun while I snort a bit of crack. Oh, you're too kind!'

'Martin, you're being really obnoxious today,' Eve scowled. 'What's the matter with you?'

'I think it's this place,' Martin said in his normal voice again. 'It's the presence of so many future clergy. It freaks me out.'

'Humph! Sign of a guilty conscience probably,' said Eve automatically, then was secretly horrified that she'd said it. What if Martin really did have a guilty conscience about something fairly major?

'You're probably right,' he replied in an off-hand way.

Eve breathed a sigh of relief. Boy, she'd better be careful on things like that. She knew that he was still supposed to feel guilty about Henrietta Garrett-Brown. And she hardly dared contemplate what else might be on his conscience. At least he wasn't the man in the photo, so hopefully the police were discounting him. But another side of Eve's brain reminded her that the photo might not be of the murderer anyway. She had still better be careful with Martin.

There was a knock at the door.

'Come in!' cried Eve. 'Ah, Jack, thanks for coming. This is Martin that I was telling you about. Martin, this is Jack Wintour-Thomas, who's studying here - to be an Anglican priest.'

'She just can't stop talking about me,' said Martin as he stood up and the two men shook hands.

Jack was tall and broad with short curly brown hair and an easy smile.

'So, you served some time at Dragonshead,' he said to Martin as Eve handed him a coffee.

'Briefly.'

The conversation seemed in danger of grinding to a halt right there so Eve decided to get straight to the point. She sat down with her drink.

'Martin, I told you on the phone about what the police found in Fern Harrison's cache, for want of a better word, and what Sarah said about Fern's involvement in witchcraft. That's why I asked Jack to come along. He knows a lot about exorcism and the occult and stuff like that...'

'Or the deliverance ministry, as we now call it,' Jack smiled.

'He's been in Africa and seen all sorts of amazing things - in Zaire, voodoo an' stuff. Anyway, I've told him about the latest evidence, in fact he's been helping to keep me sane while I've been reading all these weird books on the occult from Feral - I mean, Fern's room.'

'Oh, we're calling her Fern now, are we?' said Martin.

Eve looked at Jack.

'Well, it's about occult names, you see,' said Eve. '"Feral" was Fern's occult name - '

'Occult means "hidden",' said Jack.

'Yes, I know,' said Martin.

'So it doesn't make any sense,' said Eve, 'that Fern should have used her occult name ordinarily. Apparently she did it as far back as school.'

'To tell someone your occult name gives them power over you,' explained Jack. 'It was very foolish of this girl to use it as her normal name, considering the people she was mixing with. It means that any spell can work against you more easily - that's the theory anyway. The supernatural powers that are being called up have more ready access to you, as it were.'

'Isn't it horrible?' Eve shivered. 'So I don't understand why she was using her occult name in normal life. Perhaps it must have been a pathetic attempt to intimidate people, or perhaps she was 'coming out of the closet' as a witch and didn't mind people knowing.'

'I wonder how she first got involved?' Jack asked. 'Often with teenagers it's a ouija board. They think it's a party game, and they don't realise they can actually call up spirits that way.'

'So,' Martin broke in, 'you actually believe in all this - that there are actual spirits people get in touch with? Are they ghosts, or what?'

'There are invisible powers around us all the time,' said Jack in a matter-of-fact voice.

Martin sang the theme tune of *The Twilight Zone*. Jack smiled and continued:

'They're usually called angels and demons, according to which side they're on. This is the Judeo-Christian tradition, of course. Although I think Muslims believe the same sort of thing. I'm not sure about Hindus. Anyway, the demons are fallen angels. In Christian mythology, if I can call it that, even the devil started out as a good guy.'

'So we're in Milton territory here,' said Martin. 'The devil began as the archangel Lucifer - "Lightbearer" - but then got too big for his boots and wanted to take the place of God. And he took hoards of other angels down with him. "*Better to reign in Hell than serve in heaven*". You really believe this stuff?'

He looked from Jack to Eve.

Eve looked from Martin to Jack.

'Obviously Milton was using poetic licence,' said Jack, 'but he got the basics right. The biblical origins of the idea of the devil are obviously from the serpent in the Garden of Eden, who tempts mankind to disobey God. The devil tells us we're OK on our own and we can be our own god - we don't need the real thing. Much better to be in charge of our own destiny and be centred around ourselves. That was our original disaster, of course, called the Fall, that has been affecting us and the planet ever since. Even the natural world was dragged down with us, and human beings have been stumbling around in the dark ever since. That is until God took several very important initiatives to bring us back to Himself.'

'Oh great,' said Martin, 'an after-lunch sermon.'

'You did ask me what I believed,' smiled Jack. 'It's your fault.'

'Yes, I know all this stuff. I did have to go to chapel, you know. Anyway, it all goes to show you can't trust women called Eve,' Martin grinned maliciously.

'The point is,' said Eve, ignoring him, 'that this is all relevant to the case.'

'You may not believe in the supernatural,' said Jack, 'but there are an awful lot of people who do. And you don't have to go to

Africa to see it. There's a huge flood of shamanistic ideas flooding our culture under all sorts of guises, usually called the New Age movement. It includes Astrology, Divination, Spiritualism and Mediumship - what used to be called Necromancy and Sorcery. It's all as old as the hills. Paganism is back, and it's big business.'

'Did it ever really go away?' asked Martin rhetorically.

'No, just underground. But now,' said Jack, 'along with pluralism and moral relativism, neo-paganism is the Church's biggest enemy.'

'The point is,' said Eve again, 'that this is what Fern Harrison was into. And it was probably what got her killed. If we don't know about it, we won't know how her mind worked and how she functioned with people. I hate all this stuff, but we won't understand the case until we have got a grip on it. And there may be more lives at risk,' she added, 'Sarah nearly managed to top herself, and we don't know what's happened to Angela White. And you said Tony Greer has always looked close to the edge. John Harborough didn't look exactly a happy bunny either when I saw him. All sorts of people have been affected by this crap.'

'I don't know whether I'd call it crap,' said Jack. 'That implies it's rubbish and not true.'

'I suppose,' said Martin reluctantly, 'that even if people just *believe* it's true, it will have an effect on them, like the placebo effect. It could all be psychological.'

'It *could*,' said Jack, 'and anything that happens to us as human beings is bound to have a psychological component. But no, I would say that here this is primarily *spiritual*. We're talking the genuinely supernatural here. It's very annoying that when people hear the word 'supernatural' they think of ghoulies and ghosties and things to do with the occult. They seem to forget that *God* is somewhat supernatural Himself and that Christianity is nothing if it's not supernatural through and through.'

'So you believe in miracles and the virgin birth and resurrection and stuff like that?' said Martin.

'I do,' said Jack. 'But we're not talking about me here. This case involves a girl who believed she could have power over other human beings by calling on natural forces inherent in the universe and the human psyche - that on its own would be "white" magic. But there is now evidence that she strayed into the other side of it, the "black" side, as it were.'

'Like the dark side of the moon,' said Martin.

'The shadow side,' said Eve.

'Whatever,' said Jack. 'She had books of spells and may well have actually called on evil spiritual power to help her achieve her purpose.'

'She was into channelling as well,' added Eve.

'So she was actively offering herself,' Jack interpreted, 'as a channel for alien spirits to take over her personality...'

'Hold on a minute,' Martin burst out. 'This is giving me the creeps! I thought you two were Anglicans. I didn't know you actually believed in this stuff.'

Jack laughed.

'You'd be surprised how many "stuffy" Anglicans believe in this stuff! Have you heard of the 'Charismatic' movement in the church?'

'I think so,' said Martin. 'I think I saw an article about it in *The Times*. Is that all that speaking in tongues and laying hands on people so they fall over?'

'That can be part of it,' said Jack cautiously. 'The main point is that since the sixties a section of the Church has gone back to basics and rediscovered the more obviously supernatural part of its own faith. And that has been a rediscovery of the New Testament emphasis on prayer for healing, prophecy, and what are called "words of knowledge", that's God revealing information to somebody that they don't naturally know.'

'Sounds psychic,' said Martin.

'Yes, it does,' agreed Jack. 'And that's what I meant by the other side seeming to have a monopoly on the supernatural. The Church has let its own heritage lie dormant for so long that it's let the other side get away with counterfeiting these "gifts of the Spirit", as they're called.'

'It's like Nature filling a vacuum,' said Eve. 'If the Church isn't doing it's stuff in the obviously supernatural, then bogus crap from the other side floods in to fill the gap!'

Martin pursed his lips as if assessing what they were saying.

'I can see from your point of view this makes sense,' he said. 'You're positing this cosmic battleground of spiritual forces, and human beings can tap into the good guys or the bad guys.'

'Almost,' said Jack cautiously. 'Christians believe that we should only ever tap into God's spirit. We don't directly communicate with the good angels. They can communicate with us if God wants them to, like Gabriel telling Mary she was to have Jesus at the Annunciation. But getting in touch with the spirits of the dead or fallen angels is strictly no-no. The Bible forbids it.'

'So you're saying,' said Martin, 'that when someone like Fer - Fern thinks she's tapping into some force of nature, or channelling a spirit of an ancestor, or something, she's actually in touch with these evil spiritual forces in disguise.'

'Yes. And the Church is now taking this a lot more seriously.'

'But the Church has taken it pretty seriously in the past,' said Martin. 'What about Salem and all the burning of witches in the middle ages...'

'Ah,' said Jack. 'That was not the Church at its best.'

'You can say that again!'

'That was another symptom of the Church having forgotten or buried its own heritage. Instead of tackling a spiritual problem with spiritual weapons, it used the intellect...'

'And sheer prejudice!' Eve burst out.

'And sheer prejudice,' continued Jack. 'It should have been a purely supernatural battle, fought with supernatural weapons, as it were. But because the Church had forgotten how to use its own spiritual weapons, it resorted to Reason and physical force.'

'And it was a good excuse to get rid of a lot of troublesome women that it hated anyway,' said Eve. 'There was a lot of sexism involved - men wanting to hold onto power. And because women weren't allowed legitimate spiritual power at the time - seen in terms of the priesthood - then women resorted to illegitimate spiritual power, the power of the occult.'

'Like we saw in Malory,' said Martin, catching on. 'Remember how many of the women in that are casting spells and using love potions all over the place. And speaking of Malory, I think I've identified the scene from the photograph. I think I can guess what Fern and her mystery man were re-enacting. Can I tell you now?'

'I wondered what you had in that plastic bag,' said Eve. 'Oh dear, it's the big navy book again.'

'Perhaps it's time for me to leave,' said Jack. 'Helen's waiting for me.'

'Oh, your fiancee!' cried Eve. 'Don't let me keep you. I had no idea she was here.'

'Long weekend,' smiled Jack. 'Bye, Martin, good to meet you. I hope it was of some help.'

'Yes, thanks. Bye,' said Martin politely.

As soon as Jack had left the room Martin resumed, eagerly pointing to a place in Malory:

'Here it is. Launce and Guinnie having it away one night while Art's away. But of course it's a trap - Arthur wanted to see if his wife could actually be faithful to him for one night. Big mistake. "L" and "G" are caught by Arthur's men. Launcelot kills a few of them in his escape but manages to leg it, leaving his love to be burnt at the stake...'

'But we know this already,' Eve burst in bad-temperedly. 'We know this from watching *Camelot* - what more does this add?'

'Alright, don't get nasty. I just thought you might like to hear the original in Malory, that's all. Authenticity an'all that.'

'Read my lips - N.O. - no.'

Eve was banging the washing up around in the small sink in the corner of her room. Why was she feeling so angry? Was she feeling embarrassed at showing her true colours to Martin, showing her own belief in the supernatural - a faith that he would despise as simplistic? Or was it because lunch in general had felt like a disaster?

Martin seemed to silently take the hint as her back was turned to him.

'Mmm, perhaps I'd better go,' he said, standing up. 'Lots of work to do.'

'OK.'

'OK.'

'Bye then.'

'Bye. Oh, see you at *Princess Ida* tonight.'

'Don't remind me,' grumbled Eve.

'I won't say "break a leg" because you probably would and then you'd blame me. Oh, by the way,' Martin added as he opened the door to leave, 'if I'm not there tonight, I've been arrested.'

'What!' That got Eve's attention. 'For the murder?!'

'Don't be silly. No, only for theft. I nicked the CDs of The Prat Downstairs last night,' Martin grinned round the door. 'He foolishly left his door unlocked while answering a call of nature or something and I grabbed my chance. No more booming out crap at midnight for him!'

'Tut! Well, don't expect me to give the police a character reference!' Eve could feel a smile creeping across her face against her will.

'Would you believe,' Martin added, 'the Prat had everything wired up to give electric shocks like his pal Jeremy East. They're both headcases.'

'I bet he's had a shock - to find his CDs gone.'

'I neither know nor care. As long as he doesn't kick up a fuss before tonight, I don't mind. See you, my princess.'

Martin closed the door and was gone.

Eve sat down with a sigh. She looked at her watch. Three hours to go till supper - her stomach rumbled as if on cue. Friday's lunch really was meagre. Should she nip out to the shops to get something to eat? Otherwise there was no way she was going to survive. But then she realised it was only four hours till she had to be at the Union for her first public performance as Princess Ida. Instantly she felt as if she couldn't eat a thing. Did she know her part well enough? Should she listen to the music one more time? Or should she do some work? Friday afternoons were so awkward - it was still the week but had begun to feel like the weekend...

She was saved from an immediate decision by a phone call. It was DS Woolston. Jeremy East had been attacked last night and was now in hospital. His home had been broken into and ransacked. Jeremy had been hit on the head with a hammer. It was not yet known whether this was linked to the murder of Fern Harrison or whether this was a completely random attack. Regardless,

DS Woolston had been directed by DI Andrews to inform her of the fact and to instruct her to take the utmost care with her own security for the foreseeable future.

CHAPTER THIRTY SIX

"...IT WAS A MISTAKE TO MAKE THEM LONGER AND TO SPREAD THEM OUT INTO TWO ACTS. THE FUN GOT TO BE TOO LONG DRAWN OUT. WHEN THERE WAS BUT ONE SHORT ACT YOU HAD NOT TIME TO THINK OF ANYTHING BUT HOW FUNNY IT WAS. BUT WHEN YOU HAD TO WAIT BETWEEN THE TWO ACTS AND COULDN'T PREVENT YOUR MIND RUNNING ON IT, YOU BEGAN TO DOUBT WHETHER IT MIGHTN'T ALL BE NONSENSE."

[EDWARD BURNE-JONES ON GILBERT & SULLIVAN, 1898]

"OH, I LOVE THE JOLLY RATTLE
OF AN ORDEAL BY BATTLE,
THERE'S AN END OF TITTLE, TATTLE,
WHEN YOUR ENEMY IS DEAD.
IT'S AN ARRANT MOLLEY CODDLE
FEARS A CRACK UPON HIS NODDLE,
AND HE'S ONLY FIT TO SWADDLE
IN A DOWNY FEATHER BED!"

[GILBERT AND SULLIVAN, *PRINCESS IDA*, 1884]

Things were getting serious. It was now the evening of the Friday of Seventh Week - the first night of the Gilbert and Sullivan Society's performance of *Princess Ida*. Martin knew he was cutting it fine by having friends back to his room for coffee after supper. He'd be really pushing it for getting to the Union on time. And his friends were definitely outstaying their welcome. There were about eight of them crammed into Martin's room, all talking loudly over the music, drinking coffee and eating biscuits, and largely ignoring Martin who was doing a last minute check on his lines for the opera and humming to warm up his voice.

'Hey, Martin,' one of them yelled, 'this had better be good tonight, seeing as we didn't get free tickets.'

Others agreed who were also coming to the performance.

'Of course it will be good,' said Martin bad-temperedly. 'Now will you please all drink your coffee and leave, I've got to go soon.'

The noise continued unabated. No one showed any sign of leaving. Martin looked hurriedly at his watch. Only five more minutes before he really had to leave, and he still had half the opera to scan yet. God, it was impossible to concentrate with all this noise!

Martin then had an idea. There was a brilliant way of clearing the room ready to hand. He went to his wardrobe and took out one of Robert Baker's CDs. The cover depicted a muscular winged demon playing a guitar. That looked seriously heavy metal. A few blasts of that at full volume should have his guests running out of the room howling in pain with bleeding eardrums.

Martin stopped his computer from playing one of the Brandenburg concertos, put in the heavy metal CD, turned the volume way up and waited for the blast. For a few seconds there was just the babbling of Martin's friends, then:

'I'M BUSY. GO AWAY!'

A huge voice boomed from the speakers on his desk. There was nothing for a few more seconds, then:

'I'VE CHANGED MY MIND. I CAN'T COME TO THE DOOR, I'M IN THE MIDDLE OF SOMETHING!'

Martin's friends shrieked their protests at the noise.

'What the hell is that?'

'A bit minimalist, isn't it?'

'Are you trying to deafen us?'

Martin turned the volume down anxiously. What the hell was this? He picked up the CD cover. It was supposed to be a group called Planet Demon. The first track was supposed to be a song called 'Rape'. Was this it? The voice was continuing:

'I'm busy, I'll see you later.'

Now the voice was quieter it was starting to sound familiar.

'Get out, all of you,' said Martin, 'I've got to go.'

His friends eased themselves out of their chairs or off the floor and left muttering protests.

On his own at last, Martin stopped the CD and started it again. He then tried to play some of the later tracks. But the CD was a blank. After the first ten or so phrases, there seemed to be nothing else. The only thing it contained was someone shouting that he was busy and couldn't come to the door.

'Oh my God,' said Martin, running his hands through his hair. He looked at himself in the mirror for a few moments. He had got to perform that night. He couldn't let them down. He had got to tell Eve.

Martin threw a few things into a bag, including the libretto and the CD, put on his coat, and hurried out of his room, down the stairs and out into the cold evening. It was so cold he could see his breath. It might snow before the night was through. Hopefully it would put off the punters and they'd have to cancel so he could do something more important. Oh no, he was miserably late - they'd kill him. He half-ran, half-walked up St Aldates and Cornmarket until he came to the small alley way that led to the side door of the Union building.

The great gothic building looked warm and inviting to Eve as she approached from St Michael Street. All the lights were on, the huge windows showing the lively bar packed with students drinking, a sight as incongruous as seeing a booze-up through the majestic windows of a cathedral. But Eve had no time to appreciate the atmosphere - she had to hurry to get changed into costume (a long white grecian style pleated dress with twining vine leaves up her arms and in her hair).

This was no sooner done than there was panic spreading like a flame amongst the assembled cast.

Martin hadn't turned up yet and he was on in the First Act. As all the characters gathered in one of the small rooms on the ground floor of the Union to warm up their voices together, there was agitated murmuring about him. Albert Singh, the Director, kept looking at his watch and cursing under his breath, which made everyone more nervous.

Someone came in and reported that it was a full house. Two hundred people were packed into the Union Debating Hall which had been converted into a theatre. The audience were now freezing their butts off on wooden benches waiting for the orchestra to warm up. It was time for the cast to go over to the Debating Chamber and wait for their cue.

As Eve and the others made their way out and waited in the corridor, the orchestra began to play the Overture. The first crashing notes made everyone jump and then laugh. The atmosphere lifted immediately as the loud and merry music galloped along.

But where the hell was Martin? When the Overture was finished and King Hildebrand and Florian and Chorus had set the scene, Hilarion was supposed to make his entrance and sing his first ballad. The cast had removed their watches so as not to clash with their medieval clothes.

Just as the anxiety was becoming unbearable, Martin could be seen haring over from the Union in tunic and tights. Thank God for that! It wasn't a moment too soon. He was due on any minute. As Martin slid down the corridor in his pointed shoes and was slapped on the back by the cast, he hissed at Eve:

'I know who did it!'

'What?'

'The murder! I know who did it! I don't know how yet, but there must be a way.'

Martin was then practically pushed on stage. Eve was left to sit through the rest of the First Act in an agony of confusion and excitement. What on earth was Martin talking about?

As soon as she could, Eve cornered Martin during the first Interval.

'What are you talking about? Who are you talking about?'

Martin pulled Eve down the corridor, out of ear shot of the rest of the cast.

'I'm not sure,' he said with a worried frown, 'I can't work out how he did it. I've been singing with half my mind on that, half on the songs. I think it was Robert Baker. And I think I've got the only bit of real evidence - here, look.'

Martin opened up his tunic and showed Eve the CD.

'What a revolting picture!' she exclaimed. 'What's a CD got to do with it? At least, that's what it is, I assume.'

'It's got Rob Baker's voice on it. I'll swear it's his. I didn't recognise it straightaway 'cos the volume was too loud.'

'Is this one of the ones you stole? How come it has his voice on it?'

'I don't know - he must have recorded it.'

'OK,' said Eve. 'but I still don't understand what it means.'

'That morning,' said Martin impatiently, 'the Saturday of the murder. Well, Baker was supposed to be in his room at the time, right? Damn it, I was providing the alibi for the bastard! And Jeremy East.'

'Jeremy East? He's still unconscious in hospital - he was attacked, did you know..?'

'This CD has the words on it that Baker yelled through the door to me...'

'But surely you saw him. Wasn't there a slit at the side of the door where you could see through, you said.'

'I know!' said Martin impatiently. 'It looked as if he was sitting at his computer...'

'The dummy!' cried Eve. 'That mannequin-thing they found in the river. Don't you remember? That could have been it. Or did you see him move?'

Martin paused, running his hand through his hair.

'I can't remember seeing him move. I think I just assumed he could because the computer screen had stuff moving and changing on it. It looked as if he was clicking his mouse.'

'But doesn't he do Electrical Engineering, like Jeremy? Wouldn't rigging up his computer to do that on its own be possible?'

'You tell me,' said Martin. 'I don't see why not. But how would this CD work? Could it have been on some kind of timer? No, that wouldn't work. How would he know that I'd be there? But turning the volume of his music up or down on a timer might work. But how would he know when I was there?'

'Did he do that on the Saturday morning, during the murder?'

'Yes,' said Martin. 'After I'd told him to turn it down, he did about ten minutes later.'

'EVE!' Albert called down the corridor. 'You'll be on soon. Warm up. And you, Martin!'

'Oh, Martin, what should we do?' Eve whispered.

'I don't know...'

'There's the armour,' said Eve. 'Could he have stolen that on the Friday night?'

'Yes!'

'And did he know Feral at all? Oh, the photo! Robert Baker without his glasses!'

'Or anything else!' exclaimed Martin. 'Oh Eve, I think we've cracked it!'

And Martin gave her a hug that knocked all the breath out of her.

'There's a long way to go yet to actually proving it,' she said.

'EVE!' cried Albert. 'Get down here NOW!'

'We've got to go on,' said Eve. 'For God's sake don't lose the CD.'

'Absolutely not,' said Martin, tucking it back inside his tunic. 'I'm not letting go of this sucker in a hurry.'

Eve waited in agony for her moment of entrance onto the stage. She was desperately trying to concentrate, to be aware of the exact moment of her cue. The other 'maidens' in Castle Adamant were to sing:

> *Mighty maiden with a mission,*
> *Paragon of common sense,*
> *Running fount of erudition,*
> *Miracle of eloquence!*
> *We are blind, and we would see;*
> *We are bound, and would be free;*
> *We are dumb, and we would talk;*
> *We are lame, and we would walk.*

Eve may have felt like a maiden with a mission, but was beginning to feel that walking and talking were probably beyond her when she felt a gentle shove and found herself in front of a darkened audience and a spotlight. Like magic, the words of her opening song floated from her lips as if someone else had taken over her body. This continued as the scene became even more surreal - as Prince Hilarion and his two friends Cyril and Florian dressed up in women's clothes to invade Ida's women-only college. There was more banter and singing and flirting between the women students and the disguised men, up until the point where Ida discovers that they are really male and tries to eject them from the premises ('Man-monsters!'). At this point Eve had to lose her footing and pretend to fall into a river or moat around the college and suffer the indignity of being rescued by Prince Hilarion. It also meant the indignity of having a bucket of tepid water thrown over her to represent her plight. She hoped this didn't make her dress see-through in the lights (Alf's assurances to the contrary had been less than convincing). She tried not to think of the possible irony of being rescued from death in a river by Martin.

Princess Ida, spluttering, then calls for the binding of the deceiving men, who of course sing, protesting their love for the women:

> *A loveless life apart from thee*
> *Were hopeless slavery,*
> *If kindly death will set me free,*
> *Why should I fear to die?*

Then King Hildebrand (Hilarion's father) and his soldiers arrive to storm the college and try to force a marriage between Hilarion and Ida. Their singing gives just enough time for Martin and Eve and the others to change into their armour - Eve's a light plastic silver breastplate and helmet with a Britannia-type plume, Martin's heavier and darker with chain mail and a gold circlet round his head to denote royalty. This was in order to appear waving swords defiantly around the cardboard battlements at the end of the Second Act. Big Crescendo. Applause. Break.

Eve and Martin met panting in the corridor again. Martin looked in agony.

'I can't do this,' he said. 'I can't go on with this hanging over me. I think we should go and confront him.'

'But the show will be finished soon...'

'It'll be another hour at least!' protested Martin. 'And Baker must know his CDs are missing by now. He'll put two and two together pretty quickly. He'll know someone has the CD with the incriminating stuff on it, although he won't know whether they've listened to it or not. It is disguised in another cover. He might even realise I have it. I did threaten him a while ago with stealing his CDs if he played his music loud again - or perhaps I said I'd smash them. I bet he knows it's me!'

'But he doesn't know that *you* know...'

'Not yet.'

'Oh! Oh!' cried Eve. 'Jeremy East! I bet that was Baker too. What if he thought Jeremy had taken his CDs? What if Jeremy already suspected Baker and confronted him with it? Baker would probably have thought Jeremy took them - that's why he tried to break into Jeremy's house too, because he wanted to get his CDs back!'

'Bloody hell, and I've got them instead. I hope he doesn't try and whack me over the head with a hammer on the way home...'

'Oh, don't! We'll go straight to the police when the performance is over. And we'll get other people here to escort us...'

'I'm going now,' said Martin, and began to walk to the door.

'You can't!' Eve cried after him. 'What about the final Act?'

'I hate to point out the obvious,' said Martin holding the door open, 'but this is it. Are you coming or not?'

Eve ran after him to protest at his leaving but instead found herself having to run to keep up with him as he headed for Cornmarket.

'He could have scarpered already,' Martin panted as they ran down the street. 'Now he knows it's missing...'

'I don't believe we're doing this,' panted Eve as passers-by began to stare at them as they ran past in their medieval clothes and armour.

At least being with Martin was preferable to staying behind and facing the wrath of Albert Singh and the rest of the cast when they found out Martin had gone missing. At least, that's what Eve told herself, until Martin ran past the police station despite Eve's protests and made straight for King Henry Hall.

'We haven't got the time,' he yelled as they ran through the entrance and through the main quadrangle. There were lots of comments and laughs from other students as Martin and Eve flew past in their outlandish costumes.

They reached Staircase H of Sanderson Quad and ran up the stairs.

'Oh God, help,' was all Eve had time to say before Martin, after a deep breath, was knocking on the door of Robert Baker's room.

There was silence.

'Perhaps he's not in,' Eve whispered, trying to get her breath.

'Perhaps he's gone already,' Martin muttered, then knocked on the door again. He tried to push it open but it was locked.

'Baker, if you're in there...' Martin shouted. 'This is Martin Massey, you're friendly upstairs neighbour! I have something that might interest you!'

Again there was no sound.

'Damn!' said Martin under his breath. 'I hope we haven't missed him. I shouldn't have turned up tonight at all. I should've let an understudy do it. But I hadn't worked out what it meant...'

'We still haven't really,' said Eve.

Martin tried again.

'Robert Baker, I have your CD! I know what's on it. I've heard your voice. I want to talk to you about it. It's only Martin Massey. Please let me in.'

They waited a few moments longer.

'Damn. We've missed him. He could be anywhere. Let's ask around college who's seen him.'

As they began to walk away down the stairs there was a noise behind them. The lock on Baker's door was being turned. To Eve's amazement, the door opened and there stood Robert Baker. He only opened the door the width of his body. He seemed calm enough at first but then registered surprise at the sight of them.

It must have been the medieval costumes. Baker was wearing a zip up jacket and looked very ordinary. He blinked at them from behind thick glasses and said politely:

'You'd better come in.'

Martin and Eve slowly climbed up the stairs and walked towards him. Although Baker seemed calm enough on the surface, Eve felt as though the atmosphere was charged with energy. She felt very nervous going past him into his room. He was holding the door out for them and they had to brush past him to get in.

'What interesting costumes,' Baker said.

Again it seemed calm and polite on the surface, but Eve felt as if there was a hundredweight of hidden meaning attached to every word and look. They all knew. Eve and Martin were standing in the middle of the room. Eve only had time to take in the fact that the room was fairly bare - there was a desk and a computer, two chairs, a Tolkien poster on the wall in front of her...

'I'll have to go and get some milk,' Baker said from the doorway.

'But...! said Martin, as Baker disappeared out of the door.

Martin and Eve stood in stunned silence for a few seconds as if frozen.

'He can't be making us a drink, surely,' Eve hissed.

'I bet he's going to scarper,' said Martin.

'He had his coat on - he was wearing a... oh, what the heck do you call those things - a zip up bag thing, bum bag – we call them a fanny pack! Around his waist. It looked full...'

'The bastard! I'll get him. He was getting ready to leave all along,' said Martin and ran out of the room. Eve followed.

They ran down the stairs and out into the quad. There was no sign of Robert Baker.

Martin swore loudly. He then began to ask other students if they had seen him.

It took a couple of minutes before they could get the information they needed. Baker had been seen walking at a fast pace into the old stone corridor that led to the river.

'Good God, he could've taken a scull,' said Martin as the two of them ran in that direction. 'That will move him bloody fast. He could get out at any point and get away to the road. If he's got money with him, we're done for...'

'Credit cards, though,' said Eve, 'they can be traced.'

Their footsteps were now echoing in the old stone corridor with a strange clatter.

'Have you got your key?' asked Eve anxiously.

Martin didn't reply but instead frantically unlocked one of the sculls and threw it's chain onto the ground.

'You're not going to...' Eve began, but it was pointless to finish the sentence.

'Here, take this,' said Martin throwing her the CD. 'Take it to the police.'

Martin was now in the scull and was angrily locking the oars in place.

'Give me a push off,' cried Martin, 'these other boats are in the way.'

Eve did as she was told, sliding on the mud of the bank and almost falling in the icy water for real this time. She then had to stand and watch as Martin manoeuvred himself down the canal way. She wanted to yell 'Be careful!' but instead murmured it. She watched until the sight and sound of Martin was swallowed up by the night.

CHAPTER THIRTY SEVEN

"'Most people, if you describe a chain of events to them, will tell you what the result would be. They can put those events together in their minds, and argue from them something that will come to pass. There are few people however, who, if you told them a result, would be able to evolve from their own inner consciousness what the steps were which led up to that result. This power is what I mean when I talk of reasoning backwards, or analytically.'"

[Arthur Conan Doyle, *A Study in Scarlet*, 1881]

"You'll remain as hostage here,
 Should Hilarion disappear..."

[Gilbert and Sullivan, *Princess Ida*, 1884]

Eve was standing again on the bank of the river at the back of King Henry Hall. Two policemen were with her and she was wearing DS Gavin Woolston's green waxed cotton jacket over her medieval dress and armour. It was now snowing quite heavily. Eve was praying for Martin's safe return (especially as Woolston had unhelpfully begun to share how in the 1920s a decaying Victorian boat had been found up a side stream on the river containing two skeletons). How could Martin see anything out there? Hopefully he wasn't stuck somewhere, unable to get back. And what if he caught up with Robert Baker anyway? What on earth was he going to do with him? Eve had bizarre images in her mind of Martin and Baker tussling with each other on the water like in a 1950s B-movie.

Eve had dashed into St Aldates police station as soon as Martin had disappeared from sight. She was still in her medieval costume and so had a bit of a problem getting herself taken seriously by the officer behind the desk. But then she asked to see DS Woolston and he vouched for her and got the police hunt under way. A heat-seeking helicopter would be sent up to track Martin and Baker on the river as soon as the weather allowed. Meanwhile officers with dogs would search the banks of the river on both sides. Extra officers were being called up to take part in the search. Eve had wanted to get back to King's as soon as possible to keep her vigil. If Martin returned and she wasn't there, he wouldn't know where she was.

As she stood peering into the darkness and getting soaking wet, at last she saw someone in a scull steering himself into the narrow canal way. It was Martin and he was alone. He was slouching at the oars and looked completely exhausted. With his wet hair plastered down and streaked over his face, he was barely recognisable. Eve and a police officer helped him out of the scull.

'God,' said Martin, 'I should have taken the armour off first.' He was rubbing his shoulders under the armour-plating. 'It's going to be bloody sore tomorrow.'

'You didn't see him?' Eve asked.

'What a callous disregard for my welfare. No. Well, I thought I did at one point, but if it was him, he was way ahead of me, and then he just disappeared. Could have gone down one of the side streams - I don't know. God, I'm knackered.'

'Don't worry,' said DS Woolston, 'we'll carry on looking. You two get indoors and dry off. We'll get statements from you in the morning. We've got the CD. Eve, I've called up your uncle so he should be here soon. But he'll kill me if you catch pneumonia hanging around by the river.'

'Are you sure you don't need us?' Eve asked anxiously.

'Absolutely,' said Woolston. 'You get off into the warm. Let us do the dirty work. You've both done more than enough for one night. And this young gentleman looks fit to drop.'

'Gentleman!' said Martin. 'I haven't been called that for a long time, if ever.' He gave a huge yawn as if completely starved of oxygen and then shivered. 'Oh God, yes, come on Eve, I can hear cocoa calling me, preferably with a large slug of something alcoholic. Oh, I'm going to be in agony tomorrow!'

'I think it's tomorrow already,' said Eve as they hurried through the snow and deserted quadrangle to Martin's room.

They both had a moan about the situation - Martin about the anticlimax of not catching up with Baker, and Eve about them ruining the first night of *Princess Ida* and that they'd never be able to show their faces again. Martin stumped off for a hot bath leaving Eve to make the cocoa spiked with Cointreau for his return. Running bath water at that time of night was strictly forbidden, but Baker at least was not in his room to protest at the noise, and Martin was feeling too worn out to care what anybody thought. Martin said Eve could change into any of his clothes that fitted her so she could get dry too. He had turned on the gas fire full blast and so Eve sat wringing her clothes and her hands, wondering what would happen next. Would they have to go to court? Would they be on the news? What would her aunts say? Her gran?

But then, as she chose which of Martin's clothes to change into, it suddenly occurred to her - *it's not Martin, the murderer isn't Martin!* And there's proof at last. What a relief! But how come she had only just thought of it? Did that mean she had never seriously thought it was Martin at any point?

But then another side of her brain began to ask awkward questions that she was forced to try to answer.

Could Martin have faked the CD in some way? Could he have recorded Rob's voice when he was shouting through the door? Seemed unlikely. How would they know it was Rob's voice, though? Friends could testify. But Rob's main, if not only, friend was unconscious in hospital, fighting for his life. But the police could get Rob to shout and test his voice pattern... but what if Rob was not found alive? What if there really had been a B-movie fight on the river and Rob would be found sunk beneath his overturned scull (a skeleton in fifty years' time - no, don't think that...)?

Eve shook herself and sat closer to the fire. She was wearing a loose grey and beige ethnic sweater and baggy grey trousers that she had never seen Martin wear. They looked surprisingly good. The waist was a bit big on the trousers but they were about the right length. She had taken off the pointed medieval shoes and instead was wearing some of his thick grey socks.

Oh, this is ridiculous, she thought. I can't still suspect Martin. Baker's relatives will be able to identify his voice, surely. What relatives did Baker have? Eve had no idea. Look well if he had no living relatives...! Now Eve rebuked herself again. Rob's tutors - all sorts of people - would be able to identify his voice.

But shouting? Do people's voices alter when they shout? What if people listen to the CD and they still aren't sure?

Eve, get a grip!

But even if it is Baker's voice, how could they prove he played the CD on the morning of the murder? And how could the CD have been activated? It would take an electronics expert to figure it out - it was beyond Eve. The police would surely figure it out.

Eve jumped as Martin came into the room behind her. He was only wearing a towel round his waist.

'Make way, woman,' he said, 'I'm dying of cold. I'm not drying off in that bathroom, it's freezing! All there is is a little heater over the door so all the heat goes up through the ceiling. It's ludicrous. The heat never hits you at all. Oh, is that my cocoa? Oh, cold, thank you.'

'I'll make you another,' said Eve getting up.

'Well, you'd better avert your eyes regardless, 'cos I'm whipping my towel off and getting dry. You can pass me some clothes. Oh, you're in mine already! You look better in them than me.'

'That's not saying much,' said Eve automatically.

'Ha ha. Root around in that top drawer, will you, and get me some socks and stuff. You must be intimate with the contents of my drawers by now.'

Eve did as she was told and warmed up the cocoa with some hot water. Martin complained about it being made with half-water but Eve said there was hardly any milk in the communal fridge unless he had wanted her to make it with a carton with the initials 'R.B.' on it. Martin saw her point.

Eve carried on talking to try and hide her nerves. She sat at Martin's desk and tried to forget that Martin was standing naked behind her. She couldn't help the thought invading her mind... the photograph - the naked Feral and the pale young man with short brownish hair... the glinting armour on the floor.

Eve turned her head slowly. She looked down to her right. There was a pile of discarded armour reflecting the glow of the gas fire.

'So,' she began, 'it must have been Robert Baker on that photograph with Feral.'

'Yes, I suppose it must,' agreed Martin. 'Of course, having only seen him with his glasses on, it's hard to compare. Do you remember when I pointed him out to you one lunchtime here? Well, you said then that he might be quite good looking without his specs. Perhaps Feral thought so too.'

Martin's hair, thought Eve. Was it his hair in the photo? But Martin's hair looked different every other day...

'Anyway,' said Martin, 'Angela White's got a lot of explaining to do, wherever she is. She must have known it was Baker on the photo. She must have known about the re-enactment between Feral and Baker since the summer, for God's sake. Why the hell didn't she say? She must have known Baker was the prime suspect for being Launcelot.'

Eve tried to get her mind onto the other track - where Martin was innocent and Baker was guilty.

'Oh,' she sighed, 'perhaps she thought Rory would be protection for her. Remember he threatened Feral when he thought she was a danger to Angela. He's twice the size of Baker. Possibly Angela thought Rory would protect her - until Rory himself started knocking her about. Then she realised she was on her own and ran off.'

'Assuming nothing's happened to her, of course.'

'Yes, assuming that.'

'Right,' said Martin happily, 'I'm decent again. You can look round now. I'll try not to feel jealous that you've nicked my best clothes and I've got to make do with these.'

He was wearing black jeans and his old ratty green jumper that was coming undone at the edges.

'I thought that was your favourite outfit,' said Eve.

'It is. Do you want something to eat? I'm ravenous after all that rowing. God, I could wolf a Chinese. I don't suppose they do them at - what time is it? Oh, our watches are at the Union. Oh, I'll never be able to see Albert again! They must want to kill us. We've ruined their first night.'

'Yes,' said Eve wearily, 'I think we can safely say we are not popular with the University Gilbert and Sullivan Society. I wondered if they carried on with the understudies?'

'At least we were doing something worthy. If this gets all over the news, we might actually have won them some good publicity. 'University Production of *Princess Ida* Delayed by Murder Hunt!' 'Murderer caught by Prince Hilarion in dramatic boat chase while Princess Ida looks on weeping!' It could actually boost ticket sales!'

'You're in a fantasy world,' said Eve. 'They're more likely to murder us.'

'What an unfortunate phrase. Anyway, at least we shouldn't get any more letters from Sir "L".'

'Oh yes. I'd been dreading that,' said Eve in a dull voice.

'It's great that Rory's off the hook,' said Martin knocking back his cocoa. 'He really must have been hypo-whatnot on that Saturday morning. And Guy will be very relieved to know it's all over. He's been panicking that Araminta will give him the push if he's involved in anything sordid. I wonder how... Oh yes, Baker must have sent the pink letter to Guy after Feral's death. He must have had a few lurid letters from Feral himself and either sent an old one on to Guy to try and implicate him in the whole thing, or Baker by that point could imitate Feral's handwriting and bought similar paper. Wow, devious bastard.'

How convenient, thought Eve, that this means that none of Martin's good friends are in trouble. They'll all have reason to be very grateful to him.

'Poor John Harborough,' she said.

'Oh, him. Yes. I wonder how long he'll continue putting flowers by the river.'

'If he's unemployed, it must cost him a bit, coming up to Oxford from Brighton every week,' Eve sighed.

'Mmmm. Oh, talking of poor sad sods, Tony Greer won't have to have his nervous breakdown now - or Sarah Zorginsky.'

'What a way to talk! They had good reason to feel awful. I think I would if I had Feral or Rowan after me.'

'I suppose you're right,' Martin laughed. He thought for a moment, then said more seriously: 'Do you think Feral was trying to blackmail Baker with that photo? I mean, he might never have seen it and not know how innocent it was. He might have thought reproductions of his private parts were going to be plastered all over the university. Feral could have told him anything about it. He would just have been lying on the bed with her and whooshh! Angela nips out from behind a screen and flashes him.'

'How do you know she was behind a screen?'

'I don't. I'm just using my imagination. You *do* have one, I suppose? Although, I suppose if you were deprived of vital nutrients and stimulus in your early years, you might be imaginationally-challenged...'

'I can assure you,' Eve interrupted bad-temperedly, 'that my imagination is on bloody overtime right now, thank you!'

'Wow, I got you to swear! And in English - how wonderful! Your halo's slipped. Here let me re-adjust it...'

'Don't touch me!'

'Alright, alright, there's no need to be so jumpy. And you're in my jumper too - "Jumpy in my Jumper" - that ought to be a song...'

'Oh, *please*. Spare me. You've got no right to be so bloody perky after what we've been through.'

'Perky! I assure you, this is pure hysteria - the adrenalin must still be coursing through my veins at mega-speed. Unless you've put something extra in my cocoa.'

'I wish I had. Something to knock you out.'

'We must be very different as people,' said Martin meditatively. 'All the way through this, everything that I've considered very exciting and stimulating, you've regarded as an ordeal to be endured. I don't think you've enjoyed it half so much as me.'

'Of course I haven't enjoyed it!' protested Eve. 'It's you that's sick, that's all.'

'You could be right,' said Martin with narrowed eyes.

There was silence for a while apart from the quiet roar of the gas fire.

'God, I'm so hungry,' said Martin. 'I think I'll have to nick someone's bread from the kitchen and we can make some toast in front of the fire.'

He left the room to carry out his task.

Meanwhile Eve ran through all the suspects in her mind. She was feeling so tired she wondered if she could cope with much more. But she must think it through and make sense of it. In no particular order, she went through the list:

Tony Greer off the hook - was with a man he picked up in a club. Sound alibi after all.

Rory Ablett - had motive but was in bed with massive hypoglycaemia attack. The real murderer had stolen his bracelet and left it with the stolen armour to implicate him. Alibi must have been true.

Angela White - motive, but seemed to have a cast iron alibi, unless her friend at college and her caller from abroad were lying.

Sarah Zorginsky - according to the police she had a good alibi and not a good enough motive.

Rowan Hunter - ditto.

Guy Fastness - motive, no alibi. Finding the real murderer would be the only thing to take him out of the picture.

Martin Massey?

CHAPTER THIRTY EIGHT

"He seemed to me another Lancelot-
Yea, twenty times I thought him Lancelot.'"

[Tennyson, *Idylls of the King*, 1859]

Martin at that moment came back into the room humming happily. He smiled at Eve and then sat cross-legged in front of the fire and put the stolen bread on a toasting fork.

Martin Massey, Eve forced herself to think. Think, girl, think. Martin Massey - motive? Possible. Alibi? Tenuous, and provided by someone who at that moment was missing.

'Get the Marmite and marmalade, will you?' Martin was saying. 'They're in that cupboard. Don't look so surprised - I do put things away sometimes.'

'What? Oh, yes, sure.'

'You're on another planet. Want to go to sleep? Or do you want to eat first?'

Eve wondered where she was supposed to sleep.

'I'll eat,' she said.

'I'll have that brandy down as well - can you reach it? Great. I need all the help I can get. I'm completely wired.'

'I suppose a plate is too much to ask.'

'There's a clean knife on the cupboard, what more do you want? Pretend we're medieval and use the bread as a trencher. You use the bread as a plate and then eat it as well.'

'I know.'

Eve ate in silence for a while, then said:

'It's quite a coincidence...'

'What is?'

'That of all Robert Baker's CDs, that was the one you picked to put on.'

'Yes,' agreed Martin, 'Weird, isn't it. It must be - what do you call it - synchronicity? You're the one who's into psychobabble, you should know. It must be my subconscious that's been secretly working on the case and mystically guided my hand!' He laughed.

'Mmm,' said Eve dubiously. 'I find it incredible that anyone could kill another human being. I mean, how could Robert Baker do it? Even if Feral, Fern, whatever, wasn't very nice to look at and was sending you nasty letters...'

'Oh, and casting spells on you and threatening you with all sorts of things, like exposing your naked bod to one and all! If Baker is the classic nutty loner, then Feral definitely chose the wrong man to experiment on.'

'Do you think he was?'

'He was certainly a loner. I mean, apart from yelling at each other through the door every so often, we hardly ever spoke and we're on the same staircase. And I'm the social hub of King Henry Hall, so if *I* didn't know him...'

Martin shrugged as if that was proof enough.

'So Baker only had one friend we know of - Jeremy East,' Eve continued. 'And he was an outsider too, but more obviously a social misfit. He was someone that you *noticed* was a misfit, whereas Baker was someone that no one seemed to notice, anonymous, slipping in and out of situations easily because no one could care less about him.'

'Oh!' interrupted Martin, 'that reminds me of something Rory said ages ago. He said that he'd seen Baker going back to Guy's room on the Friday night when the armour was stolen, when everyone was milling round because of the fire alarm. Wow, I'd forgotten about that. Baker must have been going back to steal the armour! I bet he hid it in a couple of plastic bags from Guy's room in the cubby hole outside and then came back to pick it up later. Crafty bastard!'

'So Rory could testify to that?' said Eve. 'That's good.'

'Is it?'

'It helps to make the case more watertight.'

'I suppose so. But I would have thought we had enough on Baker already. Talking of watertight, I wonder where he is now? If he's still on the river he must look like a drowned rat. I bet he's got off at some point near the road and got on a bus somewhere. He could be on a plane by now if he's got credit cards and enough money.'

'Gosh,' said Eve wide-eyed, 'I never thought of that. I wonder if the police are checking the airports.'

'And the Channel Tunnel, etc, etc. I'm sure they will be,' said Martin, although he looked slightly worried.

'Oh, if he escaped now, after all this!' Eve exclaimed.

'Well, I'd be pissed off for a start,' said Martin, 'after I risked life and limb in the pursuit. If the police bungle it now... God, I'd be speechless!'

'Huh, and that's saying a lot.'

'Thank you.'

'My pleasure. But seriously...' Eve paused as if uncertain how to go on.

'Yes?' Martin prompted.

'Oh, I don't know. I think part of me doesn't want him to be caught. I hate the idea of someone spending their life in prison...'

'Well, at least he won't be hanged or electrocuted. Or would you prefer that?'

'No,' said Eve. 'I don't approve of the death penalty.'

'So what's your problem? He'll probably only serve ten years of a life sentence anyway.'

'Well, what do you think should happen?'

'I think...' he said, then more slowly, 'I think that the murderer should be given a way out - you know, like in all those old Agatha Christie stories - these Brits with stiff upper lips being left on their own with a gun and then you just hear a shot from the room and you know they've done the decent thing.'

'Assisted suicide?!'

'Why not? Saves the state a lot of expense.'

'You're a throwback to another age, aren't you,' said Eve contemptuously. 'Don't you think there's a chance for change? That even a murderer can repent and change his ways?'

'Possibly,' sighed Martin. 'But why should we all pay for his upkeep while he takes years to make up his mind. And who knows whether the leopard can change his spots. Did you ever read Evelyn Waugh's story "Mr Loveday's Little Outing"?'

'No.'

'It's about an old man who's released from prison after years and years inside. He was originally imprisoned for killing a young woman - a bit like our friend Baker. Anyway, he's the model prisoner for years and everyone thinks he's reformed. So when he's old and grey, they let him have a day out in the community. And what's the first thing he does?'

'Let me guess - murders a young girl.'

'That's it. Are you sure you haven't read it?'

Eve glared at him.

'I still don't understand... the murderer,' she said.

'Why should you? Perhaps you'd have to be one yourself to understand. God, you've got me sounding like a trick cyclist now.'

'A what?'

'Psychiatrist - trick cyclist. Surely you must have heard that? Wow, what a sheltered life you've led. Do you have television where you come from?'

Eve burned red in the face.

'We don't have one, actually. But that's by choice.'

'Oh, the studious little girl upstairs doing her sums and reading great books instead of watching drivel. Good for you. Made you the Oxford undergrad you are today, no doubt.'

Eve chose not to say that the over-riding passion of her youth had been a longing for a television so she could be the same as the other girls at school.

'Oh, that reminds me,' said Martin, 'I had a programme I was going to show you, to help with the case. But I suppose it's superfluous now.'

'Oh? What was it about?'

'King Arthur. Attitudes to him throughout history, and all that. I thought it would help us understand these nutters in the Launcelot and Guinevere Society.'

After a pause, Eve said:

'Didn't you say that you had been along to some of their meetings?'

'Only once or twice. When there was free booze.'

'So you must have met up with some of them. You must have known some of them already before we even started.'

'I wouldn't say I *knew* them. I'd talked to a few in an alcoholic haze.'

'Feral?'

'No, I don't think I ever spoke to her...'

'But you recognised her when we found her in the boat.'

'Well, she was at my college. What is this, you're sounding like the police all of a sudden!'

'Sorry. I was just trying to imagine... things.'

'I can hear the little cogs grinding away from here.'

'I was wondering, um, if *I* was in the Society, which character I would like to be. I suppose Guinevere is one of the best ones to be.'

'For most of it, perhaps,' Martin agreed, 'but not at the end. I mean, she lost her husband, her lover, and ended up dying in a convent.'

'I suppose you'd call it a full life though.'

'I don't think you had much choice in those days. If you were a woman you were being raped, or married, or widowed every other day, and for the men it was kill or be killed on a daily basis.'

'Exciting, though. Which character would you be?'

'Me?' said Martin. 'Oh, well, I wouldn't want to be Arthur. He starts off as the hero but then is cuckolded and makes an ass of himself. I suppose it would have to be Launcelot. He's the hero throughout, really, even when he's naughty. Yes, definitely Launcelot. And what about you? We still haven't decided on a suitable one for you.'

'Ummm, I'm not sure. You pick one.'

'I can't imagine you as any of them.'

'Oh, go on. You're not trying.'

'People usually say I'm very trying - arf, arf. OK, then I accept the challenge. I think, if you were transported back into Malory's world, you would be... Morgan le Fay.'

'What!'

'Yes. A powerful woman, very feminine, into the supernatural, a bit weird and otherworldly...'

'But she was a witch! She was on the wrong side!'

'But there weren't any powerful spiritual woman on the right side in his story - they're all dabbling in the occult. I seem to remember it was you who pointed out that it was the only way that woman could gain power then...'

'Yes, but...!' Eve was speechless. How could he say that?

'Don't be offended. It's a bit of a compliment, really. It means I see you as a very powerful woman.'

'It's not exactly flattering!'

'You didn't ask to be flattered.'

Eve sighed.

'So, that makes us Launcelot and Morgan le Fay.'

'I suppose it does,' said Martin looking surprised as if he had only just thought of it. 'What a coincidence.'

'Only because men stereotype women, and have done for centuries. You can't be a powerful woman without being called a witch! It's ridiculous. And I'm not even powerful. You're the one with all the wealth and privilege...'

'Hey, hey, hold on. Don't take it personally...'

'You've just called me a witch!'

'I haven't. Don't be silly...'

'And now you're being patronising!'

'Oh my God,' groaned Martin. 'I can't win. Let's just go to sleep, shall we? We're both completely strung out and *we'll* end up killing each other if we're not careful!'

Eve sat on the floor stubbornly. She could hardly bear to look at Martin, she felt so insulted.

'Well, where on earth am I going to sleep?' she said bad-temperedly.

'On the bed, of course,' said Martin, sounding just as annoyed.

'Then where will you sleep?'

'On the bed. And don't look like that, I'm not up to anything. I couldn't even raise a smile at the moment. Believe me, if you were Marilyn Monroe, I wouldn't try anything. Especially as she's dead. Even if, some of Malory's characters were into necrophilia, I'm not.'

'Oh, how reassuring,' said Eve sarcastically.

'Look, I'm not walking you home at this time of the morning. I haven't even got the energy to get you a taxi, so it's put up or shut up.'

'OK, OK,' said Eve.

She walked reluctantly over to Martin's bed. She did feel incredibly tired and Martin's bed did look very inviting. The duvet looked cosy and welcoming. She did suddenly just want to keel over and be in oblivion.

'Shall I get under the duvet?' she asked dubiously.

'You can just lie on top if you want.'

'Won't that be cold?'

'I'll leave the fire on.'

Martin switched out the light as Eve lay down on the bed.

'Didn't you say there was something wrong with your fire?'

'Stop worrying. Good night. Sleep well.'

'But it's on full.'

'Ssshhh.'

Martin was now lying next to her on the bed. Eve felt very tired and tense. But when Martin didn't make any move towards her, she began to relax. She had rarely felt so chronically tired, as if every part of her was screaming for sleep. And Martin was in love with someone. She must remember that. Martin loved Henrietta. So that was alright. She was safe with him. Eve gave a huge sigh inside. She felt as if she couldn't move if she tried, as if she'd been doped. The room was so warm and cosy. Martin smelt nice. His hair smelt faintly of shampoo. How strange that they were lying there together, after all this time. Like when she fainted when the body was found in the river, she'd been on his bed then too...

What if Martin was the killer? No, no, musn't think that... that's Fern gone... and Angela... and Robert.. and probably Jeremy. That's serial... serious.... Martin's mother could write the story, crime ran in the family...

Launcelot and Guinevere... Launcelot run mad...Launcelot scrabbling like a dog on Guinevere's grave... Launcelot and Feral lying together on the bed at last, together forever... the room so warm with the fire on, overpowering... left alone to do the decent thing...

CHAPTER THIRTY NINE

"Is it Lancelot who hath come
Despite the wound he spake of, all for gain
Of glory, and hath added wound to wound
And ridden away to die?"

[Tennyson, *Idylls of the King*, 1859]

"A man is but an ass Who fights in a cuirass,
So off, so off goes that cuirass.
These brassets, truth to tell. May look uncommon well,
But in a fight They're much too tight,
They're like a lobster shell!
Those things I treat the same (I quite forget their name.)
They turn ones legs to cribbage pegs
Their aid I thus disclaim."

[Gilbert and Sullivan, *Princess Ida*, 1884]

Eve and Martin were awakened by loud music crashing up through the floor. Martin leapt off the bed as Eve sat up groggily. The digital clock at the side of the bed said 7.15am.

'What the hell...!' shouted Martin.

They looked at each other in amazement.

'It can't be Baker back, playing music, surely,' Martin said in confusion.

'It could be,' said Eve sleepily. Her mind was fighting to catch up. She was on Martin's bed in his clothes. Last night. *Princess Ida* ruined. The CD. The chase...

'I'm going down,' said Martin and headed for the door.

Eve got off the bed and stumbled after him. Meanwhile the music stopped. Then it started again as abruptly as before. Then the volume gradually slid down to a more acceptable level. What on earth was going on?

They sped down the stairs and arrived at Baker's room. Martin hammered on the door. A voice called out from inside:

'Go away! I'm busy!'

'Bloody hell, it's Baker's voice,' said Martin.

He tried the door. It opened. They went in.

'Oh, what a relief!' said Martin.

Inside were Detective Inspector Andrews, DS Woolston, and three other police officers they didn't recognise.

'Oh, you're *both* here!' said Andrews.

Eve hoped he wouldn't notice she was wearing Martin's clothes. But why should he? Although it was pretty obvious she'd stayed the night.

'What are you doing - a reconstruction?' she said.

'Our own little re-enactment,' grinned Andrews frostily. 'It was handy you knocked on the door just then - saved one of us doing it. Now we know it works, at any rate.'

'It's all very easy. We didn't even have to break any security codes or passwords – Baker had left the computer on standby when he fled,' said a black guy who was introduced as Sergeant Ben Njuku - 'our technical wizard', according to Andrews.

He was obviously experimenting with Baker's computer.

'It doesn't seem easy to me,' said Eve.

'Nor me,' said Andrews. 'But Baker had all the necessary stuff here in his room. We set Ben here the task of seeing if he could make this work with what was to hand. Apparently Baker had programmed the computer himself. His program was written to detect sound picked up from this small microphone attached to the back of the door. When anyone knocked on the door it would trigger the computer to operate the CD, starting or stopping it for set lengths of time, as well as adjusting the volume for the music. This CD in this old CD player here has several tracks with Baker's voice pre-recorded and it's all connected to the computer. Phew!' said Andrews, 'did I get that right?'

'You did indeed, sir,' said Sergeant Njuku. 'That's what happened just now – a sound sample from the CD of Baker yelling.'

'How does it work?' asked Martin.

'We'll show you,' said Andrews, 'if you get out of the way of my men searching the room. That's right, Jim, get behind the wardrobe, take up the floor, I want it thorough.'

The officer thus ordered began to move furniture. Another began levering up floor boards near the bed.

Ben Njuku began to explain Baker's system to everyone.

'You see this wire at the back of the computer? Well, the wire from the microphone is connected to the sound card...'

'So that's the music going on and off, and up and down, explained,' said Eve, 'but why is Baker's voice on a CD?'

'On this old CD player is the CD that you found with his voice recordings on,' said Ben. 'Presumably Baker didn't want to implicate himself by having his voice stored on the computer's hard drive - no matter how well encrypted it was we would have been able to find it and decode it. But there's no way we would have been looking for the evidence in his old music CDs.'

'Ah!' Eve suddenly exclaimed. 'The Retrotech Society! Look at the 1980s stuff in his room - phones, CD player, that little keyboard-thing. I bet he was into that as well. Although I can't remember noticing it before. Perhaps it was hidden somewhere.'

'Retrotech - really? You must tell me all about it. Yes, this old technology was hidden in the wardrobe and that cupboard over there. Anyway, in this scenario, all the computer has to do next is wait for a signal from the tiny microphone on the door...'

'But weren't there coats hanging on the door? Wouldn't they cover over the microphone?' asked Eve.

'All the better,' said Ben. 'These tiny mics only pick up very localised sound. If it was muffled inside the room, it would only pick up sound from the door itself. That's ideal for Baker's purposes. The sound of anyone banging on the door or shouting outside would be picked up by the microphone. The computer program that has the music timings on, also monitors the signal from the microphone via the sound card, so any loud sound or knocking on the door triggers the computer to play Track One of Rob's voice. The second signal will play Track Two, etc. But Baker only has about fifteen sound samples of his voice on here. The rest's a blank. He had planned for the music to be turned down before he needed any more.'

'He certainly planned it well,' sighed Andrews. 'It looks as though he'd had the scheme planned for a while. It was just fortuitous circumstances that meant he could put it all into action so early in term.'

'But...' said Eve, then stopped.

'Yes?' said Andrews.

'Nothing.'

Now was not the time for Eve to ask about her other suspicions. As Ben had been talking, it had occurred to her that this whole set-up could be something that Baker had intended to use for all sorts of occasions. Why couldn't it have all been a practical joke on Jeremy East? It was the sort of thing those geeks would do to each other. Jeremy liked wiring up his room too. What if Baker had rung Jeremy to ask him to turn up at a ludicrously early hour that Saturday morning as a joke, and Baker could have been somewhere else all the time - perhaps stealing something from Jeremy's house to prove he'd been there?

Or what if Baker hadn't used the program that morning at all?

'The program ends,' Ben was continuing, 'at 8am, so that means that Baker himself wouldn't have set off his own voice when he returned.'

'Apparently all this is really easy for students nowadays,' said Andrews with a sigh. 'It makes me feel like a dinosaur.'

'I shouldn't worry,' said Martin. 'None of us are Renaissance men now. Everyone's so specialised. I haven't got a clue about any of this. I know how to do word-processing and play my music but that's about it.'

'Perhaps future generations will know computers inside out,' said Eve.

'I doubt it,' said Ben Njuku. 'Just think how long TV's been around, and do you know how it works? No. Even the generation that's grown up with it. We only know how to switch it on and off because that's all we need to know. We get an engineer to do everything else. Anyway, even Baker was using old-fashioned technology here. He didn't want the latest form of data storage – it was crucial for him to use a CD to record the data so it could be hidden with his music CDs and look innocent.'

'True,' sighed Andrews. 'So this was baby level stuff for Robert Baker. He and his mates could do things like this in their sleep. So now we know everything we needed to know for our reconstruction and we know it all works.'

'So you think,' said Eve, 'that Baker had his alibi planned for a while, he was just waiting for the right moment?'

'I think so. He certainly had the mic and program and so on ready, although he could have used those anytime, as you say. We know he sent Fern a letter on the Friday. We found that in her room, telling her to meet him at Dawn the following morning. We're not sure how he got the letter to Fern...'

'Oh, it must have been in her pigeon hole,' said Martin.

'How do you know?' said Eve. 'We don't even know yet whether it was his writing.'

'Because, - and I've only just remembered this - several people in Hall had mysterious brown envelopes in their pigeon holes that day,' said Martin, 'all with their names in calligraphy. But there was nothing inside the envelopes, apart from Feral's of course. Baker must have done it as a blind, so no one would think he was just putting a letter in her pigeon hole. It would just look as if he was handing out several innocuous brown envelopes for a society or committee or whatever, which anybody could do.'

'Possibly,' said Andrews. 'Anyway, this set up the meeting with Fern which was to be at approximately 7am the next morning, the Saturday of Noughth Week. Apparently it is quite normal for the Launcelot and Guinevere Society to do re-enactments at such outlandish hours - for Authenticity - and for Fern's group 'Black Dawn' to do things at, er, dawn, believe it or not. The moment before dawn was supposed to have been a particularly powerful time for their occult activities - don't ask me why.'

'But on the Friday night,' Andrews continued, 'quite by chance, Baker found he could steal the perfect disguise. He was one of the many people in Guy Fastness' room...'

As was Martin, thought Eve feverishly.

'...admiring the Sir Edward Chichele armour that the JCR President had persuaded the porter to leave in his room temporarily. There is a surprise fire alarm. What a gift! The room clears. But Baker notices that Fastness does not lock his door - he is scatty...'

'Ha!' interrupted Martin. 'Understatement of the year.'

'...and he cannot find his key. As everyone is milling around in the corridors, Baker is able to walk back to Guy's room...'

'Yes,' Martin interrupted again, 'Rory Ablett saw him going back.'

'...and he removes the - oh, what are they?'

'The bascinet, greaves, sabatons and gauntlets, boss,' said DS Woolston smiling.

'Thank you. Those bits. He puts them in a couple of strong, large plastic bags that are lying around Guy's floor from his unpacking. He takes them out of the room and hides them in the cubby hole opposite...'

'I found that out!' cawed Martin.

'Yes, thank you. Baker now joins the fire drill in the quadrangle outside as if nothing's happened. He was ticked off on the list as present. When Guy Fastness finally returns to his room and finds his key, the black cases are still there so he has no idea that some of the pieces of armour are missing. Baker probably couldn't believe his luck! He must have combined them with a breastplate and chainmail from elsewhere - we still haven't found those or know how he had access to them. He certainly seems to have had them last term, as there is discarded armour in the photograph of him and Fern, erm, on a bed together. We suspect that under the armour, Baker wore a grey tracksuit with the hood up as padding, and tan leather gloves - traces of these were found by forensics.'

'I wonder what was going through the murderer's mind that night,' said Eve.

'He was most probably setting up the computer in here,' said Ben Njuku.

'I bet he didn't get much sleep,' said Martin, with a sigh and a yawn.

'On the Saturday morning,' said Andrews, 'Baker was already at the scene of crime by 7am to meet Fern. That means he must have left here at around 6am, in order to get to the old boathouse and change. But we have no sightings of him to confirm that, although he was seen later near the boathouse when he had already changed into the armour. We know he used a King Henry Hall boat to get there, as that was found later and had fibres of his grey tracksuit caught in the seat.'

Did Martin have a grey tracksuit, Eve found herself wondering? She'd never seen him in one, but of course he could hide it.

'Meanwhile, all the equipment here was primed to act out a little drama of its own, at exactly the same time as the murder itself. Rob's friend, Jeremy East, had been told to come to Rob's room for 7am as well, to help strengthen the alibi. Rob is virtually Jeremy's only friend and easily dominates him. They had both been involved with the Launcelot and Guinevere Society - Jeremy very much so, Rob only on the fringes to the extent that he is hardly remembered by anybody there.'

'Really?' said Eve.

'Yes, we checked up on him and Jeremy in that respect quite a while ago,' said Andrews. 'Anyway, Jeremy faithfully fulfils his charge and comes and knocks on Rob's door at 7am-ish. That sends a signal via the microphone on the door, and Rob's voice yells out...'

'I'VE CHANGED MY MIND, I'M BUSY! I'M REALLY INTO SOMETHING HERE!' Rob's voice dutifully cried out, activated by Sergeant Njuku on the computer. It still made everybody jump.

'Of course, Jeremy thought that he could see his friend Rob through the gap at the side of the door...'

'That's right!' said Martin. 'Same here, when I came to the door. It looked as if someone was sitting at the computer, and of course there was a program running.'

'But it wasn't Rob,' said Andrews, 'it was a shop dummy that Rob later dismembered and threw in the river.'

'I remember it well,' said Eve.

'Jeremy leaves very disgruntled,' Andrews continues, 'after another burst of shouting and knocking - it's alright, Ben, don't put it on, I don't think we want to jump out of our skins again. Then Jeremy was seen leaving at the right time.'

'What about that note from him, boss,' said DS Woolston. 'The one we found this morning?'

'What note?' said Eve.

'All ripped up in Baker's bin,' said Woolston eagerly. 'We think it's from yesterday. It was signed Jeremy, and it was making fun of Baker because his CDs had been stolen.'

'Oops,' said Martin. 'That was me.'

'We know,' said Andrews. 'Eve told us when she gave us the CD here. Baker probably thought Jeremy had stolen them as a result, and we think that might be why Baker went round yesterday and walloped poor Jeremy with a hammer and tried to steal them back - although of course, they weren't there. But if Baker thought Jeremy had this incriminating CD, you could understand why he went crackers.'

'If it was Baker who hit him,' said Eve.

There was silence.

'Why wouldn't it have been?' said Andrews.

'Oh, er, no reason,' said Eve, feeling flustered. 'It just could have been anybody, that's all. We don't know, while Jeremy's still unconscious and unable to talk.'

'Yes, I suppose we don't know for sure, but it seems pretty bloody likely,' said Woolston stubbornly. 'It all fits in.'

'Yes, I suppose so,' said Eve, looking at the ground, aware that Martin was frowning at her.

'Anyway,' said Andrews, clearing his throat, 'to continue with our re-enactment, reconstruction, or whatever. Fern has meanwhile rowed to the place in the woods stipulated in the letter. She takes a photograph of this amazing sight - with old technology again, hmmm, that's quite a theme - giving us two photographs - of the medieval knight in gothic armour, emerging from the trees in the mist. All very romantic.'

'Row-mantic,' joked Martin. '"R-o-w"? Oh sorry, that was on automatic.'

Andrews sighed.

'She docks the boat at the muddy bank. Perhaps he helps her out. She leans up towards him. This is so much better than she was expecting! Where on earth did he get the armour from? He's her Launcelot and they are supposed to be re-enacting a scene that she knows well and feels safe with, presumably, otherwise she would never have turned up. We don't know what they say to each other, if anything, but pretty soon he has grasped the camera strap around her neck and is trying to strangle her with it. Now we have the camera, we know that the strap made the marks on Fern's neck. But when this doesn't work, Launcelot resorts to his gauntlets. He's now up to his knees in the water - there was mud and weeds right up the shins on the... on the...'

'Sabatons, boss,' prompted Woolston.

'Of course there is now Fern's blood on the gauntlets too. When he is convinced she is dead, he lays her out in the boat with her arms crossed over her chest, like a mock medieval tomb. Then, as a final act of malice or form of revenge, he rips off the false eyelashes he must have hated so much - something that many people have said they disliked about her and that were her most memorable feature - apart from her slight limp, of course. But the gauntlets are big and clumsy and very sharp - her eyelids are ripped off as well. At least we are assuming that was a mistake.'

'That was one of the worst bits,' said Eve, 'about finding the body.'

'At least you didn't have to see her up close,' said Martin.

'What are you talking about, you enjoyed every minute!' said Eve.

'What?'

'Sorry, I'm tired,' she apologised immediately.

Andrews looked at them both quizzically before continuing:

'We're pretty sure he then tried to push the boat further away, perhaps hoping it would float away from the scene of the crime, but it was pretty much stuck in the mud of that shallow side stream. He then walked - backwards because of the feet thingies...'

'Greaves, sir,' said Woolston.

'...tut! - through the trees to the boathouse, leaving us plenty of juicy tracks to puzzle over, until this boy genius here...'

'Thank you,' said Martin with a bow.

'...figured it out. Meanwhile, at 7.15am, Rob's loud heavy metal music is switched on by his computer. By the way, if Martin has nicked all of Baker's CDs, whose was the one we played earlier?'

'Er, mine, sir,' said Ben Njuku, looking sheepish.

'Bloody awful row it is too,' said Andrews. 'So, not surprisingly, this has Baker's neighbours complaining in turns and hammering on the door which sets off the recording of Rob's voice, telling them in various ways to push off.'

'Yes, that's what I heard,' Martin confirmed.

'But by 7.25am the music is turned down to a more bearable level - giving the impression that Rob is in his room to control the volume, and making sure that no one is annoyed enough to get the porter - which would be disastrous as the porter has keys to all the rooms and could open this one up and find, lo and behold, a mannequin instead of Baker. Meanwhile at the old boathouse, Baker washes off the armour as best he can. He puts the Chichele pieces in strong plastic bags again and presumably jogs across two fields, via a couple of paths, to hide them under a pile of leaves where they were later found. But he has also put a bracelet inside one of the gauntlets. He may not even have known who it belonged to, but he must have found it around King Henry Hall where Rory Ablett lost it. It did have the intriguing name of 'ANGEL' on it, which perhaps appealed to him. But equally he may have known it was Rory's and delighted in pointing the finger of suspicion at him, particularly as Rory had threatened to kill Fern in the JCR the night before. Couldn't be much better. Baker now jogs back to the boat that he has hidden near the old boat house. He probably rowed part of the way back to college, judging from where we found the boat abandoned, and then jogged the rest of the way. We know someone wearing a grey tracksuit with the hood up was seen jogging over Folly Bridge in the direction of King's at the right sort of time on the Saturday morning. And it would seem that Baker had removed his glasses for this as he collided with someone's bike near the entrance to King's. The person concerned only noticed the grey tracksuit and didn't recognise Rob.'

'Wow,' said Eve. 'He must have been nervous at being found out.' But all the time she had been thinking - it could have just as easily been Martin...

'He must have been high on adrenalin,' said Martin.

'We think by about 8.50am Rob was back in his room,' Andrews continued. 'He locks the door, perhaps hides the dummy under the bed for the time being, and takes apart all his fancy equipment.'

'It's really not that fancy,' said Ben.

'OK, OK. It isn't to you.'

'I wonder what he did then?' said Eve.

'Slept the sleep of the innocent,' said Woolston.

'I certainly slept another hour or so after that,' said Martin, 'then Charlie Boscombe woke me up at about nine, then we called for Eve. The rest you know.'

'Oh, sir,' said the officer who'd been taking up floorboards systematically. 'I think we've found what we're looking for.'

CHAPTER FORTY

"'Mervayle nat,' seyde Merlion, 'for hit ys Goddis wylle that youre body sholde be punysshed for your fowle dedis.'"

[Sir Thomas Malory, *Le Morte Darthur*, 1485]

"Most noble Lord, Sir Lancelot of the Lake,
I, sometime called the maid of Astolat,
Come, for you left me taking no farewell,
Hither, to take my last farewell of you."

[Tennyson, *Idylls of the King*, 1859]

The policeman had moved Baker's bedside cabinet and had taken up the floorboards underneath. It had been very easy as they were already loose and seemed designed to be used as a hiding place. The policeman pulled out something grey in a clear plastic bag.

'Grey tracksuit!' he announced with pleasure.

Everyone was smiling. Eve closed her eyes in relief.

'Tan leather gloves!' was the next announcement.

DI Andrews looked as if he would like to break into applause. There were appreciative noises all round.

'We've nailed the bastard,' said DS Woolston in satisfaction.

'Hmmm, pity we didn't do this a few weeks ago,' said Andrews. 'But we had no way of knowing at that point we should be tearing up this particular room.'

'I wonder how long it's been there,' said Eve. She then looked round, almost as if she was wondering who had said it.

'Since Saturday of Noughth Week, I should think,' said Martin sharply.

'Oh, um, of course,' said Eve, looking down, feeling stupid. Hopefully it would look as if she'd just made a silly mistake. Thank God there were no eyelids with false lashes kept there. That would have been the ultimate sickness, to keep them as trophies.

But what it... what if... what if? Had anyone else had access to Baker's room to plant the evidence there? How did they know the tracksuit and gloves were Baker's? What if someone else had known there was an easy way to hide them in Baker's room? What if someone had a similar room (upstairs), identical in every respect, and knew that it was easy to hide something in that spot?

Had Martin ever had access to Baker's room?

Yes. At least once.

Everyone knew that he had stolen Baker's CDs. He had been inside Baker's room in the last twenty four hours.

DI Andrews' radio crackled. It was a call for him from the helicopter crew. They had found an upturned boat on the river. The heat-seeking equipment had been no use during the night because of the snow and the fact that there seemed to be no body in sight. It was only now that it was daylight that the upturned scull could be seen. Officers on the ground could be there within minutes.

There was silence in the room as if everyone was holding their breath. Everyone had heard.

'I wonder what's for the best,' said Andrews.

Eve knew what he meant. Was it better for Baker to disappear by escaping from his scull to who knows where, to be caught later and made to serve life imprisonment? Or would it be better for all concerned that he should be found in the water underneath his boat? The phrase 'Doing the decent thing...' came back to Eve from the old detective stories.

'I think we're all finished here, then,' said DI Andrews. 'Eve, would you like a lift home? You must be tired.'

'Um, yes,' said Eve, 'yes, I am.'

She looked across at Martin, but he was chatting to Ben about the computer program and she could not catch his eye. He seemed to have lost interest in her.

'PC Jarvis can take you home,' said Andrews. 'I'd do it myself, but I'll be needed at the river. The sooner we get this thing wrapped up, the better.'

Woolston radioed for a car for Eve. Andrews and Eve walked down the staircase. While Eve picked up her things from Martin's room and got changed in thirty seconds flat, another message came through on the radio for the Detective Inspector. There was no sign of Baker's body near the boat. He wasn't underneath it, or anywhere near it. In fact, there were tracks away from it in the mud, heading towards Donnington Bridge and the road.

'So,' said Andrews grimly, 'the little bastard's alive and on the run. That's a turn up for the books. I could have sworn we'd got another body in the river there.'

'Yes, it was looking that way,' agreed Eve.

'At least we've got more chance of proving who did it with him alive rather than dead,' said Andrews. He then looked at Eve seriously. 'You've been through a lot with all this. You go and take it easy for a bit. You don't look very well to me.'

'Oh, I'll be alright,' said Eve. But she didn't dare say what she was longing to ask - did her uncle also still suspect Martin? Is that why he wanted Baker alive?

There was no chance for further speech as Eve's lift arrived outside King Henry Hall and she got inside PC Jarvis' car.

'What a night, eh?' said the policewoman, as she drove over Folly Bridge towards Donnington Bridge. 'We're all doing double-shifts. We're all shattered.'

'Oh, it's very kind of you to give me a lift then.'

'Oh, I do whatever the boss says. Anyway this is a holiday compared to slogging round the river in the snow in the pitch dark. It's a wonder more of us haven't fallen in, and it's bloody cold in the water.'

'I'm sure.'

'Anyway, hopefully we'll catch the little bugger before the day's out.'

'Mmmm.'

Eve was feeling slightly sick in the car. It had a new plasticy sort of smell mixed with petrol. She was also incredibly hot. She felt her forehead. She was burning up! She must have caught 'flu again. She was feverish.

Eve was so grateful to see the boring solidity of St Frideswide's as the car drove up the short driveway and parked outside. She was told again to look after herself, which she again promised to do, and walked on unsteady legs towards the main door and then her room.

It was still only ten o'clock in the morning. What on earth was she going to do with herself all day? She flung down her bag and switched on the radio. A cheery voice said:

'From Venetian Vivaldi to sensational Stravinsky, this is Classic FM!'

There then followed such cheerful music that Eve switched it off again immediately. She needed to think. She knew she had to carry on playing the 'What if...?' game a bit longer, except that it was deadly serious for a game. The fact that Baker was probably still alive made no difference at all, if he wouldn't confess. Eve then tortured herself with thinking that *even if he did* confess, it still might not mean he'd done it. There were all sorts of cases of people confessing to crimes they hadn't committed, especially notorious ones. If Baker was a bit unstable, and by now Eve was quite willing to believe that he was, then his confession might not mean anything. What if there was a much cooler customer behind the scenes, quite prepared to let the unbalanced Baker take the rap?

Come on, Eve, she told herself, you really are being too imaginative now. Why not just let the police get on with it and let sleeping dogs lie?

But if it was Martin...!

There were only three people saying that Robert Baker yelled at them through the door at the time of the murder.

Well, what if he really did?!

What if Robert Baker had been in his room all the time, merrily playing with his computer and turning his ghastly music up and down to his heart's content? What if the mannequin in the river was nothing to do with the case at all, or had been put there by someone else as a decoy? If Martin had been planning to frame 'the Prat Downstairs', as he called him, for some time, then he could have easily done that. Martin and Jeremy may well have been able to see the *real* Robert Baker sitting at his desk that Saturday morning through the gap at the side of the door.

Eve felt as if her burning head was about to explode. She had all sorts of aches shooting around her muscles, making her feel about ninety. She sat at her desk and tried to think. She picked up a pen and began to write. At least then she couldn't forget anything.

There were really only three alternatives:

(1) Robert Baker genuinely used the CD containing his voice and the computer program to cover for him while he committed the murder;

(2) Robert Baker used the CD and computer program on that Saturday morning, but only as a practical joke on Jeremy East - using it as a decoy while he went to East's home to steal from him, or whatever - making someone else the murderer;

(3) Robert Baker didn't use the CD. He really *was* in his room using his computer that morning and was genuinely yelling at people through the door - also making someone else the murderer.

All of these begged the question: how could they *prove* beyond doubt that Baker used the CD that morning? If it couldn't be proved in some way then it was just another piece of inconclusive circumstantial evidence.

Eve threw her pen down in disgust. Her head was throbbing. She'd better take some Tylenol or something. She downed a couple with some cold water from the sink. Suddenly the thought of tea or coffee made her feel sick. That *definitely* meant she was ill. It was hardly surprising that she'd succumbed to something, after hanging around on a snowy river bank at night in a flimsy costume doused in a bucket of water. Her aunt would have a fit if she found out.

Eve sat at her desk again and forced herself to think the unthinkable. Martin. Crispin Martin Alexander Xavier de Beauchamp-Massey. What if...?

How had Charlie first introduced Martin? (Hard to believe it was only seven weeks ago.) He'd called him 'the best Hamlet the University had ever seen'. That meant at any rate that Martin was a very good actor. Eve had seen the comic side of that for herself - he was superb as Prince Hilarion. But if he was the cream of Oxford university's actors, why was he slumming it with the Gilbert and Sullivan Society? They were definitely more downmarket than other university drama groups. Martin could have been hitting the headlines and building a career for himself with talent scouts who were always on the lookout. Had he suggested G and S because he knew Eve had a good singing voice and it would be a way for them to meet up each week in the same production? That way, Martin could keep an eye on the person who had found the body with him and had a rather convenient tie with the police, ie. her 'uncle' Andy Andrews.

He could also imitate people's voices very well and do all sorts of accents. (Good grief, the CD! Was he good enough to imitate Robert Baker's voice? He could have heard Baker shouting several times.) Martin could also look very different from one day to the next, according to what he was wearing or how he'd combed or gelled his hair. Even the colour seemed to veer between brown and varying shades of auburn and red.

Was he the man on the bed with Feral?

He knew Malory. He had claimed he had only skim-read it last year for his studies, but he certainly seemed to have an intimate knowledge of Arthurian legend and all of its characters. And he had a suit of armour. He hadn't worn it this year at his birthday party, but perhaps that was because he didn't want to draw attention to it. With his hair straight down to below his ears, he would look exactly like the popular image of Sir Launcelot.

Why had Martin obsessively followed the case? Charlie, who had also found the body, hadn't wanted to, nor had Eve. She had only given in to constant pressure from Martin. She had allowed herself to be manipulated. She had let herself be the Watson to his

Holmes, the Harriet Vane to his Lord Peter Wimsey. Huh, vain was the word! How could she let herself be made such a fool of? She'd been his foil, his stooge, his dupe all along!

Oh God, help, Eve thought, I'm getting paranoid. It can't really be as bad as this. Martin's so nice! Well, when he's not being obnoxious. How on earth was she going to be able to be objective about someone she had been so close to and been through so much with during her first vulnerable term at university? Good grief, she'd even ended up on a bed with him, like Feral!

Well, not *quite* like Feral, she reminded herself. At least she had been wearing clothes. Yes, but *his* clothes. The discarded armour, too, had been next to the bed. Perhaps Fern Harrison had started off in Martin's clothes...

No, no, she was feverish, this was all too ridiculous! What on earth would Martin and Fern Harrison have in common?

Perhaps they didn't need much in common. Perhaps Fern had just been lonely and vulnerable - easy prey for a strong personality. (But surely it was Feral who liked to prey on people? To the point they had breakdowns.) But surely, as far as women were concerned, Martin was in love with someone. Charlie had said so. Martin was in love with Henrietta Garrett-Brown.

But Henrietta Garrett-Brown had nearly been killed, and Martin had been involved. She'd had a breakdown, nearly managed to kill herself. But how? What had Charlie said about it? Come on, Eve you must remember! They had arranged to 'do it' at the same time in the same way. But was it in the same place? Was there some way that Martin could have made sure that he survived... and Henrietta didn't? She had been saved, but perhaps only just - Eve had no idea of the facts of that case. What if Henri, despite the beauty on the surface, was deep down lonely, hurt and vulnerable - easy prey. Perhaps she had been open to Martin's charm and manipulation. Just like me, thought Eve with a sense of shock.

It was mounting up.

What had Martin said about himself once? He had joked about having 'multiple selves' who would perhaps go off and do things without him knowing about it. That was called Multiple Personality Disorder. Eve remembered reading a semi-serious article in a magazine once about how all writers and actors are supposed to be only one step away from this serious mental disturbance. The ability to 'become' other characters... what if one or more took over? Martin Massey, Crispin to his family, Crisp or Crispies to his friends, Hamlet, Prince Hilarion...

Eve sighed. This was all way beyond her, even on a normal day when she wasn't feeling awful. She went and lay down on the bed. The Tylenol was kicking in and she was feeling very dopey. Was her door locked? She felt too tired to check. She had come full circle. Seven weeks ago to the very day she had been lying here on the bed with the 'flu when it had all started. What if Martin came round to play? To play? To play what? How childish. She thought of the bin in the bathroom. Her hair clippings were still in there. From when she had cut her fringe. Feral would like to collect those...she would find them very useful...

There was a knocking sound inside her head, throbbing and banging. No, it was someone at the door.

'Eve, are you in there?'

'Mmmm,' Eve grunted automatically and sat up. That was a mistake. All the blood seemed to drain from her head and she almost fell sideways with the giddiness.

'Gosh, it's all dark in here! What on earth are you doing? Have I woken you up?'

'What time is it?' said Eve mournfully.

'It's about four o'clock,' said the ever-cheerful Marion, switching the light on, which made Eve go 'ouch!'.

'You can't have a hangover at this time of the afternoon,' Marion said.

'Wow, I must have been asleep for... *six hours!* I must be really ill.'

'Oh, not again! You've been succumbing to every bug in the Thames Valley this term. You should have been inoculated with some of the vapor before you came down here.'

Eve smiled wanly.

'Oh, I have a phone message for you,' said Marion, 'that's why I've disturbed your beauty sleep. It's from your uncle, that police inspector. Apparently your phone's switched off so he rang the staircase.'

'Oh?' Eve felt suddenly alert.

'Yes, I'm afraid it's bad news. Someone you know has been in a car accident.'

'Who?' said Eve sharply.

'His name's Rob.'

'Oh, so they've found him!'

'Yes, he's in hospital apparently. I'm afraid I don't know where, I didn't ask. I'm sure you can ring back and find out if you want to visit.'

'Oh, no, I won't be visiting.'

'Oh.' Marion was obviously mystified. 'There was another odd bit to the message. I didn't understand this bit at all. It sounded as if this Rob chap was wearing false eyelashes, but that can't be right!'

'What?! Show me!' Eve grabbed the piece of paper from Marion's hand on which she had taken down the phone message.

'Your handwriting's terrible,' said Eve impatiently, 'what the heck does that say?'

'It says "Tell Eve that Rob had the eyelashes on him". That was what he told me to tell you. He said "just in case she still thinks it's someone else". I have no idea what he was talking about.'

'Oh!' cried Eve. 'Oh, thank God!'

Marion was even more confused that such an odd message should have Eve bursting into tears. But the motherly Marion didn't let a little thing like that bother her and she hugged and rocked the weeping Eve, made her a cup of tea she didn't want, and very kindly left without asking any questions when Eve said she wanted to be on her own.

So her Uncle Andrew had known that she still suspected Martin. And perhaps he had too. But it was all over now. The murderer had his trophies. The whole thing had fallen into place. They knew how he had done it. They now had all the proof they needed.

As Eve eased herself off the bed she had a sudden memory - of waking up with Martin that morning, when he had jumped off the bed ahead of her and she had followed.

His arm had been around her in his sleep.

She hadn't registered it before. But for a split second she had known, until the craziness of the morning had begun to take over.

Would she see Martin again? She walked over to her desk in a daze and looked out of the darkened window. But in the strong light of her room all she could see was her own reflection looking back at her. She looked down. Her desk had a pile of books on it ready to write an essay. The essay title was there too: 'Is Death the End? Give a Biblical and Theological Survey of this Question.' She had already marked a few passages in some of the books - St Paul's imagery of death as 'sleep', the idea of the intermediate state between this life and the next, of limbo, of paradise, of the vigil of the souls in wait for final judgment, of Hades, of the Great White Throne, and the Lake of Fire, of the New Jerusalem coming down as a bride from heaven.

Next to these theological texts rested a medium-sized navy book with the crest of Oxford University embossed on the front. It was Martin's copy of Malory. He had insisted on leaving it with her for further study the day before. Eve now opened it up. It still contained Martin's many markers. It fell open at the last page, before the many pages of 'Notes and Glossary' and at the end of the section 'The Dolorous Death and Departing Out of this World of Sir Launcelot and Queen Guinevere'. Martin had marked the last paragraph with heavy black lines in the margin:

> *I PRAYE YOU ALL JENTYLMEN AND JENTYLWYMMEN THAT REDETH THIS BOOK OF ARTHUR AND HIS KNYGHTES FROM THE BEGYNNYNG TO THE ENDYNGE, PRAYE FOR ME WHYLE I AM ON LYVE THAT GOD SENDE ME GOOD DELYVERAUNCE. AND WHAN I AM DEED, I PRAYE YOU ALL PRAYE FOR MY SOULE.*
>
> *'FOR THIS BOOK WAS ENDED THIS NINTH YERE OF THE REYGNE OF KYNG EDWARD THE FOURTH, BY SIR THOMAS MALEORE, KNYGHT, AS JESU HELPE HYM FOR HYS GRETE MYGHT, AS HE IS THE SERVAUNT OF JESU BOTHE DAY AND NYGHT.*

Eve sighed and took the hint. She prayed for the 'good delyveraunce' of all those potential eternal souls wrapped up in this strange case.

Eve was only later to find out that Angela White had been in touch with her parents and was safe and well. She had taken the photograph of Feral and Robert Baker on the bed. Jeremy East regained consciousness in hospital but was never able to return to his studies at the university. But he was able to confirm that it had been his 'best friend' who had attacked him so viciously. He was also able to inform the police that Baker did indeed have his own suit of armour. It had been bought after a school production of *Ivanhoe* and been auctioned off and eventually bought by Baker. It had been hidden since the murder at his parents' home in Basingstoke. Baker had not deigned to wear it for any public gatherings of the Launcelot and Guinevere Society as it had not been the right period and not 'authentic'. He had only made the exception the once for the assignation with Fern Harrison, when she had egged him on to be Launcelot to her Guinevere. But Feral had chosen to prey on the wrong man.

Robert Baker was to die in hospital without regaining consciousness. He was found to be wearing Feral's eyelashes (and lids) in a small gold locket under his shirt. It was the sort of thing that nineteenth century lovers would use to capture a lock of a loved one's hair to wear next to their heart. What had it been for him? A murderer's trophy? A lover's memento? A sorcerer's talisman? Counter magic? There was no one left alive who could say.

But all that knowledge lay in the future. It was all part of the usual police procedure that was known by the cliché of 'mopping up'. All Eve had to do now was to recover from 'flu and try and get her work done.

And try not to think about Martin. Would she see him before the end of term? A note had been left for her saying not to bother turning up for 'Princess Ida' - they could manage with the understudies from now on, thank you very much. Obviously the production team didn't yet know of the rather dramatic and perfectly valid reasons that she and Martin had had for their fleeing of the Final Act. But it did mean she had no good excuse for getting in touch with Martin again. Admittedly she could give him the Malory back, but she could just as easily leave that in his pigeon hole at college. Did she actually want to speak to him at the moment? If Andrews had realised that she had still suspected Martin, then perhaps Martin had realised too. Would he ever trust her again? It was a pretty devastating thing to do to somebody who's supposed to be a friend.

She knew Martin was going skiing in Switzerland over Christmas. Eve would be going home to her aunt's in Massachusetts. Probably their very different worlds would just swallow them up again as if nothing had ever happened. It would probably be one Michaelmas Term they would all be glad to have behind them.

Maybe some day she would see Martin in the street, by chance, in a year or so's time. He would be coming up to Graduation - maybe he'd be about to go touring with the Royal Shakespeare Company for the summer. She'd be going to South America to work in a ghetto. He'd be engaged to Henrietta. She'd be...

Eve didn't want to think about it anymore.

She took two more Tylenol, switched off the light, and lay down on the bed in the darkness. The headlights of an occasional car skimmed over the ceiling. There was the noise of someone running down the stairs outside.

Martin hadn't come to visit.

She had ended how she had begun, lying on the bed with 'flu. Somehow the amateur detectives in books were always a lot more keen than that. Dynamic.

Eve crossed her hands over her chest and closed her eyes. At least she now understood one thing about the teaching of St Paul and the legend of King Arthur and the Knights of the Round Table. The desire to be left in peace and allowed to sleep for an indefinite period of time.

THE END

Jeanette Sears was born in Nottingham, England, and has a PhD from the University of Manchester. She was a Kennedy Scholar at Harvard and has worked as a kitchen maid, a bank teller, a bookshop manager, a teacher in the UK and US, and a college lecturer at a seminary. She has been a student and an Anglican priest in Oxford and lived there for ten years. She is currently a full-time writer and speaker, particularly on C S Lewis, J R R Tolkien, and Dorothy L Sayers.

www.jeanettesears.com

A Murder in Michaelmas is also available as Kindle and Epub downloads.

Lightning Source UK Ltd.
Milton Keynes UK
UKOW040308271012

201283UK00001B/2/P